Paradise

Falls

Talia
johangvas.com

Books by Jonnie Jacobs

Kali O'Brien Legal Suspense

Shadow of Doubt
Evidence of Guilt
Motion to Dismiss
Witness for the Defense
Cold Justice
Intent to Harm
The Next Victim

Kate Austen Suburban Mysteries

Murder Among Neighbors
Murder Among Friends
Murder Among Us
Murder Among Strangers

Non-series books

The Only Suspect

Paradise

Falls

JONNIE JACOBS

ISBN-13:978-1481922913
ISBN-101481922912

:

ACKNOWLEDGMENTS

Several years ago I had a conversation with two young women who opened my eyes to the tensions, and unexpected joys, of blended families. While the events of this story in no way reflect their personal stories, their experiences spoke to me both as parent and writer, and eventually provided the germ of the idea that became Paradise Falls. A special thanks to Rita Lakin, Margaret Lucke, Camille Minichino, and Deborah Schneider for their insightful comments and suggestions on earlier drafts of the book. And finally, my heart goes out to all parents who've lost a child to crime.

CHAPTER 1

Caitlin Whittington hunched forward under the weight of her backpack and pulled her jacket tight across her chest. The wind whipped strands of chestnut brown hair across her face, stinging her eyes and catching in her mouth. The warmth her body had generated during volleyball practice was long gone. She shivered and checked her watch.

Her dad was late. No surprise there, he was always late. Then he'd spend twenty minutes making excuses, which was really just a way of reminding her how busy and important he was.

It wasn't like she actually wanted to spend the weekend with him, anyway. It was boring at his place, away from her friends, from her home, from everything that was hers. He never seemed particularly happy to see her either. Especially now that Starr had moved in and all she wanted to talk about was their upcoming wedding.

Caitlin had tried explaining this to her mom but she must not have done a very good job because her mom had just shaken her head sadly and said, "Really, Caitlin, is a weekend now and then really so much to ask? He's your father, after all."

And Caitlin knew that her mom and Carl liked having the time to themselves. She'd noticed that her visits to her father's always coincided with the weekends Adam and Lucy, Carl's kids, were with their mother. With no teenagers around, her mom and Carl would have the house to themselves.

Caitlin checked her watch again just as Traci Redding walked past, one hand holding a cigarette, fingers of the other looped through Leo Johnson's rear belt loop. Traci waved with the hand holding the cigarette.

"Hey, Cate. Thanks for the study help in Algebra. I got a C-plus on the test." Traci sounded pleased, although Caitlin thought a C-plus was nothing to get excited about.

"Good for you," she called back. "I bet next time you'll do even better."

Caitlin's words were drowned out by the sudden, deafening beat of rap music emanating from a car that screeched to a halt in the student parking lot. Traci and Leo jogged toward it and climbed in.

Traci was one of the divas, a group of girls Caitlin had once held in disdain. But that was before she got to know them. She and Fern had started calling them divas behind their backs, making private jokes about them, none really funny even though once they'd laughed so hard that Fern wet her pants and had to pretend she'd gotten her period so she could go home and change. Then at the end of last year Fern's dad got transferred, the family moved clear across the country to New York, and Caitlin somehow found herself dating Ty Cross, who everyone said had the cutest butt in the whole school. All of a sudden, the divas were Caitlin's new best friends.

Sort of.

And now . . . well, Caitlin wasn't sure what was going to happen. What she wanted to have happen even. Sometimes Caitlin wasn't so sure she even knew who she was anymore.

A gust of wind stirred the dust and litter at her feet. Caitlin was growing impatient. It was practically night already, the campus almost deserted. She pulled out her cell phone to call her dad and saw that the battery was dead. Shit. He couldn't have reached her if he'd tried.

Caitlin was freezing. One of the wettest winters on record and it showed no signs of letting up, even though it was the middle of March and the buds on the crabapple trees were ready to burst. At least today it wasn't raining. She could walk home and call her dad from there.

As she headed for the football field and the shortcut along the river to her house, she saw Lucy sitting on the wall by the flagpole, probably waiting for her mother. No way Caitlin would ask Mimi for a ride, although the thought of braving the cold for three-quarters of a mile was almost enough to tempt her. Lucy was okay, even as a stepsister, but her mom was something else. Caitlin had no trouble understanding why Carl had divorced her.

Ducking her head against the relentless cold, Caitlin skirted the flagpole and headed home.

CHAPTER 2

How was it, Grace wondered, that life's pivotal moments could sneak right by and you wouldn't blink an eye. Looking back, they might flash in neon, but right then, when destiny was making a hairpin turn, you were usually thinking of something else.

Caitlin, for example. Grace's love for her daughter was so all-encompassing it sometimes hurt, as if Grace's heart wasn't big enough to hold it. But motherhood, decidedly the most momentous change in Grace's entire life, had begun with a late period she'd passed off as a side effect of the flu—even though, as a nineteen-year-old sleeping with a guy who clearly had no interest in commitment, she shouldn't have been so naive. The fact that she might be pregnant hadn't crossed her mind.

By the time Caitlin was born, Jake had stepped up to the plate, as he was fond of putting it, ignoring altogether the fact that he'd stepped away six years later. When he moved out—another pivotal moment—he'd been absent so long in spirit that Grace barely noticed he was gone.

And then Carl. Who would have thought the careless act of spilling her latte onto the lap of a stranger three and a half years ago would have opened the door to such happiness? Grace couldn't imagine her life without him.

Now, as the waiter brought their salads and refilled their wine glasses, she smiled across the elegantly set table at the kind and boyishly handsome man who was her husband, and wondered how she'd gotten so lucky.

Carl reached for her hand. "What are you thinking?"

"That we don't do this sort of thing often enough."

He laughed and the corners of his hazel eyes crinkled. Grace loved that about Carl, the way he laughed easily and with genuine pleasure. When he was angry or hurt, those emotions played out on his face with equal candor, which further endeared him to Grace. There was nothing phony about Carl. No posturing or guile or manipulative innuendo.

"That's what makes weekends away such a treat," he said. "If we made a habit of it, they wouldn't be as special."

"You always put a good spin on things, don't you?"

Carl was a glass-half-full kind of guy. His attitude was such a change from Jake's that it had taken Grace awhile to get used to it.

The flicker of candlelight against the white tablecloth made Grace think of Caitlin's favorite childhood book with its illustrations of fairies dancing under a full moon. Grace remembered how the magic of the story had been a tonic for the bleakness she'd felt about her own life at the time.

"There you go, lost in dreamland again," Carl said.

"Sorry." Grace sipped her wine. "Do you want to get an early start tomorrow or sleep in?" They were planning a leisurely bike ride along a scenic, back-road route that had been written up in Sunset Magazine not long ago.

Carl grinned. "Depends on whether or not you wear me out tonight."

"I didn't think that was possible," she tossed back.

"Is that a challenge?"

Grace's cell phone chimed in her purse. She wanted to ignore it but was worried it might be Caitlin. "Sorry," she said, slipping her hand from Carl's to retrieve the phone.

She glanced at the readout. "It's Jake." Annoyed at her ex for intruding on their evening, she wondered if he'd timed the call out of some petty sense of being burdened with their daughter for the weekend.

Carl sighed. "You'd better answer it."

Grace hit receive. "Hi," she said softly, so as not to disturb the other diners. "I'm in a restaurant so I can't really talk."

"Where's Caitlin?" Jake asked without prelude.

"Isn't she with you?"

"Not exactly."

"What does that mean? Either she is or she isn't."

He sighed. "I was tied up in a meeting so Starr went to pick her up after volleyball practice."

"Then she must be with Starr." Grace glanced at Carl, whose set jaw and narrowed eyes betrayed a sense of irritation she knew he would never admit.

"Starr had car trouble," Jake continued. "By the time she got to the school, Caitlin was nowhere to be seen."

"Have you tried Caitlin's cell?" Grace felt the first tingle of alarm.

"She's not answering. I was hoping maybe you'd know where she is."

Grace and Carl were two hours away at a bed and breakfast on the Oregon coast. Why did Jake think she'd know where Caitlin was? "What about the house?" she asked with growing concern. "Have you called there?"

"No answer. And the inside is dark. Starr drove over there to check." Jake's tone was clipped. "I'm going to be really pissed if this is her idea of sticking it to me."

"Why would you even think such a thing? You know Caitlin isn't like that."

He ignored the question. "She's probably gone off with some friends. Wasn't there some boy she was involved with?"

"Ty? That's over."

"Whatever. Are you sure she understood I was going to meet her at the school?"

"Absolutely. We talked about it this morning. Five-thirty, when volleyball practice got out. She was going to wait for you at the flagpole on the oval." Grace hesitated. "How late was Starr?"

"Not that late. Forty minutes maybe."

"Forty minutes!" Grace was appalled. How could Starr have been so irresponsible?

"Why don't you call a couple of Caitlin's friends," Jake said. "See if they know where she is. I can't expect Starr to hang around Paradise Falls all night."

After the divorce, Jake had changed jobs and relocated fifty minutes away to Portland, which in Grace's mind was a foolish move for a man with a child. "Where are you now?" she asked.

"I'm at home. But I don't know who her friends are or how to reach them." Jake's voice became softer. "I feel bad about bothering you on a weekend away, but I'm kind of stuck. I don't know what else to do."

"No, I'm glad you called." Alarm had swelled to panic. Her chest felt tight. Grace had to remind herself to breathe. "I'll see what I can find out and get back to you."

It wasn't like Caitlin to go off without telling anyone. Even if she'd gone to a friend's house when Starr hadn't shown up, she'd have called to let them know where she was. Her daughter was resourceful and responsible. Mature beyond her fifteen years. Grace was sometimes tempted to shake her and tell her to loosen up. Have some fun before she grew up and stepped into the adult world for real.

"What is it?" Carl asked, sounding worried. "Has something happened to Caitlin?"

Grace bit her lip. It had to be a misunderstanding. They'd all get a good laugh about it later. "Caitlin wasn't at school when Starr arrived to pick her up. I need to call some of her friends." The restaurant was one you had to make reservations for weeks in advance. They'd both been looking forward to this dinner for a long time. "I'm sorry," Grace said. "I'll just be a minute."

Carl reached a hand across the table to touch her arm. His amber-flecked eyes probed hers. "Can I help?"

She shook her head, trying to keep it light. "Just save me some wine."

Grace stepped outside to make her calls. She didn't know every one of Caitlin's friends, and she didn't have the phone numbers of all she did know. But she managed to reach three girls, and through them got the numbers of two more.

No one had seen Caitlin since that afternoon.

Grace's hand was shaking by the time she called Jake back. "I think you'd better notify the police," she told him.

"Don't you think that's a little premature?"

Grace couldn't believe her ears. "Do you?"

"It's just that I hate to make a scene for no reason."

"A missing daughter isn't reason enough?"

To his credit, Jake relented. "Okay, if you think that's the way to go."

"We'll be home as soon as we can. Probably a couple of hours." She imagined Carl's face when she told him they had to leave. He'd be worried, but he'd also be disappointed, as she was, that their weekend had been cut short. Carl was wonderful to Caitlin, but Grace knew there had to be times he resented her. It bothered him that he lived with Grace's daughter twenty-four-seven, and saw his own children not even half that often. If it turned out Caitlin had simply gone off without telling them, there'd be hell to pay.

"I'll meet you at your place," Jake said. "Call me when you're close to home."

CHAPTER 3

The detective assigned to meet with them was a woman named Rayna Godwin. She was slender, with short, honey colored hair, and looked to be a few years older than Grace. Grace had seen her on the news last fall when Karen Holiday went missing. She supposed she should be happy the dispatcher hadn't sent out some wet-behind-the-ears patrolman, but when she'd opened the front door and seen Detective Godwin standing there on the porch, Grace's knees had buckled.

Now they were seated in the living room, all five of them perched on the edge of their chairs as if eager to be somewhere else. Grace could sense the discomfort in the room. Jake because he didn't like emotion-ridden situations of any sort. Starr because she had no interest in any part of Jake's life that came before she arrived on the scene. Carl because he was feeling helpless, and Grace because she knew with a certainty born of more than dread that something truly terrible had happened to her only child.

Even the detective seemed to wish she was anywhere but there.

"Which of you are her parents?" the detective asked.

"I'm her mother," Grace said. "Carl Peterson is her stepfather."

"And I'm Jake Whittington, her actual father," Jake added. "Starr is my fiancée."

Detective Godwin seemed puzzled. She addressed Grace. "You've kept Whittington as your last name?"

Grace nodded. "I wanted the same last name as my daughter." She'd expected Carl to balk at that when they'd decided to marry, but he'd taken it in his stride. "You can call yourself whatever you'd like as long as you call me your husband," he'd told her. That easygoing manner was typical of Carl and one of the things that so endeared him to Grace.

"When was the last any of you saw Caitlin?" the detective asked.

Grace glanced at Jake, who narrowed his dark eyes back at her. He was still in his business suit but his tie was crooked and there was a smear of Starr's bright pink lipstick on his collar.

"This morning," Grace said, "before she left for school. I've talked to her friends. I know she was still at school around five-thirty, waiting to be picked up." Grace tried not to shoot daggers at Starr.

"I had a flat," Starr said, twisting a strand of golden hair around her pink-tipped index finger. "I wasn't late on purpose. Sometimes things happen."

Grace was angry that Jake, who didn't spend time with his daughter all that often anyway, had delegated picking her up from school to a twenty-six year-old bimbo. Sometimes things did just happen, but Grace was in no mood to be forgiving.

"Have any of you tried calling her?" the detective asked.

Jake spoke up. "I did. The minute Starr told me she was going to be late. That was probably a little before six. Caitlin didn't answer."

"I've called a couple of times since then," Grace added. "It rolls right into her mailbox."

Detective Godwin adjusted her position in the chair and rubbed her palms over her knees. "Tell me about Caitlin."

"She's a typical fifteen-year-old," Jake offered with a shrug. He stole a glance at his watch.

"She's an honor student," Grace added, annoyed that typical was the best Jake could do. "A good athlete. Well-liked by her classmates. She sings in the school chorus and volunteers with Habitat for Humanity. She earns spending money walking neighborhood dogs."

Carl had been silent until now, sitting glumly at Grace's side. "Caitlin's a great kid," he said with emotion. "I have two of my own about the same age, so I've got a bit of perspective.

The kids get along, in large part I'm embarrassed to admit, because Caitlin makes a real effort. She's friendly and upbeat and goes out of her way to keep things on an even keel."

Their blended family wasn't quite the rosy fantasy Carl made it out to be, but Grace was grateful for his show of support. And he was right that Caitlin was the peacekeeper. In that regard, she was more like Carl than her. Grace sometimes found herself tensing up around Carl's kids, especially Adam. She told herself that was because he was a boy and she'd only had experience raising a daughter, but the truth was that Adam wasn't the easiest person to get along with.

"Where do your kids live?" Detective Godwin asked Carl.

"My ex-wife and I share custody. They're here maybe three days a week."

"Any chance Caitlin might be with them?"

"I've already checked," Carl said.

For anyone who knew the people involved, it was an outlandish question anyway. Mimi would never have allowed it.

The detective rubbed her temple. "I have to ask, what about drugs and sex?"

"Caitlin? No way." This was Jake, finally getting beyond typical.

"I'm sorry," the detective said. "I know these questions are difficult for you."

Not half as difficult as having your daughter disappear, Grace thought.

"Does she have a boyfriend?"

"She was seeing a boy at school," Grace explained. "A senior named Ty Cross. It ended a few weeks ago."

"Who ended it?" the detective asked.

"I think she did, but . . ." Grace recalled the muffled sobs coming from Caitlin's room in the days before the breakup, the hollow look in her daughter's eyes. "I got the feeling it wasn't easy."

"You didn't talk to her about it?" the detective asked.

"I tried but Caitlin wasn't open to discussing it with me." Which had hurt Grace more than she'd let on. She and Caitlin had always been close, something Grace had never had with her own mother.

The detective jotted a few lines in her notebook. "Has your daughter ever run away before?"

"No, and she hasn't run away now," Grace protested. "I know Caitlin. I'm certain that's not what happened."

"How can you be certain?"

Because I know my daughter.

When Caitlin was entering kindergarten, the principal had informed Grace that Caitlin's test scores were so low she was recommending special education classes. Grace insisted that there had to have been a mistake, that Caitlin was more than capable of holding her own in a class of five-year-olds. She'd argued until she was blue in the face. The principal had finally agreed to retest Caitlin, at which time she admitted there'd been an error. Caitlin had been assigned to the gifted program.

Grace felt the same urge to argue now. She knew her daughter better than some self-righteous police detective, but there was no challenge in Rayna Godwin's tone. If anything, the detective seemed pained at having to ask.

So Grace gave serious thought to her question. Was there any chance Caitlin had simply run off?

She'd threatened to run away once, when Grace announced she was marrying Carl. It had been just the two of them for so long—mother and daughter—that any change was bound to be upsetting. But they'd talked it out, roughly and painfully at times, and in the end, Caitlin had written Carl a letter, welcoming him into their family. As it turned out, she was probably closer to Carl than to Jake.

But there'd been nothing out of the ordinary this morning. No gripes or threats or indications of displeasure. Caitlin had downed a glass of orange juice, grabbed a granola bar and her backpack, and with a quick hug, told Grace to have a good weekend.

"As certain as I can be," Grace told the detective.

"How about enemies? Anyone mad at Caitlin, or at any of you? Mr. Whittington, you're an attorney, right?"

"Tax attorney," Jake replied. "And no, I can't think of anyone who'd harm Caitlin to get back at me."

The detective looked at Grace.

"I work part-time at the college. Administrative assistant, which is a fancy word for secretary. Most of the people I deal with don't even know who I am. Carl teaches there, but anyone upset with him would go after his daughter, Lucy, not Caitlin." Grace cringed inwardly, as if by voicing the idea, she was somehow tempting fate to put Lucy in harm's way.

"If anything comes to mind, be sure to let me know." The detective closed her notebook. "I'd like to look in Caitlin's room, if I may."

"What for?" This was Jake, and it wasn't even his house.

"It might help locate your daughter."

Grace wasn't happy about the idea of a stranger pawing through Caitlin's things either, but she understood how it might be necessary. "I'll show you the way."

"It would be helpful if each of you would agree to a polygraph test," the detective said, rising from her seat.

"A lie detector test?" Jake asked, incredulous. "Whatever for?"

"Family is always suspect. We'd like to be able to rule you out right away."

"Oh, brother," Jake said, shaking his head. "It's no wonder you guys can't find the real criminals."

Grace wasn't sure she trusted her legs to hold her, but she got out of her seat and led the detective upstairs to Caitlin's bedroom. They'd bought this house when she and Carl were first married, not because they'd fallen in love with it, as Grace had the small cottage where she and Caitlin had lived after the divorce, but because it was large enough that each of the children could have a bedroom. Caitlin's room was the largest, but Carl's kids had agreed that was only fair since Caitlin lived here full-time while Adam and Lucy spent half their time at their mother's.

Caitlin's room was also the neatest. Whereas Lucy and Adam tossed their clothes, clean and dirty, onto the floor along with their books, binders, and dirty dishes, Caitlin was obsessed with order. She'd bought plastic drawer dividers and bins for her closet, and tucked everything away in its proper place. Her posters were framed rather than simply tacked to the wall, her dresser was topped with an artful array of lacquered jewelry boxes, and the books on her wall unit were arranged by size.

Now, as the detective opened drawers, glanced at the titles on the bookshelf, the awards pinned to the bulletin board on the wall, the carefully made bed with its sage green coverlet and trio of patchwork pillows, Grace felt nothing but the emptiness of the room, as if every nook and cranny cried out for Caitlin's return.

"Does she have an Internet connection in her room?" the detective asked.

Grace nodded. "The whole house is on a wireless network."

"We'll probably want to take the computer, or at least copy the hard drive."

"I don't think you'll find anything."

"You never know."

The innuendo annoyed Grace. She knew her daughter and resented the implication that she didn't. She followed the detective out of the room. At the top of the stairs, she paused.

"What's happened with the Karen Holiday investigation?" Grace asked, her voice little more than a whisper. It had been all over the papers last fall when Karen disappeared but Grace couldn't recall hearing anything in the last few months. "Do you think there's a chance she's still alive?"

"That's our fervent hope." The detective's tone was anything but hopeful.

"Do you have any idea who took her?"

Detective Godwin's expression darkened. "Not yet."

"But you have leads, right?"

"A few."

"And you're following up on them? There's progress being made?"

The detective looked at her feet, then raised her gaze to meet Grace's. "Mrs. Whittington, you need to remember that every case is different. The Karen Holiday investigation has dragged on longer than any of us would like. That doesn't mean we won't find Caitlin."

But it was an ominous sign.

The only real crime the town had seen in five years and the cops had nothing. Grace felt desperation descend on her like heavy, thick smoke. She struggled to fill her lungs with air.

Caitlin was gone. Grace might never see her daughter again. Every parent's worst nightmare, and here it was staring her in the face.

CHAPTER 4

At the station house, Rayna Godwin locked the door to the women's lavatory, leaned back against it, arms clutching her chest, and bit back a sob. She couldn't do this.

Correction, she didn't want to do this.

Not again.

In the five months since Karen Holiday disappeared, not an hour went by that Rayna didn't think about the missing girl and mentally comb through the details of what little they knew about her final hours.

For all the good it did.

Despite her assurances to Grace Whittington, they'd made pathetically little progress in finding Karen. By now, the chances of finding her alive were so slim to be almost nonexistent.

Rayna had been attracted to the job in Paradise Falls precisely because it was the sort of small, safe community where violent crimes were rare. Nestled in the forested hills of northern Oregon at a bend in the river, it was far enough from Portland that the town's character was distinctly its own—an interesting blend of lumbering and agricultural interests overlaid with the cultural crosscurrents of a college environment and the tourists who visited for fishing and boating.

Oh, there were plenty of altercations and burglaries, an occasional sexual assault, and even an armed robbery at the bank the year after she arrived. But the last homicide in town had happened before Rayna's time, when Billy Granger shot the man his wife was having an affair with.

Until Karen Holiday, that is. And Karen wasn't officially a

homicide since they didn't have a body. But Rayna knew it was only a matter of time. One of these days, some hiker or fisherman or high school kid with a hot date and a six-pack would stumble on a jumble of scattered bones and alert the authorities. They'd have their body then, but still no viable suspect.

That's what had been gnawing at Rayna these past few months. She was begrudgingly willing to accept that Karen Holiday had been murdered, but it galled her to know that the person responsible would get away with it.

That wasn't right. And it wasn't why she'd gone into police work when she could have just as easily found a nine-to-five job in a plush office with carpeting. Rayna had taken the job in Paradise Falls because she'd burned out on the urban violence of San Jose and her own personal tragedy, but she hadn't lost her passion for ridding the world of bad guys. Which was part of why her failure to close the Karen Holiday case weighed so heavily.

And now, Caitlin Whittington.

Rayna pulled the girl's photo from her pocket. It was a wallet-sized school photo—the kind that came in a packet containing more copies than most parents knew what to do with. Probably none ever imagined one of those copies coming in handy when their child disappeared.

There was a knock on the door. "Hey, Rayna. You fall in or something?"

Leave it to Hank to overlook the possibility that a lady might actually require some extra time in the bathroom. "I'll be out in a minute."

Hank ignored her and pounded again. "It's important. We got the press on the line."

"Already?"

"They monitor the scanners."

"Who is it?"

"Seth Robbins."

Just what she didn't need. "Tell him I'm not available."

"You want me to tell him you're in the can?"

Jesus, there were times Hank was a little too rough

around the edges. "Forget it. I'll be right there."

Rayna ran the water and splashed it on her face. You can do this, she told her reflection. Focus on the facts. Don't let the rest of it get to you.

But the face that looked back at her wasn't her own. It belonged to Karen Holiday. Caitlin Whittington. And, always, her own daughter, Kimberly.

There was no shortage of girls to grieve for.

Media coverage could be an asset, particularly in missing persons' cases. The more word got out, the better the chances of finding a witness who'd actually seen something important. But Seth Robbins was the last person Rayna felt like talking to right then. He'd led the charge against her with his editorials questioning her competence in the Karen Holiday investigation. And he'd kept it up long after most of the town had moved on to other things.

Still, as she talked to him now on the phone, Rayna was careful to be polite, taking her time to give him as much information as she could about Caitlin Whittington's disappearance.

"You think we've got a serial killer on the loose?" he asked the minute she finished.

She leaned back and the chair squeaked beneath her. Time for another squirt of oil. "Nothing says the two cases are connected."

"The girls went to the same school," he pointed out. "I can't remember the last time we had a teenage girl disappear, and now we've got two. Seems to me like they've got to be connected."

"We'll certainly be looking at the possibility," Rayna conceded. "But we're not jumping to any conclusions."

"It would be nice to get a conclusion of any sort."

"Right." Did he think she liked leaving a case unsolved? The man was so busy stirring up dissension, he didn't stop to think.

When she hung up, she turned to Hank, who'd been on another line with the supervisor of the bus depot. "Anything?"

she asked.

"Nope."

Rayna hadn't expected there would be. Caitlin had been waiting at school shortly after five-thirty, expecting her dad to pick her up. It didn't make sense that she'd have suddenly decided to take off by bus. And if someone took her, well, he wasn't likely to hightail it out of town on public transportation.

"See what you can dig up on the parents," she told Hank. "The mom and stepdad were out of town, so I'm hard pressed to see how they'd be involved. But it's a divorce and remarriage situation—always sticky—and anything is possible. I'd like to get a better feel for the girl's relationship with each of them."

"Okay."

"And alert the bank. We want to know if there's any activity on her ATM card."

"Will do." Hank's long, angular frame was hunched over his desk. When she'd first met him, Rayna assumed his gawky awkwardness was an act, but she'd since decided he simply had more bone than he knew what to do with. And while the country bumpkin side of him irritated her at times, it amused her at others. Bottom line was that she couldn't think of many people she'd rather work with.

"I'm heading over to the school," she said.

"It's nighttime."

"I know."

"Won't be anyone there."

"I want to look around anyway. See if just maybe there's something that will point us in the right direction."

"You want me to come along?"

"No. Finish up your calls, then go home and get some sleep. We've got a busy weekend ahead of us."

Rayna scanned Caitlin's photograph into the computer and sent it to Seth Robbins at the newspaper. She called the television and radio news stations in Portland and the surrounding towns, and repeated the information she'd given Seth. She sent them all copies of the photo, as well. Then she drove out to the school.

The Paradise Falls high school and junior high operated independently, but they shared a campus, much to the dismay of many junior high parents who considered the older students a bad influence.

Located about half a mile inland from the eastern bank of the river, the high school was a sprawling, single-story facility with open hallways and patios. A large parking lot faced the street. The athletic facilities and sports fields were to one side and the rear. Rayna had spent weeks on campus following Karen Holiday's disappearance, meeting with students and teachers, hoping against hope she'd learn something that would help them find Karen.

Now, as she got out of the car and pulled her jacket tight against the cold March wind, she felt her earlier failure like a weight on her shoulders.

The parking lot and hallways were well-lit—for safety reasons and to deter vandalism. Rayna walked around the area at the front of the school where students waited to be picked up at the end of the school day. She noted the usual litter, but nothing that struck her as telling. She wandered the hallways, as well. A group of students drifted toward her from the direction of the auditorium.

"You're all here late on a Friday night," she said, both a friendly greeting and an unspoken question.

"Rehearsal," said one of the boys. "And we've got to be back again first thing tomorrow morning."

As if on cue, they all groaned in unison, but none of them seemed particularly unhappy about the prospect.

Rayna asked about Caitlin. Only a couple of the kids actually knew her and neither of them had seen her that afternoon. Nor had they noticed anyone suspicious around the campus.

Rayna made a sweep of the other block of hallways, where she found Truman, the after-hours custodian, sitting on the edge of his cart enjoying a cigarette. When he saw Rayna, he jumped to his feet and ground the cigarette out under his heel.

Rayna eyed the edge of the butt near his shoe.

"Busted," he said, with a toothless grin. "I promise I won't do it again, okay?"

"Just not on school grounds. You know the rule." And as far as Rayna could tell, he made a habit of ignoring it.

He nodded. "Yes, ma'am."

"Were you by any chance here this evening around five or six?"

"Yeah." Truman sounded cautious. "I woulda been here then."

Rayna showed him Caitlin's picture, asked if he'd seen her.

He shook his head. "I've seen her around, but not today."

"Did you see any strangers on campus? Anything suspicious?"

"No ma'am, I sure didn't."

"Keep an eye out, okay?"

"Sure thing." He shook his head, weary with the weight of the world. "Another one missing," he said with a low whistle. "That ain't good."

It was well after midnight when Rayna crawled into bed. She was exhausted but keyed up at the same time. She knew sleep would be a long time coming.

Karen Holiday. Caitlin Whittington. Were the two disappearances related? The girls attended the same school, but were two grades apart. According to Caitlin's parents, they hadn't known one another. But that didn't rule out the possibility that their paths had crossed at school.

Karen had disappeared in October, Caitlin in March. The girls shared a youthful energy, but aside from that they were nothing alike. At least on first impression. Caitlin's coloring was dark, Karen's fair. Caitlin was an honor student while Karen ran with a crowd that liked to party. Drugs, sex, and rock and roll. Not that any of them were really bad kids.

Karen had disappeared on her way home from a friend's house in the middle of a late night storm. Her car was found broken down by the side of the road. Caitlin had last been seen at school in the early evening. Still, the parallels were strong enough to grip Rayna's heart like a vise. Had her failure to apprehend Karen's killer led to his taking a second girl?

And if she didn't find him soon, how many others would there be?

CHAPTER 5

Grace was cold. Freezing, even under the heavy down comforter. She scooted closer to Carl and pressed her back against the cocoon of his warmth. Without waking, he draped an arm loosely across her middle, and Grace hugged it around her like a cloak.

Carl hadn't complained at all about their spoiled weekend plans. He was shocked and maybe a little hurt that it had even crossed Grace's mind.

"Good God," he'd told her. "Caitlin's my stepdaughter. How could I be anything but worried about her? She's part of my family. You and Caitlin, along with Adam and Lucy."

He'd tried to comfort Grace, too, but she could tell he didn't buy into his reassuring platitudes any more than she did. She saw the distress in his face, and knew it bothered him that there was nothing he could do to make things right.

Carl was a fixer. If there was a problem, he looked for a solution. When there were no solutions, he sought a patch. Tonight, he'd been able to offer neither. After the others had gone, he'd spread his hands bleakly, then held Grace tight and cried with her. Even if he couldn't magically bring Caitlin home, Grace took solace in knowing he was there, sharing her pain.

She knew that Jake was worried, too. It was just that he was, by nature, so self-absorbed he was incapable of reaching out. Instead of fixing things, he fixed on himself. But he had to be feeling the same desperation and dread Grace felt.

When Caitlin was born, Jake was too busy studying for law school exams to take off more than the day of delivery—and even then, he'd left the hospital once Caitlin had been pronounced healthy. But Grace had woken many a time in the following months to find him standing silently by Caitlin's crib, smoothing the dark fuzz on her head and singing to her softly. While he hadn't been as involved in Caitlin's life over the years as Grace—and Caitlin, although she wouldn't admit it—would have liked, Grace never doubted he genuinely loved his daughter. She hoped Starr had some inkling of what he was going through right now.

Beside her, Carl rolled onto his back and began the ragged, uneven breathing that would soon erupt into full-blown snoring. Grace eased herself out of the bed. She slipped into her robe and padded down the hall to Caitlin's room, where she pulled back the covers and slid between the sheets, breathing in the scent of Caitlin's apricot shampoo.

Grace's heart felt so heavy she thought she would die under the weight. A part of her welcomed the prospect. Death would put an end to her pain. She couldn't imagine going on, day after day, stumbling through the bleak fog of despair. The small sliver of hope that Caitlin might be returned to them was all Grace had to hold on to.

She was still awake an hour later when Carl looked in on her with a cup of herbal tea. "I thought you might be able to use this," he said softly.

He'd pulled on his boxers and the ratty old sweatshirt that served as a robe substitute on cold nights. His hair stood in tufts on the left side of his head where it had been pressed against the pillow.

Grace sat up and held the steaming mug in both hands. "Thank you." The warm liquid soothed her throat and eased some of the tension from her body.

"Did you sleep at all?" Carl asked.

"Not really."

He sat on the bed next to her and began rubbing her neck and shoulders.

Grace closed her eyes. "I keep wondering where she is right now. Is she alive? Hurt? Cold? Scared? And if she isn't alive—"

"Don't go there, Grace. It doesn't help."

"And if she isn't still alive," Grace continued stubbornly, "what were the last moments like for her? She must have felt so alone. So terrified."

"Don't torture yourself like this. There's nothing to be gained."

Grace shook her head. "I can't help it. I can't not think about her."

"No, I guess not. I just wish—"

She put a finger against his lips. "I know."

"I put myself in your shoes. If it was Lucy—"

"There's nothing either of us can do right now except wait and pray." Grace didn't believe in a God who answered personal prayers. There was way too much turmoil and tragedy on this earth for that. Nonetheless, she'd been pleading with God all night for Caitlin's safe return.

Carl kissed her hand. "I wish I could bear this burden for both of us. I'd do anything to make it easier on you."

Even if it meant Lucy was missing rather than Caitlin? Grace doubted Carl's love, genuine as it was, went that far.

Over coffee the next morning—neither of them had the stomach for food—Carl looked at her sheepishly and said he thought he should spend time with his kids.

"I hate leaving you alone," he explained. "Even for a short while. But Adam and Lucy need me, too. They were pretty upset last night when I told them what had happened."

Grace nodded. Though part of her resisted, she understood. Carl's kids had been part of Grace's life for three years now, part of her household for over two. There were rough edges to being a stepparent, but there were soft spots as well. She knew they must be reeling from the news of Caitlin's disappearance, and despite her own pain, her heart went out to them.

"Should I come along?" she asked, mostly because it seemed the right thing to offer.

Carl's face softened. "I'd love it. But only if you want to."

The local paper had run the story about Caitlin's disappearance on the front page, along with speculation about a predator in Paradise Falls preying on teenage girls. Grace knew that friends, curious acquaintances, and reporters would be calling the house throughout the day. She'd already talked to her closest friend, Sandy, who was organizing volunteers. The phone call, and the shared tears, had been therapeutic for Grace. But the others would be a burden, more than she could face right then.

"I do want to," Grace said. "I think it would be good for all of us to be together."

Carl finished the last of his coffee and rinsed the cup. "I'll call over there in a bit and see what their plans are. I don't want to wake them."

Grace felt a lump form in her throat. While Adam and Lucy were comfortably ensconced in dreamland, Caitlin was. . . where? Not comfortable and not safe. Possibly not even alive.

"We might as well get that polygraph out of the way, anyway," Carl said. "Having us take the test doesn't make much sense, but I guess I can understand why the cops think it's necessary."

"Why don't you call the station and see if they can fit us in this morning." At least then Grace would be doing something about her daughter's disappearance.

Detective Godwin was out, presumably doing what it took to find Caitlin, but she'd made arrangements for the polygraph test. Grace went first, while Carl waited in the tiny reception area of the police station. A uniformed cop opened the wide door next to dispatch and led Grace to a room at the end of a short hallway. It was a small room, but not unpleasant, furnished with three straight-back chairs and a table. Inside, a heavyset, balding man was fiddling with a machine that reminded Grace of the EKG machine that had monitored her mother in the days following her heart attack.

"I'm Sergeant Moran." He gestured to a chair next to the machine. "Have a seat." When she'd settled in, he strapped a cuff to her arm.

"You comfortable?" he asked. His tone was pleasant without being especially warm.

Grace nodded.

"I'd like you to answer my questions verbally, please."

"That was a test question?" When he didn't respond, Grace said, "Yes, I'm comfortable."

"Tell me your full name."

"Grace Ann Whittington."

"How do you feel about being here today?"

How did she feel? Like she'd been skinned alive. "My daughter is missing," she said. "I'm worried sick."

"When did you last speak with her?"

"Yesterday." Grace cleared her throat. "Yesterday morning."

"Are you married?"

"Yes." The questions continued. Ask. Answer. It wasn't so bad, Grace thought. They couldn't possibly suspect her anyway. The test was just a formality.

"Have you ever lied to get out of trouble?" Moran asked.

The question threw her. Grace couldn't actually come up with an occasion when she had, but she must have, right? Didn't everybody lie at some point in their lives? And what did he mean to get out of trouble? It had to be a trick question.

She hesitated, then mumbled, "No."

The examiner didn't blink. Maybe no was the correct answer.

"Are the lights on in this room?" he asked.

"What?" Was this another trick question? Grace felt herself begin to sweat. "Yes, they are," she replied.

"What kind of relationship do you have with your daughter?"

That caught her by surprise. It was the first question that struck Grace as being relevant, and there was no simple answer. "Overall, we get along very well. But she's a teenager. There are times I have to say no. Times when she's angry at me or I'm angry at her." Grace swallowed. "She's the most precious thing in this world to me. I think . . . I hope, she knows that."

"Is she open with you?" Moran asked, his eyes on the wiggles of the readout rather than Grace.

"Open?"

"Does she talk to you about her feelings? About what's going on in her world?"

"Yes." Grace saw the arm of the machine jump. Had they caught her in a lie? "Usually," Grace qualified. "But, like I said, she's a teenager. She wants her privacy."

In fact, Caitlin had grown less open in the last couple of years. Since Grace's remarriage. That was what happened as kids got older, wasn't it? It wasn't something that made Grace happy, but her friends told her it was normal.

"Do you ever wish she hadn't been born?"

"My God, no." Grace felt as if the wind had been knocked from her. "Never."

Moran took a moment to adjust the roll of paper in the machine. "What's her relationship like with her father?"

"Decent. He lives about fifty minutes away so he only sees her on occasional weekends."

"And her stepfather, your current husband?"

"They get along very well. In many ways, she's more like Carl than either Jake or me."

Moran gave her an encouraging smile. "We're almost finished here."

"Okay." Grace was beginning to feel pressure in her bladder. She needed to use the restroom. She probably needed a shower as well. Her underarms and chest were clammy with perspiration.

"What was your daughter wearing the day she disappeared?"

To her horror, Grace realized she didn't know. But admitting that sounded wrong, like she wasn't a very good mother. "Jeans," she said, nodding her head to affirm what was only her best guess. Caitlin often wore jeans, so it wasn't a complete stab in the dark. "I think she was wearing Jeans. And a T-shirt. Also, her red parka." Caitlin had been wearing the parka as she left the house, Grace was sure of that.

"Did you have anything to do with your daughter's disappearance?"

"No," Grace said emphatically. At last, a question that

was as clear-cut as it appeared. "Absolutely not."

Lucy and Adam arrived half an hour after Grace and Carl returned home. Grace was watching from the front window as Adam pulled the car into the driveway. Both kids had house keys, yet they hesitated at the front door, and she realized they were unsure of expectations now that they were on uncharted territory. Caitlin was missing and they had no idea what that meant for the family.

Grace saved them the awkwardness by greeting them at the door. "I saw you drive up."

Adam held back, looking at his feet. He was a gangly kid, not unlike his dad. Only Carl's body had filled in and softened with age, whereas Adam was all angles. He tugged at the baggy cargo pants and fidgeted before raising his gaze to meet hers.

Lucy hesitated only for a moment, then flew into Grace's arms. "You must feel so terrible," Lucy wailed, and started to cry.

She was a bit on the chubby side, soft and cuddly like a downy puppy. Her body molded into the arc of Grace's arms, and Grace felt the grip of her own panic recede, if only for a moment.

CHAPTER 6

Detective Rayna Godwin set the brake and turned off the car's engine. She pressed a palm to her forehead where she felt pressure building.

She was tired. She hadn't slept well, her mind racing with worry about Caitlin Whittington's disappearance and her own culpability in failing to find the monster who'd taken Karen Holiday. If he'd struck again . . .

The prospect made Rayna's stomach turn. She closed her eyes to stop the thoughts.

Blaming herself wasn't going to do any good. There was no saying the cases were even related. Caitlin Whittington was her focus right now. Find the girl, assuming she was still alive. Track down her killer if she wasn't.

Either way, the answer was lodged somewhere in Caitlin's life—friends, family, and associates —or at the juncture where her life intersected Karen Holiday's. Two very different scenarios, but in terms of investigational ground, there was a lot of overlap. It meant Rayna would need to be vigilant about keeping an open mind.

The dull pressure in Rayna's skull was turning into a full-blown headache. She reached into the glove compartment for the Motrin and popped two with the dregs of yesterday's bottled water.

Too bad today was Saturday. It was much easier to talk to kids on campus, even under the watchful eyes of the school administration, than to track them down at home. Half the time when she showed up at a kid's house, the parents went ballistic. Cooperation was a rare thing. Too many cop and lawyer shows on television. Or maybe parents didn't really trust what they knew about their children. But Rayna couldn't afford to wait until Monday. She ran her fingers through the feathery wisps that had curled so nicely at the hairdresser's but never since, then climbed out of her car and headed up the walkway to the Cross residence.

She didn't recall interviewing Ty Cross during the Karen Holiday investigation, and doubted she'd be able to pick him out of a crowd, but she knew the name. Ty was captain of the school's winning football team as well as an ace hitter for the less successful baseball team. He was one of those kids whose name everyone knew, even if they'd never met the boy. Rayna had heard his name bantered around the station, too, but again it had been third-hand. Ty had been picked up once for reckless driving, and while there was some talk of open beer cans having been tossed from the car before it was pulled over, Ty's reputation as a local sports hero, along with pressure from his politically connected father, had led to charges being dismissed. Rayna recalled several other incidents as well, but none had been serious enough to warrant a detective's involvement.

The Cross home was in one of the better neighborhoods of Paradise Falls. It stood on a small knoll with a view of the raging river in the distance. A sprawling single-story house with an abundance of brick work and carefully manicured landscaping. Rayna faced the carved, double-entry door and rang the bell.

The woman who answered wore gray wool slacks and what Rayna guessed was a cashmere sweater. The sort of outfit Rayna might wear for a special luncheon date but certainly not around the house on a Saturday morning. Not if she had any hopes of saving the outfit from a trip to the cleaners.

"Mrs. Cross?"

"Yes."

"I'm Detective Godwin of the Paradise Falls Police Department." Rayna flashed her ID. "I'd like to speak to Ty."

"Is something wrong?" Mrs. Cross's mouth twitched but her face remained expressionless.

Botox or too much Valium? "I don't know if you've

heard," Rayna said. "Caitlin Whittington is missing."

"Yes, it was in this morning's paper. Has there been a new development?"

"No, nothing yet."

A man appeared from somewhere inside and stepped in front of Mrs. Cross. "George," she said, addressing him, "this is Detective Godwin. She's looking for Ty."

"He's not home." George Cross had a broad forehead and strong chin. His tone was curt.

"Where might I find him?" Rayna asked.

"What do you want with him?"

"It's about Caitlin Whittington."

"That's over. He knows nothing about her being missing." Cross stepped back as if preparing to shut the door.

"Did he tell you that?"

"He didn't have to tell me. I know my son."

"I'd like to ask him myself."

"Ty's upset enough already. Maybe he and Caitlin weren't together anymore, but he dated her for six months." Cross softened some. "This is hard on him."

"I understand that. I'm hoping he can give me some insights."

"Insights?"

"About her routines and habits and the like."

Cross scoffed. "What good's that going to do? There's a madman out there targeting young girls. Shouldn't you be looking for witnesses or something?"

"We're doing that, too."

"I'll have Ty call you if he thinks he can be of help." This time the door closed.

Rayna sighed. Monday seemed a long time to wait.

She had better luck with Traci Redding's mother, maybe because she was acquainted with Mrs. Redding from the Karen Holiday case. The woman had been one of the parents involved in setting up a reward fund. The reward offer was still outstanding—ten thousand dollars. It had elicited pitifully few calls, and no useful information.

"I've heard about Caitlin," Mrs. Redding said without asking why Rayna was there. "It's just so terrible. How can this be happening in our quiet little town?"

"That's a question we're all asking," Rayna told her.

"Do you think it's like what happened to Karen? The same person, I mean."

"It's too early to say. Do you know Caitlin?"

"Not really. I know she's a friend of Traci's—only for the last couple of months, though. I've never exchanged more than a 'Hi, how are you?' with Caitlin."

"Is Traci in?"

"No, she's helping post flyers around town. Isn't the police department organizing some sort of search or something?"

Rayna nodded. "We didn't actually organize it, but we're coordinating the effort." Hank was there now, in fact. "Are other students volunteering, as well?"

"I think so. There was quite a bit of phoning back and forth."

Better even than trying to interview kids at the school. And Rayna wouldn't have to wait until Monday. "Does Traci have a cell phone? Maybe I can catch her there."

"Cell phones and iPods." Mrs. Redding rolled her eyes. "How did we ever grow up without them? Let me write down her number for you."

Traci and another girl were waiting for Rayna in front of the Starbucks on Grant Street. Despite the overcast sky and brisk winds, both girls were dressed in low-rise blue jeans with pullovers short enough to leave their midriffs bare. Rayna tugged at the back of her jacket, grateful that her own blouse was long enough to tuck solidly into her waistband. The mere thought of chilly air on the exposed skin around her middle sent shivers down her spine.

"This is Jenna," Traci said, introducing her friend. "She hangs around with Caitlin, too."

"Hi," Jenna said, extending a hand for Rayna to shake. Like Traci, she had a slender build and straight, shoulder-length hair.

"You want to go inside?" Rayna asked. "I'll treat." She noticed there were already two MISSING PERSON posters for Caitlin posted in the store's windows, one on each side of the door.

The girls exchanged shrugs. "Sure."

With their beverages in hand—black coffee for Rayna, mochas for both girls—they found a table in the corner.

"This is just too creepy," Traci said. "I saw her as I was leaving school yesterday. She was standing on the oval, waiting for a ride, I guess. We waved and I told her about my algebra test. Everything seemed perfectly normal, you know. Then I get this call last night from her mom. Totally blew me out of the water."

"Was Caitlin alone when you saw her?"

"Yeah. I mean, a few other kids were around, but she wasn't with any of them."

"You remember any names?"

Rayna wrote them down as Traci rattled off the ones she remembered. "Her dad was late picking her up," Rayna told them. "Do you think she'd have taken a ride with someone?"

"Not a stranger. Not after Karen."

"We're all real careful," Jenna added. "Even though Karen was, well, you know."

Not exactly upright and responsible. Karen might have taken a ride with a stranger, in other words. She might have done a lot of dumb stuff. Like generations of kids before her who didn't follow the straight and narrow. But very few came to serious harm.

"But if it was someone Caitlin knew who offered, sure."

"Any idea who might have offered her a ride?"

The girls looked at one another and shrugged. "Not really," Traci said.

"Tell me about Caitlin and Ty Cross."

Jenna tucked her silken, ash-blond hair behind her ear and sighed. "Ty is totally cool. I wish he'd ask me out."

This was an angle Rayna hadn't yet considered. A girl who saw Caitlin as competition? It was worth considering, although she couldn't detect any resentment in Jenna's voice.

"I understand they broke up recently," Rayna said. "Whose idea was it?"

Traci thought a moment. "Hers, I think. She didn't talk about it much."

"She was upset, though," Jenna added. "I figured they must have had a fight or something."

"Any idea what about?"

Traci sipped her mocha, wiped her mouth with the back of her hand. "Who knows. Maybe Ty was getting too demanding. I mean he is cool"—she looked at Jenna—"but he's also a bit sold on himself."

Jenna smirked. "It's not like he doesn't have reason."

"Oh, please. It's all packaging."

"Yeah." Jenna drew the word out with a giggle.

"Was Caitlin seeing any other guys?" Rayna asked.

They shook their heads. "Not like in dating," Jenna clarified. "But I saw her and Rob together a couple of times. Once Caitlin was crying."

"Rob?"

"Hardy. He's sort of a friend of Ty's. I'm pretty sure she wasn't interested in him. Not like a boyfriend. He's definitely not cool."

"But there might have been someone," Traci said. "I got the feeling he might be a bit older. Not a high school student."

Rayna's pulse quickened. "Do you know a name?"

Traci shook her head. "I could be wrong, too. It wasn't anything she said, really, just a feeling I got."

Jenna finished her mocha. "I'll be right back. I gotta pee."

"Sounds like Jenna has a crush on Ty," Rayna said to Traci when the other girl was out of earshot.

Traci laughed. "That's just Jenna. She likes guys, period."

"Any chance Caitlin ran away?"

"I don't think so."

"Or met up with this guy she had her eye on?"

Traci licked foam from her lips and thought about the question. Then she shook her head. "That's not like Caitlin. She's real grounded, sometimes too much so for her own good, in my opinion. Besides, she wouldn't have some mystery guy pick her up at school when she was waiting for her dad."

Rayna nodded. The timing was the biggest argument against Caitlin having gone anywhere voluntarily. "How did she get along with her mom and stepdad?"

"I didn't know her before they were married. We just became friends this year. But she seemed fine with them."

"And her stepdad's kids?"

"Pretty good. Me, I'd be a little weirded out about suddenly sharing my life with strangers, but I never heard her complain. I mean, sometimes about little things. Like how Lucy would borrow something without asking, or Adam would clomp around making popcorn in the middle of the night and wake her up. Stuff like that."

Jenna returned and Traci grabbed their stack of flyers. "We'd better get the rest of these distributed. Thanks for the mocha."

"I appreciate you taking the time to talk with me. If you think of anything more, give me a call." They headed for the door. Rayna glanced at the flyers. "Is Ty Cross part of the volunteer effort?"

"I saw him earlier," Traci said. "In the park where we gathered. I think he's part of the search thing."

"Thanks." Rayna watched the girls head into the pet food store next door and tried not to think about Kimberly. Her daughter, Kimberly, would be almost the same age as these girls, if she'd lived. A familiar tightness in Rayna's throat made it difficult to swallow. Four years, and it seemed like only yesterday.

"You sure you don't want one?" Hank asked Rayna through a mouthful of chili dog. "It's really good."

A steamed hotdog from a park vendor, even doused in chili, wasn't Rayna's idea of good. If she was going to consume calories, she wanted them to be for something worthwhile.

"I'm sure," she replied. She watched two boys kicking a soccer ball back and forth. "How's the volunteer effort going?"

Hank swallowed. "I don't think they'll turn up anything, if

that's what you mean. But people like to feel they're doing something useful. And you never know. There's a lot of open ground to cover in this town and the surrounding area. I just hope to God if they do find something, they don't contaminate the scene."

"You warned them about that?"

"Hit them over the head with it. And they all watch TV. They ought to know, right? Besides, we've got the uniformed guys out there with them."

Trouble was, even the professionals sometimes messed up.

Hank wiped a spot of chili from the corner of his mouth. "You got a theory yet?"

"I wouldn't call it a theory."

"So what are you thinking?"

"First, it doesn't feel like a runaway. Or a suicide, for that matter. Which means she was abducted, probably by someone she knew. I think she's smart enough not to voluntarily go with a stranger."

"Unless he was posing as someone she thought she could trust," Hank pointed out.

"Like a cop?" They'd had an episode last year. A man pretending to be a sheriff's deputy pulled over cars at night and robbed the occupants.

Hank nodded.

"That would have to mean our guy not only knew Caitlin's dad was picking her up that afternoon but that he was going to be late." Rayna worked the setup through as she spoke. "The guy shows up and says there's been an accident or something, and he's going to take her to the hospital. I don't know, it's a bit of a stretch."

"Okay, so it's not the number one theory. But you did a nice job putting it together like that." Hank ran a hand over the bristles of his receding hairline and gave her a crooked smile. "What do you have on the family?"

"The mom and stepfather passed the polygraph. Plus, they were out of town when she disappeared."

"What about the bio dad?"

"He hasn't come in for the test. I'm guessing he might be feeling responsible since he was the one who was supposed to get Caitlin."

"He and the wife only got married because she was pregnant. It didn't last—just long enough for her to help put him through law school. He's not happy about paying child support, either."

Rayna looked at him. "Is this another of your far-fetched theories? Where do you come up with this stuff, anyway?"

Hank grinned. "It's amazing the things you learn bowling and playing pool at the local bars."

Hank had an entire network of bar buddies, all local working men. He claimed it was a good way to pick up useful gossip—and in truth, he did sometimes come up with good stuff, like the name of a drug dealer they'd been trying to track down for months—but Rayna suspected it was Hank's social network, as well. When his wife of thirty years died a few years back, he'd wandered around like an abandoned puppy until he'd discovered there was an entire fraternity of lonely men out there.

"Okay, so we'll put Jake Whittington on our list of possibilities. Also, Caitlin's boyfriend. I'd like to speak to him without his dad's interference. I think he may be part of your search team."

"Could be. Couple of boys about that age took the woods east of town. You might see if he's there." Hank tossed the hot dog wrapper in the trash. "You missed out on a great lunch, Rayna."

She laughed and shook her head. Hank was a good partner and a decent man but they were as different as night and day.

CHAPTER 7

Rayna arrived at the staging area near the woods just as the volunteer search team was finishing. Seven people, including three high school boys, were milling around the patrol officer assigned to the group. Rayna singled out the tall, sandy-haired boy she guessed was Ty Cross, and approached him when he stepped away from the others.

"What's to talk about?" he said irritably after Rayna explained why she was there. "I don't know where Caitlin is. You think I'd be out searching for her if I knew?"

Rayna flashed on Scott Peterson and the multitude of other convicted killers who'd done just that. Not that she was lumping Ty together with any of them. Way too early to jump to conclusions.

"I'm trying to learn about Caitlin," she told him. "You know her. I don't. You know her in ways that even her parents don't. I need some help and thought you might be able to give it to me."

Ty picked up a stone and tossed it across the open field. He had a good arm. Years of baseball and football practice. Or maybe it was the years of throwing stones that had primed him for sports.

"What if she's being held prisoner?" Rayna prodded. "What if she is being mistreated or abused? Don't you want to help her if you can?"

Ty turned back and met her eyes. "You think that's what's going on?"

"It's possible. The only thing I'm sure about is that time is working against us."

He hesitated. "I should probably check with my dad first."

Rayna feigned astonishment. "Whatever for? I just want to have a conversation, Ty. I'm not going to handcuff you, or lock you in an airless interrogation room with a blinding white light aimed at your face." She chuckled. "That's for the movies."

He seemed to soften some.

"You're free to leave any time. What are you afraid of?"

His eyes flashed. "I'm not afraid."

"Good then. Let's talk." She started walking toward the car.

"Can't we talk here?"

"If you want. I thought you might feel more comfortable someplace where your friends wouldn't be bending their ears to hear what we were saying. You can leave the door open if it makes you feel better. Or maybe you'd rather meet me downtown."

"I don't have my car with me. I got a ride with friends." He looked at the small cluster of searchers, then back to her. "I was going to bum a ride over to the discount mart after we were finished here."

"I'll take you." The discount mart was only a couple of miles up the road and she'd have Ty all to herself for the short drive.

He shrugged. "Yeah, okay, I guess."

Ty rejoined his friends for a few minutes, then wandered to the car where Rayna waited. She leaned across the seat and opened the passenger door. "Sit in front," she said. "This is a friendly conversation."

He crawled in, his broad shoulders and long legs filling the space beside her. "Is that a computer?" he said, pointing to the display attached to the dash between them. Rayna could tell he was nervous, or at least ill-at-ease.

"Yep. We're part of the twenty-first century here." She pulled away onto the main road. "What's at the discount mart?"

"I gotta get my grandmother a birthday present."

"What are you going to get her?"

"I dunno. They got all this bath powder and cologne and stuff. It's what I get her every year."

Rayna thought of her own mother, Kimberly's grandmother, active and fit at seventy-three. "Do you like your grandmother?"

"Yeah. She's sweet." He smiled and Rayna was reminded that Ty was still in many ways just a kid. "The nicest person in my whole family."

"Why don't you get her something different this year then? Something more . . . individual."

"Like what?"

"What are her interests?"

"She likes to knit. And garden. She wins prizes for her roses. And she loves watching movies."

"There you go." Rayna fought the urge to suggest he write a personal note on the card. Maybe she was underestimating him.

Ty settled back in his seat.

"Is there anything unusual going on in Caitlin's life that you're aware of? Anyone bugging her? Mad at her? Acting in any way threatening?"

He shook his head.

"Did she seem worried or troubled?"

Ty stared out the window. "I wouldn't know. We broke up a couple of weeks ago."

"Do you mind if I ask why?"

He shrugged. "It was her call."

"But you must have some idea." There was a long stretch of silence. "Was it about sex?"

Ty looked at her sharply. "What kind of question is that!"

"Am I embarrassing you? I don't mean to. I'm just trying to get to the bottom of what happened." Rayna paused. "Were you pressuring her? Was that the problem? I'm not here to judge. It's pretty typical, if that's what happened."

"She wanted it," Ty mumbled.

Rayna held her breath, half expecting a confession. Sex that got out of hand? Some variation of date rape? They struggled and he choked her without really intending to?

"I thought she was different," he said at last.

Had Ty assumed she was willing, then become threatening when it turned out he was wrong? Rayna nodded encouragement.

"Most girls, that's all they're interested in. Then they run to their friends and brag about their conquests."

"Most girls want sex?" Boy, had she had that one backwards.

"Well, a lot of them. There's even this sort of contest at school. The girls, some of them anyway, they compete with one another. Sort of like bingo, I guess. Or a scavenger hunt. They see who can fill in all the squares first."

Rayna refreshed the image in her mind, putting thoughts of date rape aside for the moment. "The squares stand for guys they've slept with?"

"That and, you know, other stuff."

"I should think that would be just fine with guys."

He laughed. "It gets old."

"And Caitlin was playing this game, is that it?"

Suddenly Ty's mood shifted. "I don't know. Maybe she just wanted sex."

"And you didn't?" Rayna was having trouble finding the story believable. But maybe she was simply out of touch with this generation. Kimberly's generation, she thought sadly. If her daughter was alive, would she be scoring points for sex and lording it over her friends? Rayna couldn't reconcile the image with that of the rosy-cheeked eleven-year-old who was forever etched in her mind.

"Is that why she broke up with you?" Rayna asked.

Ty crossed his arms over his chest and looked out the side window. "I don't want to talk about this anymore."

"What about Karen Holiday? Did she play the game?"

"I said, I don't want to talk about it."

"Okay." Rayna backed off. "No more sex. Tell me about Caitlin."

He shrugged. "She was fun to be around. Smart. Interested in things besides the latest color of nail polish."

They were nearing the discount mart and Rayna slowed, stretching out the minutes. "Was Caitlin friends with other guys?"

"No one special."

"I heard something about her and Rob Hardy."

Ty's eyes widened. "What did you hear?"

"Rob's a friend of yours, isn't he?"

"Not really. We went to preschool together. Our moms have known each other for a long time. I don't hang with him much, but sometimes, you know, our families rent a ski condo together or something."

Rayna slowed as the stoplight turned yellow, again milking the travel time for all she could get. "When was the last time you saw Caitlin?"

"Friday. After school. I saw her at volleyball practice."

"Did you talk to her?"

"No. She was playing. I was just passing by the gym."

"But you have talked since you broke up."

"Not really." Ty's hands twisted in his lap.

"You never tried to get back together again? Never asked her reasons for breaking up?"

He gave an exasperated sigh. "We dated. It was no big deal."

Rayna pulled into the mart's parking lot. She hadn't fully stopped the car when Ty opened the door. "Thanks for the ride."

Before she could respond, he was bounding across the pavement toward the store entrance.

At the station later that afternoon, Rayna was writing up a report when Chief Stoval leaned into the alcove that was home to the detectives. "How's the investigation going?"

"It's coming along." If he wanted particulars, she knew he'd ask for them. It wasn't his style to get involved in the details of a case.

"I've got something you're not going to like," he told her.

Rayna's heart stopped. "Caitlin's body has been found?"

He shook his head. "The FBI's getting involved."

She pushed back her chair to face him directly. "You're shitting me."

"Such language. From a woman, no less."

"Who invited them?" Rayna shot back. "We don't need them. This investigation has just begun."

Stoval looked uncomfortable. "We've still got Karen Holiday. It's been five months."

"But the two cases might not even be related. The Feebs can't just come waltzing in on their own. We have to ask for their help."

"I know." He looked at his fingernails, then back to her. "I made the call."

"You?" Rayna couldn't believe it. Stoval wasn't a hands-on kind of guy. He was great at smiling for cameras and dealing with the press. And at smoothing ruffled feathers in the community. He was good at what he did and he knew enough to leave the field work to others.

"The mayor asked me to. Phone lines have been jammed all morning with concern about serial killers and madmen in Paradise Falls. Seems the general feeling is that we didn't do enough to catch Karen's killer and now he's struck again."

"Seth Robbins. He's been stirring things up, I bet."

"I'm sure that's part of it. But there's real worry in the community, too. You and I both know bringing in the FBI probably isn't going to make a difference, but perception is important. We want to look like we're on top of it."

"We are on top of it." Rayna fought to control her anger. The mayor was openly wooing voters for a potential congressional bid and rumor had it that Stoval was interested in stepping into the mayor's slot. The appearance of doing something was important to both of them but it didn't help Rayna.

"How about stalling them for another week or so?" she asked.

Stoval shook his head. "It's already arranged."

CHAPTER 8

Grace knew media coverage was helpful when a child was missing, but she'd been ripped so raw by Caitlin's disappearance she hadn't been able to muster what it took to be part of the effort. Until today. It remained a struggle, but one Grace felt she needed to make, even though Jake had already been talking to the press. She'd seen him interviewed on the Portland news last evening.

Now, in less than forty minutes, it would be her turn. Already media vans and unfamiliar cars were jockeying for position in front of the house, although not as many of them as Grace had imagined. And from what she could tell, they were all local. Grace experienced an unexpected pang of disappointment. Had she really expected there to be broader interest? Her own world had been turned on its head, but one more missing teen in a land where children were abducted with alarming regularity wasn't likely to capture national attention. She felt certain Caitlin's disappearance wouldn't even have gotten the attention it had if Karen Holiday hadn't disappeared first. Serial killer was now a household word in town.

Carl came into the bedroom where Grace was standing in front of her open closet trying to decide what to wear.

"You're sure you're up to this?" he asked her.

"It's something I have to do. The more we can keep Caitlin in the headlines, the better the chances she'll be found. Maybe the publicity will even frighten whoever took her into letting her go."

Carl nodded but his expression was strained. Grace knew he walked a fine line between giving into his own sadness and remaining upbeat for her benefit. And she could read in his eyes how unlikely he found it that Caitlin's kidnapper would simply let her go.

"I'll be there beside you." He placed his hands on her bare arms. "We'll do it together."

When Carl had gone back downstairs, Grace sat on the edge of the bed. The past forty-eight hours felt surreal. How could something so awful actually be happening to her? Tragic events were what you heard about on the nightly news, not what you lived yourself. Grace had always thought of herself as a survivor, but now she wasn't so sure.

She glanced again at the closet and pressed her fingers against her temples. She was going to be on television, pleading for her daughter's safe return. What did it matter what she wore?

She went to the closet and grabbed the first thing she found—a pair of charcoal slacks and a blue sweater. One of her standard work outfits, and comfortable. Minutes later, touching up her makeup, she remembered Caitlin had been with her when she bought the sweater.

It's a good color on you, Mom. You hardly ever wear blue and you should. It makes your eyes sparkle.

Grace's throat closed in a choke hold of emotion and she felt the sting of tears. What if she never saw Caitlin again?

Grace stood beside Carl on the front steps of their house and read the brief statement she'd prepared. The glare from the camera lights was disorienting, but she tried to look into the camera often.

"We implore anyone who has any knowledge of Caitlin's whereabouts," Grace concluded, "to come forward, and we beg whoever took her to let her go. Caitlin, we love you." Grace's voice cracked. "So much. I miss you and want you home again."

Grace pressed her lips together to keep them from trembling. Her chest felt so tight she could barely breathe.

"Do you think your daughter's disappearance is connected to that of Karen Holiday?" one of the reporters asked.

"Did your daughter know Karen?" another called out.

"They went to the same school," Grace said, "but they weren't friends. They weren't even in the same grade. As to the first question, that's something you'd have to ask the police."

"Do you think they're doing enough to find Caitlin?" the first reporter asked.

"They seem to be doing everything they can."

A woman asked, "Do you have any theories about what might have happened or who's responsible?"

"No," Grace replied. "Caitlin is a level-headed girl. She wouldn't do anything foolish."

"Do you think she's still alive?" called out a voice from the rear.

Grace had the sensation of a ball of ice rattling through her chest. She felt her lungs might collapse.

Carl put his arms around her shoulders. "That's our fervent hope," he answered for her, then led her back into the house.

Later, while Carl worked in his study, Grace wandered aimlessly through the house. She'd spent yesterday in a fugue state of denial, at some level going on as if everything were normal. If she didn't acknowledge what had happened, maybe it would go away. She'd tried instead to focus on Lucy and Adam and making sure they were okay. But inside a panther had been gnawing at her heart.

And today it was more voracious than ever.

Grace found herself now in Caitlin's room. Her gaze fell on the collage of photos Caitlin had framed on her wall. It had been an eighth-grade English assignment initially, but in typical Caitlin fashion, she'd taken the idea beyond the parameters of the classroom.

There was a photo of Caitlin and Jake taken on Caitlin's first birthday. She wore a silly party hat and had a face smeared with cake. Another photo showed Caitlin at seven in the garden with her grandmother. It had been taken soon after Grace's divorce, when her mother's small townhouse seemed like the only safe haven she knew. And one of Grace's favorite photos, a headshot of Caitlin and herself, cheek to cheek, both smiling broadly. People said they looked alike. Grace had trouble seeing that. Maybe a faint resemblance through the eyes, but Grace knew with certainly that she'd never been as lovely as her daughter.

Caitlin had put together a second photo collage more recently. It was filled with snapshots of her friends. Fern Daniels, who had been Caitlin's best friend for years before she'd moved away, and some of her newer friends—Traci Redding Jenna Priestly, and a handful of other familiar faces Grace couldn't come up with names for. And Ty Cross. Ty was a good-looking boy, what in her day had been called "a catch." But she'd been secretly pleased when Caitlin broke off the relationship. Grace was a little surprised that Caitlin hadn't removed Ty's photo from the collection.

Looking at the spread of Caitlin's life before her, Grace felt again the gnawing fear in her gut.

Caitlin had to be alive. She simply had to be.

CHAPTER 9

Monday morning, Grace went to work. Anything was better than sitting at home paralyzed with fear and waiting for the phone to ring. But the routine of her job offered no solace at all.

The Dean's office bustled with its usual activity, and although her co-workers were quick with hugs and sympathy, they eventually drifted off to share news of their weekends and families. Grace felt as though she were entombed in glass, more alone than ever.

She settled at her desk with a cup of coffee and tried to focus on the tasks at hand. Normally, she enjoyed her job. She liked the energy of the office, the rhythm of the work, the sense of teamwork. But today she found herself growing angry. Angry at her associates for having uninterrupted lives. Angry at the students for being alive and safe. Angry at the mounds of paper and multiple forms that tracked class schedules and GPAs and petitions for candidacy. She knew she was being unreasonable, but the more she tried to rein in her annoyance, the more irritated she became.

She was talking with a particularly perky, gum-chomping sophomore about a schedule change when the girl's phone rang.

"Hi, Maya," she said, cutting Grace off mid-sentence. "Yeah, I can't talk long. I'm in the Dean's office trying to get out of that sucky psych class."

Grace waited for her to hang up, but she didn't. "That's so cool," the girl said into the phone. "He really said that?"

Grace drummed her fingers on the counter. The girl ignored her. Grace ripped the request form in half and handed it back.

The girl looked startled. "What's your problem, lady?"

"You, for starters. It's rude to be carrying on a conversation with your friend at the same time you're talking to me."

"I wasn't exactly talking to you," the girl replied. She brushed her bangs from her eyes with a dismissive flip of her wrist.

"You know what you are?" Grace said, her voice rising. "You're a shallow, immature, self-centered brat."

"What did you call me?" The girl's voice had risen even louder than Grace's and the entire office was staring at them.

Grace's hands shook. She thought she might throw up. What was happening to her? It was as if some alien had crawled inside her and taken over.

Dean Johnson stuck his head into the front office. He called to one of the women, "Marcia, can you help this young lady?" Then he put a hand on Grace's elbow and took her aside.

"Go on home," he told her kindly. "You didn't need to come to work today. We all understand what you must be going through."

She shook her head. Johnson was a kind man, popular with students and faculty alike. But he couldn't understand. No one could unless they'd been there themselves.

"Take some time off," he suggested. "You've got more important things to deal with right now than the stuff that goes on here."

"I thought work would be good for me," Grace replied bleakly. The anger had suddenly dissipated, like helium from a punctured balloon. "I thought it would give me something to do. I'm so sorry, I just . . ." She felt her throat choke.

He put a comforting hand on her shoulder. "It's okay. Take all the time you need."

Outside, the day was overcast and blustery. Grace got into her car and stared blankly into the flat gray of the horizon. What was she supposed to do with herself? She thought of the

articles she'd leafed through in magazines over the years—
"How to Handle a Fussy Baby," "When Your Child Has
Nightmares," "Talking to Your Teen About Sex." Never once
had she come across advice to mothers of missing children.

Grace felt terribly alone. Her friends were doing their best
to be supportive, but they had families and jobs and worries of
their own. Even Sandy, who'd taken on the volunteer effort
and come by each day with a prepared meal, a willing ear, and a
powerful hug, couldn't slip into Grace's skin. Carl was her only
refuge, and wonderful as he was, Caitlin wasn't his daughter.
He didn't feel what Grace felt.

When Caitlin was little, one of her favorite books had
been The Runaway Bunny—the last book they read together
each night before Grace tucked her daughter into bed. One
night Caitlin, still dewy and smelling sweetly of strawberry bath
soap, had turned to Grace and, out of the blue, asked, "But
what if I'm stolen? Will you still find me?"

That such a worry should cross her child's mind about
broke Grace's heart. She'd hugged Caitlin tight and, like
thousands of mothers before, promised to go after her and
bring her home, no matter what.

Now, she wondered if Caitlin remembered and was
holding on to that promise by whatever thin thread she could
muster.

Please, God, Grace pleaded silently, Please let her be
okay.

Five minutes later, Grace still sat in her car in the parking
lot. The car radio aired an annoying commercial for a
supplement that claimed it could make you lose weight while
eating as much as you wanted. Grace changed stations, only to
land on another commercial, this time for an all-natural male
enhancement formula. Too bad there wasn't a quick fix for
grief, too. She turned the radio off and ran her hands over the
steering wheel.

What am I supposed to do?

One thing was certain, she couldn't very well spend the
day sitting in the parking lot. With no clear idea where she'd
go, Grace put the car into reverse and backed out of her spot.

Then it hit her. Someone would understand what she was going through because she'd gone through it herself. Karen Holiday's mother.

Grace didn't know the woman, but she knew where the Holidays lived—a green single-story house near the railroad tracks. The local media had perched there for several days following Karen's disappearance, just as they'd descended on Grace and Carl's home over the weekend. She drove there now with a dry mouth and a pounding heart, fervently hoping Mrs. Holiday would be home.

Grace felt as though she'd been lost at sea and unexpectedly tossed a lifeline. If she couldn't speak to Karen's mother, she'd sink into the inky blackness of despair.

Grace rang the bell, noting the pot of dead petunias by the door. That's what happened when the bottom fell out of your world, she thought. You lived in freeze-frame mode. The simplest tasks became overwhelming.

The woman who answered the door was younger than Grace expected by seven or eight years. She had a toddler on her hip and another, slightly older child, following at her heels. She wore no makeup and her dull brown hair was pulled into a limp ponytail secured by a simple rubber band.

"Mrs. Holiday?"

The woman peered at Grace cautiously. "Who's asking?"

"My name is Grace. I'm Caitlin Whittington's mother."

The toddler began fidgeting, and the woman slapped the girl's thumb from her mouth. "Keep your hands away from your face, Mary." She turned back to Grace. "I'm sorry. Do I know you?"

Grace shook her head. "My daughter, Caitlin, disappeared Friday afternoon. I thought you might have heard about it on the news."

"I don't much watch the news." Mrs. Holiday hoisted Mary higher on her hip. "What is it you want?"

Grace wasn't sure what she'd been imagining. Certainly not that she and Karen's mom would wrap their arms around one another in commiseration and become instant friends, although she wouldn't have ruled it out. Now, she wasn't sure how to respond. She felt foolish for coming.

But she was also desperate to know how another mother handled the roaring fear and despair. "I was hoping . . . I mean, your daughter disappeared, too. You suffered through what I'm dealing with, are suffering still, I know, I didn't mean to imply . . ." Grace took a breath. She was coming across like a crazy woman. "I feel so lost," she said finally, with a voice that cracked. "I thought talking to you might help."

The woman regarded her for a moment, then pushed the screen door open. "You might as well come in. My name is Beth."

The door opened directly into a small, cramped living room. The beige wall-to-wall carpeting was stained, as was the green and brown plaid recliner positioned in front of the television. Prints of the masters—Grace recognized Monet's water lilies and a Cezanne landscape—hung on the walls in cheap metal frames. Although the room was surprisingly orderly given the presence of young children, it was, to Grace's mind, cluttered with knickknacks, lace doilies, and dusty, artificial plants. The stench of stale cigarette smoke permeated the air.

The corner table next to the couch held a collection of photographs, the largest a portrait of five children, ranging in age from the toddler on Beth's hip to a slender teenager Grace recognized as Karen. All were girls.

Beth must have followed Grace's gaze.

"It was taken late last summer," she said. "Not long before Karen disappeared. It's the only one we have with all the kids. Pure luck. I had a discount coupon for that new photo place in the mall, or I wouldn't of done it. I told my husband, God musta' been looking out for us."

Her daughter had been missing since October and Beth believed God watched over her? The statement seemed absurd.

Beth hastened to clarify, probably in response to Grace's expression of horror. "I didn't mean we're lucky to have lost her or something. Goes without saying we want Karen home. I miss her every day. But after awhile, you begin to appreciate what you've got, no matter if they're small things." She repositioned the frame on the table, pausing to gaze at the faces of her children. "I'm real glad we've got this photo, you know what I mean? That smile of Karen's helps me remember the joy as well as the pain."

Grace wondered if she'd ever be able to say the same thing. Caitlin's photograph—whether hanging framed on the wall of their family room, peering out from the pages of the newspaper, or hanging on the flyers about town—did nothing but suck the air from Grace's lungs.

Beth gestured to the frayed, square-cushioned sofa. "Have a seat." Beth sat down on the far end, bouncing the toddler on her knee. The older child had wandered off into another room. "Tell me about your daughter. Kate?"

"Caitlin."

"Is she a friend of Karen's?" Beth lit a cigarette from the pack on the table near the sofa and inhaled deeply.

Is. Present tense. Did Beth truly believe Karen was still alive?

"I don't think they were friends," Grace replied. "They go to the same school but they're a couple of years apart." It felt odd talking about Caitlin as though she and Beth were simply two mothers who'd met at a school function. "It was after school this last Friday that she disappeared. She was waiting for her dad to pick her up. That's the last anyone saw of her."

Beth blew out a plume of smoke. "What do the police say?"

"Not much. They're looking for her, of course. They've talked to her friends and questioned possible witnesses. But so far, nothing."

Grace sucked in her breath. It was a mistake to have come. What had she been hoping for—a magic cure for grief?

"Karen went missing at night," Beth said matter-of-factly. "She snuck out to go a friend's house. We didn't even know she was gone till morning. It was a regular thing with her. We'd ground her, she'd find a way to get out. Got so we more or less gave up." Beth shrugged. "Kids get to be teenagers, what are you going to do?"

Not give up. Grace was beginning to realize how different she and Beth were. She doubted their lives intersected anywhere, except in the disappearances of their daughters.

"Did the police come up with any leads?" Grace asked. She'd followed the news reports, of course, but after the initial burst of publicity, there'd been very little in the press.

"At first they thought maybe she'd run off. Then when they found her abandoned car, they thought she might've met up with someone or hitched a ride with a stranger. Truth is, they don't know what happened."

"That's it? They don't have anything? No evidence whatsoever?"

"They found her purse," Beth said after a moment. "In a Dumpster out at the east end of the mall. Still had money and credit cards and everything. But the cops never did find a single person who might've seen anything."

Beth set the toddler on the floor with one of the throwaway catalogues from a pile on the coffee table. "Here, Mary, see if you can find the doggies, okay?" She turned to Grace with a softness in her eyes that hadn't been there before. "I know how hard it is, waiting and hoping and worrying."

Grace nodded, feeling the sting of tears.

"It doesn't go away," Beth continued. "But it does become . . . not easy, exactly. I guess what I mean is familiar. Like a bum knee or something. You learn to live with it."

For the first time, Grace was glad for the rawness of her emotions. The thought that she might someday lose that and become accustomed to Caitlin's absence was as frightening as Caitlin's being gone itself.

"Anyways, the other kids need me," Beth added. "I have to keep going."

"Maybe that makes a difference." Although Grace didn't honestly believe it could. "Caitlin is my only child."

"I had Karen when I was very young. Too young. The second time, I did it right and got married first."

"Your husband isn't Karen's father, then?"

Beth waved the smoke from her face with her hand. "Her father is long gone."

"How does your husband feel about Karen being missing?"

"He feels awful, of course." She frowned at Grace. "Why wouldn't he? He's a good man. Works hard to put food on our table and clothes on our back. What are you implying?"

"Nothing. It's just that I'm remarried, too. Also to a wonderful man. But Caitlin's not his daughter. He can't feel what I'm feeling."

"Does it matter?"

Grace hadn't considered that before. Carl cared about her. He cared about Caitlin, too, but even if they hadn't been close, Carl would feel sad for Grace's sake. Why wasn't that enough?

"I don't know," Grace said. "All I know is that I feel so helpless. Hollow, afraid, alone. I feel as though I can't catch my breath."

"Well, gosh yes," Beth replied. "I felt that way too. But the Lord don't give us more than we can handle."

"It sounds like you have a strong faith." This wasn't the first time Grace had envied those who found solace in religion. Unfortunately, belief wasn't something you could pick up and learn, like skiing or dancing the samba.

"Yeah, guess you could say that," Beth said. "Me and my husband both."

"Don't you ever despair?"

"More than you'd believe. Or maybe you would, being there yourself." Beth grew quiet for a moment. "Karen was a difficult child. And me being a single mom for so many years, that didn't help. But she was turning herself around, getting on the right path. That's what makes what happened even harder to accept."

Grace nodded encouragingly, although Karen and Caitlin were nothing alike. Grace could almost understand that something bad might happen to a girl like Karen, and, at the same time, she felt guilty for thinking that way.

"Karen's counselor made her enroll in that tutoring program they have at the school," Beth continued. "Kids helping each other. Her grades improved. Not a lot, but enough. She met kids who wanted to make something of their lives. Good kids, you know? Not that she hung around with them, but just knowing kids like that was a good influence."

"My stepson is part of that program," Grace told her. "Adam tutors in math. I think he sometimes gets discouraged, so it's good to hear you say it can make a difference."

"Oh, it makes a big difference." Beth's gaze followed her youngest daughter, who'd grown bored looking for dogs in a catalogue that appeared aimed at car enthusiasts. Mary had toddled over to the recliner and was trying to climb into it when she let out a howl.

In one swift movement, Beth extinguished the cigarette and rushed to her daughter. She began kissing the child's fingers. "Let's make it all better," she cooed.

"Is she okay?" Grace asked.

"She got her fingers pinched, but she'll be fine. Won't you Mary berry?" Beth turned to Grace. "I'm sorry about your daughter. I'll add her to my prayers."

"Thank you." Grace felt it would be heartless to point out that praying hadn't helped Karen at all.

CHAPTER 10

Adam glanced at the clock on the wall above the chalkboard. Fifteen minutes until lunch. By then he'd have four classes down. Two more to go in the afternoon, although he was giving serious consideration to ditching them. He was way behind in French already, and history—well, Adam was a history buff of sorts, but Mr. Tedesci could suck the life out of even the most exciting Civil War battle or congressional debate. And the exams were taken verbatim from the textbook so there was really no reason to go to class.

The next fifteen minutes might just test the limits of his endurance, anyway.

He certainly didn't plan to hang around during lunch. He'd already fielded enough questions about Caitlin to wear him down. Kids who normally didn't acknowledge his existence were all of a sudden swarming around him. Like vultures, he thought. Pecking and picking and then flying off to savor whatever tidbit they'd been able to glean. Not that he had much to tell them.

He hadn't had much to say to the cops on Sunday, either. Unlike Lucy, who'd repeated the story about how she'd seen Caitlin at the oval but didn't think Caitlin had seen her, and how she thought Caitlin might have gone back to her locker or something because next time Lucy looked, she was gone.

Big fucking deal, like that was important.

He shouldn't blame Lucy. She just wanted to help. Adam could tell by the way she'd clung to their dad when they'd played miniature golf on Saturday that she was upset. Miniature golf, if you could believe it. As if things were perfectly normal.

No, that wasn't true. The four of them had never played

miniature golf before. His dad had suggested it, and Grace had acted like it was a brilliant idea. Adam knew they wanted a "relaxed setting" where he and Lucy would be comfortable airing their fears about Caitlin, but it seemed like a stupid idea since nobody paid the least bit of attention to the game and no one but their dad had much to say.

At the front of the classroom, the clock hand ticked the last few seconds to noon. Adam timed his internal br-r-ing with the bell so he could be the first person out the door.

Heading to the student parking lot, he passed Rob Hardy, who'd obviously gotten a jump on the bell. He looked half stoned.

"Yo," Rob said, like they were buddies or something.

"Yo, yourself," Adam muttered. Rob was weird, but then a lot of kids thought Adam was weird too.

"Bad shit about Caitlin."

"Yeah."

Adam tossed his backpack into the passenger seat of his car and drove out to the river, where he parked and climbed down the rocky bank to the wooded cove, his own private retreat. The roar of the river here was deafening, thundering all around him like a powerful ancient god.

The ground felt damp, but Adam lay down anyway. He spread his arms and aimed his face toward the sky. A fine mist rose off the river. Droplets, rendered faintly violet by the refracted sunlight, danced above him. The icy wind grazed his skin with razor-like sharpness.

He remembered meeting Caitlin for the first time, over barbecued baby-back ribs at the apartment his dad had moved into after the divorce. He should have known something was up, the way his dad had been busy cleaning up the place, chortling over nothing the least bit funny.

"There's a woman I'm seeing," he'd told them casually over breakfast that morning. "She and her daughter are coming for dinner tonight."

Lucy, who was only ten at the time, turned on him like a coiled spring. "You invited strangers to dinner?"

"They're not strangers, sweetie. I know them both—"

"Adam and I don't." Lucy stuck out her lower lip. "I don't want them to come. I'm not sharing my toys."

"No one's going to make you."

"Who's the woman?" Adam had asked. He was fourteen. Not any happier than Lucy about the prospect of sharing their evening with people he didn't know (no matter what his dad said, they were strangers). But he understood the ramifications of seeing someone. Adam wondered if his dad and this woman were already having sex. He couldn't imagine his dad doing it. It would be too weird.

"Her name is Grace." The way his dad's face softened when he said her name sent a shiver down Adam's spine. "Her daughter's name is Caitlin. I think you'll like them."

Adam's initial impression of Grace wasn't anything special. She was a mom kind of woman. Not as lean and fit as his own mother, nor as talkative, but she seemed okay.

Caitlin didn't make much of an impression, either. She was twelve, right between Adam and Lucy. She wore her dark hair pulled back from her face with a yellow ribbon. She was polite and sweet, maybe a bit too sweet, like that movie he'd seen where all the women in town turned into robots, probably because she'd gone to Catholic school where they didn't let kids be kids. His mom had told him that.

His dad had iced a bucket of sodas and beer, and he steered them all outside the small yard for some refreshment. Adam wondered if his dad had turned into a robot also. He'd never heard him say refreshment before.

The conversation that followed felt stilted and uncomfortable. Mostly it was the two adults trying hard to involve the kids. Finally, Lucy took her can of soda and announced that she was going to her room.

"Can I come?" Caitlin asked. Politely, of course. And sweetly.

Lucy turned quickly, her ponytail bouncing like a rubber toy. "No, you can't."

Adam caught the chagrined look on his dad's face and came to the rescue. "I've got a model train in my room. You want to see it?"

"Sure." Caitlin smiled.

Grace and his dad exchanged meaningful glances. "I think," his dad said uncomfortably, "that's probably not such a good idea."

It felt like a reprimand, and Adam started to argue. Then suddenly he got it. Caitlin was a girl. A Girl.

Not that he knew a lot about girls. Lucy, of course, but she didn't count. He had a couple of girl cousins, but they were family. Caitlin was a girl. And Adam a boy. She didn't belong in his room.

So instead, they'd played a boring game of Scrabble and the ribs had burned.

Adam stood, brushing loose soil and debris from this clothing. He felt the need for a memorial of some sort. A farewell. Whether people said it or not, he knew Caitlin wasn't coming back.

He reached into his pocket for the mood ring he'd given her last Christmas in her stocking. It was a silly, plastic thing he'd bought at a dollar store, but it had been a big hit for a while. He found a protected spot next to a stone outcropping and buried it in the soft soil. Then he broke off a bare lilac branch from the bush nearby and planted it on top of the ring. He hoped, with all the rain, that it would sprout.

Lastly he took his pocket knife and scratched Caitlin's initials into the stone. As an afterthought, he added his own.

"Goodbye, Caitlin. I'm going to miss you."

He thought he could hear her answer him, but it was probably the wind.

It sounded like "Come on, Adam. Please."

That was the Caitlin he wanted to remember.

CHAPTER 11

Rayna entered the alcove where Hank's and her desks were located.

"Good job with the media," Hank said.

"Thanks." The press conference had gone well, she thought. Now she could only hope that the exposure would trigger helpful input from the public—someone who'd seen Caitlin or maybe had suspicions about who might have taken her.

"It will be interesting to see what Seth Robbins does with it," Rayna added. She'd seen the columnist in the cluster of reporters, standing nonchalantly toward the back, not even bothering to take notes. Not that Robbins let facts guide his diatribes.

Hank pushed aside some papers and leaned back in his chair. "Neither Jake Whittington nor his fiancée have shown up for a polygraph yet. Think we should lean on them?"

Rayna had trouble understanding how the parent of a missing child could do anything but cooperate fully, yet she'd seen it happen before. And while the odds of either Whittington or his girlfriend having been involved in Caitlin's disappearance were slim, Rayna wasn't ready to rule them out.

"It couldn't hurt," she told him.

Hank grinned. "Good. I already left a message telling them to get their butts down here."

"Not in so many words, I hope."

Hank looked hurt. "You really think I'd be that stupid?"

Yes. "No," she said diplomatically. "Of course not."

"Liar." He pointed a finger at her in a gotcha motion.

"I'd especially like to get a handle on the fiancée," Rayna

said, hanging her jacket on the back of her chair and sitting. "Have you been able to verify the timing of the flat tire?"

"Working on it. Seems a private citizen stopped and changed the tire for her. I followed up more generally, too. Doesn't appear to be any animosity between Grace Whittington and her ex over the divorce or the re-pairing. Jake Whittington is well-liked, both by the people who knew him here in Paradise Falls and his partners in Portland. He appears to be a straight arrow."

"I'd still like to see them take the polygraph."

Hank nodded. "No recent activity on Caitlin's ATM card, by the way."

Cliff Leavitt, their new IT guy, pushed his considerable bulk back from the computer he'd been working on three desks down and shuffled to the supply closet at the back of the room.

"That guy gives me the creeps," Hank said, lowering his voice. "He never says a word. Never smiles. I'm not sure the muscles in his face even move."

"Maybe he's intimidated by you."

Hank's gaze followed Leavitt. "Somehow I doubt it." He turned back to Rayna, who'd perched on the corner of her desk. "Fritz is still out at the school. He was going to follow up with Rob Hardy and a couple of others."

"Good." Rayna and Fritz Burns had been at the high school this morning to talk with teachers and students. Rayna had come away with the feeling that Caitlin was considered friendly enough but that she kept to herself and wasn't really close to anyone except Fern Daniels, who'd moved away over the summer.

Rayna knew what it was like to be outside the loop in high school, only in her case her friends hadn't left, she had. Every year her father's job took them to a new location, and Rayna ended up at a new school. At least Caitlin had had a boyfriend, which is more than could be said for Rayna. Her late husband, Marc, had been her first boyfriend and one true love. She'd thought his death was the worst thing that could happen to her, until she'd lost Kimberly.

The door opened and Hank looked up. "Speak of the devil."

Fritz grinned. "So what were you saying about me?" Fritz was young, and a bit too cocky. He was good looking and knew it. Six feet of masculine, blond, eye candy. But Rayna had no idea what was on the inside. He'd started with the department in September, a month before Karen Holiday went missing, and Rayna still felt she didn't have a sense of the man.

"Were you able to talk to Rob Hardy?" she asked Fritz.

"Yeah. A bit of an oddball, if you ask me."

"How so?" She'd seen her share of Goths and geeks and heavily pierced or tattooed kids at school that morning.

Fritz shrugged. "Just a feeling I got. Nothing specific." He slid into the chair at his desk, then rolled it closer to them. "Man, some of those high school girls are babes. You shoulda been there, Hank."

"About Rob," Rayna reminded him.

Fritz winked in Hank's direction and turned to Rayna. "When I asked him about the scene with Caitlin, he tried to brush it off, like he couldn't remember. But when I pushed him, presto, his memory snapped into sharp focus." Fritz smiled as though he'd said something clever. "He says Ty was the one who broke up with Caitlin, not the other way around. She tried to get Rob to intercede. That's what the big scene at school was about."

Rayna frowned. "Why would she go to Rob? Aren't there guys Ty's tighter with than him?" Ty had told her he and Rob were only friends because their families were friends.

"I'm telling you what the kid told me. I didn't get a sense there was anything between him and Caitlin, though. She was kind of a non-issue as far as he's concerned. Nothing anyone else said indicated otherwise. As for Friday afternoon, he says he was home messing around on the computer. In fact, he and Ty were playing some on-line virtual reality game." Fritz must have seen Rayna frown. "Real time," he explained. "On the computer."

"I know about on-line gaming. It's just that Ty told me he saw Caitlin at volleyball practice about the same time, so he couldn't have been on the computer."

Hank pressed his palms together. "We might be able to get a record of the exchange if it's important," he said. "But we'd have to get a warrant, and even then I'm not sure what we'd find."

"Probably not worth it," Rayna agreed. But there was something about the threesome—Caitlin, Rob, and Ty—that didn't sit right in her mind.

"Doesn't look like we're going to get this wrapped up in time to fend off FBI involvement," Hank said.

Rayna pushed herself off the desk. "I'm not giving up."

"You've got"—Hank checked his watch— "less than twenty-four hours."

"The Feds show up tomorrow? Where did you hear that?"

"From Stoval, less than half an hour ago."

While Rayna was holding a press conference. An end run. The chief knew she wasn't happy about bringing in the FBI so he'd announced their arrival when she wasn't around. Rayna felt a flash of anger and tried to brush it aside. Petty political power plays annoyed her. But worse, they were distracting. Better to focus on getting the job done.

The phone on Rayna's desk rang and she picked it up. "Detective Godwin."

"You are not, I repeat, not, to talk to my son again unless both my attorney and I are present."

"Who is this?" she asked, although she had the feeling she knew.

"George Cross. This is twice now you've interrogated Ty, who is a minor in case you've forgotten, without a parent present."

"I didn't interrogate him, Mr. Cross. He and I spoke Saturday and again today at school where we interviewed a number of students."

"I don't give a damn what you call it. You go through me from now on. Do I make myself clear?"

"Perfectly." Rayna paused. "Since you feel that way, why don't you both come down to the station tomorrow."

"What?"

"It shouldn't take long."

So much for ignoring power plays. But it felt good, and she did want to clarify Ty and Rob's stories.

It was close to nine o'clock when Rayna arrived home. The small, single-story bungalow was dark and cold. Not worth turning on the heat, she decided. She'd be in bed in an hour. She thought of making a cup of hot tea but opted for a cold beer instead. Sections of the morning paper were still scattered on the kitchen counter where she'd left them. Seth Robbins's column, with its insipid accompanying photo, mocked her.

"How does a teenage girl simply vanish into thin air?" Robbins had asked. "Twice now in less than a year, right here in Paradise Falls. How many more girls will disappear before the monster responsible for these depraved acts is caught? It's time to ask ourselves if our local cops, with their fat benefit and pension plans, are doing all they can. Don't we deserve that much?"

Rayna tossed the paper into the recycle bin in disgust. Did he think the detectives were sitting idly by twiddling their thumbs?

The message light on her answering machine blinked. Rayna hit play.

Two hang ups, and then Paul: "Nothing important. I saw you on the news and thought I'd say hi. Guess you must be pretty busy with the latest disappearance, but give me a call if you want to get together for dinner sometime."

Paul Nesbitt was a nice man. A county prosecutor she'd met not long after she'd moved to Paradise Falls. It wasn't his fault that Rayna wasn't interested in a romantic relationship. Not with him or anyone else. She'd been there, done that. She and Paul had dated for a couple of months last fall, nothing serious, and he claimed to have understood when she explained that it had nothing to do with him, it was her. He still called, and occasionally she succumbed to the lure of male companionship and went out with him. But it wasn't, and never would be, anything serious.

She took her beer into the den. On the bookcase by the window, Anastasia was curled up in the soft wood shavings at the bottom of her cage. As always, Rayna experienced a momentary fear that she'd discover the hamster had died. She knew it would happen at some point. No creature lived forever.

Rayna set the beer down on her desk and reached into the cage for the soft, warm, golden ball of fluff. She pulled the hamster out and cradled it in her hands. Anastasia had been Kimberly's hamster, a gift from her dad when he was going through chemo. The three of them—father, daughter, and hamster —were an instant team. One of Rayna's favorite snapshots was of Marc and Kimberly together on the old family room sofa, with Anastasia proudly displayed front and center. Marc had died six months later, Kimberly less than a year after that. Only Anastasia remained. Tears stung Rayna's eyes. How could a stupid little rodent be such a powerful reminder of all she'd lost?

Rayna returned Anastasia to her cage and filled her food dish. She brushed her tears away. She was tired, that's all. Tired and worried. She had a killer to deal with. Or at the very least, a kidnapper. Not to mention the FBI. She couldn't let herself be distracted by her own problems.

CHAPTER 12

Out of habit, Grace washed her face with the special non-drying cleanser the saleswoman at Macy's had told her helped eliminate wrinkles, then smoothed the peach-scented night cream over her face, careful to avoid getting it in her eyes. But she was only going through the motions. Her mind and heart were being held captive far away in a dark and frightening place.

Caitlin had been missing now for seventy-six long, awful hours.

The last thing Grace cared about was the state of her skin. She felt silly—ashamed and guilty even—going about her regular routine. The once familiar habits felt as alien to her as if she'd suddenly found herself in a stranger's body. Yet she clung to her nightly ritual because to abandon it would bring her face to face with chaos.

How odd, she thought, to live in parallel worlds simultaneously.

At the sink to her left, Carl brushed his teeth, splattering the mirror and dribbling toothpaste onto the faucet, as usual. Tonight, his carelessness irritated her.

"Can't you brush your teeth without making a mess?" Her tone was caustic, surprising her with its sharpness.

Carl looked hurt. "Apparently not to your standards."

His response irritated her further. "Your standards might be higher if you were the one cleaning the bathroom," she snapped.

"What put you in such a foul mood?"

Grace was dumbfounded. Had he forgotten about Caitlin? What kind of mood did he expect her to be in? Anger boiled in her veins. How could he be so obtuse? So callous.

"My daughter has disappeared," she said. "Or have you forgotten? Did you think I'd be feeling upbeat?"

This was what really bugged her, she realized. Her daughter was missing and Carl's life hadn't come to a screeching halt.

Over dinner, she'd told him about her visit with Karen Holiday's mother, tried to explain how she'd totally lost it at work. Carl's responses were appropriately sympathetic, but she knew him well enough to know that he'd been only half there. As soon as they'd finished eating, he'd headed for the television to watch a basketball playoff. He'd been distracted by thoughts of the game all along.

Carl wiped his mouth, then toweled down the faucet. "I'm sorry, Grace. I shouldn't have said what I did."

"But you did say it." Grace felt the sting of tears. "It was cruel and heartless. It was so . . . so uncaring."

"I do care, honey. I care very much. I thought you knew that. I'm worried sick, and I'm trying my damnedest to be supportive and reassuring. To give you what you need. I just never—"

"I know you are," Grace said, feeling suddenly deflated. "But sometimes I think your heart isn't in it."

"How can you say that? It's not true!"

Grace shook her head. "You're worried, yeah. But mostly you don't want me moping around and being upset."

"Of course I don't want you to be upset." Carl put his arms around her and pulled Grace close. "But I am worried about Caitlin. You must know how much I care about her. I'm worried and sick and scared. Just as I would be if Adam or Lucy were missing."

No, Grace thought, it wasn't quite the same. But the anger was no longer exploding inside her. She could hardly fault Carl for being more invested in his own children than hers. She knew that if the situation were reversed, her concern for Lucy wouldn't match his. And if it was Adam . . . well, to be honest, she'd have to dig a bit deeper to find a reservoir of compassion.

"I hate not being able to do anything," Carl said. "I feel helpless. And maybe that makes me seem less there. But I do care, Grace."

As he smoothed her hair and kissed her forehead, Grace felt her anger fully dissipate. Carl was a good man. A loving husband who embraced Caitlin as his own. Why was she turning on him?

She stepped back and kissed his mouth, which was fresh with the minty taste of toothpaste. "I shouldn't have snapped at you," she offered. "It's just that I'm so afraid, I feel I'm about to erupt."

"You can lean on me, Grace. Let me help you. I'm here for you. Always."

Grace decided this was not a good time to tell him she didn't want Adam and Lucy staying at the house this upcoming week.

CHAPTER 13

The next morning, Grace remained in bed until almost ten, long after Carl had left for work. Sleep was beyond her—had been for much of the night—but throwing back the covers to face the day took will and energy, and Grace had neither. That didn't stop her mind from reeling, however, and what finally propelled her from the soft warmth of her cocoon was the hope that movement might somehow silence the agonizing scenarios that played relentlessly in her head.

Caitlin hurt and scared. Caitlin alone and lost. Caitlin tethered to a stake in some dark, dank basement. Or locked in an airless box.

Caitlin suffering from unimaginable torture.

Caitlin dead.

Grace shuffled unsteadily into the bathroom where she splashed water on her face and brushed her teeth. She noticed that Carl had gone out of his way to wipe down the bathroom counter and faucet, and she experienced a moment of guilt over her outburst last night. It wasn't fair to take her anxieties and fears out on him. It really wasn't. Carl was a kind, generous, and loving man. He cared about her deeply. But at the same time, she couldn't help feeling an edge of resentment that his kids were alive and safe.

In the kitchen, Grace poured a cup of lukewarm coffee from the pot that Carl had made earlier, then perused the morning paper without actually reading it. She did read the news story about Caitlin, however, dismayed to find that her daughter's disappearance was no longer front-page news. And she read the editorial piece by Seth Robbins, which was, as usual, critical of police efforts. Part of her was grateful that he seemed to share her frustration with the lack of progress, but she thought he also delighted in being inflammatory. She was willing to bet he was more interested in stirring things up than in finding Caitlin. Grace had never met the man in person, but she'd seen the photo that ran with his column so often that his narrow face, bushy brows, and silly little goatee were as familiar as though he lived next door.

Stuffing the newspaper into the recycle bin, she experienced a moment of déjà vu. She shook her head to clear it.

Then she remembered. Caitlin and Adam one morning last fall, soon after Karen Holiday had disappeared. Grace had been gathering the morning paper for the recycle bin when Adam reached for the front section.

"Don't toss this yet," he said. "There's a story I want to reread."

"Karen Holiday, I bet," Caitlin taunted. "You're like a ghoul."

"I'm interested. It's creepy and fascinating at the same time."

"Like I said, a ghoul." But her tone was more playful than contemptuous. Then she'd turned serious. "Do you think she's dead?"

Adam shrugged. "Might be better than some of the alternatives."

Grace had silently agreed with Adam. Now she wasn't so sure.

Grace spent the next hour on the Internet reading every story she could dig up about Karen Holiday's disappearance. None of it was new, and none of it brought Grace any closer to understanding what might have happened to Caitlin. The two girls were nothing alike. Caitlin was dark and athletic, Karen blonde and curvy. Different grade levels, different circles. The circumstances surrounding their disappearances weren't similar, either. Was Seth Robbins barking up the wrong tree with his ranting about serial killers?

Still, two girls from the same school in less than six

months. Both gone without a trace. It couldn't be a coincidence.

Although she knew the police had been down this path before, Grace checked the list of locally registered sex offenders. There were more than Grace expected. Most, surprisingly normal in appearance. A white-haired, fatherly looking man, an attractive Latino who appeared to be in his thirties, a toned and clean-shaven man with closely cropped hair who would have looked at home in the hallways of any corporation in America.

Which might very well be the case. That thought brought Grace up short.

But it was nothing like the shock she received when she scrolled further down the page.

"Oh, my God!" Her hands flew to her mouth. It was the middle-aged mechanic at the shop where she took her car to be serviced. At least, it looked like him. The same straight, lank hair and gap-toothed smile. Lance Richter, according to the name under his photo.

The man had always been friendly and helpful, certainly not someone you'd be on your guard around. Thinking back, she tried to recall if there were red flags she should have picked up on. Nothing came to mind. But seeing his photo there on the screen along with a list of his offenses sent a nerve-jarring chill down her spine. Lewd or lascivious acts with a child under fourteen. Sodomy with a person by force. Oral copulation with a child of fifteen. Grace felt her skin itch. Had Caitlin ever gone with her to get the car fixed? She couldn't remember, though it was certainly a possibility. She wondered if Beth Holiday used the same mechanic.

Grace's hand shook as she logged off. The names and faces on the website were only the tip of the iceberg. What about the predators who didn't register or hadn't been caught? Or the drifters who might come through Paradise Falls and then move on? How could the police catch a person like that?

Panic gripped her by the throat. For the first time she considered the possibility that she might never know what had become of her daughter. As if the void of missing Caitlin wasn't unbearable enough, not to know who or how or why would be hell.

She struggled to fill her lungs with air, and then, still shaking, pushed herself away from the computer.

The police will find Caitlin, Grace told herself. They will. They will find her alive and they will catch and punish the man who took her.

It was a mantra she clung to out of necessity.

Grace needed to make a run to the store, but it was mid-afternoon by the time she could muster the energy to head out. Not that she had any interest in food. In fact, she hadn't been able to swallow more than a few bites since Friday night. But Carl, whose appetite didn't appear to be similarly affected, needed to eat, and the refrigerator was getting low on necessities. Since she'd never worked up the nerve to tell him she couldn't cope with Adam's and Lucy's visit this week, she needed to stock up on food for them, as well.

She made a stab at cleaning up the kitchen, then showered, dressed, and got into her car.

The day was gray and bleak. A solid layer of clouds blanketed the sky. Pedestrians, heavily bundled for warmth, huddled against the buffeting wind. Grace pulled into the parking lot and turned off the engine. The thought of walking through the store, filling her cart with boxes of cereal and cans of soda, overwhelmed her. And what if she ran into someone she knew? She didn't have the energy to explain once again that there were no new developments, or to respond to outpourings of concern and sympathy. People meant well, but kindness was a burden, too. Grace found it easier to simply avoid people.

Taking a deep breath, she backed out of the parking space. She would ask Carl to pick up some things on his way home. He wasn't one of those men who acted like a fish out of water in the grocery store or in the kitchen. And he genuinely wanted to help. He'd happily do whatever she asked.

Except allow his children to feel unwelcome in their home.

It would have been unfair of her to ask them to stay away. Grace understood that in her head if not her heart. On the other hand, shouldn't he know how it would pain her to have Lucy and Adam under their roof right now? It would be like drawing big arrows pointing to the hole that was Caitlin.

Instead of driving straight home, Grace headed toward the police station to tell them about Lance Richter, the auto mechanic on the sex offender list.

Until she and Carl had gone in for the polygraph Saturday morning, Grace had visited the police station only once before, to turn in a wallet she'd found in the gutter near their house. Now she was making her third trip there in almost as many days. The squat brick building and sterile lobby were beginning to feel familiar, just as the Pacific Memorial Hospital ICU had become familiar following her mother's heart attack two years ago. Not pleasant or comfortable, but familiar all the same. It was frightening, Grace thought, how quickly the human mind could adapt to adversity.

She pushed open the door and told the young male officer at the desk that she wanted to see Detective Godwin. "I'm Grace Whittington. Caitlin Whittington is my daughter."

The officer avoided looking at her directly, as if having a missing daughter were an embarrassment, like being caught on the front lawn in your pajamas. "Let me see if Detective Godwin is available," he told Grace.

A moment later, the detective strode to the lobby. "I was just getting ready to call you."

Grace's heart leapt. "You found something?"

"No, I had a few questions for you. Come on back."

Grace followed her to an internal work area with half a dozen desks. Godwin's desk, and another, were somewhat separate in an alcove to one side.

"How are you holding up?" The detective pointed Grace to a visitor's chair.

"Not so well, if truth be told. I went to work yesterday and got sent home by my boss for yelling at a student. Last night I had a fight with my husband."

Detective Godwin started to say something, then stopped

and nodded sympathetically. "I know this must be a rough time for you."

Hardly, Grace thought. How could she possibly understand what it was like to have a missing child?

"What about Caitlin's dad? How's he doing?"

"Probably better than me."

A quizzical frown tugged at the detective's brow. "You haven't talked to him?"

"Not at any length." Grace couldn't bring herself to admit how limited their contact had been.

"He hasn't come in for a polygraph yet," Detective Godwin remarked. "We can't force him to, but it would be helpful if he did."

"Sorry, I can't help you with that." Grace sat forward. Her skin prickled. "You can't think Jake had anything to do with our daughter's disappearance."

"The test is standard procedure. In cases like this we like to rule out family members. It helps us narrow the focus of our investigation."

Which meant that on some level, he wasn't in the clear.

Grace knew that family members were always suspect. Often with good reason. Men killing wives and girlfriends. Fathers killing entire families. Or kidnapping their children.

But not Jake. There was no way he could be involved. He could be aggravating at times, but he wasn't a bad person. In fact, he could be kind and generous when he thought about it.

"We're hoping his fiancée will volunteer, as well," the detective added.

Starr. Grace felt anger rising in her chest. This was all Starr's fault. If only she'd gotten to the school on time. Grace's breath caught. Maybe she had. Was it possible that the whole flat tire story was a cover-up? Starr's world revolved around Starr. Caitlin was an irritant. She was competition for Jake's affection. For his money. His time. What if Starr had picked Caitlin up and then harmed her in some way?

"Have you verified her story?" Grace asked.

"We're working on it. We really are covering all the bases."

Did Grace dare give voice to what she was thinking? Jake would be furious. But this was Caitlin they were talking about. "In terms of motive, I mean it's far-fetched, but Starr would probably be just as happy to have Caitlin out of the picture."

"We've thought of that," the detective said. "Believe me, we're looking at this from all angles. Now, what was it you needed to see me about?"

Grace spread her hands. "Can you give me an update first? I can't stand not knowing. I don't mean about a suspect necessarily, just information."

"If we knew anything definitive, we'd tell you. We've talked to your daughter's friends and classmates, as well as people who live around the school who might have seen something. And Caitlin's disappearance has been getting a lot of coverage in the news. That's good. It may be hard on you, but the more her face and name are out there, the greater the chances that someone with information will come forward."

"Wouldn't anyone with real information have come forward already?"

"Not necessarily. And the reward will help."

Fifteen thousand dollars. Money raised by friends and members of the community. It was larger than the reward offered for information about Karen Holiday, a fact which brought Grace a twisted sense of gratification, but it still didn't offer her much hope.

The detective bit her lower lip. "I did want to ask you about Rob Hardy."

Grace frowned. "I don't recognize the name."

"He's a classmate of your daughter's. A friend of Ty's."

"Still doesn't ring a bell. Should it?"

"Not necessarily. It's just that he and Caitlin apparently had a bit of an intense discussion at school not long ago. Caitlin ended up in tears and wouldn't talk to any of her friends about it."

"About her breakup with Ty, could this Rob have hurt Caitlin to pay her back for dumping his friend? Could Ty have put him up to it?" Grace rubbed her eyes.

"That's everyone's guess. But from what I can tell, it took

place before they broke up. Of course, these things are usually pretty messy for a while before they officially end, so the timing doesn't mean much."

"Do you think he's . . ." Grace swallowed. "Do you think he had something to do with what happened to Caitlin?"

"There's no indication that's the case."

But the detective must have had a reason for asking about him.

"One of her friends thought Caitlin might have been interested in an older guy," Detective Godwin continued. "Any idea who it might be?"

"What?" Grace rocked forward. "How old?"

"I don't know. Someone no longer in high school."

"We wouldn't allow that. Believe me. Ty's a senior and that was old enough for us." Which was part of the reason Grace had been secretly relieved at the breakup and hadn't pushed Caitlin for details.

"So there's no one that comes to mind? A neighbor? A teacher she's close to?"

Was it possible? Grace's stomach turned. Caitlin had been moody the last few weeks. More secretive than usual. Grace had commented to Carl about it. He'd reminded her that moody and secretive kind of went hand-in-hand with being a teenager.

Now, Grace's mind raced. Where would Caitlin meet an older male? "I guess it could be one of her dog walking clients. Most of them are families with young children—" Although anything was possible. Grace recalled stories about dads hitting on their children's babysitters. "One couple, I think they have a son who's in his late twenties. He's living with them while he goes through a divorce."

"Can you give me names?"

Detective Godwin took notes while Grace gave her the information. Then she said, "Anyone else?"

"The teacher she's closest to is the volleyball coach, but he's a real family man and, well, frankly, not very attractive." Grace shook her head. The man was approaching fifty. "Wait, there's also an assistant coach this year. An intern or student teacher or whatever. He's probably only a couple of years out of college."

And he was cute, Grace recalled. Lean and sandy-haired, with an easy smile. Caitlin spent long hours at practice every week. That's where she'd been the afternoon she disappeared, in fact. "His name is Rusty. At least that's what the kids call him. I'm not sure if it's his real name or not."

"Okay, we'll be sure to follow up. If you think of anything—"

"There is something. It's the main reason I came to see you. I was on the Internet this morning, looking up registered sex offenders. I think the mechanic at the shop where I take my car is one of them."

"That's something we looked into after Karen Holiday's disappearance but nothing came of it. What's his name?"

"Lance Richter. He works at Art's Auto Body."

"Okay. We'll follow up on that, as well." The detective's phone rang and she started to reach for it. "Was there anything else?" she asked.

Nothing that you could understand or help me with, Grace thought irritably. The detective was doing her job. But it was just that, a job. At the end of the day, she went home and her life went on. For Grace, there was nothing but agonizing loss and infinite bleakness.

CHAPTER 14

Adam lay on his bed in a shaft of afternoon sunlight and watched the bare branches of the elm tree dance in the breeze outside his window. He wondered what it would be like to be a bird, to swoop and dive through the ether of the skies. To fly away and be free. Caitlin once told him that she sometimes dreamed she was a bird. Adam had tried priming his mind with that image when he crawled into bed at night, hoping to conjure up a similar dream, but it never worked. He wondered if being dead was anything like flying.

Downstairs the front door slammed and he heard his mother's voice as she came inside. "How was your day?" she asked Lucy, dropping her briefcase on the desk in the kitchen.

"Okay." His sister's tone was indifferent.

Always the same question, always the same answer. You'd think his mother would have learned to ask it differently. Or maybe she wasn't really interested in the answer.

"Where's your brother?" Adam heard the rustle of his mother going through the day's mail.

"Lying down."

"At this hour? Is he sick?"

"I think he's upset," Lucy said.

"Upset? About what?"

"About Caitlin."

"Yes, of course. What a terrible thing to happen. It's really complicated our lives. Listen, honey, I'm going to take a shower so pick up the phone if it rings."

"Have you even called Grace?" Lucy asked.

His mother hesitated. "Why would I call her?"

"To offer sympathy."

"I'm sure your father is giving her enough for both of us."

"That's mean. How can you be so mean?"

Good for you, Adam thought. It wasn't very often his sister stood up to their mother.

"You're a child, Lucy. You don't understand about these things."

"I hate it when you say that. Why can't you just give an honest answer?"

Their mother sighed. "I wasn't trying to be mean, I was stating the obvious. I doubt Grace is interested in my sympathy, anyway."

"How would you feel if it was me who was missing?"

"I'd be devastated. That's a stupid question. But I wouldn't expect Grace to come around acting all fuzzy and warm because I was upset."

But Grace would do that, Adam thought. The differences between his mom and Grace were so stark he sometimes wondered how his dad could have been attracted to both of them.

Neither was without flaws. And they both had their good points. But they were as different as day and night. His mom was smart—a busy dentist with patients who seemed to adore her. She was slender, animated, and very pretty. But she was used to being in charge and had little patience when things, or people, didn't fall into line as she expected.

Grace was softer, both in appearance and manner. She seemed tentative at times, less certain of herself than his mom, but she radiated the kind of warmth and humor Adam associated with storybook mothers. He recalled seeing the photo of Caitlin as a toddler, nestled in Grace's lap. Grace's head was bent slightly like she was pressing her check against Caitlin's dark curls, and Caitlin's eyes were looking up toward Grace, her face alive with a chuckle about to be born. He had trouble imagining his mom ever cuddling him or Lucy in that way.

"Speaking of which, isn't this your night with your father, Lucy? Why are you still here?"

"We're not sure if we should go."

"Of course you should go. He's your dad. Caitlin missing doesn't change that. Besides, I've got company coming."

"A date, you mean."

"Who I entertain is my business, not yours."

"I guess you could hardly screw him with your children in the house, could you?"

"You've got a fresh mouth, young lady. I'm not beyond washing it out with soap."

Adam cringed. Mom and Lucy could really go at it. That was one of the worst things about the divorce. The two of them constantly at each other's throats. Or maybe it was simply that Lucy wasn't the sort of cute, sparkling teen his mom must have wanted. Lucy liked Grace and threw that in Mom's face at every opportunity, which only made his mom angrier.

He wondered if Lucy would have turned out more like Caitlin if she'd had Grace for a mother.

And what would he have turned out like?

He rolled on his side and put the pillow over his ears to block out the arguing downstairs. At one point he heard the door to Lucy's room slam and then the house turned quiet. He knew he'd have to pull himself off the bed soon. His backpack was ready. He kept clothes and books and stuff at his dad's, but never the right stuff. What a pain, living in two places, but he didn't hate it the way Lucy did.

The minute they walked through the door, Adam had the sinking feeling that Lucy's instincts had been right. They shouldn't have come. It was too soon after Caitlin's disappearance.

His dad was on the phone when they arrived and Grace tried for a cheery greeting. "Dinner's in the oven. Chicken stew. I hope that's okay."

The stew was usually kind of bland. Not the best thing Grace made for dinner, but not bad either. "Sure," he said. "Whatever."

"I didn't really feel like cooking, and this is easy."

"We could have done take-out or something," Lucy said. "I feel bad that you had to cook for us."

"It gave me something to do. And people have to eat. No matter what."

Adam could tell she was trying to keep things normal but there were dark circles under her eyes and her mouth was tight, like she'd had dental surgery and didn't want to move it.

No, they definitely shouldn't have come.

Dinner was awkward, too. Not like before when the table buzzed with conversation and laughter.

B.C. Before Caitlin's disappearance. And now . . . A.D.? After death? A shiver worked its way down Adam's spine.

Caitlin's spot at the table was conspicuously empty. At least Grace hadn't set a place there. That would have been downright creepy. He'd read about families of missing kids who kept the Christmas tree up for years waiting for them to come home. Or kept the kid's room as a shrine, even though by then the kid would have been old enough to have kids of his or her own. He wondered what would happen to Caitlin's room.

No, it was definitely not a typical meal. Before, it was sometimes hard to get a word in edgewise. Tonight, there were long stretches of silence broken by stabs at conversation. The weather. The meal. His dad's classes.

"What's going on over at the school?" Grace asked, pushing the uneaten chicken stew around on her plate.

"Same old stuff," Lucy replied. "We're reading Pride and Prejudice in English. I liked the movie better."

Grace smiled a little too brightly.

"Is the teacher any good?" his dad asked. "That's what's important. A dull teacher can ruin anything."

Adam cleared his throat. They'd both missed the point. "I think Grace meant, what are kids saying? About Caitlin."

"Oh." Lucy looked embarrassed. "I'm sorry."

"There's nothing to be sorry about," Grace said, but she shot Adam a look of gratitude. He doubted she was even aware she'd done it.

"Everyone's in shock," he reported. "And worried."

"You'd tell us if there were rumors, wouldn't you?"

"If there were any," Adam said with a self-deprecating laugh, "no one would share them with me."

"Rumors about what?" Lucy asked.

Grace didn't answer. Turning to Adam, she said, "Do you know Rob Hardy?"

"I know who he is. He's kind of a loner. A little dorky in a Goth kind of way. The kids used to make fun of him when we were younger, but now they mostly leave him alone. Why?"

"Detective Godwin said she'd heard that he and Caitlin had a conversation not long ago. Caitlin seemed pretty upset. You wouldn't know what it was about, would you?"

Adam shook his head. Rob wasn't Caitlin's type. Any more than Adam was. Caitlin went for hunks like Ty Cross. Although she'd broken that off, so who knew what she really thought?

"What about the assistant volleyball coach? Rusty something. What do you know about him?"

"Not much. He's a student teacher. He has a couple of history classes and a study hall. Kids say he's pretty cool, but I've only seen him around."

His dad leaned on the table. "What is this, Grace? Why are you grilling the kids over dinner?"

"Leave her alone," Lucy admonished. "She's just trying to figure out what happened. And we don't mind, do we, Adam?"

"No, not at all."

When they were done eating, Lucy got up without being asked and began clearing the table. "I'll take care of the dishes," she said, hugging Grace over the back of the chair. "We know you're upset. But things will work out."

"Adam, help your sister." His dad turned to Grace and picked up her hand in his own. "Let's take a walk. The fresh air will be good for both of us."

The night air was more than fresh; it was bitterly cold. Grace shivered in her coat and scarf, tucking her gloved hands into her pockets. Carl, impervious to the cold, wore a light windbreaker.

He draped an arm around her shoulder and gave a squeeze. "I'm sorry I jumped on you over dinner," he said. "I probably overreacted."

"Probably?" Even Lucy had come to her defense.

"Grace, I apologized. Give me a break. My nerves are frayed, too."

"But you haven't got a missing daughter."

"No, I haven't got a missing daughter. You act like that's a defect or something on my part. Like I'm at fault."

Grace tucked her chin further into her scarf and hunched her shoulders against the cold.

"Look," Carl said, "I just wanted a normal dinner with my kids."

"Normal? How can we have a normal dinner when Caitlin is missing?"

Carl took a deep breath. "I guess wanting to hear about my kids' day was asking too much."

There was an edge to his voice Grace hadn't heard before. "I didn't say we couldn't talk with them, Carl."

"They like you, Grace. And they like Caitlin. We're a family. This isn't easy on them. They're frightened and worried, too. Don't you think we ought to be concerned about what they might be going through?"

He was right. Grace was in such agony she'd lost sight of the fact that others might be in pain also. Good parents put their children's feelings before their own. And Carl was a good father.

"They are both trying to be understanding," Grace said, offering an olive branch. "I appreciate that. I really do."

Carl kissed her check. "I love you, Grace. You are the best thing that ever happened to me."

"After your kids."

"No, right up there with them. You and Caitlin and Adam and Lucy. I love you all. And I'm grateful you get along so well."

Grace was grateful, too. She knew of other second marriages where that hadn't happened. Where stepkids tried their best to sabotage the new marriage. Where the blended family was more like oil and water, and sibling rivalry akin to tribal warfare. She knew of stepparents who resented their new spouse's first family. Women, in particular, who did nothing but complain about their husband's children. She didn't want to be like that.

The one role in life Grace thought she was actually cut out for was being a mother. She loved the soft neediness of a baby, the ready, laughing acceptance of a toddler, the imaginative and often unanswerable questions that sprang naturally from a child's mind. The teen years, which everyone warned her about, proved to be just as satisfying. She delighted in having Caitlin's friends around and listening to their take on the world.

She'd wanted another child, or two or three, but Jake hadn't. And then he'd left, which put an end to whatever dying hopes she'd been clinging to. In marrying Carl, she'd gotten her wish. Lucy and Adam were good kids. She'd enjoyed getting to know both of them, even Adam, who was a bit more of a challenge. But now, without Caitlin, it didn't feel like a family at all. It felt like a gigantic black hole sucking her toward the void at its center.

CHAPTER 15

Rayna's head throbbed. Either the Motrin she'd taken earlier hadn't kicked in yet or it was outgunned by the monster headache. She reached into her desk drawer for the bottle and popped two more pills, washing them down with the bitter remains of lukewarm coffee from the bottom of her cup. She should probably call it a day and head home. She felt exhausted, and feared she was doing little but chasing her tail.

But if Caitlin Whittington was still alive—

She wasn't. Any more than Karen Holiday was alive. Rayna could feel it in her bones.

Pressing her palms against her forehead, she closed her eyes and rested her elbows on the top of her desk. Less than two years on the job and already she'd flubbed the most serious pair of investigations the town had ever seen.

She heard the shuffle of footsteps behind her, and then a soft drawl. "A pillow would be more comfortable."

She tensed, recognizing the voice. She opened her eyes and spun around in her chair. "What are you doing here?"

"I thought you asked for FBI assistance."

"Hardly." She didn't want help from the Feds, and especially not from Neal Cody. Jesus, could things get any worse?

"Funny," he said. "The call came in a couple of days ago. Something about a killer targeting young girls."

Neal Cody pulled up a chair next to her desk and sat, stretching his long legs out straight in front of him. She felt the gaze of his smoky blue eyes, and the rush of way too many memories, good and bad.

"It wasn't my doing," she said. "It was the chief." She

crossed her arms. "If it was up to me, you wouldn't be here."

"If it was up to me, I wouldn't be here either. So at least we're in agreement about that."

Because of her? Did he find the memories that distasteful?

"I thought you loved your job," she said. "You seemed ready to go anywhere on a moment's notice." The Neal Cody she'd known had lived and breathed the bureau. Catching bad guys was his life's blood.

"It's a long story." He rocked forward. "Now tell me about the missing girls."

"We don't know if the two cases are related."

Cody brushed the air with his hand. "That's something we'll have to figure out."

"Karen Holiday disappeared at the end of October. She was a senior, just shy of her eighteenth birthday, and given to occasional lapses in good judgment. Caitlin Whittington was a sophomore—"

"Was?"

"Is. An honor student and by all accounts responsible. She was last seen around five-thirty on Friday in front of the high school where she was waiting to be picked up from volleyball practice."

"Witnesses? Tips? Theories? Anything at all?"

"You think we've been sitting on our hands? We've got reams of stuff." Anything at all? Insulting bastard!

"And?"

Rayna sighed. "Nothing solid. Yet. The Holiday case has pretty much gone stale, not that we haven't been working it as hard as we can. Now we're looking at areas where the girls' lives might have overlapped. Caitlin's mom found out the mechanic at the local auto shop she uses is a registered sex offender. Both families have taken their cars there, so that's one avenue. The most obvious link is the school. We vetted the teachers and staff pretty thoroughly last fall, but we'll take another look." She told him about the volleyball intern and the possibility that Caitlin was interested in an older guy.

"That's definitely worth a follow-up."

"Could be whoever did this picked the girls at random. Assuming it's even the same person."

"Is it all right if I take the case files tonight? The sooner I get up to speed the better."

"Suit yourself." She didn't have the energy for a turf war, especially one she was bound to lose.

Cody gathered the files and prepared to leave. "I'm going to grab a bite to eat. Why don't you come along and we can continue the discussion over dinner."

"No, thanks. This is work, not a social event."

"I wasn't talking candlelight and fine wine. Just a burger or something. You have to eat, don't you? And I'm starving. Friggin' planes these days don't even spring for pretzels."

Rayna hesitated. She was hungry and her fridge was bare. On the other hand she looked like shit, and probably smelled that way too. It had been a long day.

What the hell did it matter? Whatever there'd been between them had ended a long time ago.

"Okay," she agreed. "But I'll drive myself."

He looked at her with surprise. "I hadn't considered anything different."

Rayna gave him directions to the Black Bear Diner in the center of town. It was a popular place, but the folks of Paradise Falls ate early and by now the evening rush would be over.

"See you in a few minutes," he said, easing out of the chair. He tucked the case files under his arm.

As soon as Cody had gone, Rayna headed for the rest room to see if freshening up was a lost cause.

Cody polished off the last of his meatloaf and mashed potatoes and ordered a second beer. He eyed Rayna's largely untouched pile of French fries.

"Help yourself," she said, inching the plate across the table toward him.

"You sure?"

"They'll go to waste otherwise." Better that than to her waist, she joked silently. The silly pun was a favorite of Hank's.

Cody snagged a handful of fries and leaned back in his seat. "So you're a lieutenant now. Big honcho chief detective."

"Until they fire me." She hadn't meant to let that slip. "It's a small department. Chief detective doesn't mean much anyway."

"Beats being a squaw."

Now she was getting bad jokes from Cody as well as Hank.

"Why would they fire you?" he asked after a moment.

"Not everyone is happy about having an outsider in charge. And a woman at that. There's also a fairly vocal element who consider Karen Holiday's unsolved abduction a glowing example of my incompetence."

"And now you've got another missing girl." He worked the label on the beer bottle with his thumb. "That's tough."

"Yeah. Especially since serious crime was almost nonexistent in Paradise Falls until I got here."

"I didn't mean just the public pressure, but the nature of the cases. You doing okay with that?"

If his tone hadn't been so gentle, she might have bristled. But it actually felt good to have someone acknowledge her own loss. Someone concerned for how she might be feeling. Few people in Paradise Falls knew she'd had a daughter, much less one who'd been murdered. She kept her private life private.

"It gets to me, sure. But I knew when I decided to stick with police work I'd run into something like this. It's why I stayed in the field. Getting the creeps off the streets is my way of getting even."

He rolled a torn bit of label into a ball. "Any new developments on Kimberly's homicide?"

Rayna shook her head. She didn't trust her voice.

Her daughter's killer remained at large. He was able to smell the honeysuckle in spring and wood smoke in the fall. He could feel the warmth of the sun on his skin, the prickle of winter's frost, the soft downiness of a puppy's fur. Perhaps even a lover's touch. Kimberly couldn't. He'd stolen everything from her. And from Rayna, who didn't even have the satisfaction of seeing him put away.

Cody put his bottle of beer aside and looked into her eyes. "I didn't cut and run, you know. Even when I was officially pulled from the case, I kept after it, scanning databases, keeping my ear to the ground, staying in touch with the local authorities. I wanted to find him. I wanted to give you that much."

She'd be damned if she was going to thank him. Cody had come onto the case when it looked as if Kimberly's disappearance might have been tied to a string of abductions in the northwest. But that killer, when caught, happily confessed to the murder of five young victims and led authorities to their graves. Neal Cody had gone back to D.C. by then to be near his wife, who suffered periodic bouts of severe depression. But not before he'd comforted Rayna by taking her into his arms, and his bed, on numerous occasions, while failing to mention that he even had a wife.

She had felt betrayed and used and taken advantage of at a time when she was most vulnerable. But when honest with herself, she couldn't say she wouldn't have willingly done what she'd done even if she'd known. The anguish and desolation had been so overwhelming, Rayna had felt as though she were sliding toward an open crevasse. Losing herself in Cody's kisses and caresses and passionate lovemaking had been all that had kept her from going over the edge. He'd been a lifeline when she needed it most.

"How is your wife?" Rayna asked.

"Better, or so she says. I wouldn't know. We've been divorced almost a year now."

And he hadn't bothered to contact her. Not that Rayna would have wanted him to. She certainly didn't harbor any romantic notions about their brief affair.

Cody's jaw twitched. "I didn't ask for this assignment," he said. "As a matter of fact, I tried damn hard to get out of it. But it looks like we're going to have to work together."

"Don't worry. I'm not going to hold your feet to the fire about the past."

A flicker of a smile touched his lips. "And here I thought

I detected a less than warm welcome."

"I wasn't happy about having the FBI involved even before you showed up. If I have any chance of proving myself to the doubters in town, I need to be in charge. My case. My perp."

"Fine by me. It's not exactly a plum assignment."

She bristled. "What's that supposed to mean?"

"Don't take it personally, Rayna, but it's a nothing assignment. Two girls in some □odunk, nowhere town—"

"Missing kids are missing kids. What does it matter where they live?" She could feel her throat grow tight. How could she not take it personally?

"The girls are important. Of course, they are. I wasn't implying they weren't. Only that it's a low-profile assignment. Especially for agents at my level."

Rayna pushed back her chair to leave. "You're disgusting. All you care about is yourself and looking good to your bosses."

Cody grabbed her arm to keep her from rising. "Didn't you just tell me 'my case, my perp'? Seems I'm not the only one who wants to look good."

His touch sent an unexpected jolt through her. Despite her anger, she could feel a tingle all the way from the top of her head to the tips of her toes. Jesus, she didn't need this.

"It's not the same," she said.

"Recognition is always a factor. But it's not the main one, Rayna. Not for me. And not for you."

She pulled her arm free. "I'll see you in the morning," she said, and left the diner without looking back.

CHAPTER 16

Rayna had just stepped from the shower the next morning when her phone rang. Hair still dripping, she wrapped the towel around her shivering body and went to answer it.

"Something here you might want to take a look at," Hank said.

Rayna held her breath. Not a body, please. And not another missing girl. "What is it?"

"We may have found Caitlin Whittington's backpack."

She exhaled. "Where was it?"

"In a Dumpster near the mall. Not the one where Karen Holiday's purse turned up, but awfully close."

Rayna felt her skin prickle. Another similarity between the two cases. "Who found it?" she asked.

"That's not entirely clear. A couple in their late teens, a guy and a girl, were trying to buy CDs at Wal-Mart using Caitlin's credit card. The clerk recognized the name and called it in. The kids claim they found it in the Dumpster. They could have dumped the backpack there themselves, of course, but my take is that they're telling the truth. Their stories match to a tee, and they even admitted to taking the twenty-three dollars inside."

"Any idea how long it might have been there?"

"Pickup is Friday," Hank said, "so the backpack could have been dumped right after Caitlin disappeared, or any time in the last four days. But the kids say the backpack was close to the top."

"So not that long then," Rayna said, thinking out loud.

"Looks that way. Kind of spooky, isn't it?"

"Right. What about the kids, do they know Caitlin?"

"They say they don't. They aren't from around here. The must never listen to the news, either, because they didn't know there was a missing girl. They live out of a ratty old VW bus plastered with liberal-left bumper stickers."

"But they were trying to buy CDs?"

"Yeah, go figure. I guess even vegan pacifists need their creature comforts."

Rayna used a corner of the towel to wipe a rivulet of water running down her neck. "Where are you? The station?"

"We're still at the mall. You want us to wait for you here?"

"Yeah. I just got out of the shower. Let me get dressed and I'll be on my way." Her hair could dry itself, although given the weather, it would be a cold process.

"I'm talking to a naked lady?"

Rayna hung up without bothering to answer.

The Dumpster in question was near the loading dock at the east end of the mall. Rayna spotted two patrol cars as well as Hank's unmarked car. Hank got out to greet her when she pulled up. Fritz Burns followed from one of the black and whites.

"We separated the couple," Hank explained. "One in each of the cruisers. Backpack's in my car. I took a quick look inside, but I didn't want to disturb any prints that might be on it."

"Any witnesses who might have seen it being tossed?"

"We canvassed the nearby shops," Fritz said. He was wearing reflective sunglasses, despite the overcast sky. "Nothing."

Hank rubbed his palms together against the cold. "It can't be a coincidence that her backpack ended up in more or less the same place as Karen Holiday's purse."

"My thinking as well. And if Seth Robbins hears about it, you can be sure he'll use that information to fan the fires."

"You think we can keep the details from the press?"

"Let's hope so."

An unfamiliar white Camry screeched to a halt next to

them. Neal Cody got out of the driver's side and crossed to Rayna with fire in his eyes. "You must have received an F in 'plays well with others' in grade school."

"I was going to tell you about it. I just didn't expect you'd be into grunt work."

Hank was giving her a curious look so she made the introductions.

"Pleased to meet you," Hank said, extending his large, bony hand. "Don't mind Rayna. Her bark's bigger than her bite."

"That so?" Cody smiled. "I'll bear it in mind."

Rayna turned to Hank and shot him a piercing look.

He shrugged. "Well, gosh, Rayna. It's true."

"Oh, for God's sake." Working with Hank was sometimes an exercise in patience. The saving grace was that he was a good cop and despite his goofy social awkwardness, she was fond of him. "What are you going to do about the young couple?"

"They're being cooperative," Fritz said.

Hank scratched the balding dome of his head. "Still, using a stolen credit card is against the law. And on the off-chance they know more than they're saying, a little time down at the station might refresh their memories."

"Good move." Rayna looked around the largely empty parking lot. Only a handful of stores were open at this hour and most of the cars were clustered around the Wal-Mart entrance, which was some distance from the Dumpster. Even later in the day when the lot was close to full, there'd be few cars parked at this end. Whoever dumped the backpack would have had an easy time going unnoticed.

Cody peered into the back of Hank's car. "Did you have a chance to examine the debris in the Dumpster around the backpack?" he asked. "Could be the guy who pitched it there also tossed something of his. A grocery receipt, maybe, or some junk mail. Not likely, but it's happened."

Rayna could tell from the expression on Hank's face that he wasn't thrilled with the idea of searching through garbage.

"We did that," Hank grumbled, "but we'll take another

look just to be certain."

"I'm going to head out to the high school," Rayna said, "unless you need me here."

Hank glanced at Fritz. "No, we've got it covered."

Pretty-boy Fritz, Dumpster-diving. That should be a sight. Rayna considered sticking around to watch. Instead, she turned to Cody. "We got an okay to search Caitlin's locker." She paused. "I suppose you want to be there, too."

Without waiting for an answer she climbed into her car, and was surprised to find Cody climbing into the passenger seat next to her.

"What about your car?"

"I'll pick it up later."

Rayna opened her mouth to protest—she hadn't intended to offer him a ride —then, feeling defeated, started the car's engine.

"Are you expecting her locker to tell you anything?" Cody asked after a few minutes.

"No, but it's worth checking."

"What about her computer? You've looked at that?"

"Yes. And yes, she's on Facebook. We've got Cliff Leavitt, our tech guy, looking into it further." After a moment she added, "Karen Holiday had Facebook, too, but so does just about every kid who's not living under a rock."

"Hey, I wasn't criticizing, just asking."

The way you'd ask a child if he'd done his homework. Well, she'd just have to get used to it. You couldn't fight the FBI. Rayna kept her eyes on the road. Cody must have picked up on her mood because he was quiet for the remainder of the short drive to the school.

Rayna parked in the visitor parking area near the main entrance. The student and staff lots were full of cars, but the hallways were largely empty. Rayna knew that would change the moment the bell rang for passing period. Probably seconds before the bell rang, if past experience was any indication.

Chuck Morgan, the principal, waited for them in his office. He was a fair-complexioned man whose face and arms were doused with freckles. Rayna had dealt with him extensively last fall when Karen Holiday disappeared. He was straightforward and cooperative, which made her job much easier.

She introduced him to Cody as they walked to Caitlin's locker, where Morgan opened it with a master key.

It was practically empty, which didn't surprise Rayna, given the load of school books in Caitlin's backpack. What did surprise her was that nestled among the few remaining textbooks and lone hairbrush was an iPod nano.

"She must have forgotten it," Rayna remarked.

"Most kids are glued to theirs," the principal noted wryly, before adding, "Of course we do have strict rules against using phones and other electronic devices during class."

Rayna leafed through Caitlin's books, turning up nothing of interest. "We'd like to talk to the assistant volleyball coach," she said. "Rusty? A student teacher?"

"Right. Rusty Hanson. I believe he's got a history class at the moment, but the period ends in ten minutes."

"We'll wait." Rayna closed Caitlin's locker. "Did Karen Holiday have Mr. Hanson as a teacher?"

"No, Rusty didn't come on board until after the winter holiday. Why?"

"Just asking." Although she was sure the principal was smart enough to figure out the implications of the question.

"What's Rusty like?" Cody asked.

"He's a good teacher. Knows his stuff and gets along well with the kids. We've had nothing but favorable feedback."

The bell rang and Morgan walked them to Rusty Hanson's classroom, the three of them dodging a steady stream of students along the way. The teacher was young and athletic looking, with thick sandy-brown hair and a square jaw. He looked like a teacher who would be popular with students. And a fantasy idol for a segment of the female population.

Morgan made the introductions and left them alone.

"What can I do for you?" Hanson asked with an easy smile. He sat casually on the edge of his desk, one leg on the floor, the other hanging free, while Rayna and Cody remained standing.

"We wanted to ask you about Caitlin Whittington," Rayna said. "I understand you coach girls' volleyball."

"Yes. It's terrible, her being missing. All the kids are upset, especially the girls on the team. And the staff, too. It's been hard on everyone."

"Do you have any theories about what might have happened to her?"

"No. I understand there was another girl last fall. The consensus seems to be that the disappearances are related."

"That's one theory," Rayna told him. "But it's far from certain." She looked around the classroom. A poster of the American presidents through Bush, a wall map of the thirteen colonies, and an enlarged replica of the Declaration of Independence. Standard fare, but there was also a bulletin board of contemporary political cartoons and slogans.

"How about Caitlin's personal life?" Cody asked. "Was there anything that raised red flags with you? Maybe something she said or a conversation you overheard?"

"I try not to get involved in the personal lives of my students. It's one of the things they warn us about in the teaching program. You want to be friendly but not too friendly." Hanson gave them an embarrassed laugh and eased himself from his perch on the desk. "Especially being a guy and all. Too many chances for a misunderstanding, if you know what I mean."

Rayna wondered if he'd raised the point in order to deflect suspicion from himself. "She recently broke up with her boyfriend. Ty Cross. What do you know about that?"

Hanson hesitated. "Nothing directly. Like I said, I try to keep a distance between myself and the kids. But I did overhear some of the girls talking. None of them seemed very sympathetic. They seemed to think Caitlin was crazy for breaking up with him, and that she had no call to be upset about it since it was her own doing."

"Was she upset?" Cody asked.

"Yeah. Maybe she was having regrets, I don't know. But she'd been upset before they broke up, too. I remember one day in particular. She was worthless at practice. She couldn't concentrate, kept missing shots, and then left in tears, saying she felt sick."

"When was this?" Rayna asked.

"A few days before the big breakup, I think."

Around the time of her encounter with Rob Hardy. Rayna clearly did not have the full story on Caitlin's breakup. Whether or not it had anything to do with her disappearance was another matter.

"We understand she might have been involved with someone older," Cody said, with a meaningful pause before continuing. "You wouldn't know anything about that, would you?"

"No, like I said, I didn't really—" Hanson stopped midsentence and looked at Cody through narrowed eyes. "What you're really asking is if I was involved with her, isn't it?"

"Were you?"

"Jesus." Hanson's jaw hardened as he looked from Cody to Rayna. "My teaching supervisors were right. Everyone's on a hunt for misconduct. I've got nothing more to say to you." He turned his back on them and began wiping the chalkboard.

"Have it your way," Cody said with a hint of implied menace. "We'll be in touch."

When they were outside in the hallway he turned to Rayna. "What do you think?"

"Testy."

"Can't say I blame him."

"He never did answer the question," she pointed out.

"No, but there's not a lot to go on, either. We don't even know for a fact that Caitlin was involved with someone older, do we?"

"There's a lot we don't know," said Rayna, worried they never would.

CHAPTER 17

Grace sipped her coffee and watched Jake stir the second packet of sugar—real sugar, not the diet stuff—into his own cup, then top it off with cream. How did he avoid gaining weight? Jake was as lean as the day they'd met seventeen years ago. Probably as good-looking, too, although she had trouble seeing him objectively. There were simply too many memories—good times gone bad, tenderness turned ugly, dreams left unfulfilled. She sometimes wondered if those glimmerings from the past colored her feelings for better or worse. Not that it really mattered. She and Jake shared a bond that overrode everything—the bond of a child.

Especially now that Caitlin was missing.

Jake looked up and their eyes held, momentarily eclipsing the strife and distance of their divorce. Grace was happy to see him, even if the meeting was something of an afterthought on his part. Jake had finally agreed to take the polygraph test and had phoned to suggest they get together for coffee since he'd be in town.

"It's hard to believe this is really happening," he said, resting the wooden stir stick on a paper napkin. They had one of the small tables along the wall and seemed to be the only people in the coffee shop having an actual conversation. The others were lost in books or busily typing away on their laptops.

"Hard to believe what's happening? The polygraph?"

Jake gave her an odd look, and Grace realized she'd insulted him. "I was talking about Caitlin. Did you really think she wouldn't be first on my mind?"

"I wasn't sure what you meant." Grace had thought he

might have been referring to the test. It wouldn't be the first time Jake put himself first.

"At times it's almost surreal," he continued. "I know she's missing but it's so totally unbelievable I can't get my mind around it. And other times it's so real, the panic grips me like the jaws of some horrible prehistoric creature."

Grace reached across the table and touched his hand, feeling a twinge of guilt for her unkind thoughts a moment earlier. She'd never doubted that their daughter's disappearance worried Jake, but she wasn't sure he felt it the way she did. To see the emotion that boiled beneath the surface, to know that Jake was as lost as she was, made her feel less alone, and in that way, stronger.

"I understand," she said, her throat tight. "I know exactly what you mean."

"It's like I'm two different people. One going about my day, taking care of business, and the other frozen with fear."

"Do you think she's still alive?" Grace asked quietly.

He picked up the stir stick in one hand and snapped it in two. "The cops asked me the same thing."

"What did you tell them?"

"That I have to think so. I can't let myself imagine she isn't."

Grace wanted to believe it, too, but she had far less control over where her imagination took her.

"You don't?" Jake asked, after a moment.

"I don't know. Sometimes, yes. Sometimes I can actually hear the sweet lilt of her voice saying `I love you, Mom.' I can picture her coming home. I can feel myself hugging her." The sensation felt so real at times, Grace was sure Caitlin had to be standing beside her. "But other times when I try to conjure up that sense of optimism, I'm left with nothing but heavy despair. It all seems so bleak."

Jake tossed the fragments of the stir stick onto the table. "I wish to God I had a sense that the cops were making progress."

She raised her eyes to his and found there a common ground forged of sorrow. "Waiting is harder than I ever imagined."

He took a sip of coffee and set the mug back on the table, gripping it with both hands. "It's been four days now and nothing. The longer she's gone—" He stopped himself, pressed his thumbs together. "What do you think happened?"

"I have no idea. I think about it all the time. It could be there's a connection with what happened to Karen Holiday. Or maybe Karen's disappearance is unrelated to Caitlin's." She traced the rim of the ceramic mug with her thumb. "I hope they're unrelated."

"Why?"

"Because the chances of Caitlin being okay are better that way. When I think of a serial killer grabbing her, I . . ." Tears welled in Grace's eyes. "I can't handle that. I can't." She reached into her purse for a tissue. "Oh, God. I can't handle any of it. There's nothing that prepares you for this."

Jake squeezed his eyes shut and was silent for a moment. Then he sighed and looked at Grace. "What do the police think? Have they shared much with you? I have trouble getting more than half a dozen words out of them."

"Maybe that's because until now they didn't see you as cooperating." The words were sharper than Grace intended and she felt bad about that, but she saw no need to apologize.

"Are you referring to the polygraph?" Jake leaned forward on the table, fixing her in his gaze. "There's a reason the results aren't allowed in a court of law, Grace. Those tests aren't foolproof."

"They must be reliable or the police wouldn't use them."

"They don't use them to eliminate people, despite what they say. They use them as leverage on those who trip up. They like nothing better than to catch a potential suspect failing the thing."

Grace had a horrible thought. It had never occurred to her that Jake might actually be a suspect. "Is that why you didn't want to take it? You were afraid they'd think you had something to do with Caitlin's disappearance?"

"Welcome to reality, Grace. That's exactly what they'd like to think."

Another cold thought struck her. "Did you pass it?"

"They didn't share the results with me, but they didn't hold me, either."

"I told them you couldn't have been involved."

"Thank you."

The comment had a sardonic edge to it, and Grace couldn't tell if he'd intended that or not. "I doubt you were ever a serious suspect," she said. "It has to have been a stranger, or someone Caitlin crossed paths with." She told him about discovering her auto mechanic on the sexual-predators website.

"Jesus. I hope the cops have him on their radar."

"I told them."

"What about the ex-boyfriend?"

"Ty? I know they've talked to him." Grace had never particularly warmed to Ty Cross, but she couldn't imagine him hurting Caitlin. In fact, she had trouble imagining anyone who knew Caitlin causing her harm.

Except maybe for one person.

"Did Starr take the polygraph test?" Grace asked.

"Why should she take it?"

"The police asked her to, didn't they? Shouldn't she be doing everything possible to help them?"

"She's been busy."

Starr ran her own personal shopping business. Grace found it hard to believe she couldn't free up a few hours to help the police.

"Don't forget that Starr was the one who was supposed to pick Caitlin up," Grace pointed out. "She was here in town. That's opportunity, isn't it?"

"You've been watching too many bad television shows," Jake said angrily. "Besides, I was supposed to pick up Caitlin. Starr was just helping out because I was in a bind."

"But she doesn't like Caitlin." Grace had started down this road and she wasn't turning back now. "That gives her motive."

"What are you talking about? They get along fine."

"Then why is Starr so critical of Caitlin? Why does she

resent the time you spend with her?" Grace decided not to raise the money issue, although she knew Starr must resent that too.

"You're being ridiculous, Grace. If we're going to start pointing fingers, maybe you should take a closer look at your own household."

"Carl? He and I were three hours away when she disappeared."

"I was talking about that boy of his." Jake leaned back and crossed his arms, a contemptuous posture Grace was familiar with from six years of marriage. "I've told you before, it's not right for Caitlin to be living in the same house with some boy her age she's not related to. That's asking for trouble."

"They are related. Adam is her stepbrother."

"That's not what I meant and you know it. It's not like they grew up in the same house. He was a complete stranger until you married his father. And he's an odd one. You've admitted that much to me."

Grace bristled. It was one thing for her to think that Adam was odd, another for Jake to throw it in her face. "Adam is not the kind of odd you're insinuating. Both of Carl's children welcomed Caitlin. They all get along really well."

Grace realized, too late, that she'd more or less parroted what Jake had said about Starr and Caitlin. In any case, she now regretted having turned what was a comfortable meeting into a session of finger-pointing. "I'm sorry for raising the issue, Jake. I wasn't implying that Starr had anything to do with Caitlin's disappearance. I just wish she'd cooperate with the police. Now that you've taken the polygraph, can't you convince her to do it?"

"Starr doesn't answer to me." He checked his watch. "I have to run."

"It was good seeing you," Grace said truthfully.

Jake grabbed his coat from the back of the chair, and brushed her cheek with a kiss. "We have to stay hopeful. If the worst happens, we'll deal with it then."

The worst. Grace didn't want to even imagine what that

might be.

A few blocks from home, Grace's cell phone rang. She retrieved it from the pocket on her purse, slowed to check the readout, then quickly pulled to the curb and flipped the phone open. Her hand was shaking. A call from the police could mean the best of news or the worst. No, not the worst, she told herself. Surely if Caitlin was dead they'd send someone out in person.

"Hello. This is Grace Whittington."

"Rayna Godwin here. I was hoping I could come by and talk to you. I tried your home number and got the machine."

Grace's heart skipped a beat and then turned to stone. "You have news?"

"No, not that kind. I'm sorry. I didn't mean to upset you. Just a few things I'd like to go over with you."

It took Grace a moment to breathe again. "Sure, I'm on my way home right now."

"I'll come by in about half an hour."

Grace disconnected. Her skin was clammy and she felt light-headed, but she needed to follow Jake's advice. Stay hopeful. Think positive. She rested her head on the steering wheel, took a deep breath, and tried to picture Caitlin happy and safe.

Half an hour later, almost to the minute, Detective Godwin sat at the farmhouse table in Grace's kitchen. Grace had put a kettle of water on the stove and she now busied herself with mugs and tea bags.

"Herbal, decaf, or full punch?" she asked.

"Anything is fine."

She filled two mugs with boiling water and set an array of tea bags in front of Detective Godwin. How could the woman find her daughter if she couldn't even decide what kind of tea she wanted?

"I understand my ex-husband finally took the lie detector test," Grace said.

"That's right." Godwin chose a peppermint tea, one of

Caitlin's favorites.

Grace waited, hoping the detective would elaborate, but she didn't. Instead, she took a minute to open the tea packet and dip it into her cup. Then she said, "We found Caitlin's backpack today."

"Where?" Grace's heart kicked into overdrive. Was finding the backpack a good or bad sign?

"In a Dumpster at the mall. A couple of drifters going through the trash found her wallet, took the twenty-three dollars inside, and tried to use her credit card to buy some CDs. The store clerk recognized Caitlin's name and contacted us."

"Do you believe them? How do you know they aren't the ones who have Caitlin?"

"From what we know, that's unlikely."

Grace felt unsteady and dropped into a chair across from the detective, her own cup of tea still on the counter. "So what does it mean? Will this help you find Caitlin?"

"We're hoping there will be something with the backpack that will provide a clue. But I have to be honest, it's a long shot. Since it was near the top of the Dumpster, we're assuming the backpack was disposed of in the last couple of days."

"That would mean the kidnapper is still in town. Or was until recently. That's a good sign, isn't it? It would mean he didn't take off with Caitlin and that you can concentrate your search efforts locally. And if someone saw him at the mall—"

Grace gripped her stomach. The mall.

Oh God, the same place they'd found Karen Holiday's purse. Beth Holiday had said the police found her daughter's purse in a Dumpster at the mall.

With the swift, cold force of an unexpected ocean wave, heartbreaking certainty crashed down on Grace, paralyzing her. Caitlin was dead. Along with Karen Holiday.

Some horrible monster was preying on young girls right here in Paradise Falls. And he had taken Caitlin from her forever.

When Grace could breathe again, she said, "Isn't the mall

where Karen Holiday's purse was found?"

The detective gave her a curious look. "How did you hear that? The information wasn't made public."

"Her mother told me. And there was money in Karen's wallet, too. Whoever took her wasn't interested in money or credit cards."

"I thought you didn't know Beth Holiday."

"I don't. But I went to see her the other day. I thought meeting her might help me, you know, get through this." Grace felt her throat grow tight and her eyes sting with tears. "I thought it would help to talk to someone who's been there."

Detective Godwin's eyes softened. "Did it?"

"Not really." Grace rose from her chair. She wanted the detective to leave. She needed to be alone. She wanted to process what she'd just learned in private.

"I have one more question," the detective said, still in her seat. "I searched Caitlin's school locker today. It seemed odd she'd leave her iPod there. Especially on a Friday. Was that something she usually did? Or do you think she forgot it because she was in a hurry or distracted?"

"What are you talking about? Caitlin doesn't own an iPod."

"Are you sure?"

"Of course I'm sure. She must have borrowed it."

"Aren't most kids glued to their iPods?"

"I guess so. I don't know. Like I said, Caitlin didn't own one." When the detective showed no sign of leaving, Grace said, "Was there something else?" She knew her tone was curt but she didn't care.

"You're upset," Godwin said, rising at last. "What is it?"

Grace shook her head. The dam was ready to burst and there was nothing she could do to stop it. She felt her chest shudder. She grabbed the kitchen counter as the tears came, then quickly grew to a flood. "I'm sorry," she said between sobs. "I'm having a meltdown moment."

"You're entitled. Is it something we talked about?"

Grace grabbed a fistful of tissues from the box on the counter, and blew her nose. "It's the backpack. Caitlin's wallet.

Her things. And at the mall. Just like Karen Holiday. I think it just hit me that Caitlin won't ever be coming home. She's really gone."

"Grace." Detective Godwin touched Grace's arm lightly. "I know it's hard to hold out hope. Close to impossible sometimes, but there is a chance we'll find your daughter alive."

Grace pulled her arm away. "What do you know?" she snapped, tired of well-meaning outsiders telling her to remain hopeful. People who couldn't begin to understand her pain. Hollow words easily delivered. "You never found Karen Holiday, and you aren't going to find Caitlin, either."

"We're working very hard to—"

"Stop the crap! I don't want to hear how hard you're looking for her and how I have to hold out hope. She's my daughter. Do you understand what that means? Do you have any idea?"

The detective stared at her like she'd been slapped in the face. In a way, she had, Grace conceded silently. But Grace's anger hadn't ebbed.

"Granted, it will be a disappointment for you," Grace went on. "But bottom line, it's just a job. When the day is over you go home to your husband or boyfriend or dog, take off your shoes and sip a little wine. Maybe you even rock your own child to sleep. For all your so-called knowledge, do you really think you have any idea how horrible it is to be in my position? How can you think for even a minute you're in any position to tell me to stay positive?"

Grace's voice had risen along with the heat in her cheeks. She took a breath to calm herself.

Silence echoed in the space between them. An eerie, electric silence.

"Just go," Grace said when the silence grew unbearable. "Please, give me time alone."

"You don't know how tempted I am."

"Do it then. You know where the door is."

Detective Godwin ran a hand through her hair, feathering it at odd angles. She sat down again in the chair she'd vacated earlier, and leaned forward, arms on the table, head in her hands. Then she looked up and fixed her gaze on Grace.

"I do understand some of what you're going through. My own daughter disappeared when she was eleven. She was missing for one year, ten months, and twenty-seven days."

"But you found her again? Safe?"

The detective's eyes half closed and the surrounding muscles tensed, as though she stared into a bright light. "Her body, what was left of it, was found at the bottom of an old well. If she'd lived, she'd be Caitlin's age."

"Oh, my God!" Grace's lungs burned with the venom of her earlier outburst. "My God, I'm so sorry." She gripped the table as she sank into her chair. "I never thought—"

"That's why I do what I do. Why I go after the bad guys. It is personal for me."

"Did they ever find her killer?"

"No. A lot of people worked on it. I was a cop, after all. At first we thought her disappearance was tied to the abductions of four other girls in Northern California. But that man was ultimately caught. He was miles away, in jail on other charges, the day Kimberly disappeared."

"Kimberly. That's a lovely name,"

"She was a lovely girl." A faint smile touched the detective's lips. "Parents always say that, I know. But she was. Funny and caring and full of life."

Memories of Caitlin at age eleven flashed in Grace's mind. The mother-daughter trip they'd taken to a dude ranch in Montana. The scarf Caitlin had knitted for her grandmother, an oddly irregular shape in bright orange. Grace's throat constricted. She'd had four more years with Caitlin than the detective had had with her daughter. If Caitlin had disappeared at eleven, Grace would never have known the spirited teenager she'd become. Just as she would now never know the woman Caitlin could have grown to be. Caitlin would now be forever fixed in Grace's mind at fifteen, just as Kimberly was for her mother at eleven.

"So your daughter's killer is still out there?" Grace asked.

"As far as I know."

"And there were no clues? No leads?"

"Nothing meaningful. The lead detective on the case retired last year, but the guy who inherited it is someone I used to work with. He and I both keep an eye out for more recent cases that might be a link. And someone I know in the FBI was involved early on. He says he hasn't given up either."

The detective had lovely green eyes, but there were dark circles under them, the kind that never really went away. Grace hadn't noticed that before. Nor had she noticed the set of the mouth that rarely smiled. Or the deep frown lines in her forehead.

"Is your husband in law enforcement, too?" Grace asked.

"He was a veterinarian. He died a year before Kimberly disappeared. Cancer."

Grace stayed quiet. Of all the things she thought to say, none felt right. She couldn't imagine how she'd cope without Carl. Even when she turned on him, he was there to support her. Jake, too. He shared her fears and heartache.

Finally, she managed, "How awful for you. How do you go on?"

"Some days I wonder that myself. There are times, less frequent now, when I'm not sure I can. But until I find my daughter's killer, I don't have a choice. I owe it to Kimberly not to give up."

"I'm really sorry for what I said earlier. I didn't know. Didn't have any idea."

"No one here does. That's part of why I came to Paradise Falls. I don't really know why I told you, but I'd appreciate it if you didn't repeat it."

"Of course. Thanks for telling me, though." She wasn't sure why, but her conversation with Detective Godwin left her feeling calmer. In some ways she felt the detective was more an ally than either Carl or Jake. She was a mother who'd lost her daughter, and a mother's loss was like no other.

CHAPTER 18

Rayna slammed the door to the car shut. What had she been thinking? What in God's name had possessed her to tell Grace about Kimberly? She gave her head a symbolic knock on the steering wheel.

Grace had her own problems, she didn't need to hear about Rayna's. It was unprofessional and besides, Rayna made it a practice not to talk about her daughter in casual conversation. Talking about what happened leveled her own personal tragedy to the mundane. Ho-hum, another murdered child.

Nobody but Rayna could ever understand the agonizing loss she'd suffered. It wasn't that people were indifferent. Rayna had endured months of pitiful stares, avowed expressions of condolence, and sympathetic whispers behind her back. People agreed that a murdered child was about the worst thing imaginable, but then in the next breath they were discussing recipes for peach cobbler or how to get oil stains out of cotton clothing.

Talking about Kimberly drained life from Rayna's memories, and the memories were all she had.

She'd been so careful up till now. Chief Stoval knew, of course—he'd hired her—but he'd agreed to respect her wish for privacy. No one else, not even Hank, knew that she'd had a husband and daughter in another life. So why had she felt the need to blurt it out to Grace?

It wasn't that Caitlin was missing. Rayna hadn't confided in Beth Holiday. God forbid. The woman scared her. No, saddened her. Beth Holiday grieved for her lost daughter, of course, but as far as Rayna could tell, Beth accepted it on some level. God's will and all that bunk. Grace's grief was so raw, it reminded Rayna of her own.

Or maybe it had something to do with the fact that Caitlin touched a nerve with Rayna in a way Karen Holiday hadn't. Caitlin looked nothing like Kimberly, who had blue eyes and fine blond hair to Caitlin's darker, richer coloring. But Caitlin seemed possessed of spiritedness that reminded Rayna of her own daughter. Caitlin was the sort of girl Kimberly might have become.

Rayna took a deep breath. Get a grip, she told herself. She had a job to do.

Back at the station she found a message that Paul Nesbitt had called and she remembered that she hadn't returned his phone call from the night before.

She dialed his number in the prosecutor's office, hoping he'd be unavailable. That way she could leave a message and be off the hook. Paul was a decent man and a good companion for those times she was in the mood. Now wasn't one of those times.

His secretary put the call through and Paul picked up on the second ring. "Hey, good to hear your voice," he said. "It's been a while."

"What's up?"

"I've got tickets for that new musical in Portland this weekend. I was hoping you would join me."

"I'd love to, but this missing girl investigation has me spinning a thousand different directions." Had the circumstances been different, Rayna might have accepted—she loved the theater and Paul knew how to dine well, a winning combination in her book

"How's the investigation going? You making any headway?"

"You know what it's like. Lots of threads to follow, most of which go nowhere."

"Yeah. At least by the time my office gets involved, we've got a suspect and a theory. Listen, take care, Rayna. And we'll get together soon."

"Thanks, Paul. I'm sorry I can't make it this weekend."

When the investigation wrapped, she'd invite Paul over for dinner. She had been a good cook at one time and she sometimes treated Paul shabbily. It wouldn't hurt to extend an olive branch.

But first she needed to find out what had happened to Caitlin Whittington.

CHAPTER 19

After Detective Godwin left, Grace lay down on the big bed upstairs. She covered herself with the red wool afghan Carl had given her last Christmas, closed her eyes, and retreated into a space that was hers alone.

Her body felt like lead—heavy and lifeless. Her mind was a murky pond. Thoughts came and went, images drifted past. Memories dropped in like uninvited guests, prickly and irritating.

Caitlin as a cooing baby, splashing in her bathing tub. Her first Christmas, her first day of school. The scraped knees and fevers, the tears and hugs and sloppy kisses. Shopping trips to Portland, quick trips to the store for everything from school supplies to shoelaces.

Grace curled into a ball. She drifted off to sleep intermittently, but always awoke to the same feeling of despair. At one point she heard voices downstairs. Lucy and Adam home from school. Water running in the kids' bathroom. The heavy metal tones of Adam's cell phone. Doors closing. Doors opening.

And then, later, Carl tiptoeing to their bedroom closet to change out of the slacks and jacket he wore to work. Grace pulled the afghan from her eyes. Outside, the sky was the murky gray of twilight. She could see the glow of street lamps reflected in the bare tree branches beyond the window. She didn't have the energy to look at the clock but knew it was time to start dinner. Maybe past time. Still, she didn't get up. And when Carl turned out the closet light and slid quietly from the room, she pretended to be asleep.

Alone again, she rolled onto her back and stared at the

ceiling, seeing nothing but the long trail of empty days before her. A lifetime without Caitlin.

Finally, she washed her face and ran a comb through her hair. I am beginning to look like my mother, she thought. Sallow skin and puffy face. An old lady already.

At the top of the stairs, she jumped when she saw the door to Caitlin's room open.

When Adam emerged, she said, "What were you doing in Caitlin's room?"

"Nothing." Adam shuffled his feet in that way Grace always found irksome.

"Why were you in there?" She looked to see if his hands were empty, and they were. Still, he had no reason to be poking around Caitlin's things. "You must have had a reason."

Adam avoided her eyes. The oversized black T-shirt hung loosely on his thin frame. "Just looking," he said.

"Looking for what?"

"Nothing. I'm sorry. I didn't know it would upset you. I miss her, wanted to be . . . around her."

"Around her?"

His color deepened and his face took on the red of his hair. "It's a way to feel in touch, is all."

Hadn't Grace done the same thing herself, many times? Hasn't she run her hands over Caitlin's collection of books, smelled the scent of her pillow, lovingly examined each item of clothing in Caitlin's closet? But that was different, Caitlin was her daughter.

And she was Adam's stepsister, Grace reminded herself. Of course he'd miss her.

But Jake's words echoed in her mind. He's not family. He's a boy her own age. An odd one.

Grace waited until Adam had gone to his own room before continuing downstairs.

Carl had already started dinner. Nothing elaborate, but all on his own he'd scrounged up ingredients for a sort of pasta carbonara and a salad. Knowing Grace's penchant for having a green vegetable with dinner, he'd even found a bag of frozen peas in the freezer and put them on to boil. She felt a surge of gratitude and love.

"How can I help?" she offered.

"I've got it under control. Why don't you have some wine and take it easy. The bottle's open."

"You're the kindest man I know. Thank you."

Carl wiped his free hand on his apron, tilted Grace's chin, and planted a kiss and a soft nibble. "Cooking dinner is the least I can do." He stirred the pasta with a long-handled wooden spoon. "It's actually nice to be able to do something for you. I hate feeling so helpless."

"You do a lot for me." Grace poured herself a glass of merlot and topped off Carl's glass.

"You looked pretty wrung out upstairs," he said.

She sipped her wine. She hadn't eaten all day, could feel the warmth spread quickly through her body. "Detective Godwin came by this afternoon," she said, leaning against the counter. "They found Caitlin's backpack in a Dumpster at the mall near where Karen Holiday's purse was found. I think that's when it hit me. It's not speculation anymore. There's tangible evidence. Whoever took Karen took Caitlin, too. Suddenly it all seemed so clear, so certain to me that she must be dead."

Carl stopped stirring the sauce and looked at her. "It's not certain at all, Grace."

"Maybe not certain, no. But fairly likely if you look at it objectively." He opened his mouth to speak but she cut him off. "I know I'm supposed to stay optimistic. And I'm trying, I'm really trying to stay hopeful. I'm her mother, for God's sake. I'm the last person who should ever give up hope. But I've never been very good at sticking my head in the sand."

"There have been cases where kidnapped kids escaped. Sometimes the kidnapper doesn't even hold the kid by force, just convinces her to stay. That girl in Salt Lake City, remember? It turned out she was with some religious nut as one of his wives. She had been brainwashed but not physically restrained. She's back home now, doing fine."

"Caitlin would never stay with someone like that voluntarily. I don't think anyone could brainwash her to that extent."

"And some guy locked another girl in a closet. For a couple of years, as I remember. But she managed to escape. And those boys who were kidnapped by some guy named Tree Frog or something. Lived in a bus, I think. It took years, but they escaped."

Years of being held prisoner in a closet or the confines of a bus. Was that the golden ray of hope she was supposed to cling to for Caitlin?

"That's not the norm, though," Grace pointed out. She brushed her hair from her face. "Anyway, I'm doing better now. I mean, not better-better, but I crawled out from under my blanket."

To Grace's relief, Carl didn't push his point. She knew he'd only been trying to boost her spirits. He was too much of a realist to buy into the happily-ever-after fantasy he'd been peddling.

"Whatever the future brings," he said, "we'll face it together. You're not alone, Grace."

She thought of Detective Godwin losing her daughter so soon after her husband's death. "I know that. And it means the world to me."

"Dinner's almost ready. Why don't you tell Lucy to set the table?"

"I'll set it myself." Grace laid the red checkered placemats on the kitchen table, her heart wrenching anew as she skipped Caitlin's usual seat. "Detective Godwin's daughter was murdered four years ago. It took almost two years to discover her body. They never found the killer."

"Jesus. She told you this?"

Grace nodded.

"Why? It's not very encouraging."

Logically, Carl was right. Detective Godwin's experience was anything but heartening. Nonetheless, Grace felt consoled by it. "I think I goaded her into telling me, Carl. I accused her of being unable to understand what parents of a missing child go through."

"I don't care what you said to her, she shouldn't have told

you." Carl poured the pasta into a ceramic bowl. "It would have been different if her story had a happy ending."

"She also told me her husband died of cancer a year before their daughter's disappearance."

"Seems to me the detective's got issues with boundaries."

Grace didn't see it that way at all. Maybe it was because women shared in ways men couldn't understand. "It was helpful, really." She moved into Carl's arms. "I couldn't go through this without you. You're the only thing that keeps me from drowning. Detective Godwin had to do it alone."

Carl kissed her mouth, her eyes, her forehead. "We hold each other up, Grace. We're a team."

"All right already," Adam said from the doorway, then loudly cleared his throat in case they hadn't heard him. "Can't you wait until after dinner for that?"

Grace thought he was teasing but she couldn't be sure.

"No," Carl said, one arm still around Grace's shoulders. "Some things are more important than food."

Over dinner Grace relayed the information about Caitlin's backpack to Adam and Lucy.

"Is it a good sign or a bad one?" Lucy asked, echoing Grace's earlier question to Detective Godwin.

"I'm not sure," Grace told her.

"Isn't the mall where you said Karen Holiday's purse was found?"

"Yes, but not the same Dumpster."

Lucy's eyes widened. "The location's got to be significant, though."

"The mall would be an obvious spot for dumping anything," Carl pointed out. "It's central, it's public, it gets a lot of traffic. I wouldn't read too much into it."

Adam hadn't said a word. Nor had he taken more than a bite once the conversation turned to Caitlin. He seemed content to push the food around on his plate with his fork. Grace debated saying something about seeing him emerge from Caitlin's room. It still bothered her, but she knew there were reasonable explanations and that Carl would gravitate to them without a moment's hesitation.

Once again, Jake's comment echoed in her mind. An odd one.

Lucy shook her head. "I bet it is important," she said, clearly agitated. "And it doesn't sound good. Some crazy killer is out there picking off teenage girls. Any of us could be next."

"There's no need to get hysterical about it, honey." Carl patted his daughter's arm. "I think you want to be careful, as always. Don't go off alone. Keep alert. All the stuff we've talked about before. But don't let it rule your life."

Adam pushed back his chair.

"Where are you going?" Carl asked. "You've barely touched your food."

"I'm not really hungry."

"You were the one who was prodding us to get dinner on the table."

"I ate as much as I want." He carried his plate into the kitchen and then tromped upstairs.

"What got into him?" Carl asked.

"He's feeling bad about Caitlin," Lucy said. "He doesn't have many friends and Caitlin was"—she looked at Grace—"is a friend."

Grace again debated telling Carl about seeing Adam in Caitlin's room, but clearly this was not the place or time.

"Can you help me with my science report, Dad?" Lucy asked.

"Honey, you know I'm clueless about science. You should ask your mom."

"But I'm asking you."

Carl sighed. "You waited until the last minute, didn't you?"

"Maybe I can help," Grace offered. She'd been through the eighth-grade science project assignment with Caitlin only a couple of years earlier.

She expected Lucy to rebuff her offer. Instead, she got a grateful, "Are you sure? I don't want to be any trouble. I mean, I know you've got a lot on your mind."

"It will be good for me to think about something else for

a bit." And she knew her relationship with her stepdaughter was important to Carl, just as his with Caitlin had been to her.

Lucy's eyes lit up. "Thank you. Thank you so much."

She really was, or could be, a cute girl, Grace decided. If only she'd lose some weight and do something with her stringy hair. Maybe, at some point, Grace could make a few artfully gentle suggestions.

CHAPTER 20

The small conference room was barely able to accommodate the seven of them crowded around the pockmarked laminate table. Rayna was wedged between Hank and Cliff Leavitt, their computer expert. Fritz Burns and another uniformed officer who'd been working the case sat on the far side of the table. Neal Cody and the chief were positioned at either end. The sense of frustration in the room was thick enough to cut with a knife.

"It will be one week tomorrow," Rayna informed them, although she knew the time line was firmly etched in everyone's mind. One week since Caitlin Whittington had gone missing, and they didn't have a single solid lead.

"I don't need to remind any of you," Chief Stoval added somberly, "the longer she's missing, the less likely it is that there'll be a happy outcome. So let's go over what we've got. Maybe with a second look, something will click."

It might be a "second look" for him, Rayna thought irritably. The rest of them had thought of little else during the past week.

"Let's start with the backpack," Rayna said, taking back the reins. "Anything more from the couple who found it?"

Fritz shook his head. "Their story didn't change, even after a night in jail and the threat of prosecution in connection with the stolen credit card."

"It's only a threat?"

"The DA doesn't want to follow through. They've got clean records and the boy's family is well connected."

"So either the person who took Caitlin tossed the backpack in the Dumpster," Rayna said, "or a third party found it elsewhere and tossed it there."

"Without removing her credit card or the twenty-three dollars that were in it," Cody pointed out. "You'd think a random stranger would try to return it or contact us rather than simply dumping it."

"Or he'd at least keep her credit card and the cash," Hank added.

Cody nodded. "It's almost like someone wanted us to find it."

"Which supports a serial killer theory," the chief said in disgust. "Someone who enjoys rubbing our noses in it."

"In that case, the backpack ought to be our best bet for evidence." Rayna didn't like the fact that it had been Cody who pointed out the obvious, something she'd overlooked. She turned to Fritz. "What does forensics say? Any prints? Hairs? Fibers?"

"Nothing useful. Unless we can find a witness who saw it being tossed, I'm afraid the backpack isn't going to help us."

"Let's run through the time line of the evening she disappeared," the chief said, rising with marker in hand and flipping to a clean page on the large newsprint tablet that hung near his end of the table. "She was seen on campus around five-thirty, waiting for her ride home, right? And that's the last we know anyone saw her."

"Correct," Rayna said.

He wrote the time on the tablet. "And the witness is reliable?"

"There were several. All friends of hers. And her stepsister, Lucy. One theory is that she decided to walk home."

"And maybe she got a ride along the way." Chief Stoval wrote "RIDE?" on his chart.

"Or was forced into a vehicle," Hank pointed out.

Stoval added Hank's comment to his list. "What about potential suspects? Anyone look promising?"

The detectives exchanged glances. "I'll give it a shot," Rayna said. "The rest of you speak up with thoughts and opinions. One of the people we looked at was a mechanic at the shop where both Grace Whittington and Beth Holiday have taken their cars. He's a registered sex offender, but he was at work until six Friday evening. It would take him another fifteen minutes to get over to the school."

She waited for the chief to make a mark on his chart, but he merely rolled the pen between his palms. "There was also some talk that Caitlin might have been interested in an 'older guy,' whatever that means. There's a student teacher who caught our eye. He coaches the girls' volleyball team, which Caitlin played on, and he's pretty friendly with the kids. He's new this semester so there's no connection to Karen Holiday, and he's got good, solid recommendations, but he's still a possibility. We know he would have been leaving the campus about the same time Caitlin disappeared."

"Name?"

"Rusty Hanson."

This time Stoval wrote the name on his board.

"Another area we looked into were clients in Caitlin's dog walking business. Hank, you handled that."

"We interviewed all of the men," Hank said, "including an adult son living at home. There's one guy in his forties, divorced, who's a bit strange. Says he was in San Francisco over the weekend. Left Paradise Falls Thursday afternoon. We haven't been able to verify it, but a neighbor remembers hearing the dog whining and whimpering like it was alone and hungry, so my guess is the guy's telling the truth. Also, for what it's worth, Caitlin's father finally took the polygraph and passed."

"But his fiancée has yet to volunteer," Rayna pointed out. "And she's the one who was closest to Caitlin in proximity. Cliff, why don't you bring us up to date on the computer stuff?"

"Caitlin has a web-based email account we haven't been able to access." Cliff tended to mumble when he spoke, pulling his chin toward his sizable frame. And he rarely made eye contact. But Cliff hadn't been hired for his gregariousness. In the realm of tech, he was tops.

"We're working on it," he added. "She also has an account on Facebook. Caitlin has a lot of 'friends,' which we all know aren't actually friends at all. One in particular piqued my interest—a guy who calls himself Romeo. He's sent her a few Instant Messages, general stuff asking about her life, her day, that sort of thing. But the tone is a little too friendly. Full of flattery and compliments and ways of telling her how special she is."

"What do we know about him?" the chief asked.

"Nothing, so far. He's got a Yahoo email address. But he appears to be posting from somewhere in Oregon."

"There was an iPod in her locker," Rayna noted. "Her mother says she doesn't have an iPod. I called the school to see if anyone had reported one missing, and they hadn't. Seems like the kind of gift a predator might give a girl he was trying to seduce."

"You're thinking maybe he picked her up from school?" Stoval added Romeo to his list.

"Possibly, except everyone seems to agree that Caitlin is a mature and level-headed girl."

"Means nothing," Cody said. "I've seen teens, especially girls, who managed to pull the wool over everyone's eyes before. I've also seen mature adults make horribly bad decisions. I say this Romeo is worth pursuing."

Rayna shifted in her chair. "We also need to keep looking at Ty Cross and Rob Hardy. There's something there that doesn't add up."

"Hardy's a bit of a nerd, is all," Fritz said.

"Those are the kind you need to keep an eye on sometimes," Hank said, with a quick glance at Cliff Leavitt. Rayna wondered if Hank was even aware of what he'd done.

"Cross is the boyfriend, right?" Stoval asked. "His father's paid me a couple of visits."

"Ex-boyfriend," Rayna corrected. "And Rob is a family friend of the Crosses. He and Caitlin had a discussion of sorts where Caitlin ended up in tears. Ty claims he only knows Rob because of the families, but Rob makes it sound like they are close friends."

Two more names added to the big board.

"Any point of overlap between the two missing girls?"

Stoval asked.

"Social networking and school. That seems to be about it. Different types of girls, different classes, different crowds."

The chief turned to his chart and drew a big X through the information. "No real suspects, no leads, no new developments, no plan of attack." He twirled the pen in his hand. "Not acceptable, folks. We've got two missing girls, most likely dead. And nothing to show for our efforts. It's a disaster. People move to Paradise Falls because they want a safe place to raise their families. They want a police force that protects them." His face reddened as he stabbed the chart with his pen. "I hope I've made myself clear."

Another stab of the pen and he left the room.

"Jesus," Fritz mumbled. "Does the guy want us to pull a rabbit out of a hat?"

"I realize you guys are putting in long, demanding days on this," Rayna said, wanting to soften the chief's harsh reproach. "It's hard not to feel discouraged. But diligent work will pay off in the end."

The meeting broke up. As Rayna gathered her notes, she heard Cody say, "You feel like grabbing a beer or something after work?"

"Sorry, I can't."

"Can't or won't?"

Caught off guard, Rayna blurted the first thing that came to mind. "I have plans to go out with Hank."

She hadn't seen Hank behind her, and she heard the surprise in his voice when he said, "Yeah, it's kind of a private thing or we'd ask you to join us. Come on Rayna, I'll walk you to your desk."

As they neared their alcove, Hank said, "I'm tied up tonight, Rayna. Bowling, with Earl."

Earl's name had come up frequently in recent months. He was part of Hank's circle of lonely male pals. The men spent evenings bowling or playing pool or simply drinking beer. Earl also fished, which especially endeared him to Hank.

"That's okay. I needed an excuse. Sorry to put you in a bad spot like that, but thanks for covering it."

"Cody seems like a nice enough guy. Maybe you ought to give him a chance."

"It's complicated," Rayna said. "And personal."

"Look, why don't you come with me and meet Earl. He's interested in you."

"That's absurd. He's never even met me."

"Guess he's heard me talk about you. Probably saw you on TV, too. He's a nice guy, Rayna. A widower. His wife and kid died in some horrible accident a while back. I think you'd like him."

"I appreciate your looking out for me, Hank. But I'm really not interested in dating, or even meeting men."

"I figured you'd say something like that, but I thought I'd give it a shot. You need to get out more. And Earl does seem interested."

Rayna shook her head in befuddled amusement. Hank was a golly-gee kind of guy without a lot of sophistication, but he had a good heart and good cop skills. As irritating as he could be at times, she counted herself lucky to have him as a partner.

At six o'clock Rayna decided to head home. She stuffed the reports she still wanted to read into a manila folder. Outside, the sky was inky black and rain had begun to fall. She'd finish her reading at home, curled up on the couch.

As she left the building, she crossed paths with Neal Cody.

"What happened to your plans with Hank?" he asked.

"He forgot he had a conflict."

"Offer's still open. A night like this, some pleasant company might be nice."

She wasn't sure if he was talking about himself or her, but either way, she realized he was right. It was a miserable night following a miserable day.

What the heck, nothing was waiting for her at home but more of the same. "Okay," she said.

On Rayna's recommendation they headed to Logger's Loop, a popular and noisy tavern near the station. They managed to snag one of the few tables. It was near a wall, which she remembered was Neal Cody's preferred location.

"I don't suppose they make a fine martini here," he said, taking in the boisterous, mostly blue-collar crowd.

"Not even a fine wine. I'd suggest you stick with beer."

He went to the bar and returned a few minutes later with two bottles of Pacifico, along with a dish of nuts and pretzels.

"This the local cop hangout?" he asked, sliding into his seat.

"Cop and everyone else. Options are limited in Paradise Falls. If you're willing to include seedy, you have a somewhat wider choice."

He laughed. "You like living here?"

"It has its pluses and minuses." She actually liked the town, and the job, more than she'd expected. At the time she'd moved here, her focus had been more on leaving the bad memories.

Hooting erupted from a raucous game of darts near the bar, and Cody turned to look. "People seem to be enjoying themselves." He turned back to her, picked up his beer, and clinked her bottle in a toast. "Is the chief as much of an asshole as he seems?"

"He's all right, really. I think he's just feeling the heat."

"Like you." Cody watched for a moment in silence. "How are you holding up?"

"I'm doing just fine, thank you." She bristled inside. "Did you think I might not be up to the job?"

"I don't have any doubts about your abilities, but I know it's got to be hard on you personally."

"It's a hard job."

"You don't have to pretend with me." Cody's voice softened. "I know you, Rayna, remember?"

She glowered. "You think you know me. But you don't know shit."

"You're angry with me." He sounded genuinely surprised.

"I don't care enough about you to feel anger. Or anything else."

He wrapped both hands around his beer bottle and

studied it in silence for a moment. "I'm sorry, Rayna," he said, looking into her eyes. "More sorry than you can imagine."

She looked away. "I'm not interested in apologies."

"I can see how you might feel I was thinking only of myself, but that's not the way I saw it at the time."

"Oh, please. It's been years."

"And I've kicked myself ever since. I hurt you, and for that I'm sorry. But I hurt myself, too. I loused up something that was good and I regret that."

"You never called after your divorce." Rayna hated herself for sounding so pathetic.

"I was embarrassed and ashamed. For misleading you. For leaving you."

"For using me."

"I didn't use you. Please, you have to believe that." Cody leaned forward. "What I felt for you was real."

Rayna shook her head in disgust.

"I couldn't do anything about Kimberly, and that's another way I failed. I wanted so much to bring you some answers. I haven't stopped trying."

Rayna's throat grew tight. "Spare me," she said, looking away. "I don't need this crap from you."

"It's not crap."

"You want to make nice? Find Caitlin. And the creep who's terrorizing Paradise Falls." She pushed her chair away from the table. "I've got to head home."

"Can't we work together like civil adults?"

"I am being civil. I've got a big day ahead." She grabbed her jacket from the back of the chair and headed for the door without a backward glance. She was afraid if she hesitated, even for a moment, she'd never make it to her car.

It was a night of exhausting dreams and broken sleep. Rayna woke to her alarm, turned it off, and closed her eyes again. Half an hour later, she bolted out of bed, cursing herself for the late start. She scanned the newspaper over a quick cup of coffee. Caitlin's disappearance was no longer front-page news, but the discovery of her backpack warranted a short article on page three. She was halfway to the sink to rinse her coffee cup when she reached the back section. Seth Robbins's column stopped her cold.

Lead detective in missing girls cases no stranger to tragedy.

There, in black and white, Robbins had laid out her entire past. Her husband's death. Kimberly's disappearance, recounted in agonizing detail, along with quotes from Rayna and a five-year-old photograph of her tear-stained face. The discovery of Kimberly's body, the leads that went nowhere. A case gone cold. Robbins concluded by asking if the ineffective investigation of the Paradise Falls disappearances might not be clouded by the detective's personal and emotional blinders.

To the casual reader, it might appear that Robbins was offering a sympathetic analysis. Rayna knew better.

But what hit her like a cannonball to the gut was the nagging question of Robbins's source. Who'd told him about her past? Grace? Cody? The chief? They were the only people in town who knew. Of course, Robbins, being a reporter of sorts, could have taken it upon himself to dig for information. Still, she felt betrayed. As well as ripped raw.

She was so intensely occupied with the column that her phone's ringing didn't register at first.

She answered, still distracted. It was Chief Stoval.

"Better get down here right away," he said. "We just got a report of a body. Couple of hikers stumbled on it when they got off the trail a bit. Looks like it's a young girl."

CHAPTER 21

Grace had volunteered to type out a draft of the science report she and Lucy had worked on last night. The gesture was wholly out of character for her. Grace believed that teenagers needed to take responsibility for their own work. Normally she limited herself to offering an explanation and maybe a suggestion or two (not that Caitlin had asked for either in a long time), but these were hardly normal times.

She settled at the computer with a fresh cup of coffee and began typing. Outside, the day was overcast and dreary. The rain and wind from the night before had given way to an icy drizzle. Grace was glad to be inside, and grateful to have a mindless task to keep her occupied.

She heard the mailman drop the day's mail through the slot, and as soon as she finished the report she picked it up. She set aside a couple of envelopes she knew would be notes of sympathy and support from friends. It was an effort to read them. Junk advertising, a few bills, and a Seventeen of Caitlin's. Grace took the magazine to Cailtin's room and set it on her desk, next to the package from Amazon that had arrived the day before.

Caitlin's purchases from Amazon were mostly CDs and DVDs. Grace wasn't strong enough to face the rush of emotion she was sure would come if she opened Caitlin's order. The memory of her daughter's soft voice singing along with whatever song she was listening to, something Caitlin regularly did with heartwarming abandon, was painful enough. Besides, Grace had always prided herself on respecting her daughter's privacy.

And then, as though the ground had shifted beneath her

feet, Grace again came face to face with the dizzying certainty that Caitlin was never coming home. She would never know if Grace had opened her mail or not.

Heaviness tugged at Grace's heart. She missed Caitlin so much, loved her so fiercely, the anguish was almost unbearable. She longed to keep her daughter close in whatever way she could. Grace picked the box up, shook it gently, and then looked more closely. It was a standard Amazon box, but the address label was handwritten. And there was no return address. Not an Amazon order after all.

With a newfound sense of urgency, Grace found scissors and cut the sealing tape. Inside, surrounded by plastic peanuts, was a square package wrapped in purple tissue paper and tied with a gold ribbon. Purple, Caitlin's favorite color. There was no accompanying card. Grace debated, gave in to the pressing need to know, and ripped through the wrapping.

It was a web cam, factory sealed. Grace knew a number of people who had them. Adam had one on his computer at home. Caitlin had showed Grace the slightly fish-eyed view of Adam waving at her during an Instant Message exchange. And Grace knew a woman at work who had installed one in order to check on the nanny. It wasn't the camera that struck Grace as odd but the fact that it was a gift. From whom? And why? Caitlin's birthday wasn't until July. Grace again checked for a card, then examined the postmark. She couldn't make out the town but it was definitely Oregon. One of Caitlin's friends? Ty, maybe? Or maybe the older guy Caitlin might or might not have been interested in.

When the doorbell rang, Grace put the camera aside, mentally rehearsing how she'd explain the opened package to Caitlin. Then she caught herself. Explaining would be a blessing. It would mean Caitlin had come home.

Grace opened the door to Sandy, who greeted her with a soup pot. "It's homemade minestrone," Sandy said. "The weather is so awful, I thought soup might fit the bill."

"You don't have to keep doing this," Grace said, taking the container from her friend's hands and heading for the kitchen. "You have your own family to take care of."

Sandy followed. "I want to do it. I have to do something. Just reheat it when you're ready."

"Thank you. I'm really grateful, not just about the food, but for your friendship."

"Where would we be without friends? You've certainly done a lot for me."

Grace put the soup in the fridge. "You want some coffee?"

"Sorry, I can't stay. Zack has an orthodontist appointment. I'm on my way to the school to pick him up."

The simple, everyday acts of mothering that were no longer a part of Grace's life. She experienced an unexpected surge of sorrow.

"I might be able to come back later this afternoon," Sandy hastened to add. "If you'd like company."

"No, I'm fine." Grace leaned back against the cool tile counter.

"You don't sound fine."

Grace swallowed hard. "They found Caitlin's backpack yesterday. It was in a Dumpster at the mall. That's where Karen Holiday's purse was found, too. I think it's a bad sign."

"Oh, Grace." Sandy embraced her in a hug. "It might not mean anything. You can't let your fear take over."

Grace could recall numerous times when she'd done just that. The time Caitlin got lost in the crowds at Disneyland when she was five. The time she'd been hospitalized with meningitis, and more recently, the night she'd been over an hour late coming home from a date with Ty, who was driving. The first niggle of worry had exploded into full-blown panic. Every time, Caitlin had been okay, but this was different.

"You sure you don't want me to come back later?" Sandy asked.

"I'll be fine. Don't let me keep you. I know you need to get going."

Grace walked Sandy onto the porch. In the distance, she could hear the pulsating thrum of a helicopter circling overhead.

"Thanks for the soup."

"My pleasure." Sandy gave Grace a final hug. "Don't put too much stock in finding the backpack at the mall."

"That's what Carl says."

"Well, he's right. As usual. You've got a good one there, Grace."

"He is, I agree."

Sandy made a dash to her car through the rain. Grace waved goodbye and glanced up at the sky, annoyed. There ought be a law against those things!

Inside the house, the thumping of the helicopter continued to aggravate her. It was circling a mile or two in the distance, now joined by a second chopper.

A moment later it hit her.

Had they found Caitlin?

Heart racing, Grace flipped the radio on to the local news talk station and caught the wrap-up of a newscast.

"Again, for those of you just joining us, there's late-breaking news that a body, possibly one of the two missing girls, has been found in the mountains west of town."

Grace felt her stomach drop.

A Body.

No. Please, no.

She frantically searched the stations, enduring commercials, snatches of discordant music, and lame discussions on both ends of the political spectrum. Nothing more about the grisly discovery in the mountains.

She called the radio station where she'd caught the news, but the lines were apparently jammed. She sat through one round of "Your call is important to us, please stay on the line" before hanging up and racing to the computer to check the station's web site. There, under the news heading, in smaller print than a teaser for most popular video downloads, was a short blurb. Police were on the scene investigating the discovery of a body in an isolated area used for logging operations. Although authorities were remaining tight-lipped, sources close to the investigation had indicated that the body was that of a young woman, possibly one of the two missing girls from Paradise Falls.

Grace's head pounded and her chest tightened. Caitlin or Karen? Did she really want the answer? Was it better to know for sure or to hold out hope?

With a shaking hand, she called Carl, although knew he was in class and would have his phone turned off. When the ringing rolled over into voicemail she hung up without leaving a message and dialed Jake. She had to talk to someone.

"It's important, please," she told his secretary. "I have to talk to him right away."

Amazingly, she was put through.

"Jake, I just heard on the news. They've discovered a body. In the mountains outside of town. Possibly Karen or Caitlin."

"My God." Jake was full of questions, none of which she could answer.

"That's all I know," she wailed. "Oh, Jake. What if it's Caitlin?" For all her supposed certainty that Caitlin was dead, Grace now confronted the possibility anew. She hadn't given up hope, she realized. Not really. Not at all.

"Have you called the police, Grace?"

"No."

"I'll call on the other line. Don't hang up."

"I won't."

He was back on the line in no time. "They won't tell me anything. The detectives aren't available."

"I'm going to drive out there."

"It won't do any good."

"I have to go. I can't just sit here."

"Wait for me. I'll go with you."

"You're almost an hour away."

"We'll go together. I'll leave this minute."

"No. I need to go now. I'll call you as soon as I learn anything."

The rain fell in a steady gray drizzle. Traffic within the city inched along, slowing for puddles and poor visibility. Grace kept the car radio tuned to the news station. They repeated the earlier broadcast, adding that they had a reporter on scene but no further details were immediately available.

They must know something, Grace thought. They had to have more information, if only unofficially. The slowly passing minutes were measured by the thump-thumping of the windshield wipers. Grace gripped the steering wheel so hard, her hands ached.

By the time she arrived at the scene fifteen minutes later, the two-lane road leading to the staging area was lined with official-looking vehicles. She noted a crime scene investigation van and another marked "coroner."

Grace parked behind a news truck and sat in the car a moment, hugging herself in an attempt to quiet her shaking body. Do I really want to know? She asked herself again. A meaningless question. She had to know.

As she approached the dirt road leading off to the right, a uniformed officer said, "Sorry ma'am, you can't go that way. The area is closed."

"Please." Grace braced herself against the icy wind. "I'm Caitlin Whittington's mother. Please tell me what's going on."

"Ma'am, I'm sorry, but—"

"I heard on the news, there's a"—Grace had trouble saying the word—"a body. They said it might be one of the missing girls."

The uniformed officer, P. Richards, according to his tag, was a heavyset man in his fifties. His weathered face pulled tight as she spoke, but his eyes softened. "I wish I had something to tell you, but I don't know any more than you."

"What about Detective Godwin? Is she here?"

He nodded slowly. "I'm sure she'll be in touch when she can."

"Have they brought the body out yet?" This time Grace got the word out with frightening ease.

"Ma'am, Mrs. Whittington, why don't you have a seat in my car? Out of the elements. You can wait there. I'll be sure to let the detectives know that you're here."

Inside the back of the patrol car, Grace rubbed her hands together to warm them, then used her jacket sleeve to wipe the fogged window clear. Neither heated nor comfortable, the car offered Grace a better view than her own vehicle, so she stayed.

A second uniformed officer had joined Officer Richards. A man and woman with blue Crime Scene Investigation jackets spoke to Richards, then headed down the rutted dirt road behind him. Another man jogged from the direction they'd gone, climbed into the coroner's van parked nearby, and slowly began inching it forward, past the uniformed officers. The cluster of reporters who'd been huddling off to one side moved in to get photos. Seth Robbins was the only face among them Grace recognized, and she turned away as his gaze drifted toward the car where she sat.

Then she saw Detective Godwin and two men emerge from the road behind the front lines. They appeared wet and muddy and cold. The reporters moved en masse toward the threesome. At the same time, Grace slid from the car and hustled in their direction. Detective Godwin looked up and caught Grace's gaze. She said something to the men, then left them to handle the reporters while she directed Grace to a black sedan.

"Let's get inside," the detective said. She turned on the engine and the heat, took a terry towel from the rear seat, and dried her hair and face.

"Is it her?" Grace asked in a voice barely above a whisper.

"We don't have a positive ID yet and probably won't for another day or so—"

"Oh, God, it is, isn't it? Please." Grace reached for the detective's hands. They were icy cold, her fingertips white. "Please, you have to tell me."

Godwin chewed her bottom lip. "I don't want to give you false hope," she said at last, "but I don't think it's your daughter. From all appearances, our victim has been deceased for more than a few days."

As the detective's words sunk in, Grace could feel her insides melt. Relief made her weak.

"You're sure?"

"I'm not sure about anything." Detective Godwin pulled

her hands free and held them in front of the car's heater vents.

"Do you think it could be Karen Holiday?"

"It could be anyone."

Grace could tell from the look in the detective's eyes that she thought it was Karen.

"You should go home," Godwin said, more kindly. "There's no reason for you to be here."

"It's just that I heard the news—"

The detective cursed under her breath. "Damn newsmongers. Let them try living in a fish bowl."

Grace reached for the door handle. "Thank you, Detective. Thank you. I've never been so scared in my life."

"Nothing to thank me for."

Grace caught the leaden dullness in the detective's eyes, the tension in her jaw, and thought about what it must have been like for her to have asked a similar question years earlier and had it answered affirmatively. It's your daughter's body, Detective. And now Beth Holiday would be in that same place.

Grace remained upbeat all evening. Strangely manic, almost. Caitlin was still missing, Grace still felt fearful and anxious, but she brimmed with relief at having dodged the ultimate bad news.

For now.

The six o'clock news showed footage of the coroner's van, a flash of Grace dashing to greet Detective Godwin, a short Q & A with the detectives that had apparently taken place after Grace left. Human remains had been found about a quarter mile in by hikers, the reporter announced. No details were available at this time. Police would hold a news conference in a day or two, or whenever they had more information.

Grace's elated mood held through dinner. It must have rubbed off on the others because the atmosphere was lighter, the conversation more plentiful than on the previous night. Grace had two glasses of wine. Adam told a joke he'd heard that day. Carl related a tale of political irony having to do with the university president. Only Lucy was unusually quiet.

"You okay?" Grace asked her as they cleared the table.

"It's all so frightening. I'm glad it wasn't Caitlin today, but she . . . she's still missing." Lucy bit her lip. "I'm sorry. I didn't mean to remind you."

"You didn't remind me. It's something I never forget. Not even for a minute."

And she hadn't forgotten. She was simply desperate enough to grab hold of anything that resembled hope. But the fleeting sense of relief she'd enjoyed earlier was gone.

After Carl went off to bed, Grace opened the notes and letters that had come in the mail that day. The first, from Grace's college roommate, offered sympathy and encouragement but was also filled with news of her own three children. The second was from an old family friend of her parents, the scrawling handwriting difficult to decipher, but Grace was touched by her heartfelt compassion. The third letter was from Fern Daniels, who'd been Caitlin's best friend and constant companion from fourth grade until she'd moved to New York with her family in August. Fern, a down-to-earth animal-loving vegetarian, was so different than the popular girls Caitlin had been hanging out with lately. Grace missed Fern almost as much as Caitlin did.

The envelope was thick, and when Grace opened it, she understood why. Besides the card and note, written in Fern's familiar, angular penmanship, there were numerous pages of printed emails. Grace read the card first.

Dear Mrs. Whittington, I don't know what to say or how to begin. I wanted to call but was afraid I might disturb you. I can't imagine what it must be like for you right now. Caitlin is such a special, special person. She's been the best friend to me ever, and this last semester was really hard without her. I miss her so much just being far away, I know it must be thousands millions of times worse for you. Know that you and Caitlin are in my thoughts and prayers. We are all hoping there's a happy ending.

P.S. I'm enclosing some of Caitlin's emails. My mom says if she was in your place she'd like to have them, kind of as a way to stay close. I don't know about that so I hope I'm not making things worse for you.

Grace smiled. She could almost hear Fern's voice. She

started to read the printed pages from the beginning, Caitlin's first day of fall semester without Fern. It was typically teenage stuff—who said what to whom, gossip about the teachers, and later talk of Ty. Grace suspected Fern had sent her an edited collection of emails, since after "You'll never believe it! Ty Cross asked me out!!" there was a large gap in time.

Exhausted, Grace decided she'd read the emails in more detail tomorrow. For now, she skimmed them, looking for Ty's name.

Instead, what jumped out at her was "Adam."

I caught him watching me again, Caitlin wrote. And in another email, I found him kind of cuddling the cardigan I tossed on the table. I told you he's strange.

And several weeks ago, I think you're right, he must like me. Now there's something to contemplate! He's sort of sweet really, and not at all like Ty. But weird, too, as you know.

Grace went back and searched every page for Adam's name. There were only those few references, but once again Jake's words echoed in her mind. Adam was a bit odd, she conceded, and he'd been inside Caitlin's room only two days ago.

Grace was still tired, but she suddenly felt as though she'd taken in a triple shot of caffeine. Sleep would be a long time coming tonight.

CHAPTER 22

Although she awoke early the next morning (in fact she wasn't sure she'd ever fallen asleep), Grace waited to get out of bed until Adam and Lucy had left for school. Then she went straight to Adam's room.

It was sparsely furnished, his choice, with a rumpled and unmade twin bed, bare walls, a dresser, a desk, and a small television. The floor was strewn with clothes, the closet largely empty. Next to his laptop was a stack of DVDs and an array of empty soda cans and dirty glasses.

She started with the laptop even though she was afraid she'd mess something up or leave evidence of her snooping. Well, if Adam wanted to confront her, let him. She might just beat him to the punch.

She searched his files and his browser history. Like Caitlin, Adam used a web-based email program so she couldn't check his messages. There was nothing she could find elsewhere in his files about Caitlin. Nothing out of the ordinary, or what passed for ordinary among teenagers these days. Grace examined Adam's drawers next, lifting the liners and poking into corners and crevices. Again, she came up empty-handed. She wasn't sure what she was looking for—an article of Caitlin's, maybe, or a diary. Something that would lend credence to the uneasy thoughts that were beginning to take root in her mind. When the closet yielded nothing but smelly socks and a broken tennis racket, Grace decided that maybe she'd overreacted. Jake had planted a seed of doubt, and because of his suggestions, she'd probably read more into Caitlin's emails to Fern than was warranted. She took one last look around Adam's room and went downstairs to make herself a cup of coffee.

Over breakfast, she read the morning paper with its headline coverage of yesterday's grisly discovery. Authorities had apparently identified the body as that of Karen Holiday. While the announcement wasn't really surprising—Detective Godwin had more or less indicated that's what she suspected—Grace was struck with the finality of knowing for sure. Poor Beth Holiday. As little as Grace had in common with the woman, she felt a tremendous empathy for her loss. She recalled tidbits of their conversation and hoped the faith Beth had professed would give her strength in the awful days ahead.

Rinsing the dishes, Grace continued to muse over her conversation with Beth Holiday only days earlier. Caitlin and Karen were so different. How was it that this maniac in their midst had picked these two girls? And why?

She stopped cold when she remembered that Karen had received study help through the peer tutoring program at school. The same program Adam was involved in as a tutor.

So what? The kids were all students at the same school. Their paths crossed, their lives intersected. But she couldn't stop the misgivings. Adam was a loner. A misfit, if she wanted to be mean about it. An aloof, asocial, sometimes surly teenage boy. Karen and Caitlin, though very different, were both lively and attractive girls. It wasn't so far-fetched to imagine a boy like Adam harboring secret fantasies. What if he'd tried to act on them?

Grace dried her hands and headed back upstairs to give Adam's room a second look.

Fifteen minutes later, after she'd again convinced herself she was off the mark, she accidentally kicked over a stack of music magazines. At the bottom was a copy of Playboy, and wedged inside were several photos of Caitlin. Her school photo from last fall, a couple of recent snapshots, and one slightly grainy—and very disturbing—picture Grace had never seen before. Caitlin, in her pajamas, was sitting cross-legged on her bed, twisting a strand of hair around her finger while concentrating on the book in her lap. Had Caitlin known she was being photographed? Impossible. Then Grace remembered the web cam. Well, maybe. Besides, there was something about the pose that wasn't entirely candid. But whether she'd posed or been caught in her room unawares, the scenario was unsettling.

Could Adam have been involved in Caitlin's disappearance? Grace's heart began to hammer.

No way! Adam might not be the stereotypical All American Teenage Boy, but he wasn't violent.

How well did she know him? And wasn't deviant behavior often well-hidden? Weren't news accounts of arrests frequently accompanied by quotes from disbelieving friends and neighbors? He was a nice kid. He was always polite and helped me carry in my groceries. I don't believe it, there must be a mistake.

She shook her head. No, it wasn't possible. Carl's son. His flesh and blood. Her own stepson.

A sourness rose in her throat and mouth. She went into the bathroom and rinsed her mouth with shaking hands. What should she do? She couldn't talk to Carl about this.

She tried to think how she'd react if the situation were reversed. If Carl were to come to her with suspicions about Caitlin. The idea was so far-fetched her mind wouldn't even go down that path.

Detective Godwin? That would mean going behind Carl's back. She couldn't do that, either.

She went to the phone beside her bed and called Sandy. When her friend didn't answer on the home phone, Grace tried her cell. Sandy wasn't someone who talked mindlessly and endlessly on her cell phone. It was for emergencies and brief messages from her children. Grace hated to intrude, but she felt desperate.

"I'm sorry to bother you," Grace said. "Are you somewhere where you can talk for a few minutes?"

"There's news about Caitlin?"

"No, not exactly."

"I'm on my way home from the store, but I've got a little time. You sound upset."

Grace's mouth was so dry she had trouble moving her lips. "Oh, Sandy, I think maybe Adam might be behind what's happened. To both Caitlin and Karen Holiday."

"Oh, my God! What gave you that idea?" A horn blared loudly in the background. "Asshole. Look, let me run these groceries home to the fridge and I'll be over there in less than fifteen minutes."

Grace greeted Sandy with a cup of coffee, but felt too nauseated to have any herself.

"Now tell me what's going on," Sandy said, taking her customary seat at the kitchen table.

Grace started with having seen Adam coming out of Caitlin's bedroom the other night. She told Sandy about Fern's emails and how Caitlin had said that Adam had her sweater.

"Cuddling it, was what she said," Grace explained. "And then today I found photos of Caitlin stuck inside a Playboy magazine of Adam's. Here, take a look." She pushed the photos across the table.

Sandy examined them one by one, then said, "There's nothing out of the ordinary about any of them."

"The one of Caitlin on her bed. How did he get that? What was he doing there?"

"We don't know that he took it. It might have been taken by a girlfriend of hers at a sleep-over. Or even Caitlin herself. All cameras have remote timers these days."

"And what about the fact he had them hidden inside Playboy?"

"I have sons, Grace. You don't. Playboy is pretty mild actually." She sighed. "I'm not saying you're wrong here, I'm just playing devil's advocate because, to tell you the truth, nothing that you've told me seems to have crossed any lines."

Sandy wasn't one to rush to judgment. She didn't go off on tangents or get hot under the collar for no reason. It was a quality Grace appreciated. But, at the moment, she would have welcomed a little less logic.

"Adam must have known Karen, too," Grace added. "She got extra class help through that peer tutoring program the school has. Adam is a math and science tutor. And he was really interested in Karen's disappearance. I remember that because Caitlin called him a ghoul."

"Like I said, I'm not saying you're wrong. It's just such a ticklish situation."

"What am I going to do?"

"What can you do?" Sandy cradled her coffee mug in both hands. "Confronting Adam isn't going to get you anywhere."

"You're probably right." Besides, Grace wasn't eager to take on Adam face to face.

"What about Carl?"

"I won't get any answers that way, either."

"That leaves going to the cops."

"Behind Carl's back?"

"I don't see that there are any other options. You can't just sit on what you've discovered and say nothing. Even if there are innocent explanations, it will eat at you if you don't do something."

"You're right." She'd have to deal with Carl one way or the other. The prospect made her ill.

"Give the detective a call," Sandy said. "Or better, go see her. Do you want me to come with you?"

"Thanks, but I can handle it."

"Go now, Grace. The sooner you get this over with, the better. Get it off your chest and let the detectives investigate."

Half an hour later Grace entered the now-familiar police station with a resolve that faded with each step. What was she doing? Could Carl ever forgive her?

I have to do this, Grace thought. As Sandy had pointed out, she didn't have a choice.

Detective Godwin's greeting was cool. "We're really backed up here with a homicide investigation. I'm afraid I don't have a lot of time."

Cool and slightly off-putting, Grace thought. But having come this far, she wasn't backing away now. "I might have information that can help."

"What is it?"

"Is there somewhere we can talk?"

"Follow me." Godwin led Grace to a small, windowless, stuffy room with a small table and four metal chairs. She pulled out one and sat. "Like I said, I don't have much time. You said you have information?"

The detective's abrupt manner was puzzling, especially following what Grace had considered a shared personal moment when Detective Godwin had told her about her own daughter.

It must be the added stress of finding Karen's body.

"I'm not sure where to start," Grace said.

"Give me the bottom line first."

Bottom line. That was the hardest part for Grace to accept. "I think my stepson, Adam Peterson, might be someone you should look at in connection with both girls."

The detective finally looked interested. "Why's that?"

Grace again laid out her suspicions. Spoken out loud in the grim, unwelcoming cell of a room, they didn't sound convincing. "It's mostly a feeling I have," Grace added lamely.

Godwin folded her hands on the table. "Tell me about his relationship with Caitlin."

"Well, they get along but they don't have a lot in common. Adam is often sullen and grouchy. Caitlin is upbeat. She'd tease him sometimes. He seemed okay with it but you never know. He'd even tease her back sometimes."

"Did anything change recently?"

"Not that I noticed." She thought for a moment. "Except, I think he stopped teasing her as much."

"Did he ever mention Karen Holiday?"

"No, not until she disappeared. I'm not even certain he knew her." Grace wished now she'd paid more attention to Adam's reaction when Karen disappeared. At the time, she'd been more focused on the story of the missing teen than her stepson's response.

"What about when Karen went missing, any change in Adam's behavior?"

"He seemed obsessed with the newspaper stories. I

remember Caitlin called him a ghoul."

"Anything else?"

Grace shook her head. She'd just unleashed a potentially powerful time bomb, and it had taken less than five minutes. "What are you going to do?"

"We'll talk to Adam again. After that, I'm not sure. Your information is far from conclusive."

"He's at our house for the rest of the week. He usually gets home around three."

"We'll try to get out there today. If you think of anything else, give me a call." Detective Godwin stood but she didn't move toward the door. She put her hands on the back of the chair. "Did you see Seth Robbins's column yesterday?"

"I don't remember. Why?"

"He seemed to know all about my daughter. The stuff I told you in confidence."

Grace leapt to her feet. "You don't think I told him, do you?" Obviously, the detective had thought that. No wonder she'd sounded so cool. "I had nothing to do with it, I swear. I'd never do that."

But she had told Carl, Grace remembered. And Adam had been hanging out in the doorway at the time. Another thread added to the web of suspicion that had taken hold in her head.

CHAPTER 23

Rayna reached into the left-hand drawer of her desk and grabbed a handful of trail mix, the kind with chocolate and nuts. It was an old habit, one she'd pretty much given up since taking the job in Paradise Falls. She'd succumbed, intermittently, during the initial phases of the Karen Holiday investigation, but it was only this last week, with her anxiety escalating daily, that she'd found herself reaching into the drawer on a regular basis. Her waistline was already feeling the effects.

And now this.

She didn't know what to make of Grace Whittington's suspicions about her stepson. The evidence was far from conclusive. On the other hand, cases often turned on less. Rayna had trouble believing Grace would point her finger at Adam unless she believed there were grounds for doing so. And while intuition might have been a big part, that didn't mean Grace was wrong.

As soon as Grace had gone, Rayna reread the notes of her earlier interview with Adam. Nothing had raised any red flags. Now, popping a walnut into her mouth, she called up a mental picture of the boy. Tall and lanky with straight red hair that hung limply around his face. He'd appeared more listless than nervous about the interview, and had answered her inquiries largely in monosyllables. Teen behavior, but not necessarily criminal.

"Oh-oh," Cody said, startling Rayna by coming up behind her. "I see it's back to nervous eating."

"Not that it's any of your business."

Untouched by her cool response, Cody opened the

drawer and helped himself. "Same drawer. You're a creature of habit, Rayna." He threw a handful into his mouth. "At least it's healthy stuff."

"Except for the chocolate."

"Chocolate's good for you. The dark stuff you like, anyway. It's good for your heart." Cody pulled up a chair. "You were a thousand miles away a minute ago."

Rayna eyed him levelly. If Grace Whittington wasn't the source of Robbins's information, it had to have been Cody. Rayna was angry enough to spit but she was afraid he'd find her ire amusing.

"Grace Whittington thinks her stepson might be responsible for what happened to Karen and Caitlin. He might have tutored Karen Holiday. And Grace has recently become aware of suspicious behavior on his part toward Caitlin."

"Like what?"

Rayna summarized what Grace had told her. "None of it means much in itself, but I don't think she'd have come forward if she didn't feel fairly strongly."

"Do we know where the kid was when Caitlin disappeared?"

"Home. Alone." It had come up when she'd interviewed him, but Rayna hadn't thought anything of it at the time. "And then out later that evening." He'd supposedly taken his laptop to a local hotspot coffee shop, then to a video store to look at video games. All perfectly logical, but nothing that could be substantiated.

"What's he like?" Cody asked.

"Quiet. A little geeky. He's never been in any trouble with the law as far as I can tell. I spoke with the principal about an hour ago. Adam is a straight A student, but not an easy kid to have in class because he's always challenging the teachers. Probably brighter than half of them. He doesn't have many friends. In fact, the principal said kids sometimes pick on him, but Adam mostly ignores them so it's never been an issue."

"Except to Adam, maybe." Cody reached for another handful of trail mix. "You know, what you just described pretty much fits the profile of a kid who might do something like this. Loner, alienated, bright. Probably never had a girlfriend."

Rayna bristled at the ease with which Cody had injected himself into her investigation. "That's a rather broad generalization," she said.

"On target, nonetheless. But you sound skeptical."

"I am."

"Want to tell me why?"

"Besides the usual, you mean?" Rayna asked pointedly. Cody already knew she thought profiling was over-hyped. "There was nothing I picked up on when I talked to him," Rayna explained, countering Grace's intuition with her own. "He's never shown any signs of aggression or antisocial behavior, but supposedly he abducts and kills two girls, one of whom is his stepsister? It doesn't make a lot of sense."

"Serial killers don't think like the rest of us."

Neither did profilers, she added silently. "I'm not convinced the crimes were committed by the same person, Cody. We aren't even certain what's happened to Caitlin."

"You have to admit there are striking similarities."

"The Dumpsters at the mall, you mean?"

"Among other things."

"What kind of killer would dispose of articles from both victims in the same place?"

"A really stupid one. Or one who wants to rub your face in the fact that he's done it again."

"It could just as easily be coincidence." Rayna nibbled on a chunk of dark chocolate. Did she really want Cody brought into this? Especially after he'd leaked personal information about her to the press. "There's something else. After Karen Holiday disappeared, I found a small stuffed dog in my mailbox."

"A what?"

"A child's toy. Kimberly had quite a collection." Rayna still had every one of the animals in a box on the shelf of her bedroom closet. "At first I thought some kid dropped it and a passerby, trying to be helpful, stuck it in my box. But then yesterday, after we found Karen's body, I got another. A bunny this time."

"And when Caitlin disappeared?"

"Nothing."

"You gave the bunny to forensics?"

"No," she said sarcastically. "In Paradise Falls we destroy everything that might be considered evidence."

"No need to get snippy." Then he held up his hands, palms facing her, and muttered, "Sorry."

Rayna ignored his apology.

"Okay," Cody offered. "For argument's sake, different crimes, different perps. All the more reason to look at Adam in connection with Caitlin. There must be some interesting dynamics in that family. I can't imagine any teenage boy who wouldn't find it a little unnerving to suddenly have a girl a few years his junior as a new sister."

"Hank and Fritz are at the school now. Then they're going to talk to Adam's mother. I'm planning to talk to Adam this afternoon." She looked at her watch. "He should be home from school any minute now."

"You want me to come along?"

"Do I have a choice?" Rayna narrowed her eyes his direction. "Besides, your buddy Seth Robbins must be eager for the latest installment."

"Who?"

"Don't play dumb with me."

Once again, Cody held up his open palms. "I am dumb. Who the hell is Seth whatever?"

"He's a columnist with the Paradise Falls Tribune."

"And?" Cody seemed genuinely bewildered.

"You didn't feed him private information about my past?"

"Rayna, honey, I've only been in town a few days. How would I hook up with some local columnist? And why the hell would I want to tell him about you?"

"I don't know." To Rayna's chagrin, she felt her eyes tear up. Oh, God, she wasn't going to do the female thing. Not here, not now.

Cody leaned forward and took her hands in his. "I don't want to hurt you, Rayna. I care about you."

The phone rang. She pulled her hands free, nonchalantly brushed the back of her hand across her eyes, and answered.

"Rayna, it's Hank. One of the kids here at school, Rob Hardy, told us Adam likes to hang out at a spot by the river. It's an isolated place, kind of his own nest. We took a look there and found Caitlin's initials scratched in a boulder, along with Adam's. And, get this, a ring. Nothing expensive, but it's the sort of thing a girl might wear for fun."

Rob Hardy was on Rayna's "something doesn't square" list. She wasn't sure she trusted him. But evidence was evidence. "Let's see if we can get a warrant to search Adam's room at both his mom's and dad's places, as well as his school locker. Meanwhile, I'll interview him."

So much for her skepticism about profiling, she thought. She turned to Cody. "Let's go. Adam just got more interesting."

CHAPTER 24

The minute he walked into his room, Adam knew that someone had been there.

Grace.

It had to have been her.

She sometimes came in to "straighten up a bit," as she put it, but today his room was as messy as ever. It's just that this was a different mess than the mess he'd left that morning. Which meant that Grace had been in here snooping. He could tell she'd been freaked out to find him coming out of Caitlin's room the other evening. Not that he really blamed her, but it didn't give her the right to pry.

This was why he kept so few things at his dad's house. His mom never set foot in his room at home. Probably less out of respect for his privacy than simple lack of interest—his mom was pretty focused on her own life—but whatever the reason, it suited Adam just fine.

Well, now that Grace was into snooping, he'd have to be more careful. He dumped his backpack on his unmade bed and trotted downstairs for a snack. Lucy was at a friend's house and Grace had left a note saying she'd gone out to do errands, so Adam had the house to himself. No big deal. At home, his mom was never there in the afternoons, although she usually left instructions for him to do the laundry or start dinner.

The doorbell rang as Adam was scanning the fridge for possibilities. He grabbed a can of Coke. When he opened the door, he recognized the lady cop who was looking for Caitlin. A man he'd never seen before stood next to her.

"Grace isn't home," Adam said. "She's out doing errands. Didn't say when she'd be back."

The woman—Detective Godwin, he remembered now—gave him a friendly smile. "That's okay, Adam. We have a few questions for you. May we come in?"

He'd taken a swallow of Coke and coughed as it went down. "Uh, sure. But why me? I told you what I know."

"It's a routine follow-up and clarification." Detective Godwin gestured to the man next to her. "This is Agent Cody with the FBI."

"Hi." Adam sure as hell wasn't going to offer his hand and say, "Pleased to meet you," the way his dad would have. FBI had an onerous sound to it.

He knew better than to leave them standing in the entryway, however, so he led them to the kitchen.

"Is Lucy around?" Detective Godwin asked.

"No. She's at a friend's. Do you want me to call her?"

"Not necessary. It's you we want to talk to."

So much for their routine follow-up. Lucy was the last person to see Caitlin, so why would they want to talk to him and not Lucy? Adam could feel his armpits dampen with sweat.

The FBI agent pulled out a bar stool from under the kitchen counter and perched on it sideways, casual and cool. "Tell me about Caitlin."

"What do you want to know?"

"You worried about her?"

"Yeah, of course." Was the guy serious? "The whole thing sucks."

"Isn't it a pain, having a fifteen-year-old stepsister? Girls like to be in charge, if you know what I mean."

"Nah, Caitlin's cool."

"Or maybe she wasn't a pain at all." The guy gave Adam a little man-to-man smirk. "Having a hot chick living under the same roof must be kind of . . . well, fun."

Hot chick? FBI Man sounded like he'd stepped out of some low budget '60s movie. Still, Adam felt his pulse race. He had a glimmer of where they were heading.

"I didn't really think about it that way," he said.

"Hard not to when you're a guy." Another smirk.

Adam's hands shook. He set the Coke can on the counter.

"Do you have a girlfriend?" Detective Godwin asked.

"I've got friends who are girls." What Adam actually had were classmates and acquaintances, but he wouldn't have wanted most of the girls in Paradise Falls for friends, anyway.

"How about a boyfriend?" the detective asked.

Adam laughed, despite his jitters. Was this guy for real? "Definitely no boyfriend."

FBI Man eased off his stool and looked at the family snapshots that Grace kept on the front of the fridge. "How well did you know Karen Holiday?" he asked.

No reason to feel nervous, Adam told himself. But he did. The cops were clearly trying to back him into a corner about something.

"I talked to her sometimes."

"In the tutoring program or otherwise?"

"Mostly tutoring. She wasn't assigned to me or anything, but we have people in the library on Wednesday and Friday afternoons if kids need help. That's where I'd see her mostly."

FBI Man turned abruptly and faced Adam. "Where were you in the early evening on the Friday Caitlin disappeared?"

The question caught Adam off-guard and he swallowed so hard he almost choked on his own spit. "I already told her." Adam gestured toward Detective Godwin. "I was home. At my mom's house."

"What time did you leave school?"

"Around two-thirty. I have last period free but I hung around some to check on something in the science lab."

"Who else was at the house?"

"No one. My mom works until six or six-thirty, and my sister was doing something after school."

"So you can't prove you were home?"

Adam's throat constricted. "What's this about, anyway?"

Detective Godwin leaned forward, slid her arms across the counter and spoke softly. "Adam, Grace found pictures of Caitlin tucked inside a Playboy magazine today. In your room."

So he'd been right. Grace had been snooping in his room. Adam could feel his face flush. "They're just pictures. I don't see the big—"

"And Caitlin's emails to her friend Fern Daniels said you made a habit of watching her. Looking at her all the time. She said she found you cuddling her sweater."

"Why would I do that?" His voice squeaked, embarrassing him.

FBI Man said, "Because you had the hots for Caitlin?"

Adam swallowed then tried to moisten his mouth which had gone very dry. "You're both nuts."

"What did you do, finally come on to her? Tell her how you felt? Or did you just go after her plain and simple?"

"No," Adam said. "It wasn't like that."

"Maybe you didn't mean to harm her," FBI Man continued. "Maybe she resisted, called you names or said hurtful things. Girls can be such bitches sometimes. Believe me, I know."

Detective Godwin positioned herself between FBI Man and Adam. "Tell us what happened, Adam. There are lots of ways things can get out of hand. If you didn't mean to hurt her, then you need to tell us that. Otherwise we might assume it was intentional."

Adam shook his head. Unfortunately, his whole body was shaking as well. "No, you've got it all wrong. I didn't—"

"Her initials, Adam, scratched into a rock by the river. In a spot you are known to frequent. Along with a ring. When we do a more thorough search, what are we going to find? Evidence that you forced Caitlin there?"

"She wasn't . . ."

"Wasn't what?"

He needed to shut up. He understood enough to know that he could easily dig himself into a hole he'd never get out of. They were leaning on him because they didn't have proof of anything. They were trying to get him to give them the story they wanted to hear.

"I don't have anything more to say to you," he said with as much confidence as he could muster.

"We're going to have plenty to say to you." FBI Man stepped forward so that his face was only inches from Adam's.

"And the circumstances will be far less pleasant than they are now."

Detective Godwin put her hand on FBI Man's arm and he retreated. But the thrust of his message wasn't lost on Adam.

"If you didn't do anything wrong, you have nothing to hide," Detective Godwin said. "Cooperate with us and everyone wins."

Adam bit his tongue and remained silent.

"Do you know what happened to Caitlin?" she asked softly.

Adam shook his head, afraid to look at them, afraid he might start crying, sure they didn't believe him.

CHAPTER 25

As difficult as it had been for Grace to go to Detective Godwin with her suspicions about Adam, telling Carl what she'd done would be much, much harder. The prospect tied her stomach in knots.

It had been her intention to go to the college directly after leaving the police station. Instead, she'd gone home and thrown up. Then she'd taken a long, hot shower and left a little before Adam was due home from school.

She knew she couldn't back away now, but that didn't stop her from second-guessing herself. Had she made a mountain out of a molehill? She felt guilty and sad and frightened all at once.

She had to speak to Carl before he arrived home. And she needed to do it in person. Which was why she now stood outside Morrison Hall where Carl taught his afternoon American Lit seminar, with nerves as jumpy as if she were awaiting her own execution.

The air was damp with mist but the heavy rain that had pounded them earlier that day had moved on. Singly and in pairs, students scurried past, eyes forward, faces determined. At the bottom of the steps a young couple exchanged a quick kiss before moving off in opposite directions.

The chimes of the bell tower across campus sounded, marking the top of the hour, and a fresh stream of students poured through the wide doors of Morrison Hall. Several minutes later Carl emerged, accompanied by two male students. One of them said something and Carl looked toward the sky and laughed. He had a wonderful laugh—rich and all-enveloping. The boys laughed also. Then Carl looked over and saw Grace. His expression shifted immediately, and he hurried toward her, anxiety imprinted on every feature.

"Is there news about Caitlin?"

A sharp sense of loss drilled into Grace's chest, like a screw turning. She loved Carl, and more importantly, he loved her. Yet she knew that nothing would ever be the same between them.

He reached for her hands. "Tell me, Grace. Is it good news or bad?"

"Not news, not really, but we need to talk."

Confusion mixed with the worry in Carl's eyes. "What's this about?"

"Please, can we go somewhere private?"

"My office?"

She nodded and they walked the short distance to Carl's office in awkward silence. When they were inside and he'd shut the door, he put his hands on Grace's shoulders. "It must be serious. You're not usually one for such drama."

"Oh, Carl." She leaned against him and pressed her check against his chest. She could hear his heart pounding beneath the rough wool of his sweater. She longed to bury herself in the comfort of his embrace. Instead, she pulled back and looked up at him. "I'm afraid you're going to hate me."

"Why? What's happened?"

Carl's office wasn't large, but he'd made the space his own. Comfortable and distinctly academic at the same time. A photo of the five of them on a trip to the coast last summer sat prominently on his desk. The family that no longer existed.

Grace sat in one of the two chairs designated for students. "I'm not sure how best to explain, but I made some discoveries."

Carl sat on the edge of his desk, facing her. "What is it, Grace?" Alarm underscored each syllable.

"A little background first." Grace cleared her throat and pressed her thumbs together in her lap. "Last evening, before I came downstairs to help you with dinner, I saw Adam coming out of Caitlin's room. I know that doesn't mean anything in itself, but it bothered me. And then later, after you'd gone to bed, I opened the letter Fern Daniels sent. She included printouts from some of Caitlin's emails. Mostly chatty girl stuff. But at one point Caitlin said Adam was always watching her and it made her uncomfortable. She also said she'd seen him 'cuddling' her sweater."

Grace had been talking to her hands but now she looked at Carl. "Today I found photos of Caitlin in Adam's room. They were tucked inside a copy of Playboy. One of the photos showed Caitlin in her pajamas, sitting on her bed."

"What are you suggesting?"

"I don't know, maybe nothing. But what if . . . I mean it might be possible that he . . ." She couldn't bring herself to say the words out loud. "It's something we should at least consider."

"You think Adam is responsible for whatever happened to Caitlin?" Carl's voice had none of its usual resonance. The tone was sharp and biting. And etched with disbelief.

"He probably had contact with Karen Holiday, too," she said, sidestepping the question. "Karen got study help through the Students for Students program where Adam tutors."

Carl stood up and stepped forward, towering over her. "Have you lost your mind?"

Maybe she had. Grace didn't know what to say.

"Do you really mean to accuse Adam, my son Adam, of being a murderer? I simply don't know what to say. This whole conversation is ludicrous."

"I'm not accusing him of anything, Carl. But his behavior raises questions."

"Only because you're looking for them."

"Caitlin is still missing and Karen Holiday is dead. You can't expect me to ignore what I've learned simply because Adam is your . . . is part of our family."

"What you've learned? And what is that, exactly? That he had a few snapshots of his stepsister? That Caitlin thought Adam was looking at her funny? And so what if he had her sweater. 'Cuddling' is a loaded word. For all we know, he could have been moving it from the table or something. You don't even know what Caitlin says is true. You don't know anything."

Carl's reaction was close to what she'd expected. Denial and rationalization. And certainly hurt, too, although that was less obvious. Grace was glad she'd gone to Detective Godwin this afternoon. If she hadn't, she felt certain Carl would have talked her out of it. He was right. She didn't have much to go on.

"If Adam doesn't have anything to hide, then there's no problem, is there?"

Carl paced to the window and back, running his hand through his thick brown hair. "I can't believe you're even entertaining this ridiculous notion. I know you're upset and not thinking clearly, but honey, you've gone off the deep end."

Grace studied her hands again. The swell of emotions inside her brought tears to her eyes. She felt as if she were being buffeted about a windswept sky.

"Look," Carl said with forced civility. "I'll talk to Adam, okay? We'll see what he says."

"There's one more thing." Grace swallowed. "I spoke with Detective Godwin this afternoon."

It must have taken a moment for the meaning of Grace's words to register because Carl didn't respond immediately. Or maybe he was simply dumbstruck.

"You told the police that you suspect Adam had something to do with Caitlin's disappearance?" he said, his voice icy.

Grace looked up at him. "I don't suspect Adam. I don't know. I don't know anything."

"How could you not come to me first?" The anger in Carl's voice was honed and hot, and pierced Grace's heart like a bolt of lightning. "He's my son, and you didn't have the decency to talk to me before you ran to the cops?"

"I did what I had to do. You can't stick your head in the sand and refuse to consider the possibility that Adam might be involved. I'm not saying he was. I don't know, but you don't know either."

"I know my son. I thought I knew you, too."

Reluctant to face the firing squad for the second time that day, and wanting to give Carl and Adam a chance to talk privately, Grace returned home slowly. It was almost six when she pulled her car into the driveway.

She entered the kitchen, where the family sat around the old wood table. Hateful stares and stony silence greeted her. Adam got up and brushed past, clipping her shoulder roughly. Lucy stared at Grace the way she might a particularly repellant bug, then also left the room. Carl, alone, met her eyes, but with such intense displeasure his glare burned, and Grace looked away.

"The police were here this afternoon," Carl told her. "They talked to Adam." He rose, scrapping the chair harshly across the plank flooring. "They sure didn't waste any time acting on your suspicions."

"What was I supposed to do? Did you want me to ignore what I'd learned?"

"Don't you realize that with no leads, the cops will take whatever comes their way? They're eager to arrest someone and be done with it."

"Just because they talked to Adam, it doesn't mean they're going to arrest him. It doesn't even mean they suspect him."

"What world do you live in, Grace?"

Adam returned, wearing his jacket. Hitching his backpack onto his shoulders, he said, "I'm going back to Mom's."

"Adam, please." Carl wove his fingers through his hair. "There's no need to run off."

"Yeah?" Adam glared pointedly in Grace's direction.

Carl sighed. "You'd better check with your mother first. Make sure she doesn't have other plans."

"It's my home, too."

"As is this," Carl said.

Adam shot Grace another nasty look. "Not so's you'd notice lately."

"I'm no happier about what Grace did than you are, Adam. I told you that and I mean it. I know you didn't hurt Caitlin. I'm sure in her heart, Grace knows that too. But these are anxious times. People under stress sometimes do foolish things."

"She doesn't like me," Adam said. "She never has." He slammed out the door on his way out.

His words took on weight in the silence that followed. "That's not true," Grace protested finally. "And this has nothing to do with liking him or not. If he had nothing to do with Caitlin's disappearance, there's no reason for him to be upset."

"You think he might be involved, Grace. I'd say that's plenty of reason."

She had never really considered that her opinion might matter to Adam. He was Carl's son. Part and parcel of the marriage. Not that she hadn't tried to build a relationship with him. With both Carl's children. She'd had slightly better luck with Lucy. Adam hadn't sought out Grace's opinion or approval, and she'd assumed Adam had considered her an interloper.

"What did he say about the photo of Caitlin on her bed?" Grace asked, in part because she wanted to know, and in part because she wanted to deflect the spotlight from herself.

Carl sighed wearily. "That Caitlin gave it to him."

"And you believe that?"

"Grace, it's just a photo of Caitlin reading, right? She's not posing in a suggestive way or doing anything provocative, is she?"

"It's not just that photo," Grace explained. "It's everything taken together. And I'm not saying it proves anything, only that it raises questions."

A lot of what made Grace uneasy defied rational explanation. Maybe it had to do with body language or reading between the lines or plain old intuition. Or maybe she really was going off the deep end, but it didn't feel that way. "What did Adam say about being in Caitlin's room the other night?"

"I didn't ask."

"I thought you were going to talk to him."

"We did talk."

"You don't want to know, do you? You don't really want the truth."

"Enough, Grace! I've had it. I've tried to be understanding. I know how hard it is for you right now. But that doesn't give you reason to turn on my family."

Mine. Yours. Obviously, blended families existed only when times were good.

"I'm going to call Mimi," Carl said. "I should let her know what's happening."

"Especially with Adam on his way there," Grace agreed. "She might be in the, uh, middle of something."

Carl crossed his arms. "Haven't you attacked my family enough for one day?"

What? How had his ex-wife become part of Carl's family? She was about to lash back when the phone rang.

Carl grabbed the receiver, and Grace could hear Mimi in an uproar on the other end.

"The police are here with a search warrant," she screamed. "They want to look in Adam's room. What the hell is going on?"

"Is Adam there?"

"This is one of your nights, Carl."

"He decided he wanted to be there, instead."

Without so much as a glance in Grace's direction, Carl took the phone into the den and shut the door.

CHAPTER 26

The coffee tasted thick and bitter but Rayna took a second swallow anyway. And although it left an unpleasant aftertaste in her mouth, she knew she'd finish the entire cup. She'd managed to grab only intermittent sleep over the weekend, and even that had been far from restful. She was counting on the kick of caffeine to clear her head.

"I want this handled correctly," Chief Stoval said, addressing the three of them gathered in his office. "Absolutely by the book."

Rayna chafed at his tone. Did he think they usually flew by the seat of their pants? "We're proceeding carefully," she replied.

Hank chirped in with, "Right. We're not rushing into anything."

Cody remained silent. Rayna could see him out of the corner of her eye, slouched in his chair and frowning at the chief.

"Do we know how Adam obtained those photos?" Stoval asked. Though he didn't say which photos, Rayna knew he was referring to the dozen or so snapshots they'd found on Adam's computer at his mother's house. Grainy digital shots of Caitlin naked in the shower and of Caitlin in her bra and panties.

"We're assuming he took them himself," Rayna explained. "From the angle, it looks like he climbed onto the overhang outside the bathroom window. It wouldn't be difficult to do."

The chief ran a hand through his thinning hair. "Jesus. His own sister. Okay, stepsister. Why didn't he just stick to Playboy?"

It wasn't, thankfully, a question that required an answer.

"Anything more on the necklace?" Stoval asked. They'd found the thin silver and onyx chain in a drawer in the basement of Mimi's house when they executed the search Friday night.

"Definitely Caitlin's," Rayna told him. "I checked with her mother."

Grace had held the necklace like an injured sparrow, in the palm of her hand, and her eyes had welled with tears. "It's Caitlin's," she'd whispered. "It was a birthday gift from Carl."

Rayna had found the look on Grace's face hauntingly familiar. When your child was missing, everything she'd ever touched became sacred.

"Looks like the kid's obsessed with the girl," Stoval muttered. "Just the sort of juicy case the public eats up. Anything else at the spot down by the river?"

Rayna looked to Hank, who'd been overseeing the search of the area. "Not so far," he said, looking chagrined. Hank liked to make the chief happy.

"Well keep at it." Stoval rubbed his cheek and addressed Rayna. "I assume you've been in touch with someone from the DA's office?"

"McKenna's got the case." Rayna had been relieved to know that the prosecutor was someone other than Paul Nesbitt. With one girl still missing and the other dead, Rayna's emotions were already tangled and close to the surface. Throwing an occasional lover into the mix might have been more than she could handle.

"Good. At least we've got someone with solid credentials."

"He's not sure there's enough evidence to convict," Rayna said. "Now that we have a possible suspect to focus on, though, the other pieces might come together." It was always easier to connect a victim with a known suspect than to pull a suspect out of the realm of infinite possibilities. With luck they'd find what they needed to fill in the gaps and build a strong enough link to satisfy the DA.

"Forensics is taking a second look at the backpack and contents of the Dumpster," Hank said, "and we've got officers following up with witnesses at the mall. We want to know if anyone remembers seeing Adam there within our time frame."

"Still no word on his whereabouts?" Stoval steepled his fingers and tapped his mouth.

"Not yet," Hank replied, "but we've got an APB out on the car. We'll find him."

Adam was AWOL, missing for two days. He'd left his father's house Friday night, allegedly heading for his mom's, and no one had seen him since. Cody offered the theory that his mother was hiding him but Rayna didn't buy it. Mimi's distress over her missing son seemed genuine. Best bet was that she and Cody had spooked the boy by questioning him. In retrospect, she wished she'd handled it differently.

"From where I sit," the chief said, "flight is a strong indicator of guilt. I can't understand why McKenna doesn't think we have enough to arrest the kid. They can plug the holes between now and trial." Stoval slapped his palms on his desk. "Maybe it's time I put in a personal call to Ray McKenna."

As the district attorney for Jackson County, McKenna wasn't likely to welcome a phone call unless it offered personal or professional benefit to himself. More to the point, Chief Stoval had forgotten his remark only moments earlier about playing by the book.

"I'd hold off on that," Cody said, speaking up for the first time. "I understand you want results. But there are advantages to building a case before the lawyers get involved."

The chief regarded Cody from under hooded eyes. "The DA is on the same side we are."

"But he knows he's got to make his case in court. No disrespect, sir, but I come down with the DA on this. First off, we don't know that Adam has fled. He could be a victim himself. I gather his parents are frantic. Or he could be scared silly. Even if he did have a thing for Caitlin, that doesn't mean he had anything to do with her disappearance."

Stoval scoffed. "He was sneaking photos of her in the shower for Christ's sake. Her necklace was hidden in the basement of his mother's house. He doesn't come across as a

Boy Scout."

"I was a teenage boy once. I suffered a lot of angst, not to mention an abundance of raging hormones. To tell the truth, I don't find anything in Adam's behavior that's outrageous enough to suggest he killed her."

Rayna looked at Cody, who shot her a half smile. She'd be willing to bet his escapades would make for interesting listening, not that he'd ever share them with her. But none of those girls had turned up missing or dead.

Stoval didn't appear amused, or persuaded. "He sure as hell looks guilty to me. And the sooner we get this wrapped up, the better for the town."

And for Stoval's reputation, Rayna added silently. The chief had to be feeling pressure from the mayor as well as the public. Not an enviable position for a man who had political aspirations.

Rayna's cell rang. She checked the number. "Forensics. I better take this," she said, and stepped away into a corner.

"Detective Godwin here."

"This is Al James. I've got something you might like."

Conversation in Stoval's office stopped while the others listened in.

"We took another look at the debris in the Dumpster where we found the backpack," James continued. "There were some paper towels. The same kind I saw in the kid's mom's house when we searched it yesterday."

Connecting the dots required a bit more than the same brand of paper towels, Rayna thought. "Anything that positively IDs the towels as coming from that household?"

"No, but these aren't your standard paper towels. They've got Garfield printed on them. You know, the cartoon cat? I've never seen anything like them in the stores."

Neither had Rayna, not that she'd looked. But they were the sort of specialty item a dentist whose practice included children might use. "Check with medical supply companies, see if they carry towels like that."

"I already did. And they do. We're running tests on the towels. There are some stains that might be blood."

Rayna felt the punch of adrenaline. "Thanks. Keep me posted." When she hung up, she relayed the information to the three men who'd watched her expectantly.

"I knew we were on the right track." Stoval slapped his desk again, this time with glee. "Now we need to find Adam."

It was stupid to have run, Adam realized. He hadn't planned to, but when he'd arrived at his mom's and seen the cop cars in front, he'd acted without thinking. He'd kept right on driving, past the house and out of town, stopping finally at a secluded forest campground, deserted this time of year.

And now he didn't know what to do. He was tired, hungry, and most of all scared.

His dad said he believed him, but Grace didn't. She'd accused him of hurting Caitlin. When push came to shove, he didn't know which side his dad would take. And who knew what his mom would think? One thing he knew for certain, she'd be pissed. He could hear her now, going on about how he'd upset her life and humiliated her in public. How many parents would feel comfortable sending their kids to a dentist whose son was a murder suspect?

But showing up at school wasn't an option, either. He had visions of the cops hauling him off in handcuffs and all the kids laughing. He'd watched enough TV to know it looked better to go to them than to have them come after you. And, depending on what they'd found when they searched his mom's house, he might be able to explain. He had to remember to keep it simple and not get tripped up.

After spending a couple of cramped, cold nights sleeping in the front seat of the car, more running wasn't really an option, even if he'd wanted to. Not without money.

Time to take action!

He checked the dashboard clock. Ten o'clock on a Monday meant his mom would be with patients, his dad in class. Assuming they'd gone to work. His mom probably had. She was a big believer in routine, and canceling her day's schedule would only highlight the mess her son was in. He wasn't sure about his dad. They'd both left messages on his cell, but neither of them had said more than "call me."

He sent Lucy a text message: "What's the score?"

"Whre r u?"

"Scrwed. M/D wk or hme?"

"Dad hm. Mom dnt kn."

It was his dad, then, by default. But the cops might have the house under surveillance, so he called his dad. They might have tapped the phone, but he'd have to risk it.

His dad picked up on the second ring. "Adam? Is that you?"

Good old caller ID. "It's me."

"Are you okay? Are you safe?" Adam could hear relief and worry in his dad's voice.

"Yeah, I'm fine. For now. The cops were at Mom's Friday night, so I just kept going."

"You had us so worried. You should have called, you should have—"

"Dad!" The last thing Adam needed was a lecture.

"Sorry. I didn't mean to yell. I'm glad to know you're okay."

Okay was a relative thing. He was alive, but far from okay. "What did the cops want at Mom's?"

"They had a search warrant. I don't know what they found."

The comment was open-ended, waiting for Adam to fill him in. Adam didn't.

"They're looking for you," his dad finally said.

"I figured as much."

"Let me help you, Adam. I'll find an attorney. We'll work this through. Come home."

"Are the police at the house?"

"I don't know. I don't think so. I could come pick you up."

Adam caught the blur of movement in the rearview mirror. A car slowly cruising the campground's spur roads. "Oh, shit."

"What's the matter?"

A patrol car pulled up behind him. "Cancel that, Dad,

they're here."

"The police? Let me talk to them."

Adam could see two cops approach, guns drawn. "I don't think it works like that, Dad."

"I love you son. I'll—"

Adam shut off the phone and turned to meet the cops with his hands in the air.

CHAPTER 27

G race pulled the wide-brimmed rain hat down low on her forehead and kept her gaze on the ground until she was well past the man with the golden retriever. Although she didn't really know him, he was a familiar face from her regular walks around the neighborhood. Usually they'd nod or exchange a few words about the weather or the dog. This morning she wanted to be left alone. It was why she'd worn the hat, even though it wasn't raining, and why she kept her chin tucked into the plaid woolen scarf tied around her neck.

The fresh air and exercise were helping clear her head, but nothing could ameliorate the misery that howled and gnawed inside her. What had she done?

Adam had run off. Carl was beyond livid. Her marriage appeared to be in shreds. And none of it had brought Caitlin home. She had destroyed so much of what she held dear, and to what end? She brushed the tears from her eyes with the back of her hand. She'd lost Caitlin, and now she'd lost Carl, too.

He'd been cold and distant all weekend, avoiding her except for intermittent bursts of raging anger. He'd moved out of their bedroom, taken to showering and brushing his teeth when she wasn't anywhere near the bathroom, and seemed to make a point of leaving a room the moment she entered.

First it had been the police, then the search warrant and Mimi's hysterics, and finally Adam, who hadn't been seen or heard from since leaving their house Friday night. And Grace was at the root of it all.

Except she really wasn't, Grace protested silently. She kicked a loose stone on the sidewalk and sent it sailing into the street. Adam was the root of it.

Grace's phone rang. She checked the readout and was surprised to see Lucy's number.

"Hi, Grace. I hope it's okay to call. Am I disturbing you?"

"Not at all." At least there was still one member of the family who was speaking to her.

"Has anyone heard from Adam?" Lucy asked.

"Not that I'm aware of, but then I'm probably the last person who would know."

"Yeah, I guess so. It's your fault Adam's in trouble."

It crossed Grace's mind that Lucy might have called simply to give her a hard time. Being on speaking terms could be a mixed blessing. "What is it you want, Lucy?"

"I wouldn't have called you except that I can't reach my dad or my mom."

"What do you need?"

A moment's hesitation. "Adam sent me a text message."

Grace reacted with a jolt. "When?"

"The middle of English class, about half an hour ago. I've been calling my dad ever since class ended, but he's not picking up."

"Is Adam okay?"

"I don't know. He sounded okay, but he didn't say much. And he doesn't answer when I call him." Lucy sounded agitated. "Where's my dad?"

"He was at home when I left for my walk."

A sigh. "I hate asking, but could you come get me at school?"

"Now? The day's not over."

"I can't stay here," Lucy wailed. "It's totally awful. The kids know the cops are looking for Adam. One of the boys in my mom's neighborhood saw the cops at the house. It's all they're talking about. And I'm worried about Adam. Please, Grace."

Lucy's distress tugged at Grace's frayed emotions. "Sure. I can be there in about twenty minutes."

"I'll wait for you at the oval."

The same spot where Caitlin was last seen.

~~~

Grace's stomach twisted into a knot as she pulled into the drive-thru at the front of the school. Her pulse raced and her hands felt clammy. How many times over the past several years had she driven here to pick up Caitlin? It was one of those familiar rituals, unremarkable in passing, that now felt as if it was carved into her consciousness in bold relief.

Lucy opened the door before Grace had brought the car to a full stop. She flung herself inside, dropping her backpack to the floor and slouching low on the seat. "Let's get out of here."

The histrionics caught Grace by surprise. Lucy was not, generally speaking, a drama queen.

She glared at Grace for a second before turning her face forward and crossing her arms. "Where's my dad?"

"I don't know." When she'd returned to the house from her walk, Carl's car was gone and there was no note. "Why don't you try calling him again?"

"I did, just before you got here." Lucy's tone was curt. "Maybe Adam reached him," she said finally, and more softly. "I hope he's all right."

"I do, too."

"No you don't." Lucy cried, quietly wiping away the tears with the back of her hand. "Everything's a mess and it's all your fault. I'm trying hard not to hate you."

"That's charitable of you," Grace replied with only a hint of sarcasm.

Grace expected belligerence, but instead, Lucy appeared chastised. "Thank you." She took a deep breath. "I'm sorry about what I said, it's just all so confusing and upsetting."

Grace pulled the car to the side of the road and set the brake. She turned to Lucy. "You need to understand why I did what I did. I'm not out to 'get' Adam. But I do need to learn the truth about what happened to Caitlin."

"By accusing Adam?" It was an indictment more than a question.

"Some of his behaviors are, frankly, suspicious."

"Like what?"

Partial knowledge was a dangerous thing, Grace thought. But she didn't feel comfortable sharing everything she'd learned with Lucy. "He seemed kind of fixated on her."

"That doesn't mean he killed her!"

Grace's breath caught. "You're assuming she's dead."

"She is, and you know it. After they found Karen's body, you can't have any doubt."

"I can hope."

"Oh, God." Lucy wiped her nose on her sleeve. "I wanted to be like Caitlin. I envied her so much. She was"— Lucy shot a quick glance at Grace—"is so pretty and confident and smart. Perfect, and I'm none of those things."

"Caitlin's not perfect," Grace said, although she found Lucy's description of her daughter accurate. "And you're you. You've got your own strengths and admirable qualities."

"Please, I'm not stupid. You're just saying that to make me feel better. Caitlin was . . . is so lucky. She has everything. Looks, good grades, a boyfriend, a good life. She has a home."

"You have a home, Lucy. You have two of them."

"That's what I mean. Two houses but neither one really feels like home."

Grace leaned over the gear console and gave Lucy an awkward hug. "We'll have to work on that. As for the rest of it, you're pretty too. Good grades come with hard work, and the boyfriend will come with time."

Lucy shut her eyes. Grace could see tears under her lashes.

"You're so nice to me sometimes," Lucy said, looking at Grace again. "I wish . . . I just feel . . ." She took a deep breath. "Everything that's happened, it's awful." She flung herself into Grace's arms.

"Yes," Grace said, smoothing the back of Lucy's head with her hand. "It is. Just awful."

Everything was awful, and as far as Grace could see, there was no end of awful in sight.

Adam huddled in the caged backseat of the police car, his hands cuffed behind his back. He was more frightened than he'd ever been in his life. The thick-necked officer in the front passenger seat had grinned as he put the handcuffs on, jerking the sharp metal so that it dug into Adam's wrist. The spot still hurt. And he'd given a shove as Adam was getting into the car, sending him headlong toward the far side door. His shoulder throbbed where it had cracked against the frame.

Not real brutality, but the rough treatment left him badly shaken. He was used to being the butt of mean-spirited pranks from some of the kids at school, but finding himself at the mercy of grim-faced men in uniform was something far worse.

The silence inside the car was broken only by the crackle of the police radio and brief staccato interludes of conversation between the two officers. Early on, Adam had tried asking for an explanation. He'd been told in so many very curt words to shut up. And so he had.

How had this happened? Never in a million years could Adam have imagined himself in such a situation. Even the familiar countryside outside the window felt foreign and unfriendly.

When they approached the police station, they pulled up alongside an unmarked door at the rear. Adam was hauled from the car, through a narrow hallway, and into a small room with a table and three molded-plastic chairs. The thick-necked officer pushed him down onto one of the chairs.

"Detectives will be with you shortly," he said.

When the door opened again, it was another uniformed officer. An older man with a mustache who told Adam he was there to photograph and fingerprint him. The man uncuffed one hand at a time, leaving the other end chained to the chair, while he pressed Adam's fingers, one by one, against a small computerized device.

"The joys of technology," he told Adam. "No more need for that messy ink. You got lucky, no?"

Adam couldn't tell if the man was trying to be kind or sarcastic so he didn't say anything.

When they'd finished, the officer had Adam stand, and he patted him down again, just as the officers who'd brought him in had done. Only this guy was slower and more thorough.

Adam gritted his teeth to keep from reacting.

Then the officer picked up a camera and shot two pictures of Adam, straight on and from the side.

"Okay, you can have a seat again," he said.

"How long?" Adam was cold and hungry and he had to pee.

"How long, what?"

"How long do I have to stay here?"

The officer chuckled and packed up his fingerprint kit.

Adam counted on his father to show up and do something. Had he made it clear over the phone that the cops had pulled up behind him on the road? He had been so scared—

"Is my dad here yet?"

"I wouldn't know."

"Don't I get a phone call?"

"This isn't camp, kid."

The door shut and once again Adam was alone.

It's going to be okay, he thought. His dad would get here and clear everything up.

But what if it wasn't okay? What if he went to jail? Stood trial? Was convicted? He started shaking.

After what seemed like an eternity, the two detectives who'd talked to him Friday afternoon showed up. The guy was with the FBI, Adam remembered. He remained standing by the door whereas Detective Godwin moved closer.

"Hello, Adam." She took a chair and smiled at him as though they were old friends. "I guess you can tell things have changed a bit in the last couple of days."

No kidding. Friday he'd been a high school senior on the honor roll whose biggest complaint was that he had no friends. Today he was handcuffed in a police station. "Am I under arrest?"

She looked pained. "I'm afraid so, Adam."

"Why?" He could feel the threat of tears.

"I have to do the small print stuff first," she said, pulling a card from her pocket. Again she smiled at him as if to say what a pain this legalese is. In a bored monotone, she read him his rights from the card. "You've probably seen that on television enough to know what it all means, right?"

"Yeah."

"Okay." She put the card away. "What was your question again?"

"Why did you arrest me?"

"Because we have reason to believe you did something to harm Caitlin."

Adam shook his head. He didn't trust his voice.

FBI Man spoke up. "Did you rape her, Adam? Did you take her prisoner somewhere? What did you do to her?"

"No, I'd never—"

"Is she still alive?" Detective Godwin asked, leaning closer to Adam.

"I don't know."

"You don't know if she's alive? Tell us where she is and maybe we can help you."

"I don't know where she is. I didn't do anything. I swear."

Detective Godwin leaned back in her chair, crossing her arms. She sounded disappointed in him. "You had pictures on your computer, Adam. Pictures of Caitlin naked. Pictures of her in the shower and in front of the mirror. We found them."

"You can't have," Adam blurted without thinking. "I deleted them."

FBI Man sauntered over to where Adam was sitting. "I thought you were supposed to be smart, Adam. You must know deleting files doesn't get rid of them."

The tears no longer merely threatened. Adam could feel them spill from his eyes and down his cheek. "It's not what you think. I'd never hurt her."

"Why not tell us what it is, then," Detective Godwin encouraged.

"It's just that . . . I mean . . ."

"We're waiting, Adam."

"You wouldn't understand. I liked Caitlin, she was a friend. A special kind of friend."

"Sneaking those photos of her was pretty clever," FBI Man said. "How'd you do it?"

The door opened. A uniformed officer and a short man with a large belly and a mustard stain on his shirt plowed through.

"Sorry, detective," said the officer. "This man is the boy's attorney."

"Your father called me," the attorney said to Adam. "He's outside now." He turned to the detectives. "No more conversations with my client unless I am present, is that clear?"

FBI Man grunted in disgust. "There goes your chance for us to work this out cooperatively, kid. Once the lawyers get involved, it's hardball."

"We have some questions for your client," Detective Godwin said.

"I need to talk to him first. Alone."

The detective gave Adam a long, hard look before she and the FBI agent left the room.

"My name's Sandman," the attorney said. "And I hope I don't put you to sleep."

CHAPTER 28

Rayna closed her eyes and slipped lower into the tub. The piping hot water eased the tension. She'd scented the bath with rose oil, and now the fragrance carried her far away to those lazy summer mornings when she'd worked in the garden, Kimberly at her side, chattering away like a little bird.

Mommy, why don't we like weeds? Look, a butterfly. Why can't people fly, too? Why do roses have thorns? Oh, here comes Daddy. He's bringing us lemonade!

Marc used to joke that he couldn't tell a daffodil from a dandelion, but that watching his wife and daughter putter in the garden was one of his greatest pleasures. At which point Rayna would gently remind him she wasn't puttering, she was gardening, and he would brush a dusting of dirt from her cheek or a leaf from her hair and hug her, and Kimberly, in one of his playful family hugs.

Rayna felt a tear track down her cheek. Maybe the rose oil hadn't been such a good idea, after all. The vivid memories the scent stirred were not as easily ignored as the steady dull pain that had become her unfailing companion in recent years.

She opened her eyes and splashed clear, cold water from the spigot on her face. She wasn't going to allow herself to sink into maudlin despair. She'd worked too hard to get past that, desperately afraid that any crack in her resolve would open the floodgates to more than she'd be able to withstand.

Instead, Rayna forced herself to focus on the events that had culminated in the arrest of Adam Peterson this afternoon. Two deputies had spotted Adam's car in a seasonal forest service campground, and taken him into custody. He'd gone with them peacefully, thank goodness. Unfortunately, the kid's lawyer had showed up before she and Cody had a chance to finish questioning him.

But at least they'd made an arrest. They had a suspect in custody. A killer off the streets. The citizens of Paradise Falls would rest easier, the captain would stop breathing down her neck, and the media would turn their spotlights elsewhere. So why this nagging sense that something was missing?

Was she unwilling to accept the fact that these crimes had been cleared while Kimberly's killer remained at large? Had Seth Robbins been onto something when he wrote that she allowed her personal history and emotions to get in the way of doing her job?

Her phone rang in the other room and Rayna let the answering machine answer. She wouldn't climb out of a hot bath for anyone. She dipped deeper into the water so that it came up to her chin, wetting the ends of her hair. They would curl the wrong way unless she spent time with the blower, but the luxury of enveloping herself in warmth was too enticing to pass up.

She wondered how Grace Whittington was holding up. For reasons she didn't understand, Rayna felt a kinship with Grace that she hadn't with Beth Holiday. Perhaps because she could envision that, under other circumstances, the two of them might have been friends. Or maybe Caitlin seemed a lot like a girl Kimberly might have grown to resemble in spirit, if not appearance. Adam's arrest wouldn't be easy for Grace, even though, or maybe especially because, Grace had brought Adam to their attention.

Stepfamilies were an intricate web of relationships Rayna couldn't begin to understand. One she'd been determined to avoid. After Marc had been diagnosed, when it became clear his time was limited, he'd told Rayna he wanted her to feel free to remarry. He wanted Kimberly to have a family, maybe even a brother or sister. The idea of being with anyone but Marc had been far from Rayna's mind, but she'd known even then that a second marriage would be in no way like her first.

She'd started dating Marc for all the wrong reasons—because he was sexy and fun and drove a BMW. But she'd fallen in love with him for all the right reasons. He was honest and direct and caring. He made her laugh. He made her feel special. She knew he was a man she could trust with her life and her heart. They were—although the term made her cringe—soul mates. Marc was her best friend as well as her husband, and when he died, a part of her died. She'd not even looked at another man until Neal Cody.

And what a mistake that had been.

The water began to cool. Rayna lingered until it was almost tepid, then stepped out of the tub and dried her body and hair with a towel. She put on sweatpants and an old T-shirt, and poured herself a glass of brandy. She was debating whether to curl up on the couch with a DVD or crawl into bed with a book when the doorbell rang.

She rarely had unannounced visitors. Her little house was secluded at the end of a sparsely traveled road, and the few people in town she knew, including Paul Nesbitt, weren't the type to drop in unexpectedly.

Peeking through window, she saw Cody standing under the porch light.

He had never played by her rules.

She didn't have to answer the door. Just because someone rang didn't mean you were obligated to open up. But it would be obvious to him that she was home, and there was no real reason not to answer it. She looked down at her faded and misshapen clothing, ran a hand through her damp, unruly hair, and after a moment's hesitation, opened the door.

"You're the last person I expected," she said.

"You're expecting someone else?"

"No, I meant you surprised me. What are you doing here?"

"I wanted to say goodbye. I'm leaving in the morning."

"Leaving?" A blast of cold, damp air blew into the house. She stepped back. "Come inside so I can shut the door."

Cody stamped his feet on the mat to clear his boots of mud, then stepped inside. "There's no real reason for me to be here anymore, and they need agents in Las Vegas for a big fraud case."

"I didn't know you worked white collar crimes."

"These days I work whatever they give me." He didn't sound happy, but he didn't explain, so Rayna let it go.

"I just poured myself a little brandy," she said. "Would you like some?"

Leaving. The word hadn't registered right away. She hadn't wanted him here in the first place—not the FBI and especially not Neal Cody—but now that he was leaving she felt inexplicably sad.

"As long as I'm not disturbing anything . . ."

Rayna looked down at her clothes and laughed. "Hardly. But shouldn't you have thought of that before knocking on my door at this hour?"

He smiled. "Maybe I wanted to find out if I was."

Same old cocky, self-serving attitude. She remembered again why she'd tried to forget him. She handed him a glass and the bottle of brandy, and let him pour his own.

"Good stuff," he said, serving up an ample snifter.

Rayna's living room was a mess: papers and magazines and a half-finished quilting project she'd begun months ago. Without a fire in the fireplace, it was also gloomy on early spring evenings. So they sat at the table in the kitchen, which despite its 70s decor was Rayna's favorite room.

"I guess," she said, taking in a whiff of brandy from her glass, "you must be happy to be onto something better than this 'nothing assignment in some podunk, nowhere town.' "

He looked surprised, then chagrined. "I'm sorry I said that. I didn't really mean it."

"Then why say it?"

He ignored the question. "What's coming is no better, even if it is Vegas." He paused to sip his drink. "I'm not exactly a popular guy with the higher-ups right now."

"What did you do?"

"I called my boss a jerk in front of his boss, for starters."

"I can see how that might not have endeared you to him." She couldn't help but smile. Cody didn't suffer fools lightly.

"During my divorce, I kind of lost patience with everything and everybody. I did some stupid stuff and it's only right I be held accountable. But the thing that really got me in trouble was not following procedure to the letter. Never mind that the case had a good outcome, that a sick pervert is in prison and two little boys have the chance to grow up in good homes."

"The end justifies the means?"

"Sometimes it does. Petty rules should never get in the way of doing what's right."

"So why stay with the Bureau?" She knew he'd chafed under their regulations in the past.

He looked into his glass, as if expecting to find an answer there, before turning his gaze back to her. "What else would I do? Besides, I'm working my way back into their good graces. And bottom line, I love what I do. Feeling sorry for myself and taking it out on everyone else was dumb. Not following procedure wasn't smart, either, but publicizing the fact was what got me in trouble."

"It's always good to learn from our mistakes," she said mildly. She would have liked to know more but thought better of asking.

"Thanks, Mom." Cody met her eyes for a moment and then looked back down at the glass in his hand. "I really didn't want this assignment, but not because I thought it was unimportant. Truth is, I was nervous about seeing you."

"How so?"

"I figure sometimes it's better to let bygones by bygones. Easier, anyway. Less painful. These past four years have been . . . well, there are things I regret."

He stood up and crossed to the open shelves by the small kitchen desk. Rayna kept her small collection of cookbooks there, as well as a glass salad bowl that was too large to fit anywhere else, various bills and letters and flyers that needed her attention, and other odds and ends that hadn't found a permanent place yet in her house.

"I was going to say it's good to see you doing so well, but I know that's not the whole truth, even though you jumped on me a couple of days ago for suggesting otherwise."

She'd jumped on him because of his presumption that he

understood her. And because she was angry at him for the way he'd treated her. Tonight, whether it was the brandy or the hot bath, or the fact that he was leaving, she felt less inclined to take offense.

"I'm doing okay," she said. "All things considered."

He ran his fingers along the spines of the cookbooks. "Thai, Indian, Italian—you must be quite a cook."

"Mostly I just think about cooking." At one time, she had been a decent cook. An adventurous one, at any rate. Now she favored quick and easy.

"Cute little bunny," Cody said, picking up the stuffed toy on top of the stack of bills.

"That's the stuffed animal I told you about. The one I found in my mailbox the day after we discovered Karen Holiday's body. Forensics found nothing. They don't even think it's tied to the case."

Cody set the little rabbit back down. "Are you looking at Adam for Karen Holiday's murder?"

"Looking, yes. But there's no solid evidence that says he did it."

"You think the two disappearances are unrelated then?"

"I don't know what to think. In some ways, I worry that Adam's arrest this afternoon was premature."

"The chief must be pleased, though. Despite his 'proceed carefully' lecture the other day, he seems to have a bee in his britches about demonstrating that the department's on top of things."

"That's pretty much his style, but you're right that he pushed for the arrest." Rayna had argued for treating Adam as a person of interest rather than a suspect, but she'd been overruled. And maybe it was just as well. Rayna wasn't sure she trusted her own judgment anymore.

Cody came back to the table and sat down. "At least the arrest ought to get that Seth Robbins guy off your back. What's his agenda, anyway?"

"I don't know." Rayna's eyelids were feeling the exhaustion of the day. She yawned. "I've only met him once, at a civic function. He's a scrawny little guy, and a bit pompous.

An oddball who delights in being odd and getting a rise out of people."

"Someone who enjoys power, from the sound of it."

"He seems to take pride in the fact that he calls it like it is, but in truth, he's all over the map. He got on his high horse about Karen Holiday's murder and hasn't let up. Why didn't we have a suspect right away? How come we weren't doing more to find her? I was a total fuckup who only got where I was because I was female. That sort of thing. I think he can't tell the difference between reality and a one-hour television crime show." But he had managed to dig up information about Rayna's past.

"Everyone's an expert these days."

Rayna agreed. Pointing out the mistakes and discrepancies in crime shows was a favorite cop pastime when she'd worked in San Jose. Thankfully Hank's viewing habits tended more toward sports.

She eyed Cody's empty glass. "You want more brandy?"

"I should be going." He made no move to leave.

She could persuade him to stay, Rayna realized. It would take only a word or a look. She hated herself for being tempted. The chair scraped the linoleum as she pushed it back and rose.

Cody followed suit, shoving his hands into his pockets. "Despite everything, it was good to see you again."

"Stay in touch," she said.

He looked surprised. "You mean that?"

She'd spoken without really thinking, but now she nodded. Maybe she hadn't resisted temptation entirely. That didn't mean she was ready to succumb to it, but she didn't want Neal Cody to disappear from her life forever.

At the door he hesitated and Rayna wondered what she'd do if he tried to kiss her. She needn't have worried. He smiled, let his gaze linger for a moment, and then trotted down the steps and into the night.

Exhausted, she decided to forget both the book and DVD and head for bed. As she slid between the sheets, she remembered the phone call she'd received during her bath. She hit play on the machine.

"Hello, Rayna." The voice sounded male, although it was difficult to be sure. The caller spoke slowly, drawing out each syllable. "Have you been enjoying your fifteen minutes in the spotlight? It's not over. In fact, the fun has just begun."

CHAPTER 29

Grace sat motionless on the living room sofa, as she had all afternoon, waiting for the sound of Carl's car pulling into the driveway. She was half afraid he would storm past without acknowledging her. Half afraid he'd confront her with his fists, although Carl was in no way a violent man. But he'd been so upset with her, so furious over Adam's arrest, she no longer knew what he was capable of doing.

Last night had been a long, horrible night on the heels of an equally horrendous weekend. Carl had gone to the police station immediately after getting Adam's call, but they hadn't let him see his son. He hadn't returned home until after eight. Hadn't even called until Grace, who, frantic to know where Carl had gone and frazzled from dealing with an overwrought Lucy, had phoned his cell so often he finally answered. Not then, and only with some difficulty once he'd arrived home, had Grace been able to pull the details from him.

Adam was under arrest, in jail. If convicted, he might be there for the rest of his life.

Through the recommendation of one of the secretaries at the college, whose own son had a history of legal missteps, Carl had been able to locate an attorney to take on Adam's case. The attorney, a man by the name of Norm Sandman, didn't seem particularly interested in Adam's guilt or innocence, Carl told her. Didn't seem particularly empathetic to Adam's plight, either. But the secretary had told Carl that Sandman was a good attorney, and what other choice did he have?

Carl had no idea how his son was holding up. Mimi, however, was hysterical. And again, it was all Grace's fault.

She had lain awake all night, alone in the large king-size bed while Carl slept downstairs in the den.

A single refrain pounded in her brain—what had she done? It wasn't so much a question she asked intellectually— she understood why she'd done it and knew that if she had it to do over again, she'd do the same thing. But emotionally, the question reverberated without end. I've destroyed my marriage, Grace thought. I've betrayed Carl. Betrayed Adam. I've lost everything that matters to me. And to what end?

What if she was wrong? What if Adam had nothing to do with Caitlin's disappearance? What if she'd started this free-fall calamity for no reason? Grace's stomach turned. No, she couldn't let herself think that.

Carl had returned to the jail early this morning for some sort of meeting with Sandman and the DA. It was now late afternoon and she'd been sitting on the sofa, waiting for his return, since the moment he'd driven off.

She had visions of a trial. Carl and Mimi and Lucy on one side of the courtroom, herself alone on the other. No, not alone. Jake would be there. And Starr. But that image brought Grace little comfort.

What have I done?, she asked herself for the hundredth time. What in God's name have I done?

When Grace heard Carl's car in the driveway, she panicked. She wanted to know what had happened at the jail. She wanted Carl's arms around her, and yet she feared facing him. She felt she might shatter under the force of his anger.

Carl blew through the door like an icy gale. He went straight to his end of the sofa, where he dropped down without saying a word, without so much as glancing in her direction. He had the weary, dazed look she'd seen on the faces of people who survived major catastrophes. She wanted to reach out and touch him but she didn't dare.

"What happened?" she finally asked.

Carl pulled air into his lungs with heavy, labored breaths, then said, "They released him. For the time being. Into Mimi's custody." He turned to Grace. "They didn't consider releasing him to me because of you."

How was she supposed to respond to that? I'm sorry didn't quite cut it. Besides, she wasn't. "So he's free?"

"They decided not to charge him right now, but that's not the same as free. Sandman explained that several times. It's good news in the short run, but he warned us not to get our hopes up that this would all go away."

Grace studied her hands.

"Twenty-five hundred up front," Carl said, sounding a bit more like himself. "It could go a lot higher. I don't even know if the guy's any good."

"He got Adam out of jail, didn't he?"

"I'm not sure he had much to do with it." Carl stood and began pacing the room. "I don't know, maybe he did. But I'm trusting my son's future, maybe his life, to this guy and he looks like someone you'd see at the hardware store and figure he worked there."

"That doesn't mean he's not a good attorney."

"Well, he doesn't inspire confidence." Carl walked to the window and looked out, his back to Grace. "Jesus, how can life fall apart so quickly?"

"I did what I thought was right, Carl. What I had to do. You understand that, don't you?"

When he didn't answer, she continued. "I don't want Adam to have been involved. I hope to God he's not. I'd like nothing better than for the police to clear him." Then maybe we can go back to being a family, she added silently, although she knew that would never happen. "At least tell me you can understand why I had to tell them."

Carl's mouth and chin were tight. "It's not just what you told them, Grace." He returned to the sofa and leaned forward, palms pressed against his temples. "There's more. Sandman learned the police found photos on Adam's computer when they searched Mimi's house. Photos of Caitlin in the shower and . . . and such."

Grace choked. She thought she might be sick. "And such?"

"I didn't see the photos, Grace. I'm only telling you what

Sandman told me."

She had once taken a yoga class. She'd never mastered even the most rudimentary poses but she'd learned to breathe. She reminded herself now to breathe.

"That necklace of Caitlin's they showed you? They found it at Mimi's. They also found initials scratched in stone down by the river. A spot where Adam supposedly likes to go."

"Initials?"

"Caitlin's and Adam's."

"Oh." Grace's heart raced. On the one hand, she was glad they'd found evidence that supported her suspicions, but she took no pleasure in hearing the details.

Carl closed his eyes and took a breath. "And they found some paper towels in the Dumpster with Caitlin's backpack. They're special towels that Mimi buys for her dental practice."

It took a moment for Grace to make the connections. Caitlin's backpack linked to Adam.

"My God!" Grace's mouth felt dry. "What does Adam say?"

"I haven't had a chance to talk to him alone. Sandman was there the entire time. He didn't want Adam answering any questions. And then, after they released him, Mimi hurried him off like I was a viper or something."

"Oh, Carl. How awful. I can imagine how terrible you must feel."

"Can you? I doubt it, Grace. I doubt it very much." Carl dropped his hands to his lap and looked at her, the anger gone, replaced by anguish. Tears formed in his eyes. "God, Grace. What if Adam did harm Caitlin?"

She knew this was a delicate moment. A moment of grave importance. But she didn't have the slightest idea what to say.

Rayna hadn't slept well. The message on her answering machine had frayed her nerves and kept her awake until dawn. She'd finally slept a little, but her day had started off with spilled coffee (thankfully, she'd managed to miss her keyboard) and the news that Adam Peterson was being released. Then she closed the file drawer on her thumb. So it was only fitting she'd run into Seth Robbins in the elevator on her way to meet the DA.

"Care to comment on this morning's hearing?" he asked, raking his fingers through his pointy little beard.

"No."

He whistled under his breath. "That was succinct."

Rayna kept her eyes forward, wishing she'd taken the stairs and avoided the obnoxious twerp.

"Do you have other suspects in mind?"

She bit her tongue.

"Is the Peterson kid someone you're still interested in? Should the townspeople be worried that he's free?"

The elevator dinged its arrival and the doors opened. Rayna stepped forward, but Robbins blocked the exit.

His face was inches from hers. She smelled stale coffee on his breath. "How will you feel if another girl disappears?"

"You're in my way," Rayna said.

"Or maybe, detective, missing girls give you some perverse satisfaction. Do cases like this help remind you that you aren't the only one who's lost a daughter?"

"You're full of crap," Rayna snapped.

Robbins smiled and stepped aside.

Rayna stormed down the hallway to McKenna's office, muttering under her breath.

Ray McKenna was a balding former defense attorney with the face and bark of a bulldog. He was hard to read, short on explanations, and totally without a sense of humor. He looked up from his desk as Rayna entered the room, then continued leafing through the papers in front of him.

"Be right with you," he said. He found what he was looking for, buzzed his secretary, then turned to Rayna.

"If you're here to gripe about this morning, don't waste your breath."

"I don't intend to gripe. But I'd like to understand what else we need on Adam Peterson to make the charges stick."

"A body would be nice," McKenna said.

"But not absolutely necessary."

"Not in the abstract, but in this case, pretty damned close.

We can't charge Peterson with Karen Holiday's murder. There's nothing solid linking him to it. And until we have concrete evidence that Caitlin Whittington is dead, we can't charge him with her murder."

"Her backpack and wallet were in a Dumpster," Rayna pointed out.

"Doesn't mean diddly."

"Only if what you're most concerned about is your conviction rate."

McKenna leaned forward and looked Rayna in the eye. "He's a juvenile. If we charge him as a juvenile, he'll be out in short order. To do this right, we need to charge him as an adult. And without irrefutable evidence, a jury is going to resist convicting a seventeen-year-old kid who's a straight-A student and never been in a lick of trouble before."

"What if he goes after another girl?" She hated that she sounded like Seth Robbins.

"That's a stupid argument," McKenna said, "and you know it. We can't lock people up because they might commit a crime. Besides, Caitlin isn't some random girl. You've focused on Adam because of his supposed infatuation with her."

These were all thoughts Rayna had had herself, but once they'd made the arrest, and even though she wasn't entirely behind it, she wanted it to stick. The DA's refusal to charge Adam made the police look bad. Made her feel incompetent. And she worried that it might cost another girl her life.

"Maybe he was infatuated with Karen Holiday, as well," she said. "And who knows, he may have another girl in his sights."

"Find me something, then. You're the detective. My office can only work with what you give us. If you want the charges to stick, give us the tools to make it happen."

Walking the two blocks back to the station, Rayna got doused with a spray of muddy water from a passing car. The day was not turning out to be one of her finest.

At her desk, she blotted the mud stains with tissue and considered the direction of the investigation. It was time to regroup. They had good reason to believe Adam was involved in Caitlin's disappearance, less to connect him to Karen Holiday—nothing, in fact, aside from the tutoring program. They needed to look at the Holiday investigation anew, with Adam in mind, but for the moment, she wanted to focus on Caitlin.

Trouble was, she found it difficult to focus at all. The call on her machine last night had shaken her more than she cared to admit. A prank? Or something more sinister? Caller ID had been useless—unknown name, unknown number. The phone company trace hadn't helped. The call had come from a disposable cell phone.

She tapped her pen against the pad of paper on her desk and forced her mind on the task at hand.

Working backwards, they needed to find the evidence that would prove Adam guilty—a fairly standard strategy. Not a good one, though, and Rayna had resisted it for most of her career. The better approach was to follow the evidence with an open mind. Granted, that had led them to arrest Adam Peterson in the first place, but the evidence was the place to begin. At the same time, they'd take a fresh look at other possible suspects. Eliminating them would bolster the case against Adam.

Opening the file, Rayna read through it, page by page. She made notes, laid out charts, wrote questions to herself in the margins. She had a crick in her neck and a stiff back by the time she'd finished. Unfortunately, she hadn't come up with any brilliant insights or clear plan of attack.

Hank returned to his desk as Rayna was stretching her cramped muscles.

"Anything?" she asked. He had been following up on the most recent tip from their abduction hot line. The calls had poured in after Caitlin's disappearance, then tapered off until the discovery of Karen Holiday's remains. None of the calls had proved useful, but each needed to be looked into.

"Not unless you think there's a chance space aliens are involved."

"I think that's about the only thing we can rule out with

absolute certainty. Everything else is pretty much open for consideration. You heard that Adam Peterson was released?"

"Yeah, I caught it on the news. Some days I wonder why we bother to bust our butts bringing in a suspect." Hank hung his rain jacket on one of the hooks near their desks. "Guess Neal Cody shoulda' stuck around after all."

Rayna knew she should call Cody and tell him about Adam being released, but since she hadn't asked for FBI help to begin with, she figured she wasn't officially obligated to keep him up to date.

"What's next?" Hank asked. "Dig up more on Adam Peterson, or are we back to the beginning?"

"Both. I want us to go through the list of possible suspects one more time. Look at each one with an open mind. Also see if there's any way to connect Adam to Karen Holiday's murder."

"Right." Hank sounded anything but enthusiastic. "Was Cliff able to get an ID on that Romeo guy who contacted Caitlin on-line?"

"Not yet. He probably pulled back when we focused on Adam."

"Romeo seems like a good bet, though. When I started in the business, there was no such thing as an on-line predator. Now it seems like they're everywhere. What a world we live in, huh?" He colored slightly, looked at his feet. "Guess I don't need to tell you, of all people, about the dangers."

Part of the reason Rayna had kept her past to herself was to avoid this sort of awkwardness. Since Seth Robbins's column, Hank seemed unsure how to deal with her, as if she suddenly needed to be treated with kid gloves.

"I'll check with Grace Whittington and see what she knows about who Caitlin might have been in contact with."

"What do you want me to do?"

"See if you can shake something out of Ty Cross or Rob Hardy. And I guess we'd better see if we can dig up a new name or two, someone with ties to both Caitlin and Karen."

"If it was that easy, Rayna, we'd have done it already."

"Have you got a better idea?"

"No," Hank conceded.

Rayna thought again of the phone call she'd received last night. The fun is just beginning. She hadn't told Hank or the chief about it because she didn't want to be considered part of the problem. But she couldn't keep it to herself forever.

They needed to figure this thing out. And soon.

CHAPTER 30

Adam doused his scalp for a second time, pouring on the shampoo until he had a full foamy lather going. He washed his body a second time, as well, scrubbing his skin raw with some of the gritty exfoliating gel Lucy kept in the shower. He was desperate to wash away every trace of the past twenty-four hours.

Jail. He'd actually spent the night in jail. He shivered under the stream of hot water.

It had been worse than he'd thought. The thin, slightly damp mattress on the narrow bottom bunk. The scratchy, moth-eaten blanket that did a miserable job of keeping him warm. The filthy open toilet. The snores and phlegmy coughing fits of his cellmate, a heavily tattooed man with bulging biceps who was, he'd told Adam proudly, most likely on his way back to prison for good. Adam hadn't dared ask the man what he'd done. He'd tried to say as little as possible. He'd tried to make himself invisible.

Relieved to be back home at his mom's, he tried to focus on that and not dwell on the harrowing experience of being locked up. But the attorney had told him it wasn't over, and that thought kept pounding in his head. What if he was sent back to jail, or worse, to prison? He couldn't do it. He couldn't. Whatever it took, he wouldn't spend another night behind bars.

The water began to run cooler. He must have gone through the whole tank of hot. If not for that, he would have stayed in the shower forever. Even though his mother was waiting for him downstairs.

He'd slept most of the afternoon, or pretended to. He just

wanted to be left alone. But she'd knocked on his door half an hour ago to tell him dinner would be ready soon. You didn't mess with his mom's schedule, especially since she'd taken the entire day off. Canceled patients, just because of him. And he knew she'd want an explanation about jail.

She was in the kitchen, a sure sign that life wasn't normal. His mom wasn't a kitchen kind of person.

She hugged him, smiling and cheery, like they were in some feel-good family TV show. "You holding up okay?"

"Yeah, I'm fine."

Her smile brightened. "I'm glad. This whole thing is absurd. Totally uncalled for." She busied herself with salad greens. "I made lasagna for dinner," she said over her shoulder. "Your favorite dish."

It had been one of Adam's favorites in fifth grade. He wasn't sure they'd had it since.

His mom was attractive. His friends said so. She was tall and slender, with dark red-brown hair that fell below her shoulders, and green eyes with long lashes. Adam had gotten her lashes and her build, as well as the red hair. Lucy took after their father, who was stockier. His mom was focused and accomplished and sure of herself. Neither of her children had inherited those qualities.

He was proud of his mom, but never felt completely comfortable with her. It was like he'd lost the instruction manual on being her son. He was never quite sure what she expected of him.

"Dinner isn't ready just yet," she said, "but I put out a bowl of chips. And I've got Coke. You like Coke, don't you?"

Lucy was the big Coke fan, but Adam nodded and accepted the glass she poured for him, then made a show of setting the kitchen table.

"It must have been quite an adventure," his mother said, "spending a night in jail."

"I survived." Instead of looking at her, he concentrated on putting the silverware on the placemats in precise alignment. He wished Lucy was there to provide a buffer, but his mother had thought it would be better if she stayed with Dad.

"Oh, honey, I can't imagine—"

"It was okay," Adam said, waiting to put an end to the discussion.

She handed him a basket of sliced French bread for the table. "Were you . . . I mean nothing really terrible happened, did it?"

"I'm fine, I told you that."

"Right, you did."

He sat at the table, sipping Coke and reading the funnies from that morning, while his mom finished up last-minute dinner preparations. Finally, she took the lasagna from the oven and served it. She handed him a plate and then sat down at the table with her own portion.

"How is it?" she asked after Adam took a bite.

"Good." It was so hot he'd barely tasted it.

She watched him eat then set her fork down. "Now tell me what this is all about."

"You know what it's about."

"I'd like to hear it from you, in your own words. Until Friday, when the police showed up here looking for you, I didn't know a thing. They took me totally by surprise."

He pushed a blob of melted cheese around on his plate. "They think I had something to do with what's happened to Caitlin."

"You didn't, did you?" The sharpness of her tone made Adam flinch.

"No."

She leaned back in her chair. "I didn't think so."

"Then why did you ask?"

It was the sort of remark that usually elicited a glare—his mother didn't like to be challenged. But this time she seemed to give the question serious consideration. "I guess I just wanted to hear you say it."

He would have liked to hear her say she believed in him without his having to ask. In fact, he wished she'd stop all the questions and simply hug him. When he was young, she'd hold his face and kiss his cheeks and tell him she loved him. He used to pull away and make a big deal of being embarrassed, but secretly he loved it. It had been a long time since she'd done any of that.

"I wasn't accusing you," she said. "I just wanted to know."

She must have had her doubts, he thought, or she wouldn't have asked.

"They had some photos though," she continued. "Some from your dad's house and some they found on your computer here at home." She made it sound like a question.

"The attorney said not to talk about it."

"But I'm your mother." For the first time since she'd brought him home from jail, she sounded uncertain. "I understand teenage boys, Adam. You don't have to pretend with me." She paused. "You have a crush on Caitlin, is that it? It's nothing to be ashamed of."

"Mom, please." Crush was such an adolescent word. It didn't begin to describe what Adam felt. He wasn't sure he understood it himself.

"It would be perfectly understandable and normal."

"I don't have a crush on her," he said. Crush, like he was some lovesick little boy.

"Then why did you take those photos?"

"I just did, okay? It was stupid, or whatever. Let's talk about something else."

She took a small bite of her lasagna. "This is all Grace's fault, you know."

"She's worried about Caitlin," Adam said. "That's not so hard to understand. You'd be worried too, in her place."

"I have to say, your dad's done a great job of brainwashing you."

"He didn't brainwash me."

"You don't have to be so accommodating, Adam. What Grace did was inexcusable. I should think you'd be mad as hell, that you'd hate her."

To his surprise, he didn't hate Grace. It would be easier if he did, but he could understand why she'd done what she had.

Besides, he liked Grace. What he felt mostly was sad. He'd disappointed so many people lately, most importantly Caitlin. He'd made such a mess of everything. And there was no one he could talk to about any of it.

He pushed his food around on this plate for a bit, and forced down another couple of bites.

Finally, his mom sighed and said, "There will be rules now. You go straight to school and come straight home afterwards. I'm responsible for you and I don't want any more complications."

"Do I have to go to school? Why can't I do some kind of home study?"

She shook her head. "You're an outstanding student, Adam. I'm not going to let you jeopardize your chances of getting into a top tier college for something that's not your doing."

"I wasn't talking about forever."

"Hold your head up, Adam. Stand strong. If you go around acting guilty, that's what people will think. You can do that, can't you?"

People were going to think he was guilty, no matter what he did. "Yeah, fine," he said. "I guess I'd better go do some homework then." He pushed back his chair and fled. There was no way he'd be able to concentrate on school work, but it was a handy excuse for getting away.

Upstairs, he called his dad, just like he promised he would. Grace answered the phone. "He's napping," she said. "Would you like me to wake him?"

"No, that's okay. I'll talk to him later."

"Adam, I know you must . . . I'll tell him you called."

Face down on his bed, he wondered how his life had become such a fucked-up mess.

CHAPTER 31

"I friggin' can't believe it!" Jake said the next morning. "What in God's name were they thinking, letting him go?"

Grace held the receiver away from her ear. Jake had been yelling at her for five minutes, a virtual blitz of fury and venom. She understood that he was upset about Adam's release, but she wasn't feeling exactly chipper herself.

"I warned you," Jake continued loudly. "I knew Carl's son had something to do with it. And now, Jesus, how could they let him go?"

"They didn't think they had enough evidence," she said for the second or third time. "But he's still a suspect. They just need more before they can charge him."

"He's not going to get away with it. I swear, I'll even the score myself if I have to."

"Jake, stop it. You sound like an idiot."

"You're siding with Carl now?"

"This isn't about sides!" In fact, Carl was horribly conflicted. She'd seen the chink in his armor last night, and although they'd discussed it only briefly, sidestepping around the rawest emotions, she knew that his doubts about Adam were tearing him up.

"My daughter is missing," Jake snapped, "and whatever happened to her is someone's fault. That makes two sides, Grace, whether you like it or not."

"All I care about right now is Caitlin."

"That's what we both care about." Jake's voice had lost some of its venom.

"It's so hard . . ." Grace could tell she was on the brink of tears. Her chest and throat were tight, her eyes stung. "What if we never see Caitlin again? Oh, Jake, I couldn't bear it."

"That's why Adam is going to pay." There was a click on the other end of the line and Jake said, "I've got an incoming call. Let me know what's happening. And remember, you're living in the enemy camp."

Grace felt drained and agitated all at once. And sad. The sadness had become so all-pervasive, like a dank, gray mist that settled into every corner and crevice of her being, that it was a part of her now. Sad was who she was.

When the phone rang and she checked the caller ID, she saw the now familiar number of the Paradise Falls Police Department. For a moment the air left Grace's lungs and her blood turned to ice.

She picked up the receiver. "Hello?"

"This is Rayna Godwin. I'm not calling with news, Grace. I just wanted to touch base."

Grace began breathing again. "Thanks for understanding about phone calls from the police." And then she realized that, of course, the detective would understand. She'd lost a daughter herself. "Is it about Adam?"

"Not exactly. I'm sorry about the way it was handled. A lot of it is out of my hands."

Grace wanted to ask if they'd learned anything by questioning him. If he'd given them any clues or new directions. She wanted to know why and how he had photos of Caitlin. But she knew that if Rayna were free to tell her, she would.

"I have a few more questions," the detective said. "We can do this over the phone, but if you have time it might be better face to face."

"I have time." Grace had nothing but time, and it stretched before her like a long bleak stretch of barren desert.

"Shall we meet for coffee, then? I could use a break from the acid that passes for coffee around here. How about the Java Mill? It's not far from the station. Does half an hour from now work for you?"

"I'll be there," Grace said.

The coffee shop was small, with only a few tables, but the detective had one of them staked out when Grace arrived. She greeted Grace over a cup of frothy cappuccino.

"I would have bought coffee for you, but didn't know what you liked. I got an extra muffin, though."

"Thanks." Grace hung her jacket over the back of the chair, stood in line to get her own coffee, and returned to the table.

Rayna Godwin slid a muffin across the old wooden table, took another sip of her coffee, and licked the foam from her upper lip. "Thanks for agreeing to meet me."

"You're one of the few people speaking to me these days."

"Sharing your suspicions about Adam couldn't have been easy."

"It wasn't. I just hope what I told you helps find Caitlin. That's what matters most." Grace looked into her coffee. "I don't suppose Adam said anything about what happened to her?" Grace didn't really expect an answer. "Do you think he did it?"

"Did what, is the question. The DA isn't ready to charge Adam with any crime, much less a specific crime." The detective set down her cup and looked at Grace. "I don't want to cause you more pain, but there's a good chance that Caitlin is dead, and you should prepare yourself for that outcome."

The words struck Grace like a lead weight, although they didn't come as a surprise. Her fingers felt sticky and she realized she'd picked a piece of muffin to crumbs.

"We're still looking at Adam," Goodwin continued, "but we're also looking at other possible suspects. That's why I wanted to speak to you."

"I'm afraid I don't have any new ideas."

"Caitlin has an account on Facebook. Some of the photos and comments she made were probably not what a mother would want to find. But more importantly, she'd been corresponding with someone who calls himself Romeo."

"Someone she met online?"

"It appears that way. Remember the iPod we found in her locker? You said your daughter didn't own one, but when we checked with kids at school, they said she did. Maybe it was a gift and she didn't bring it home because she'd have to explain."

"A gift from this Romeo?" Grace felt light-headed. "Who is he?"

"That's what we're trying to find out. She never said anything? Even something in passing? Something that didn't register at the time?"

Grace swallowed hard. "Caitlin received a package a few days ago, a web camera, one of those little things that can broadcast your live photo. It was wrapped like a gift, but there was no return address, and no card."

"Do you still have the package?"

"It's at home."

"I'll send someone by to pick it up. There's a good chance it came from 'Romeo.' "

Grace experienced a momentary flicker of hope. If Caitlin had simply run away to be with this man—

"You had no idea Caitlin was active on Facebook?"

"Not in the way you're saying. I knew she had an account, but I assumed it was just a teenage thing with a few friends."

Grace felt like an idiot. How could she not have known what her daughter was doing? How could she not have insisted on knowing? Caitlin had been upset recently, but Grace had assumed it was over her breakup with Ty Cross. Why hadn't she prodded more? "This Romeo could be anyone, right?" she asked.

"I can't say with any certainty that 'Romeo' had anything to do with what happened to Caitlin. He could be a young man smitten with a cute girl. He could even be Adam."

Grace shuddered. Could Adam have stalked Caitlin in that way? The photos, the initials the cops had found carved into a boulder, Caitlin's necklace. Dear God, had this really been happening right under their noses?

She couldn't help thinking that if she'd never married Carl, Caitlin would be safe.

"Can I ask you a personal question?" Grace hesitated. "About your daughter."

Rayna's expression was suddenly guarded. "What is it?"

"Do you ever wonder if somehow it's your fault? If only you had done this or that differently, she'd be alive?"

"I'm not sure what you're asking."

"I should have protected Caitlin," Grace said bleakly. "That's what mothers do. Whether it was Adam or Romeo or Ty Cross, if I'd been more diligent, more careful, this never would have happened."

"You're not to blame for what happened to Caitlin."

"What if she's never found? What if she's, like you said, dead? How can I live with myself? How can I not feel responsible?"

The detective drained her cup and slid it aside. "There was a homicide I was involved in almost a year before Kimberly disappeared. A little girl my daughter's age. The two of them were nothing alike, but because of their ages and the close timing of their deaths, the case has haunted me more than most."

"What happened to her?"

"I got involved initially when the mother got a restraining order against Bethany's father. Bethany was the little girl. She was eleven. The father was a junkie with a temper, but the mother wasn't a whole lot better. I think she really wanted to do right by her daughter, but she was a high school dropout who'd gotten pregnant with Bethany at sixteen and had never really gotten her life on track. She made one bad choice after another. Anyway, the dad repeatedly ignored the restraining order and got little more than a slap on the wrist for it every time. Then he snatched Bethany and took her to the fleabag hotel where he was living. He threatened to beat her if she tried to get away, and then finally locked her in the closet. When we found her she was dehydrated and filthy and her body was covered in bites from bedbugs. The father claimed he was trying to protect her, but the law finally stepped in and said he'd kidnapped her. He went to jail."

"Sounds like that's where he belonged."

"That's what I thought, too, although he didn't end up doing much time. Still, I felt pretty good about the whole thing." Rayna seemed to retreat into herself for a moment. "Two months after he went to jail his wife and daughter were dead. The mom's boyfriend shot them both, and then killed himself."

Grace inhaled. "My, God. Why?"

"He'd lost his job and speculation was that the mom was breaking up with him, but we'll never know for sure. Bethany's death hit me hard. She was a quiet little girl with big eyes who never had a chance in life. I couldn't help but compare her situation to Kimberly's. My daughter had lost her dad, but she knew he adored her. And she had me. I'm not holding myself up as an example of perfection, but I thought I was a good mother and although it wouldn't be easy, Kimberly would do fine. In the end it didn't make any difference. Kimberly is as dead as Bethany. Being a good mother doesn't make you Superwoman."

Maybe not, Grace thought, but she still should have been able to protect Caitlin.

CHAPTER 32

The school bell rang and Adam gathered his books slowly, waiting for the room to clear. Last period, he'd tried bolting for the door first thing, but so had half the class, so he'd ended up right in the thick of where he didn't want to be. Curious glances, antagonistic stares, muttered obscenities, all directed his way. And those were the "good kids." In every class so far there'd been at least one self-appointed crusader who'd led the charge of overt humiliation and hostility. The DA might not have had enough evidence to charge him, but the same wasn't true for public opinion.

As soon as the room emptied out, Adam darted for the door before Mrs. Hall could corner him. The teachers were almost as bad as the students, although they couched their uneasiness in phony displays of concern.

He really, really didn't want to be at school today. Not today or tomorrow or any time in the future. It was better than being in jail, but that was the only good thing to be said about it. School was part of the deal, though. And not just his mom's deal. His mom, his dad, his lawyer, all agreed that he needed to carry on as usual. Act normal, go to school, stay out of trouble, don't do anything that might make him the center of attention. As if showing up in class wasn't already making him the center of attention.

Fighting a powerful urge to flee, he entered the crowded lunchroom with grim resolve. He knew he'd never find an empty table, but he hoped to spot an isolated seat at the fringe. Normally he left campus during the lunch break, but part of the normal deal was staying on campus, even though that wasn't normal at all. Because of the rain, a lot of other kids who usually left for lunch had also decided to stay put, so the lunchroom was packed.

Adam stood just inside the doorway, eyeing the room. Suddenly, the din of conversation dropped to near silence. From everywhere, eyes were directed his way, boring through him like lasers. The energy of those stares made Adam dizzy.

He turned quickly and bolted from the lunchroom.

He took his backpack to the library. He couldn't eat in there, but he'd rather skip lunch than go back to the lunchroom. He sat at a table in the back, near the encyclopedias no one ever looked at anymore, and pulled out his iPod. This "carrying on as normal" wasn't going to work. He'd have to convince his parents to let him take his courses by independent study or something. He'd drop out of school if he had to.

Closing his eyes, he lost himself in music. The solitude of his own mind was the only safe place he knew, and even that wasn't as comfortable as it had once been. He missed Caitlin. More than he expected to. The funny thing was, she would have understood what he was going through. Maybe not completely understood, because there was no way someone who hadn't been through this could know what it was like. But she was the one person who could have made Adam feel less alone.

Why, oh why, had he ever taken those photos? It was stupid. He'd known it at the time, but she was so beautiful, so perfect, so unique. He'd dreamed about touching her so many times, and then—

He felt movement next to him. He opened his eyes.

"Hi." Claire Anderson sat down next to him. She was a senior, like he was, and a member of the Students for Students tutoring program, but he hardly ever talked to her. She was editor of the newspaper and had already received early acceptance at Harvard. She was also blond and curvy and very popular. The sort of girl who usually walked by him without a flicker of recognition. The sort he didn't even bother to dream about.

He removed the iPod earbuds from his ears. "Do you

want something?"

"I want to talk to you." She pulled out a chair and sat next to him.

"Why? No one else does."

She gave him a sly smile and flipped her hair over her shoulder. "I'm not a sheep. I don't do what everyone else does. Neither do you."

Adam sat up a little straighter. Maybe everyone wasn't against him, after all. "How do you know what I do?" He tried for a tone of playful banter.

"Just, you know, my impression." Another smile. She inched closer. "So tell me, what's it like having the cops all over you?"

"It's no fun." Adam managed a tangled laugh.

"I bet. It must have been really frightening being hauled into the station like a criminal. Did they do that good cop, bad cop routine the way they do on TV?"

"Sort of." In truth, it was all a haze in his mind. He remembered the inconsequential details—the stale rankness of the air, the cold draft from the overhead vent, the unevenness of the legs on his chair.

"I bet you figured out exactly what they were doing." She cocked her head. When he didn't respond, she leaned forward and lowered her voice. "Did you have a, like, body search?"

He felt himself blush. "I'd rather not talk about that."

"Please, I really want to know."

"Sort of halfway," he said, and looked at his feet.

"Did they make you strip?"

Claire was so close, he could feel the heat of her breath on his cheek. He squirmed in his seat.

"It must have been awful," she said softly.

He nodded. Maybe there was more to Claire than he'd thought. She was the only one in the entire school who seemed sympathetic.

"You spent the night in jail, right? Tell me what that's like."

"I really don't want to talk about it. About any of it." He looked at her and then away. "Sorry, I just don't."

"Are you guilty? Is that why you don't want to talk about it? Did you do something bad to Caitlin?"

He could feel a pounding in his head. "I'm not supposed to answer questions unless my attorney is present."

"Oh, right. That's like on TV, too." She crossed one leg over the other. "Even though it's just me. I mean, we're not in court or anything. I'm not even wearing a wire." She touched her chest and laughed at her own joke. "I'd really like to hear what it was like."

"I can't." He especially didn't want to talk about it to someone like Claire. He was grateful to her for caring, but he was also embarrassed.

Claire leaned back in her chair, her rose-pink lips pursed in a decided pout, and crossed her arms. "Why not? Don't you want to get your story out?"

"My story?"

"Right. For the newspaper."

So that's what this was all about. Adam felt like a fool. "I've got to get going."

"Wait." Claire put a hand on his knee. Her nails were the same shade of pink as her lipstick. "I understand what you're going through. Kids at school look at you funny. They're talking behind your back. I'm not saying this to be mean. I'm sure you know it. Don't you want to say something in your own defense?"

"It wouldn't matter."

"It might. I'd like to hear about your experience. I want to interview you."

The pounding in his head grew worse. "Interview me?"

"It's a chance to tell your side of things. Set the record straight. Why let the cops have all the power?"

"Sorry."

"Please. Just a few questions. I'll give you a hand job."

Adam stared at her. He couldn't believe he'd heard her right.

"Okay, a blow job. Is that better? Adam, I really want this story."

He could barely breathe. "You're demented."

Claire sat up straight. "I'm a journalist. The story is everything."

The story. Adam thought his head might explode. He needed air. He needed to be alone. He stood up quickly, knocking Claire's hand from his leg, and rushed for the door.

A story. That's all he was. A curiosity. A living soap opera. An animal in the zoo. His body was shaking. How would he get through the rest of the day? The rest of his life?

Ty Cross, Caitlin's old boyfriend, stopped him in the hallway. "Hey, bro. Bummer about the cops and all."

Here we go again, Adam thought. He took a breath. "Yeah."

"They ask you a lot of questions?"

"I can't talk about it. Advice of my attorney and such." He stepped around Ty.

Ty tugged on Adam's sleeve. "Did they ask about me?"

"You?"

"Me and Caitlin. She probably told you stuff about us, right?"

Jesus. The whole fucking student body was made up of egotistical, self-centered narcissists. Did any of them ever think about anything besides themselves?

"Sure," Adam said. "Only it was so boring and unimportant, I never listened."

To hell with school. At least in jail the other inmates had left him alone.

CHAPTER 33

After another sleepless night, Rayna decided Cody deserved an update on the situation with Adam. She'd just hung up the phone when Hank pushed back his desk chair and stood.

"I'm going out to pick up a sandwich. Can I get you anything?"

Rayna hadn't been thinking about food, but she realized now that she was hungry. And sleepy from spending the past several hours at her desk. "I could use some fresh air myself. How about I come with you? Or maybe I can pick up something for you."

"I'm ready for a break."

Rayna grabbed her purse and jacket. She wasn't sure what the weather was like outside but the clouds had looked threatening that morning.

"Anything new on that teaching intern, Rusty Hanson?" Hank asked as they crossed the street. They'd spent the morning tying up loose ends in the investigation, hoping to discover some heretofore missed piece of evidence that would send them off in a new direction. Or provide fresh momentum.

"He appears clean," Rayna said. "He wasn't even in the area when Karen Holiday disappeared, and there's no indication that he's made inappropriate contact with any of his students. Besides which, he's got a live-in girlfriend."

"That wouldn't stop a dedicated predator."

"I don't think Hanson fits the bill." Rayna shoved her hands into her pockets. They'd gone only two blocks and already her fingers were turning numb with the cold. "Speaking of predators, remember Lance Richter?"

"The auto mechanic who's a registered sex offender?"

She nodded. "He underwent voluntary chemical castration so he's likely not our man, either. It's got to be a coincidence that both Karen's and Caitlin's parents took their cars to that shop. It makes sense since it's the largest one in Paradise Falls."

Hank slowed to a stop at the entrance to the deli. "You know," he said, "the trouble with all of this stuff we're doing now is that there's already evidence and it points to Adam. It's not conclusive. Maybe not even compelling, if you look at it piece by piece, but there is evidence, and it's not difficult to lay out a scenario that says he did it."

"Not in connection with Karen Holiday. And until Caitlin's body turns up, we don't have proof of a homicide."

"Catch-22." Hank held the door for her and they went inside.

They got their sandwiches—corned beef for Hank and turkey breast for Rayna—and decided to eat at one of the small Formica tables by the windows at the front of the deli.

"What did Neal Cody have to say about the DA releasing Adam?" Hank asked, biting into a dill pickle quarter.

"Not much. I think he's seen it happen too many times to get upset about it." Cody was on a new assignment, with new priorities and new worries. Unlike Rayna, who sometimes felt she stood naked before the entire town. The entire finger-pointing town. As she'd expected, Seth Robbins had used Adam's release as fuel for a diatribe against departmental incompetence.

"Hey," Hank said, almost knocking over his soda. He pointed through the window. "There's Earl. He's been wanting to meet you."

Hank was out of his seat and through the door before Rayna could protest. He returned a few moments later with a bearded man in a plaid lumberman's jacket and wool hat.

"This is Earl," Hank told Rayna.

"Pleased to meet you," Earl mumbled.

"Likewise."

He was a thickset man, probably more muscular than

flabby, although it was hard to tell under the heavy jacket, and a few inches taller than Hank. He reminded Rayna vaguely of someone, but it might have been the graying beard that gave him a sort of grizzly, back-to-nature look. He was closer to her own age than Hank's and wasn't unattractive, but if Hank thought Earl was her type, he was way off base.

"I bore poor Rayna to death sometimes talking about our fishing trips and bowling nights." Hank pulled up a third chair. "Have a seat, why don't you."

Earl's gaze was fixed on Rayna. His expression was hesitant, like he was waiting for her to encourage him to join them. Or maybe he was shy.

Before Rayna could speak, Earl shook his head. "Thanks, but I need to make a quick trip to the hardware store." He stepped back and gave Rayna a sliver of a smile. "Maybe I'll see you around." Then he turned to Hank. "All set for tomorrow night?"

"Right," Hank said. "I've been bowling strikes in my head. We're going to nail them."

Earl cuffed Hank lightly on the shoulder. "That's the attitude." With another fleeting glance Rayna's way, he left.

"Tomorrow night is bowling night?" Rayna asked when they were alone again.

"Not just bowling night, tournament night. We've got our eye on the trophy. You want to come watch?"

Rayna laughed. "I don't think so."

"He's a nice guy, Rayna. A little lonely, too."

"You said he lost his wife and daughter, right?"

"Yeah." For the first time, Hank looked uncomfortable. "That was before I knew about you, that you also had a husband and daughter who . . ." He kicked at the ground with his foot. "I wasn't trying to make a match because of that. I mean, it's something you two have in common, but it's not like pity or anything." His face flushed.

"It's okay, Hank. It's not a subject you have to avoid."

"But it's touchy, you know? When Dana died, my life came apart at the seams. Emotionally, of course, but literally too. It was amazing how quickly I became a second-class citizen. I went from Hank, a can-do guy you could count on, to Hank the pathetic old geezer everyone felt sorry for."

Rayna nodded. She'd been there herself. "Have you ever thought about remarrying?" she asked.

"No, Dana was my one and only. No offense, Rayna, because you're a fine partner and I like you a lot, but most women scare me."

She laughed. "I'm sure Earl is a nice guy, but I'm just not interested."

Hank gave her a lopsided grin. "I had to try."

His phone rang. He pulled it from his pocket, checked the caller ID, and then flipped it open.

Rayna listened to Hank's largely one-word end of the conversation. Really? Interesting. Great. Then finally, Yeah, I'll be back at my desk in about half an hour.

He put his hand over the mouthpiece and turned to Rayna. "We're making progress trying to track down that Romeo who contacted Caitlin online. Facebook has agreed to cooperate."

"Great. Have them check to see if he ever made contact with Karen Holiday, as well."

Hank returned to his call. When he was done, they cleared their wrappings from the table and went back to work.

In some ways, Rayna envied Hank his ragtag circle of friends and acquaintances. She'd made few friends herself since moving to Paradise Falls. She was neither fish nor foul, neither wife and mother nor actively single. She didn't fit in, and it didn't really bother her.

She was happy for Hank that he'd found a network of lost souls to connect with. She just hoped he understood that she had no interest in being part of it in any way.

CHAPTER 34

Two weeks. Tomorrow Caitlin would be missing for two whole weeks.

Sometimes it seemed to Grace an eternity. Others, a flash in time, like a starburst. You could live a life in two weeks, Grace thought. And lose just as much.

She recalled the dinner with Carl two weeks ago when they'd been on the brink of a romantic weekend getaway. She'd been so happy. Her life was good. She had a daughter and a husband who meant the world to her, and stepchildren she enjoyed. They were a family. Her family.

Now she felt like a piece of battered driftwood bobbing alone in a vast expanse of ocean. Caitlin was missing. Carl—the man who'd held her and consoled her and carried her through those first awful days—now did his best to avoid her. Adam, well, she had to assume Adam hated her but she didn't really know. She hadn't seen him or heard about him since the day of his release from jail. Only Lucy acknowledged Grace in any real way, and Grace thought that was probably because Lucy was too confused to know what she thought.

Grace wandered from the house, where she'd spent most of the afternoon meandering aimlessly from room to room, into the garden, which was beaten and bare this time of year. The sun was setting, casting long gray shadows across the patio and empty flower beds. The landscape was as stark and uninviting as Grace's mood. But soon signs of spring would emerge. The flowering cherries and almonds would sprout buds, tulips would begin to poke green through the damp soil, and birds would again greet the morning with song.

Grace's world would remain hardened in perpetual winter.

With a sudden flash of panic she saw the bleak stretch of years awaiting her. Her throat thickened with a strange blend of sorrow and yearning.

Well, she wasn't going to give in without a fight. She didn't know quite what she was going to do, but she needed to try something.

She went back inside with a new sense of direction and started making dinner. It had been a week since she and Carl had last sat down together for a meal. The night she'd told him about Adam and what she'd done. Another marker in her descent into hell. But she was determined to begin her climb out.

Grace took chicken from the freezer and cut it into chunks. She sliced mushrooms and scallions and minced a clove of garlic. She made a salad and set the table. She knew Carl was stopping by Mimi's house after work to see Adam, but when he came home she'd have dinner waiting.

Carl burst through the door some time later and went straight to the den he now used as his bedroom.

After a moment, she followed him. "Carl?"

He lay on his back on the sofa, an arm flung over his eyes. She sat on the edge.

"Did something happen?"

"You know what happened." His voice was harsh. "You had a hand in it, Grace."

They'd been over that ground too many times already. "How's Adam doing?"

"Terribly. What did you expect?"

Could things ever again be right? "I'm sorry."

He removed his arm and looked at her. "You should be."

"I don't mean about telling the police, but I feel bad for you. And for Adam. I'm sorry everything's such a mess."

Carl closed his eyes.

"Please, Carl. Talk to me. I feel so alone. I'm hurting."

"Does it occur to you that I might be feeling those things, too?"

"Of course. I know you are. I want to help you."

Carl stared at her through half-opened eyes, then got up from the couch and walked to the window. He had his back to her.

"We can help each other," Grace said. "That's what husbands and wives do."

Carl's shoulders shook and his head was bent. "I don't know, Grace. I just don't know. I don't know what to do. What to think. I'm scared and I'm worried sick."

"About us?"

"About Adam. But about us, too. Adam won't talk to me. He won't talk to any of us. He just comes home from school and goes to his room. I'm not even sure he eats."

"And when you try to talk to him?"

"He shuts me out. I haven't heard him say more than half a dozen words since he got out of jail."

Grace stepped behind Carl and put a hand on his shoulders. Then she leaned closer and pressed her face against his back.

"I do love you, Grace, but I'm angry. And confused. I feel pulled in so damned many directions."

"I love you, too."

Carl took a deep breath. "My own son, it's like he's a stranger. I want to believe he's innocent. I do believe he's innocent and yet I can't help having doubts. And hard as I try, I can't reach him."

Grace gently massaged Carl's shoulders.

"He needs to know I'm there for him," Carl said. "He needs to know I'll stand by him. Yet I have to force myself into that space. I'm sure he senses that. How awful it must be to have a father who suspects the worst of you."

Grace slipped her arms around Carl's chest and hugged him from behind. He didn't turn around or return her hug, but he did take her hand in his and hold it to his heart.

"Could you still love me if Adam did harm Caitlin?" he asked softly.

The truth was she didn't know. She hoped so, but there was no guarantee. She said, "Of course."

They had wine with dinner. Carl had put music on and it soothed the rough edges of their silences. But the meal was not without tension.

They were eating at the same table, Grace reminded herself. That was progress.

"How is Lucy handling this?" Grace asked.

"I don't know. I've been so preoccupied with Adam, I guess I haven't paid much attention."

"She needs you, Carl. Maybe as much as Adam does."

"I know that, but I only have so much to give." His tone was short. He picked at his food.

"Adam isn't the only one not eating," she said lightly.

"Don't nag me, Grace."

Silence again.

Carl pushed a piece of chicken from one side of his plate to the other. "Mimi is having a hard time dealing with Adam. And he's there at the house alone in the afternoons. I don't think that's good for him."

"You go by after work."

"For an hour or so. It's not the same as living there, being available to him all the time."

Grace wanted to remind him that Adam wasn't talking anyway, but she had the sense to keep the thought to herself.

"Mimi thinks Adam needs me. He needs a father's influence."

"He's getting that."

"Only in bits and pieces. She thinks he needs to be with me full-time. I agree."

"How are you going to manage that?" Grace wondered if Carl was going to suggest moving back in with Mimi, except she knew that would never happen. Grace had never been jealous of his first wife because she knew how Carl felt about her, what a mismatch they were.

"He could live here," Carl offered.

"I doubt Adam would like that. I must be the last person he wants to see."

"You could stay with Sandy."

"What?" Grace was sure she must have misunderstood.

"I'm just talking a few days, Grace. A couple of weeks at the most."

"You want me to move out?"

"Short term."

"This is my house. My home."

"It's also mine. And Adam's."

Grace was aghast. She felt light-headed. Like her lungs might collapse.

Carl must have read her reaction in her face. "Okay, forget it. It was just a thought."

Only it was also much more than that. Grace couldn't believe Carl could suggest such a thing.

"I'll get an apartment," he said without looking at her.

"An apartment?"

"Nothing with a lease, just month to month." He put down his fork and raised his eyes to hers. "I need to do this, Grace. I need to do it for Adam."

Grace had lost her appetite. She felt the burn of tears in her eyes. "Have you finished your dinner?" she asked.

Carl nodded. "I guess I'm not very hungry." He poured himself another glass of wine and retreated to the den. Probably to look for apartment rentals online.

So much for climbing out of hell.

Grace scraped their untouched food into plastic containers and stacked the dishwasher. Then she grabbed a jacket and decided to go for a walk.

CHAPTER 35

It was past seven when Rayna arrived home that evening. As had become her habit these past few days, she checked the answering machine first, dreading another call like Monday's. The oddly hollow voice haunted her as much as the message: The fun has just begun. But with each passing day, she'd grown less uneasy about it. Probably some high school kid pumped up on dope or his own ego. Or maybe even Seth Robbins. She wouldn't put it past the little twerp.

After she'd changed out of her work clothes and into jeans, she made a cup of ginger peach tea and took it into the den with a grape and a leftover strand of spaghetti for Anastasia. The bulk of the hamster's diet was dried pet food and nuts, but Kimberly had insisted on supplementing that with daily morsels of human food, and Rayna made certain to carry on the tradition.

She set her tea on the desk, opened the cage, and reached in for the hamster, cuddling her in both hands. Kimberly and her dad had often laid out a makeshift playground with boxes and blocks and a sawdust "sandbox." They would also make a "legs-to-legs" pen with their outstretched limbs, and let Anastasia run free in the open space between. After Marc died, Rayna had tried to fill in for him, but Kimberly had preferred to play with her pet solo. She'd spent hours talking to the hamster and letting it run around her room. Now, Rayna managed little more than five minutes of contact a day with Anastasia.

The soft ball of fur was warm in her hands. She ran a thumb over the animal's silky smooth head and felt anew the losses that marked her life.

When the phone rang, she jumped. She put the hamster back in her cage, then checked caller ID. Private Number. Could it be the caller from Monday night?

She took a breath and picked up.

"Rayna?" Paul Nesbitt's voice.

She started breathing again. "The readout didn't show your number."

"I'm at my sister's. My phone battery's dead so I'm borrowing her phone. How have you been? I get the impression you're avoiding me."

"Not avoiding you, just busy."

"I figured that might be part of it. I guess my office didn't exactly make things any easier for you."

She responded with a humorless laugh. "Don't get me started."

"I'm glad it wasn't me who had to make the call not to proceed."

"That makes two of us."

"Then we're still friends?"

"Of course." She added lightly, "Unless you've done something unforgivable I don't know about."

"Not a chance. Listen, since we're still friends, how about dinner tonight? I'm just about to leave my sister's house. I can meet you somewhere or I can come pick you up."

"I'm not really up for dinner. I ate a big, late lunch."

"How about I stop by for a bit then? I'll bring a nice bottle of wine and maybe some cheese."

Rayna hesitated. She did enjoy Paul's company and it was certainly better than moping around all evening, feeling sorry for herself.

"I have to be in court early tomorrow morning," he added, "so I won't stay late."

No pressure about sex, in other words. "Sure that would be—"

Her pager went off and she checked the number. Hank.

"Paul, let me call you right back. There may be something going on at work. I just got an urgent page from my partner."

Grace still couldn't believe Carl had asked her to move out. That he'd wanted her out. But he'd been serious about it. Just as he was now serious about getting an apartment for himself and Adam. Leaving her.

The night air was cool and damp. Wispy clouds drifted across the sky, occasionally blocking the almost full moon. Stars twinkled then disappeared, only to emerge again minutes later. Grace turned up the collar of her jacket and shoved her hands into her pockets, overwhelmed by sadness.

So much for her earlier resolve. She'd tried, hadn't she? She'd reached out to Carl, made him a nice dinner, and what had she gotten in return? A husband who asked if she wouldn't mind moving out for a while.

She replayed their conversation in her mind, trying to understand. It was only natural Carl would be worried about Adam, even if he wasn't convinced of Adam's innocence. Wasn't Carl's love for his children one of the qualities she admired in him? She'd have lost respect for him if he'd turned his back on his son. And hadn't she gone to police about Adam because when push came to shove, Caitlin was her overriding concern? She couldn't fault Carl for supporting Adam. He hadn't chosen Adam over her anymore than she'd chosen Caitlin over him. They were both doing what they needed to do. It didn't mean they didn't still love each other.

Grace picked up her step. Exercise helped clear her head. Marriage was a rocky business, but you didn't turn away when things got tough. Through better and worse, wasn't that the vow they'd made to each other? Somehow, she and Carl would make it through this. The important thing was to remember they had each other.

She would help him look for an apartment if it came to that. He'd said it would be a temporary arrangement. One that was necessary because of Adam, not because Carl wanted to distance himself from her. An apartment made the most sense. Even if she were willing to move out, she couldn't impose on Sandy. That he'd even suggest that showed how desperate he was. But they'd work on a solution together. She'd explain all of this to Carl when she got home. She'd tell him she understood. She'd rub his shoulders and tell him she wanted to make things work. She'd ask him to come to bed upstairs.

Grace looked up at the sky and found a star. Though it was far from the first star of the night, she made a wish. Two wishes really. One for Caitlin's safe return, the other for her and Carl. She rounded the corner of her street with a lighter heart than she'd had starting out.

Because there were no flashing lights or sirens, Grace was almost home before a familiar dark sedan parked in front of their house registered in Grace's consciousness. Detective Rayna Godwin's car.

Grace ran the rest of the way home.

CHAPTER 36

Rayna had taken a seat on the sofa across from Carl when she heard the front door slam. She glanced over at Carl, who was already getting to his feet. A moment later Grace flew into the living room still wearing her coat and hat.

"What is it?" Grace's eyes were wide, her expression frantic. "You have news about Caitlin?"

Rayna had driven there straight from her own place after getting Hank's call, and had arrived only a few minutes earlier. She could tell from Carl's expression that he sensed her visit brought unwelcome news, but she hadn't had a chance to tell him the particulars.

Carl hugged Grace, then turned to face Rayna. His face was as white as Grace's.

"You've found something?" he asked in a shaky voice.

Rayna swallowed, dreading what came next. "We have a report," she said, forcing the words out. "A report of a body that's washed up along the river east of town."

"Oh God." Grace buried her head in her hands.

"It might not be Caitlin," Rayna added quickly. "But it's a girl about Caitlin's age and the description fits."

Coming here first flew in the face of standard procedure. Rayna knew she should have gone directly to the scene, but she didn't want Grace to learn about the discovery on the news as she had when Karen Holiday's body was found. Especially not this time, when Rayna feared Grace's nightmare would become a reality.

"I'm on my way out there right now," Rayna explained. "I should know more in a couple of hours. I just wanted you to be prepared. In case."

The muscles in Grace's jaw tensed as she struggled to maintain her composure. Then her mouth quivered, and suddenly she was sobbing. Her shoulders shook and she took great gulping breaths as if she were drowning. In some respects, Rayna knew, she was. Drowning in grief. Choking on a loss so overwhelming it sucked the air right out of your lungs. Rayna remembered the feeling. No matter how prepared you were for the worst, you never really were.

"I'm so sorry," Rayna said softly. "I pray that I'm wrong about this."

Grace nodded, then buried her face against Carl's chest.

Rayna plumbed the depths of her mind for something more to say, but there really wasn't anything. She let herself out.

Half an hour later, shivering in the cold night air, Rayna stopped to catch her breath. Mud sucked at the soles of her heavy leather boots, causing her to move with an unsteady gait. She'd twice slid on the uneven terrain and come close to losing her balance countless times. The dark night and heavy vegetation along the river's edge didn't help matters.

"We're not going to learn anything out here," Hank complained, scraping clods of wet muck from his work boots with a stick. "Not tonight anyway."

"You're probably right." But still, Rayna felt they needed to be there. Needed to see the spot along the shore where a body had become entangled in a jam of fallen trees. Needed to form a firsthand impression of what was, for now, being treated as a crime scene, although Rayna felt certain the victim had gone into the river farther upstream. She wanted answers for Grace, and for herself.

The body was that of a young female and appeared to have been submerged for a couple of weeks. Because of bloating and distortion from the water, and tissue damage from being dragged and pounded with the current, identification would need to be verified by dental records. Since they'd obtained Caitlin's when Karen Holiday's body was discovered, it wouldn't take long, and Rayna felt certain they'd confirm what she already felt in her gut. The fragments of clothing that remained matched the description of the hooded sweatshirt and jeans Caitlin had been wearing when she disappeared.

Rayna pulled her jacket tight against the wind. And against the thoughts that filled her head.

The beam of a flashlight flickered their way. A uniformed officer approached. "Do you have any further need for Mr. Aaronson?" he asked.

"Not tonight. He can go on home."

Aaronson, a retired lumberman who lived nearby, had been walking with his dog when he discovered what he'd originally thought was a pile of garbage caught in the branches of a log jam. The unexpectedly erratic behavior of his pooch had caused him to take a closer look. He said he could have gone a lifetime without seeing what he'd seen then.

Rayna understood. She had trouble with floaters herself. And remembering the smiling and bright-eyed Caitlin she'd seen in photographs, Rayna had had to force herself to take even a fleeting look at the corpse.

Technicians from the coroner's office loaded the body bag onto a stretcher and began the arduous climb up to the road. Rayna bit her lip to keep her emotions in control.

"You okay?" Hank asked. "You don't look so good."

"I'm fine." Rayna's tone was curt. She knew Hank meant well, but his newfound knowledge of her own personal tragedy seemed to have him treating her with kid gloves. She preferred the old blunt-spoken, rough-around-the-edges Hank.

"You going to attend the autopsy?" he asked.

"Not unless Jessup thinks I should." And she knew he wouldn't. Bill Jessup didn't like cops in his morgue. He had nothing against cops in general, but wanted to be left alone to do his job without having to answer questions or explain himself as he worked. His reports were thorough, however, and he was more than willing to answer questions after the fact. The arrangement suited Rayna just fine.

"If it's Caitlin," Hank said, "we've got our body. Do you think that will make a difference? With the DA, I mean?"

"I imagine it depends on what else we learn."

Hank looked around. "That's not going to be much. A body in the water that long . . ." He shuddered. "You know that spot Adam treated as his own sanctuary, the place where we found Caitlin's ring and her initials carved in stone? It's straight up river from here."

"There are a lot of spots straight up river from here," Rayna said. "A lot of places it could have happened."

"But none of the others have ties to a potential suspect."

Rayna nodded. It was a tenuous link, but a link nonetheless. Would it be enough to convince the DA to file charges? And assuming Adam had killed Caitlin, had he killed Karen Holiday? Rayna would like nothing more than to see both cases wrapped up and behind her.

Back in her car, Rayna called the DA's office and was patched through to McKenna.

"You wanted a body," she told him. "Looks like you may have it." She relayed what she knew about the female corpse in the river. "No positive ID yet, but indications are that it's Caitlin Whittington."

"Any signs of foul play?"

"What, you think she went swimming in the river?"

"I meant, any details about how it happened?"

"The body's so mangled I'm not sure even the coroner will get that kind of information."

"Christ!"

"So, do you have enough?"

"Enough?"

"To charge Adam Peterson."

"I need to look at the evidence before making a decision. But this does change things."

At home, Rayna showered again. She washed the muck and cold from her body, but the sorrow wasn't so easily flushed away. She knew she should call Paul Nesbitt and apologize for her quick dismissal of his invitation earlier that evening, but she wasn't up to it. He'd want to know what had happened. He'd ask how she was feeling and probably offer to come rub her feet or something. Paul sometimes wore her down, even when he tried to be accommodating.

Rayna realized the person she really wanted to talk to was Neal Cody. Not because of his forensic expertise but simply because she wanted to hear his voice. The expertise was a good excuse, however. She made herself a cup of hot chocolate, laced it with brandy, and placed the call. When she got the answering machine, she left a quick, businesslike message. The strength of her disappointment surprised her.

She wondered how Grace was doing. Horribly was a given, but how was she handling it? Would Carl try to comfort her or was the rift between them too deep? Rayna recalled the look in Grace's eyes. Denial and acceptance blending in an agonizing comprehension that this was the moment she'd been dreading.

Rayna knew how painful that moment was. She'd lived it herself. And then lived it over again in her mind more times than she could count.

It had been a summer evening and she'd been washing dishes. The scent of lemon soap was in the air. She had the radio tuned to a country-western station and Waylon and Willie had been warning mothers about the perils of letting their sons grow up to be cowboys. She'd actually been singing along.

For months Rayna had known in her head that Kimberly was most likely dead, but knowing something in your head was different than knowing it in your heart. The sound of the doorbell hadn't registered at first. It was only when a knocking followed that she realized she had a visitor. But when she ushered in the two detectives from county, she knew what they'd come to tell her before they opened their mouths.

The body found in a nearby cistern was her daughter's.

Blackness darker than any night cut her vision. The roar of the ocean thundered in her ears. Her throat and lungs were on fire. The two detectives, both men, tried to be kind but they weren't able to hide their discomfort. She'd barely listened to their words of sympathy, so eager had she been for them to leave. She'd practically pushed them out the door so that she could be alone with her grief.

No, tonight would not be easy for Grace.

CHAPTER 37

A dam was in the kitchen scooping out a bowl of rocky road ice cream when his father phoned. Although he picked up, his dad insisted that Lucy get on the extension as well. That's when he knew it was going to be bad.

"The police were just here," his father told them. His voice had wavered and he stopped to clear his throat. "They've found a body. In the river. They think it might be Caitlin."

A fire burned in the pit of Adam's stomach. He swallowed hard and could think of nothing to say. On the other extension, Lucy tossed off questions, her voice growing more and more hysterical with each one. Where did they find her? What do they think happened? How did she die?

"I don't know, honey. They'll tell us when they know more. I just wanted you to hear it from me first. I'm sure it will be in the papers by tomorrow." His father seemed unsure what to do next. "Are you going to be okay?" he asked them.

Lucy whimpered. Adam could hear her mewls and sniffles over the phone line. "Yeah, we'll be fine," he said, speaking for both of them.

"It's such devastating news. I don't know . . ." His father's voice sounded like it was short on air. "I'd like to be there with you but Grace needs me, too."

"Of course," Adam said, although he didn't see that it was really that clear-cut at all. "I'll take care of Lucy."

When he hung up, he dumped the bowl of ice cream into the sink.

Lucy cried off and on for the remainder of the evening. Adam tried to console her but gave up when it became apparent she enjoyed her heartache.

Mom took a more practical approach. "Yes, it's terrible news," she said. "But hardly unexpected." She sat with Lucy for a bit, patting her shoulder and telling her that life was sometimes unpleasant but that wounds healed with time, then retired to her bed to watch TV.

Before going off to bed himself, Adam looked in on Lucy one last time. She was curled in a ball in the middle of her mattress.

"Luce?"

"What?"

"Is there anything I can do?"

She untangled herself and shook her head. "It's like, real now."

"Yeah. I know." Adam swallowed against the dry lump in his throat. "Will you be all right tonight?"

"I'll live."

Adam wondered if she'd chosen her words intentionally.

He went to his own room and lay down in bed. But he didn't sleep. He spent the long hours of the night trying to imagine what it felt like to be dead.

Whatever flickering embers of hope Grace harbored were abruptly extinguished when Detective Godwin again showed up at their door a little after midnight.

"It was Caitlin?" Grace spoke without preliminaries, her mouth so dry she had trouble forming the words.

"I'm afraid so," the detective told her softly.

Grace's heart stood still. It was already so filled with sorrow, she'd thought there wasn't room for more, but she was wrong.

"I'm so sorry," Detective Godwin said.

Grace nodded. She couldn't find her voice to speak. The room seemed to tilt.

Carl put his arms around her and held her tight, steadying her. "Thank you, detective," he said gruffly. "For coming here at this hour to tell us personally."

Carl continued to hold Grace as he led her to bed. He

kissed her tears and shed his own. But there was no comfort to be had.

Grace stared into the black night while Carl snored fitfully beside her. The sleeping pill he'd insisted she take had given her a couple of hours sleep, but even then she hadn't been able to escape the heavy ache of loss. She'd been hoping to dream of Caitlin, to savor the joy of seeing her daughter alive again, however fleetingly and illusorily. But that hadn't happened. Her dreams were not the welcome flights of forgetfulness, only the weighty shackles of anguish she dragged with her from wakefulness.

Silent tears slid down her cheeks to her pillow. Dear God, where would she find the strength to continue living?

CHAPTER 38

Planning a funeral wasn't something Grace wanted to deal with, but Jake pointed out that it needed to be done. He picked Grace up at home and they drove to the mortuary together. Now she was seated near him in a chair covered in crushed red velvet, a fabric she found particularly inappropriate for the circumstances. Across the darkly varnished table sat the funeral director, a jowly man named Mr. Culbert.

Jake's brow creased with intensity as he studied the thick, white leather binder Culbert had handed them moments earlier. The muscles in Jake's jaw twitched and his mouth was grim, but he took his time, turning the pages one by one.

Grace couldn't look. Instead, she stared at the ornately carved wooden door that led to the main lobby, as though she could will herself back out through the lobby and into Jake's car. She shivered. The room was as chilled as a wine cellar. She didn't want to be here—not today, not ever. She wanted to pretend the detective's visit had never happened. She wanted to believe that Caitlin was alive. If only she could turn back the clock, undo these last few weeks.

"Are you thinking plain white for the casket?" Mr. Culbert asked. "Or perhaps something with pink trim?"

Grace's heart flew into a panic. She needed to escape, to run away and hide. She should have told Jake no. She should have refused to come. What was the rush anyway? While her instinct was to flee and hide her head in the sand, Jake's method of coping with adversity was to grab the reins. And that's what he'd done, setting up the appointment without even consulting her.

Jake turned to Grace. "What do you think?"

Tears welled in her eyes. "Caitlin hated pink."

"White," Jake said decisively. "And simple. None of these curlicues or cherubs."

Over the years of their marriage, Grace had often resented Jake's propensity to take charge, and while she felt railroaded into this afternoon's meeting, she was grateful to Jake for leading the way. She could not have done it without him.

As if he'd read her mind, Jake reached for her hand and squeezed it reassuringly.

Grace listened as if in a dream while Culbert guided them like lost children through the unfamiliar wilderness of planning a child's funeral. Did they have a preference for music? Or verse? Did they want to address the mourners themselves?

Jake considered each question, weighing it like a purchase of precious metal. Then he'd look to Grace for guidance. At first, the questions barely registered with her. This wasn't a wedding or a graduation or even a sixteenth birthday. Caitlin was dead. What did it matter?

But her daughter's memory did matter. It was all that Grace had left.

"This arrangement for the top of the casket," Grace said, pointing to a photograph of freesias and peonies in shades of white. "And these standing sprays of wildflowers bracketing the casket." Caitlin had loved wildflowers.

"And these," Jake said. "Baskets of lavender. Lots of them"

They left the funeral home without speaking. Without touching. Yet Grace felt Jake's strength in a way she hadn't in years. Carl had done and said all the right things last night. He'd held her and comforted her and shed tears of genuine sorrow himself, but Grace understood that Carl's grief was balanced against his more deeply felt distress about Adam. Carl cared about Caitlin, but Jake was the one who cared about her in the same way Grace did, which was ironic since Grace used to accuse him of not caring enough.

"You want to get a cup of coffee or something?" Jake

asked when they reached the car.

"I don't think I . . . I'm not really . . ."

"No, me either. But I can't just go on with my day. Not yet." He gripped the steering wheel. "Remember Caitlin's first bath?" he asked, turning to Grace with damp eyes. "We set that white plastic tub up on the kitchen table. She was so tiny, I was scared to death I'd hurt her. Or that we'd traumatize her forever."

"I was scared, too, sure I'd do it all wrong. Bathing a baby seemed such a momentous undertaking when I read about it in those baby books. But Caitlin made it easy. Do you remember the expression on her face when you set her in the warm water? She seemed to enjoy being bathed, even in the beginning."

"I remember I used to dribble the water from the washcloth over her belly. She loved that. She'd coo and laugh like she was on top of the world. And those eyes! Remember how she'd look at us with those big wide eyes, so focused. Like we were the only thing in the world that mattered."

"We were," Grace said with a sadness that was suffocating. She'd accepted the weight of that responsibility in a way that now seemed almost naive. It was only looking back that Grace could fully appreciate what a profound undertaking parenthood was.

"Well," Jake said, starting the engine. "I'll take you home then."

Home. A place where old memories and present tensions were waging a battle that left Grace unable to breathe.

"On second thought," she said, "maybe a cup of coffee isn't a bad idea."

Since the moment of his father's call, Adam had known it was only a matter of time before the police would want to talk to him again. So when his attorney and his father showed up at the house the next afternoon, he was only mildly surprised.

"I've got nothing more to tell them," Adam said, flopping down into the leather recliner his mother usually claimed for herself. But she wasn't home yet and despite the tone of casual indifference he'd managed to pull off, he wasn't sure he trusted his legs to hold him up. "They're wasting their time asking me the same stuff over and over."

Sandman cleared his throat and took a seat catty-corner from Adam, on one end of the couch. "It's not that they want to talk to you, son. There's another warrant out for your arrest."

"My arrest?" Adam's throat closed. He sat upright. "Can they do that? I mean, they tried that once before."

"But now they have a body. It's officially a homicide. We talked about this, remember? About how being released didn't mean it was over?"

Sandman had explained it. So had his dad. But Adam hadn't wanted to believe it.

"I've arranged for you to turn yourself in tomorrow," Sandman said. "Voluntary surrender. No flashing lights or rides in the back of a police car this time."

"We'll both be right there with you," his father added, coming to Adam's side and draping a protective arm around his shoulders.

Right there with him. What a laugh. They'd be with him when he turned himself in. But not after that when the cops searched him and watched him shower and hauled him off to his cell like some disgusting piece of garbage. Once he was taken into police custody, he'd be alone.

"What if I don't go?"

"You have to," Sandman said. "It will be a whole lot worse for you if they have to track you down. And they will do that."

Adam thought he'd been mentally preparing for this possibility. It was staggering how unprepared he actually was. He could feel uncontrollable trembling begin deep in his bones.

"How long before I can get out on bail?"

Sandman looked at his father then back to Adam. "There won't be any bail, Adam. Not in this case. You'll have to stay there."

"Until trial," his father added quickly. "The prosecutor

has to prove you did this. They can't send you to prison without proof."

Prison. Images from every bleak movie Adam had ever seen about life behind bars flooded his brain.

"We'll put on a strong case, Adam. I can promise you that."

Adam's mouth felt so dry, he had trouble speaking. "And if the jury believes the prosecutor instead of you?"

Sandman's smile didn't reach his eyes. "Let's not worry about that now."

Adam turned to look at his father whose hollow eyes and slack expression mirrored the raging fear inside Adam.

"Do you have any questions?" Sandman asked.

Adam shook his head. He had hundreds of questions but they weren't the kind Sandman was talking about.

"Fine. Your dad and I will pick you up tomorrow morning at eleven. I've arranged for us to go in through a rear door to evade the media." Sandman held out a hand, then reconsidered and placed it on Adam's shoulder instead. "I know this is tough, Adam. But it's going to turn out okay."

His dad stayed a little longer, but it was awkward and uncomfortable for both of them. His father made stabs at conversation, offering reassuring platitudes, trying to deflect the rank fear they both felt with mundane talk of sports and movies. Adam couldn't respond to any of it. He couldn't concentrate. There was buzzing inside his head that wouldn't stop. Finally he told his dad he needed to be alone. He lay down on his bed and stared at the ceiling.

He was going back to jail. Maybe for a long, long time. It was terrifying and yet unreal.

Jail. Then prison. Forever.

Adam walked to the window and looked out. The sky was a dreary gray, the trees bare. Wind gusts swirled debris across the yard. Everyday common events and suddenly very precious. The thought of being locked away sent Adam into a state of panic.

His father had tried to be encouraging. "Sandman's got a good reputation," he'd said. "They have to prove their case beyond a reasonable doubt." He offered words of strength and love. He hugged Adam. But he never once professed an unwavering conviction in Adam's innocence.

If his own dad thought he might be capable of hurting Caitlin, how could he expect a jury to believe any differently?

Lucy got hysterical when she heard that Adam was headed back to jail. His mother, closed-lipped and rigid. But he saw real tears in her eyes. He couldn't recall ever seeing her cry before.

He barely touched his dinner and went up to his room right after. He knew what he had to do but he wanted a little time to say goodbye first.

This had been his room for seventeen years. His crib had been over there in the corner. He didn't remember it, of course, but he'd seen photographs in his baby album. A big poster of colorful balloons had hung on the wall above the changing table. When Lucy was born, the crib went into her room and he got a "big boy" bed, the same bed Adam slept in now, despite the fact that his feet hung over the end. He had a desk instead of a changing table, and a new dresser because the top drawers on the old one had fallen apart when he was twelve. Probably because he'd hung his backpack from them.

He'd suffered embarrassments and longings in this room, worries and frustrations. But also moments of jubilation and gratification. A lifetime of memories. His memories. He wondered what his mom would do with his room when he was gone.

CHAPTER 39

Through her bedroom window, Grace watched the darkness of night begin to lift as morning emerged. Light gray sky, the silhouette of trees bending in the wind, a lone, pale star fading in the horizon. She'd taken a sleeping pill again last night but it hadn't done much good. She'd lain awake, as she had the night before, her mind filled with horrific images, her heart with stone. Sleep, which might have offered temporary escape, continued to elude her.

Dead. Her daughter was dead.

There was no more wiggle room. No more clinging to the gossamer filaments of hope. No more bargains with God.

Her daughter's death knocked not only the air from her lungs but the marrow from her bones. It clawed at her insides with the ferocity of a mountain lion and pounded inside her head like the roll of thunder. Relentlessly and without end.

And now, with Adam's arrest imminent, she was more alone than ever. Last night she and Carl had each stewed in their own private misery, the divide between them as great as the Grand Canyon. Grace knew he needed her as much as she needed him. Yet they remained on opposite rims, not even looking to the other side.

She wondered how it had happened, what Adam had done to Caitlin. Her mind raced with appalling vignettes. Her heart ached for Caitlin's fear. Her pain. What evil festered in the mind of someone like Adam? How could Grace have lived with a murderous animal and not known?

Worn out from crying, frayed from endlessly replaying imagined horrors, drained by loss, she still couldn't sleep.

She checked the clock. Five-thirty. Another half hour or

so and she could reasonably get up. To what end? Did it matter anymore?

Finally, she got out of bed to go the bathroom and heard frantic activity downstairs in the kitchen. Opening the bedroom door, she listened, then padded down the stairs. Carl was standing in front of the sink, shaking.

"What is it?" Grace asked, moving toward him.

For a moment, he didn't speak. Couldn't speak, Grace thought. She worried he might be having a stroke.

"Carl, are you okay?"

"Mimi just called. It's Adam."

"What about him?"

Carl's face crumbled. "He tried to commit suicide. He may not live."

"My God." Emotion rose in waves, leaving Grace feeling battered and beaten. Her heart raced, her stomach clenched. She fought the rush of guilt. She hadn't done anything wrong, she reminded herself. But she felt the finger of blame pointed her way. "Oh, Carl." She stroked his arms. "How terrible. Where is he?"

"Pacific Memorial. Intensive care. I'm on my way there."

"What happened exactly? When?" The kettle on the stove had begun to boil. "Sit down, I'll make your coffee. You can't go anywhere without coffee first."

Carl complied like a zombie. He pulled out a chair and sat, with elbows on the table and his head in his hands. "Mimi wasn't totally coherent, but I gather it was Lucy who discovered him. She got up early this morning and heard music coming from Adam's room. Thinking he was awake, she went in."

"Poor Lucy." It was a shock she wouldn't easily recover from. Grace felt the heat of blame intensify.

"He'd apparently taken a lot of pills. Mimi's. But only a few hours before Lucy found him. At least, that's the speculation, or what I know of it. We're lucky she found him while he was still alive, but he'd taken enough to do serious damage."

Grace brought Carl's coffee to the table and poured

herself a cup as well. She stood behind him and wrapped her arms around his shoulders. "This is just awful. Terrible. Oh, Carl. Baby."

"Mimi says they won't let us see him for more than a few minutes. One person at a time. But I'm heading over to the hospital anyway."

"I'll come with you."

The silence was palpable. "I don't think so, Grace. Under the circumstances, that's a very bad idea."

Of course. What had she been thinking? "How can I help, then? Is there anything I can do?"

He pulled away from her touch and turned to look at her. His eyes were cold. "Don't you think you've done enough already?"

CHAPTER 40

Although Rayna didn't actually need to be present when Adam turned himself in, she wanted to be there. It was her case and she was the one who'd taken the heat. For her own sake, she needed to see it through to the end. But Adam wasn't scheduled to appear until noon, which still allowed her a leisurely Saturday morning, something she hadn't enjoyed in several weeks.

She slept until seven-thirty, woke without an alarm, and then went for a three-mile run. She wasn't in the shape she'd once been in, when logging six or seven miles was as routine as brushing her teeth, but she was steadfast in her determination to fight middle age on every front.

The morning was cool and crisp, but, for a change, the sky promised more blue than gray. Her spirits were light. There was a newfound spring in her step as she left her house and headed for the two-lane country road that led out of town. She greeted each passerby with a smile and filled her lungs with the elixir of living. Even the prospect of reading Seth Robbins's column—a chronic morning irritant—didn't phase her. He was about to lose a powder keg's worth of ammunition. She grinned, imagining the obnoxious little twerp flailing at nothing but vaporized shadows.

She was glad they'd been able to work out a voluntary surrender for Adam. Not only was it somehow more humane—although she recognized that some might find the concept of humane surrender an oxymoron—it was far more private for everyone concerned. Media cameras and reporters would have to twiddle their thumbs until the department was good and ready to give them a statement.

The chief liked that. In fact, he was feeling pretty good about the entire case, and when he was happy, life was better for all of them. Of course, Karen Holiday's murder was still unsolved, but Rayna was hoping the DA might be able to pry more information from Adam as part of a plea bargain.

If it weren't for the sympathy she felt for Grace and the niggling worry that Adam didn't seem to her like a killer, Rayna would feel like she was on top of the world. She recalled Cody's cautioning them about teenage boys and lust. It was a big jump from lust to murder. But it wasn't just the photos of Caitlin, she reminded herself. There were the Garfield paper towels in the Dumpster and Caitlin's necklace hidden in the basement of Mimi's house. The DA thought they had enough. It wasn't Rayna's role to second-guess him.

She'd worked the kinks out of her muscles by the time she reached the fenced property that marked the halfway point of her run. It was one of those mornings she felt she could keep going farther, but in the interest of time she turned and headed south, where she'd pick up a secondary road that led back to town.

Teenage boys and girls. If Kimberly were alive, they'd be in the thick of it, Kimberly pushing for her freedom while Rayna agonized over every step. Or maybe not. Grace and Caitlin hadn't seemed at loggerheads. And Rayna couldn't help feeling that Kimberly would have turned out a lot like Caitlin. Once again Rayna's breath caught at the pain of her own loss—a pain that seemed sometimes less sharp than it had once been, but other times was honed like a spike through her heart.

No, she wasn't going to let herself go there this morning. Instead, she tried to imagine Cody at seventeen. She knew he'd grown up in L.A., the middle of three boys, and that he'd played first base on the high school varsity baseball team. She suspected he'd been cocky even then, but she didn't know for sure. Maybe he'd been shy and tongue-tied. Had he seen something in Adam that resonated with his own memories of growing up? Had Cody fallen prey to an unrequited teenage crush? If she had to guess, she'd have said he was more a Ty

Cross than an Adam Peterson. Not that it mattered. He was out of her life. Again. He hadn't even bothered to return her call from the previous night.

If only he'd never drawn the assignment to Paradise Falls.

Rayna tried to put him out of her mind, but instead found that she missed him, which was totally stupid. In the few shorts weeks he'd reappeared, he'd managed to handily undue the years she'd spent forgetting him.

Well, she'd done it once, she could do it again.

As was her routine on weekend runs, Rayna stopped at the Starbucks two blocks from her house for a latte to sip as she walked the rest of the way home.

Not unexpectedly, the line was long, snaking along the counter and past the pastry display. Rayna was trying to decide if she wanted to splurge calories on a scone when the front door opened.

Hank's friend Earl spotted her at the same time she noticed him. He fell into line behind her, shoving his hands into the pockets of his plaid lumberman's jacket.

"Small world, huh?" The greeting was mumbled and directed more at the floor than her.

"Do you live in the neighborhood?"

"No, I'm on my way to the lumber store. What about you?"

"I live nearby," she said. "What are you building?"

"Nothing much. Just some porch repairs."

"Are you in the construction business?" She couldn't recall if Hank had ever mentioned what Earl did for a living. If he had, she hadn't been listening.

"Guess you could call it that. I work for myself. Small jobs. More handyman than anything."

The line inched forward. Rayna decided to skip the scone.

"Do you have time to sit for a bit?" Earl asked.

"Sorry, I need to get home. Busy day and all." She couldn't put her finger on it, but there was something about Earl that made her feel self-conscious. Maybe because Hank had been trying to play matchmaker.

"Weekends can get pretty full, huh?"

There was a stretch of silence then, thankfully, the cashier took Rayna's order. Earl didn't try to pick up the conversation again, but as she left the store he said, "See you around."

She wasn't sure if it was a generic goodbye or if he actually harbored hopes along those lines. She hoped not, because she had no interest at all. She just wished she could recall who he reminded her of.

When she reached home, Rayna tossed her now empty cup into the garbage can in the side yard and picked up the morning paper. She dropped it on the kitchen table and headed for the shower. Half an hour later, back in the kitchen, she plugged in the pot for her second cup of coffee and poured a bowl of cornflakes. She thought longingly of the scone.

While the coffee brewed, she ate her cornflakes at the sink and gazed out the window at her yard. She'd lost all interest in gardening after Kimberly died, but there were enough shrubs and perennials around the patio to make the space peaceful in the spring and summer. With the winter rains and dormant plants, her yard looked less appealing. Even the pot of daffodils on the patio table, which she'd picked up at the nursery in a moment of spring longing, were bent and broken and—

Setting her bowl on the counter, she dashed outside. Sure enough, the stalks had been snapped at the base, but something new had been added: a tiny toy tiger propped against the base of the pot.

She felt a chill snake down her spine. How long had the animal been sitting there?

CHAPTER 41

When the phone rang later that morning, Grace grabbed it on the second ring, expecting the caller to be Carl. Instead, it was Lucy.

"I know this is a terrible time for you, Grace, and I'm sorry to be such a pest, but can you come be with me? Please? I'm scared and worried and I can hardly breathe."

"Where are you?"

"At the hospital. In some smelly old waiting room."

"Where are your parents?"

"With Adam. I'm here by myself. The doctors said they could stay with him for a while, but I couldn't even see him. No kids"—she gave the word a disdainful emphasis— "like I'm six years old or something. And only two people max. Adam is my brother for God's sake!" She paused then lowered her voice. "Shit, a person can't even talk around here." Then to someone else in the waiting room, "Yeah, yeah. I'm getting off now."

"I'll come right over," Grace assured her. "Where will I find you?"

"In emergency. On the main floor."

"Hang in there, Lucy. You can do it."

Grace didn't even bother with makeup. She grabbed a rumpled pair of slacks and a sweater, and ran a brush through her hair as an afterthought. She could have declined. After all, she'd learned of her daughter's murder less than forty-eight hours ago, but wallowing in her own grief wasn't going to help anyone. Lucy needed her, and Grace found it a relief to think about someone other than herself for a change.

She found Lucy curled in a chair in the corner of a very

crowded waiting room. Families with babies, worried-looking couples, an old man holding an ice pack to his forehead, a middle-aged woman, still in her bathrobe, with an elevated and very swollen foot. On an overhead TV, a cartoon bunny ran through a plowed field, chased by a pack of hounds. No one watched.

Lucy spotted Grace and raced into her arms. "Thank you, thank you. I'm so glad you came."

"Of course I came," Grace said, brushing Lucy's thick, unkempt hair from her face. "Let's go somewhere else." She put an arm around Lucy and led her toward the door. "Have you eaten breakfast yet?"

"I'm not hungry."

"How about a soda or something? There's a cafeteria on the second floor."

"Okay."

"Let me tell the intake nurse where we're going so we don't worry your parents when they come looking for you."

The designers responsible for the hospital cafeteria had clearly tried to break the mold of institutional dreary. The walls were a subtle sage and hung with soothing landscapes. Colorful round laminate tables were scattered around the room instead of being placed in rows. Classical music played softly in the background. Nonetheless, the atmosphere was anything but convivial. Hospitals were about waiting and hoping and praying, about exhaustion and nail-biting. Celebrations took place elsewhere.

Grace bought a plate of French toast and bacon for Lucy in addition to a Coke, and coffee for herself. She set the French toast down in front of Lucy.

"Any more news from the doctors?" Grace asked. It was hard to root for the recovery of her daughter's killer, so she focused instead on the fact that Adam was also Lucy's brother.

Lucy shook her head. "What if he dies, Grace? Or is like, you know, brain damaged or something?" Her eyes filled with tears. "I don't know what I'd do."

"He's lucky you found him when you did," Grace said,

walking the middle ground. "You may have saved his life."

"So he can spend the rest of it in prison? What good's that?" Her face contorted and she folded her hands across her middle as if in pain.

"Are you okay, honey?"

"I'm scared of what's going to happen to him." She looked up. Her mouth quivered. "He didn't do it, Grace. Adam would never have hurt Caitlin. She was like one of his only friends."

Love and hate, devotion and resentment. Weren't they often entangled? Grace had no trouble at all imagining how Adam might have been attracted to Caitlin and at the same time been angry enough or hurt enough or jealous enough to lash out at her. But she didn't go there with Lucy.

"That's why we have our legal system," she said. "We don't throw people in jail without proof." While her heart went out to Lucy, it held nothing but rage for Caitlin's killer. That he might be Lucy's brother and Carl's son didn't change that. "Adam has the presumption of innocence on his side," she added for Lucy's benefit.

"For all the good it's done so far." Lucy broke a piece of bacon in two, then left both pieces on the plate. "It had to be that serial killer, Grace. The one who killed Karen Holiday. He tossed Caitlin's backpack in the same place—"

"Not exactly the same."

"Close enough. Two girls from the same high school. He gets rid of their stuff in the same way. What more do the cops want? Just like that reporter said, the stupid detective doesn't know up from down."

"Reporter? Are you talking about Seth Robbins?"

Lucy nodded.

"He's hardly a reporter. He's a columnist with his own far from objective opinions."

"Whatever. He's right."

What about the photos on Adam's computer? What about Caitlin's necklace, hidden in a drawer in the basement of Mimi's house? Grace bit her lip to keep from asking. Lucy was upset enough. There was nothing to be gained by arguing with her.

Lucy traced a circle on the smooth surface of the table top with her finger. "How are you doing, Grace? I feel so sad for you."

Grace reached out and squeezed Lucy's hand. "Thank you for thinking of me."

"Of course I'd think of you!"

"I'm not sure how I'm doing. I guess on some level I'm numb. I hadn't fully realized how much I was . . ." Grace's voice broke as emotion welled up inside her. "As irrational as it sounds, how much I was clinging to the hope that Caitlin was alive."

"That seems pretty normal to me."

"I guess I'm discovering how muddled and capricious a thing grief is."

"Yeah. I think I know what you mean." Lucy pushed the bacon around on her plate some more. "Sometimes life sucks."

"That about sums it up." Although, in truth, it didn't begin to come close. "Would you like something else to eat?"

Lucy shook her head, looked toward the door. "Oh," she said and started to rise. Grace turned to see Carl and Mimi steaming toward them. It was hard to tell which of them was angrier.

"What the hell are you doing here?" Mimi said with a snarl.

Carl glared at Grace, but at least he sat down at the table so he wasn't towering over her. "I told you not to come, Grace. What are you trying to prove?"

"I wasn't trying to prove anything. I'm concerned, is all."

"The nerve of you," Mimi said, full of venom.

"I called Grace," Lucy said. "I asked her to come."

"Why?" Mimi's tone had softened some, but not much. She, too, took a seat at the table, yanking the chair with such fury that several people turned to look.

"You two hurried off to be with Adam. You left me all alone. I was scared."

Mimi's mouth thinned. "Lucy, your brother is in intensive care, and all you can think about is yourself?"

Tears filled Lucy's eyes. "I was scared because I'm worried about Adam."

Carl put an arm around Lucy. "She's right, Mimi. We did abandon her. Lucy is as shaken up by what Adam did as we are."

Lucy leaned against her dad and brushed away a tear with the back of her hand. "I didn't mean to cause trouble, it's just that—"

"Surely you could have amused yourself for a couple of hours," Mimi said. "No matter how worried you were. You knew we'd come get you."

"Leave her alone, Mimi." Carl turned to Lucy. "Sorry, honey. We weren't thinking clearly." And then to Grace, "Thank you for comforting her."

"I was happy to help," she muttered.

"How is Adam?" Lucy asked.

"He's still in a coma," Carl said. "But his vital signs are good."

"The big worry now," Mimi added with a pointed look in Grace's direction, "is liver and brain damage."

"What does that mean?" Lucy looked from one parent to the other with a stricken expression.

Mimi ignored the question and addressed Grace in a scathing tone. "Do you have any idea what you've done, Grace? Adam is a child. If he lives, if he can function normally again, if he's not imprisoned, even then his life will never be the same. You've destroyed my son. You've destroyed my family."

And what about my daughter? Grace wanted to lob back. Have you forgotten the role your son played in that? And what about Adam's decision to take an overdose of pills? No one forced him to try to kill himself. But while she was thinking how best to respond, Mimi's cell rang and she reached for it with an efficiency Grace found astounding.

"The hospital is a no cell phone zone, Mom."

"Not in the cafeteria, Lucy." Mimi's tone was dismissive. She flipped open the phone despite a few nasty looks from those seated nearby. "What? Didn't Sandman tell you? Yes,

yes, he's in the hospital. We're here now."

She looked at Carl and rolled her eyes. "Look, this is really a bad—okay, yeah, a minute." Mimi listened in silence for several moments. "A stuffed animal? What? No, of course not. He's a seventeen-year-old boy!" She sighed and turned to Carl. "Have you seen Adam with any stuffed animals lately?"

Carl looked at Lucy and they both shook their heads.

"No," Mimi said into the phone, more loudly than necessary, then quickly slammed the phone shut. "That was the detective. Why in God's name is she asking about stuffed animals?"

"I told you," Lucy said. "She doesn't know up from down. She should forget about Adam and find that serial killer."

"And we all know who's responsible for her looking at Adam in the first place." Mimi shot Grace a nasty look.

Not without reason, Grace protested silently with a glance in Carl's direction. He was looking down at the table, studiously avoiding her gaze. Grace stood up. "Well, I'd better be going."

"Good idea," Mimi said.

Carl walked her to the cafeteria door. "Thank you again for helping with Lucy."

"I'm glad she felt comfortable calling me, Carl. Lucy is a lovely girl. I care about her. Just as I care about you."

"Things are complicated, Grace. I can't begin to sort them out yet."

"You think I can? You think they aren't complicated for me, too?"

"No, of course not." Carl kissed Grace's cheek and pushed her gently into the main hallway. "I apologize for Mimi. She's not handling this well."

Of the three, Grace thought as she headed for the elevator, only Lucy seemed to have remembered that Caitlin was dead.

CHAPTER 42

At ten o'clock on a gloomy Monday morning Rayna was already on her third cup of coffee. She'd finished off her stash of trail mix before eight, and now prowled around the break room, looking for something more to nibble on.

Her stomach burned and her eyes were gritty with lack of sleep. It had been a hellish couple of days. Adam Peterson—who was to have turned himself in to authorities Saturday morning—was in a coma. The DA's office had decided to hold off charging him, and Seth Robbins was having a field day at the expense of all involved, and most especially her.

But it was the tiny stuffed tiger that bothered Rayna most.

For probably the hundredth time, she tried to sort it out. She'd found a tiny stuffed dog in her mailbox when Karen Holiday disappeared, but she'd dismissed it as a child's lost toy placed there by some neighborly passerby who'd mistakenly assumed it belonged to someone in Rayna's household. When she'd found a stuffed bunny in the mailbox after Karen's body was discovered, she'd logged it into evidence, even though she wasn't convinced it was related to the crime. No one in the department was convinced, either. In fact, she'd taken a bit of teasing over the incident.

There'd been no animal when Caitlin Whittington disappeared. And although that wasn't the only factor that led her to think the two crimes might not be related, the absence of a stuffed animal offered support of that theory. But now, with the discovery of Caitlin's body, a tiny stuffed tiger had shown up on her patio table.

It couldn't be coincidence. It had to be the killer playing with her.

Not necessarily the killer, she reminded herself. But if it wasn't the killer, who was it? And why hadn't she found an animal when Caitlin disappeared? Could she have somehow overlooked it?

The more immediate concern, though, was Adam. The animals didn't exonerate him. He could have left the tiger on her table before he tried to take his own life. And he was every bit as capable of taunting her as any other killer. But it didn't feel right. A seventeen-year-old boy fixated on girls who rejected him—again, just a theory—didn't leave gifts for the detective on the case.

Or bait her by leaving an untraceable message on her answering machine.

By all accounts, Adam was not a typical seventeen-year-old boy.

Rayna gritted her teeth. She slid a dollar into the vending machine and punched the button. A pack of peanut butter crackers clattered into the tray at the bottom.

"You must really be desperate," Hank said, coming into the break room with an empty cup. "Those things are awful."

"I am desperate."

"No time for breakfast?"

"More like nervous eating." She opened the cellophane package and bit into one of the crackers. It tasted like sawdust. "But not as nervous as I thought. These things must have been sitting around for ages." She tossed the remainder of the package into the trash.

"Jessup says we ought to have the final autopsy report by noon," Hank said, filling his cup from the communal pot. "Not that it will do us much good, I imagine. Any change in Adam Peterson's condition?"

"I checked with the hospital this morning. He's stable but unresponsive."

"That buys us time. When he comes around, assuming he does, maybe we'll have a better handle on the case."

"Let's hope so. We were ready to arrest him based on what we had before."

"My bet is he's still good for it. Forensics find anything

on that stuffed tiger?"

"No, but it's got to be connected to the murders. Just like the other two." She didn't bother to point out that the ribbing she'd taken earlier had been misguided. She'd been right to be suspicious of the toys.

"The whole thing is weird," Hank said. "Why little stuffed animals? I mean, why not a horse's head or dead roses or whatever they do in the movies? Wouldn't that be more fitting for a maniac killer?"

Rayna had asked Cody that same question when he'd finally returned her call yesterday afternoon, full of apology for not getting back to her sooner. "It probably means something to the maniac killer," she said, parroting what Cody had told her. "Maybe his sister got all the stuffed animals when he was a kid, or his mother tossed his away in a fit of anger."

"Maybe he's a sales rep for a company that makes them," Hank offered, pouring coffee into his cup. "He hates his job and he gets the creatures for free."

Rayna couldn't tell if the comment was meant as a joke or not. With Hank, it was hard to know.

"Whatever his reasons," she said, "they aren't going to help us figure this out. Maybe we were too hasty in going after Adam, maybe not."

Hank ran a hand under the collar of his shirt. "Like I said, he looks good for it to me."

"I want to interview Ty Cross again. And Rob Hardy, too. Their stories have never matched."

"You think one's covering for the other?"

"Possibly. Or they're both involved. A couple of weeks before Karen disappeared, Ty and Karen were at the same party."

"How do you propose to get past the senior Mr. Cross?"

"I don't. Let's get Ty down here this afternoon, along with his parents and attorney."

Hank laughed. "I guess now I understand the nervous eating." He headed back to his desk. "By the way, Earl is on our side regarding the news coverage. He said not to let it get to you."

"So your friend has taken it upon himself to offer me advice?"

"Don't get your knickers in a twist, Rayna. We were just shooting the breeze. He said he'd run into you over coffee. It wouldn't hurt you to be nice to the guy."

Rayna sighed. You could hit Hank over the head with a two by four and he still wouldn't get it. She wasn't interested in Earl.

"I don't understand why you want to talk to my son again," Mr. Cross huffed when he appeared with Ty and his lawyer late that afternoon. "Word has it you were ready to arrest Adam Peterson."

Rayna skirted the implied questions. She set the recorder on the table and identified those present, including Mr. Bishop, Ty's attorney. "How well did you know Karen Holiday?" Rayna asked Ty.

Ty glanced at Bishop who gave a nod. Rayna had the distinct feeling the attorney was more used to corporate negotiations than criminal interrogation.

"We were classmates," Ty said.

"That's all?"

"We didn't hang with the same crowd, if that's what you mean."

"Yet you were at a party she was at not long before she disappeared."

Ty rubbed his palms on his pant legs. "Yeah. Last fall, before I started going with Caitlin."

"Was Karen one of those girls you were telling me about? The ones who made sexual conquests into a contest."

Ty reddened. He studiously avoided looking at his father.

"Was she?" Rayna asked again.

"Yeah." The word was little more than a puff of air.

"And did you help her out?"

Ty looked sick. "Do I have to answer that?" he asked Bishop.

"No, you don't," Mr. Cross said before the attorney could speak. "You don't have to answer anything." He turned to

Rayna. "This whole line of questioning is preposterous."

Rayna doubted Mr. Cross even knew about the contest, but she didn't want to antagonize him further. She could always ask Ty again another time, although she figured she'd gotten her answer.

"How well did Rob know Karen Holiday?"

Ty laughed. "She wasn't his type, either."

"So nothing happened between them?"

"I'm sure of it."

"How can you be sure?"

The attorney cleared his throat. "I think these are questions you should ask Rob, not my client."

"Tell me again when you last saw Caitlin," Rayna said.

"At school, the Friday she disappeared. She was at volleyball practice. But we didn't talk."

"What time was that?"

"A little after five, I guess. I'd stayed late to make up a lab I missed earlier in the week."

Rayna noted the time in her notebook. "What time did you leave the school grounds?"

"I don't know. Probably around five-thirty."

"Did you go straight home?"

"I stopped to get a burrito and pick up a few things first."

"How'd you pay for them?"

"I get an allowance," Ty said, sounding a bit defensive.

"I meant, did you pay with cash or by credit card?"

"Oh. Cash."

No paper trail to verify his movements. "What time did you get home?"

"About seven."

"Was anyone one else there?"

"My mom. She was making dinner."

Rayna sat back in her chair. "How do you account for the fact that Rob Hardy says the two of you were playing an on-line video game during the time when you were out?"

Ty appeared uncomfortable, but he shrugged in what he undoubtedly intended to be an offhand manner. To Rayna it looked forced. "He must be mistaken."

"Something of an interesting coincidence that his story offers you an alibi for the time of Caitlin's disappearance. You sure you don't want to take it?"

Ty's left leg bounced up and down. He rubbed his palms on his thighs. "You've talked to him, right?"

"Of course."

Ty's father did a better job of picking up on Ty's nervousness than the attorney. "What exactly is this about?" Mr. Cross asked.

Rayna ignored the question and again addressed Ty. "How did Rob and Caitlin get along?"

"Okay."

" 'Okay' as in they were friendly, or 'okay' as in they barely knew one another?"

Bishop leaned forward. "I don't see what this has to do with my client."

Rayna ignored the interruption. "They had a big . . . I don't know what to call it exactly. An argument, a scene, whatever, about the time you and Caitlin broke up. What was that about?"

Ty looked at his feet then raised his eyes to meet Rayna's. "You think Rob killed Caitlin?" Ty's breathing had become shallow and quick.

"What do you think?"

Ty again wiped his palms on his legs. His face was flushed, his expression wary. "I don't . . . it's not . . . no. No way! I don't believe it."

Rayna found his reaction more interesting than his answer. She read his doubt loud and clear.

Mr. Cross spoke up with more conviction than his son. "Rob's family and ours have been friends for years. There's no way either boy is involved in this and I am sick and tired of your suggesting otherwise. We've tried to cooperate, but enough is enough." He started to rise.

"Rob had some interesting things to tell us," Rayna said, fishing for a reaction from Ty. If she could play the two boys off against each other, maybe she'd get to the bottom of what was bothering her.

Ty swallowed hard. "What about?"

"What do you think it was about?"

"Don't answer that, Ty," Mr. Cross said. "We're through here."

Clearly torn, Ty hesitated before rising. His gaze was fixed on Rayna and she had the distinct impression he wanted to hear if she would say more.

Mr. Cross paused at the door, impatient. "Ty, I said let's go."

Somewhat reluctantly, Ty followed his father and the attorney out of the room.

Rayna flicked off the recorder. She hadn't learned anything substantive, but she had an even stronger sense than before that Ty was hiding something. Maybe when she pressed Rob Hardy, she'd get somewhere.

Hank grabbed her in the hallway as she was leaving the interrogation room. "I was just coming to get you. We got a call. A missing person's report."

Rayna's skin prickled. God, no, not another one!"

"A sixteen-year-old girl named Terri Lowe. Last seen this morning when her mom dropped her off at the mall to do some shopping."

CHAPTER 43

Rayna took the glass of tepid tap water Mrs. Lowe handed her and drained it quickly. It was now evening and she hadn't eaten since morning. She could have used a bite of food, but she understood that the gnawing ache in her stomach was a small matter compared to a missing child.

Earlier in the day she'd talked to Terri Lowe's parents long enough to learn that Terri was home-schooled, which allowed her the flexibility to go to the mall that Monday with her mother and ten-year-old sister. They'd all had lunch, and then while the mother and younger daughter did their errands, Terri did hers. They were to have met up at the car an hour later. Terri never showed.

While this wasn't the first time Terri had pushed the boundaries of her freedom, it was unusual for her to simply ignore the plans they'd all agreed on. And Terri wasn't answering her cell phone, which was also not unheard of, but troubling under the circumstances. Still, Mrs. Lowe had initially been more angry than worried. She'd hung around for another hour, waiting for her daughter, before heading home. After she and her husband had contacted Terri's few friends and learned that none of them had heard from Terri, they called the police.

Armed with a snapshot and description of the girl, officers had blanketed the shops and restaurants in the area throughout the afternoon and into the evening. There were some possible sightings, but nothing concrete.

It was eight o'clock now and Rayna was once again seated in the Lowe's drafty living room, digging deeper into their daughter's life.

"No," Mrs. Lowe said. "I already told you. No arguments,

no fights, it was just a normal Monday, following a normal weekend. There was nothing to indicate that Terri was upset."

"What about boys?" Rayna asked.

"No boys," Mr. Lowe said decisively. "Terri knows how we feel about that. She's not allowed to date until she's out of school."

Rayna was beginning to get a feel for the seeds of Terri's hints at rebellion. The Lowes—both husband and wife—struck her as stern and regimented. Mr. Lowe worked for the postal service and Mrs. Lowe, while insisting she was a full-time mother and the girls' teacher, also worked as a bookkeeper three afternoons a week. The Lowe's house was small and dark, tidy but not particularly inviting. They had three children, all girls. Terri was the middle child. The older one lived and worked in Portland.

"Does Terri have a computer?" Rayna asked.

"There's one computer in this house," Mr. Lowe said, "for use by the entire family. I monitor it closely so I doubt you'll find any clues to her whereabouts there, but you're welcome to look."

Mrs. Lowe was anxiously clasping and unclasping her hands. "Terri didn't run away," she said emphatically, "and she didn't run off with some boy. She was kidnapped, just like those other two girls. Please find her before it's too late."

"Local authorities as well as those in neighboring towns have been alerted. The media is on it, as well. Your daughter's photo will be on the news later tonight and in the papers tomorrow morning. I understand that you are worried, believe me. I'm as concerned as you are. That's why I need to know your daughter better, to examine her habits and hope we find common ground with the other girls who disappeared. It's our best hope of finding her."

"Dear God." Mrs. Lowe had been trying valiantly to control her tears, but she finally lost the fight. She grabbed a handful of tissues. "Why Terri?" she asked between sobs. "She's a good girl. How can this be happening? What is a maniac killer doing in Paradise Falls? We moved here because it was safe."

Rayna had asked herself the same question. And she was as perplexed and frightened as the Lowes.

Rayna met up with Hank back at the station.

"Nothing," he said in disgust, tossing his clipboard onto his desk. "A clerk at a gift store thinks she remembers seeing Terri, but that's it. No one was with her at the time, and no one appeared to be following her."

"Do we know the time of the gift store sighting?"

"No. The clerk couldn't even be sure that the girl she remembered was Terri." "Has someone checked the Dumpster?"

Hank nodded. "Nothing of note."

Rayna put her head in her hands. She felt queasy. She'd skipped lunch because she'd had a dinner date with Paul, now canceled, and she hadn't had time to eat since.

"You doing okay with this?" Hank asked.

"Yeah. I'm having the time of my life." His face fell and Rayna immediately regretted her sarcasm. Hank meant well. "Sorry, I guess I'm not doing too well."

"We'll get him, Rayna."

"Maybe. But how many girls will he get first?"

"It stinks, that's for sure. We've never had anything like this before." Hank rolled his shoulders and stretched the muscles of his neck. "What did you learn from the Lowes?"

"Terri is a quiet, serious girl with a small circle of friends. None of the ones I talked to had any idea what might have happened to her, except they all agreed she wouldn't have run away. I asked about Adam Peterson—"

"He couldn't have done it," Hank pointed out.

"I know that, but I asked anyway. I ran Ty and Rob's names past them, also. Nothing. And they only knew Karen and Caitlin from the news."

"Shit!"

"That about sums it up. We might as well head home for the night. Maybe something will break by morning." Rayna didn't believe it and she knew Hank didn't, either.

After he'd left, Rayna again studied Terri's photo. Her

coloring was fair, bordering on bland, her features too small for her face. Whereas both Karen Holiday and Caitlin had been attractive girls—Karen in a voluptuous way and Caitlin with an athletic sparkle—Terri appeared mousy and dull. Why these three girls? What did they have in common? Caitlin had thick, chestnut colored hair. Karen and Terri were blonds. There seemed to be no common thread at all.

Funny that of the three girls, Rayna found Caitlin to be most like the teenager she imagined Kimberly might have become. Yet Kimberly, too, was blond, and like both Karen and Terri, she'd had baby fine, straight hair.

Rayna felt the ache of her own loss. Her eyes stung with tears. Damn, she was supposed to be stronger than this.

She leaned her arms on the desk and indulged in a few minutes of self-pity. She needed to leave this job. She'd thought she was somehow paying tribute to her daughter by going after the bad guys, but it dawned on Rayna that she wasn't doing anyone any good. She was a lousy cop. Seth Robbins had been right all along. And now it looked as though her incompetence might cost another girl her life.

She began to imagine how Robbins would gloat if she resigned. Or was fired. She blew her nose and sat up straighter. She wasn't going to give the little piranha that satisfaction. She might leave this job at some point, but she wasn't going out in defeat.

Before she left for home, she called Paul Nesbitt. It was not a night she wanted to be alone with her thoughts.

"Sorry about canceling for dinner," she told him. "I seem to be making a habit of that lately."

"It's not your fault. A missing girl isn't something you can leave sitting in your inbox for the next day."

"You're a very understanding guy."

"Tell that to my ex-wife."

"She must be nuts." Rayna knew very little about Paul's previous marriage and divorce. Just as he knew almost nothing about her past. It was what had made their relationship work. Sex and companionship, but nothing too personal. "I know it's late, but do you want to come over?"

"Tonight?"

"Yeah. And it has to be pretty soon or I'll have faded into slumber."

"Half an hour, how's that?"

"Perfect."

When Rayna arrived home, she fed Anastasia, then headed straight for the shower. Clean and fresh, she slipped into velour yoga pants and a matching tee. Her hair was still damp at the nape of her neck when she opened the door for Paul.

He leaned in and kissed her. "You smell nice. You feel nice, too."

"Ditto." Paul's signature aftershave was a fresh, gingery scent she associated only with him. She slipped an arm around the back of his neck. "I'm using you, you know. Full disclosure requires me to tell you that."

He laughed. "Do you see me objecting?"

"Just so you're forewarned." They had this exchange, or something similar, periodically, yet Rayna could never be sure Paul understood.

"I brought brandy," he told her. "Let me pour us a drink and you can tell me about your day."

Rayna followed him into the kitchen where she watched as he pulled two brandy glasses from the cupboard as comfortably as he would in his own home. She liked watching him move, easy and fluid. She liked his lack of pretentiousness.

"You're a nice guy, Paul."

"Nice guy but not right for you, I know. We've been over this, Rayna. Would you please forget it. At least for the time being." He stroked the small of her back. "Let's take our drinks into the bedroom."

"Good idea." Rayna felt better already. She didn't love him, but Paul was a good antidote for what ailed her.

She set her drink on the bedside table, pulled back the coverlet, and screamed.

Peeking out from beneath the pillows was a tiny toy kitten.

CHAPTER 44

Caitlin's funeral was Tuesday morning. Grace viewed it largely as something she needed to get through. That was the mantra she played over and over in her mind—just get through it. If she stopped to think about what it meant, what had come before, or what was happening now, she knew she'd crumble like ancient parchment.

The mortuary chapel was packed, which Grace knew should make her feel somehow comforted, but it didn't. She recognized faces—Caitlin's friends from school, teachers, neighbors. And co-workers —hers, Carl's, and even a few of Jake's, although they'd had to drive in from Portland. But she avoided making eye contact with any of them. She clutched a damp handkerchief in her hand and dug her nails into her palms. She kept her eyes focused straight ahead, warding off the reality of the moment.

She had managed to avoid breaking down completely by slowly counting backward from one thousand. Now it was almost over. Jake finished delivering an impressive eulogy and all that remained was for the minister to offer a final prayer.

One hundred ninety-three. One hundred ninety-two.

Finally, blessedly, the service ended. Grace could breathe again.

Sandy had offered to organize a reception to follow, but Grace said no thanks. She wouldn't have the strength to be gracious. And she wanted to be alone.

She walked out into the lobby with Jake, but Carl and Lucy, who'd sat to her left during the service, followed close behind. She left them for a moment when she spotted Rayna Godwin.

"It was nice of you to come to the funeral," Grace said.

"It seemed right."

"I appreciate it."

"Grace, I know how hard this is for—"

She brushed her hand through the air. She didn't want to talk about it, even with someone who'd been there before. Not now. "Please," she said. "I can't—"

"That's okay. I understand."

Grace swallowed. "The new girl, Terri something—I'm sorry my mind can't retain anything lately—the one who's missing. Do you think her disappearance is connected to what happened to Caitlin?"

"We don't know, but there are similarities."

The air left Grace's lungs. "Then it wasn't Adam?" she whispered. Ever since she'd heard the first reports about another missing girl, she'd felt choked by the ether of guilt and regret. Had she made a terrible mistake?

"If the same person is responsible for all three girls, then no, it couldn't be Adam."

"Oh, my God!" All the hate she'd directed toward Adam, and now this. She supposed she should be glad, but all she felt was a tidal wave of loss. How could she have been so wrong? "So you don't know who killed Caitlin?"

The detective shook her head. "I understand how unsettling, how agonizing, how unfair it is that whoever did this terrible thing hasn't been caught."

"Yes. Yes, it is. You'd think it wouldn't make such a difference, but it does."

"It's important to us, too."

"Adam's no longer in critical condition," Grace told her. "He's going to pull through, although there may be complications."

"Yes, I got a call from the hospital this morning."

"What have I done? I feel so responsible."

"It wasn't you who forced him to swallow the pills, Grace."

"I've been telling myself the same thing." Grace felt a knot in her throat. "It was easier when I thought he'd killed

Caitlin."

"Did you know Terri Lowe? Does her name ring a bell? Might she and Caitlin have had some common ground somewhere?"

"The name means nothing to me," Grace said. "I asked Lucy when I first heard it because I wondered the same thing. I thought maybe Caitlin might have said something to her. Lucy's younger than Caitlin by a few years, but they shared stuff."

"Lucy didn't recognize the name, either?"

"No."

The detective seemed to hesitate for a moment, then she asked, "Do stuffed animals have any special meaning for you?"

"I'm not sure what you mean. You asked Mimi something similar the other day, didn't you?"

"Right."

"If it's about Caitlin's murder, she loved stuffed animals as much as the next kid, but there's no special significance attached to them." With a sudden pang in her heart, Grace remembered Lucky, the floppy-eared velveteen dog that had been Caitlin's constant companion as a toddler.

"I'm sorry to have bothered you with questions at a time like this," Rayna said.

"It's not a problem. I'll do anything to help catch the person who killed my daughter."

Following the funeral, Carl and Lucy returned to the house with Grace. Jake, who'd all but abandoned Starr to be by Grace's side at the service, had suggested they go out to lunch, but Grace declined. The company of others required more effort than she could muster. It was as if she were half dead herself, her batteries depleted and her body hollow. Sorrow hung over her like a dark shadow, but she felt nothing.

At home, Lucy offered to fix Grace a sandwich, but she felt as though she were suffocating. She needed space to herself.

Finally, she sent Carl off to teach his afternoon seminar (having missed two classes in the past week, he offered only a pro forma protest) and suggested to Lucy that she head back to school.

"Are you sure you don't want someone around? I could stay here and not bother you."

"Thank you, honey, but I'd actually prefer to be alone right now."

"Okay." She sounded reluctant. "If that's what you really want."

Carl hugged Grace and whispered in her ear. "You need me, you call, understand?" Then he kissed her on the forehead. Caring, yet reserved. Still, it gave Grace some hope they might yet have a future together.

But it was Lucy's unrestrained hug and "please be okay, Grace," that, like an electric shock, jolted Grace back into the land of the living. Fierce emotion, painful yet welcome, rose sharply in her chest.

The moment she was alone, Grace gave into the tears she'd fought all morning.

CHAPTER 45

On her way back to the station following the funeral, Rayna stopped by the Java Mill and bought a large black coffee to go. It was hot and strong, and she hoped it would kick the cobwebs out of her head. And just maybe help her keep her eyes open for the rest of the afternoon.

She'd gotten no sleep last night. The stuffed kitten on her bed had frightened her more than she cared to admit—there'd been a madman in her house, for God's sake—but it had also fueled her anger. Now more than ever, she wanted to nail the guy.

There'd been no obvious sign of a break-in that she and Paul could find, but when the forensics team had arrived a little before midnight, they'd found the lock on the rear door had been jimmied.

"Don't you have an alarm system?" one had asked her. Guys in forensics worried a lot about personal safety.

"I do but I only use it at night, when I go to bed."

"I tell me wife to set it every time she goes out. Even to visit the neighbor. You pay the same if it's set or not, right?"

"Good point." Rayna wasn't cavalier about intruders but she found setting the alarm every time she left the house to be a nuisance. And none of the bad things that happened in her life could have been prevented by an alarm. Still, from now on she'd keep the damn thing set.

It wasn't simply that someone had been in her house, creepy as that felt. It was that the hunt was about more than murder. For whatever twisted reasons, this perp not only got off on killing innocent young girls, he needed to rub Rayna's nose in it as well.

She was nearing the station when she pulled a U-turn and, instead, drove to the offices of the Tribune. Seth Robbins had it in for her, too. Maybe if she understood why, she'd see a new angle on this animal thing.

Hell, maybe Seth was the killer. Wouldn't that be something? How she'd love to haul his ass in. She smiled at the thought.

Rayna got past the receptionist with a minimum of fuss by flashing her badge and not slowing down. It was only after she'd reached the labyrinth of waist-high cubicles in the newsroom that she asked directions to Seth's station. A sudden hush fell over the room and Rayna was aware that all eyes were on her. For once, she relished the audience.

She found Robbins talking on the phone, with his feet, in their stretched and badly scuffed loafers, propped on his desk. Smug little twit.

"Let me call you back," he said into the phone. "Something interesting just walked in."

Rayna removed a stack of papers from a vinyl-cushioned chair, dropped them without decorum onto the floor, and took a seat.

Robbins smiled, revealing pointy eye-teeth, but he took his time removing his feet from his desk. "To what do I owe this honor, detective?"

"I'd like to know what it is you have against me."

"Besides the fact that you've got your head up your ass? Nothing, really."

"Do you have a friend or relative in the department? Is that it? Someone who wanted my job and was passed over?"

He chuckled. "Afraid not, but that would be a tidy little explanation, something you might see on the big screen."

"You've been on my case from the day I got here. You did a 'meet the new detective' sort of column that was snide and belittling."

Robbins rolled his eyes. "Oh, come on. It was tongue-in-cheek. You need to work on your sense of humor."

She needed to refrain from slugging him. "You don't

believe in playing fair, do you?"

"My job is to attract readers. Nobody likes namby-pamby reporting."

"I'd hardly call what you do reporting."

He dismissed her comment with a wave of his hand. "You'd be amazed how many people regularly read columnists whose views they despise. They like to be outraged."

And Seth Robbins obviously didn't mind feeding that outrage. "You've been giving these disappearances a lot of coverage. A disproportionate amount some might say."

"Readers eat it up. I couldn't ask for better material."

"You call two dead girls and another girl missing material?"

"Isn't it?" He seemed to be enjoying himself.

"The kind of story you'd die for," she said.

"Close."

"Is it the kind of story you'd also kill for?"

The smirk disappeared, but it took a beat. "What are you suggesting? That I had something to do with what happened to those girls?"

The earlier hush in the newsroom had given way to a low-pitched murmur, like the buzzing of a far-off insect. Rayna pushed back her chair and rose. "So far, Mr. Robbins, you're the only one I can see who has anything to gain from these crimes." She expected him to be indignant, but Seth Robbins was, for once, speechless. It was her turn to smile. "I'll be in touch."

She left the way she'd come, all eyes once again following her. The conversation had done wonders for her mood.

Her cell rang as she left the building.

"We have an ID on Romeo," Hank told her.

"Who is he?"

"Jordan Buhler, twenty-six. Lives outside of Corvallis. No record."

"Close enough that he could have done it. Do you have a phone number for him?"

"Just an address."

An address was a surer bet anyway. "Do you have

anything else on him? Educational background, work history, whatever?"

"Nada. Just what we've seen on his Facebook account."

A pepperoni pizza--loving baseball fan who played the guitar, loved his black Lab and beautiful sunsets. There was a good chance none of it, including the flattering photo, was true.

It wasn't yet one o'clock. Rayna could be in Corvallis by three. If she had to wait for him to get home, so be it. "I'm going to head there now," she told Hank.

"You want me to come along?"

"I'd rather you keep digging on Terri Lowe. And do me a favor, would you? See what you can come up with on Seth Robbins."

"He's an idiot. Don't let him get to you, Rayna."

She laughed. "I'm not."

The address for Jordan Buhler proved to be an older one-story house on a street of similar homes. They appeared to be part of the development boom that had proliferated after WWII. It wasn't an upscale neighborhood, not even one particularly well maintained, although Rayna guessed it had once shone with new lawns and flower beds. A dented green Taurus was parked in the driveway.

Rayna rang the bell, thinking it likely no one was home. But a female voice responded almost immediately. A minute or so later the door was opened by a stout, older woman pulling an oxygen canister on wheels behind her. Emphysema, from the sound of her wheezing.

Had Rayna rung the wrong house? Or maybe Hank's information was wrong. "I'm looking for Jordan Buhler," she said.

The woman gave Rayna a suspicious look.

"Do I have the right house?"

"Yeah, you got the right place. How do you know Jordie?"

"I'm with the Paradise Falls Police Department. I'd like to talk to him about a case."

"Paradise Falls is a long way from here."

"Only a couple of hours."

"Far enough. What makes you think Jordie might know anything?"

"That's something I need to explain to him."

She shrugged. "Come on in. I think you're probably wasting your time, but he's a funny boy so who knows?"

"Boy?"

"He's my grandson. He'll always be a boy to me. Have a seat and I'll get him." She waddled off through an open doorway with the oxygen canister trailing after her.

Rayna remained standing, taking in what she could of the room. An older model television—the kind that still had a dial you turned by hand—a sagging sofa, a threadbare easy chair spread with a knitting project, and a newspaper folded open to the crossword puzzle. On the mantel was a photo of a slender woman in her twenties and a laughing, tow-headed toddler. Jordan and his mother? Was he living with his grandmother for financial reasons, or because she needed a caregiver? Were serial killers who preyed on young girls also caretakers?

She heard uneven footsteps in the hallway and turned, stifling a gasp.

The man who stood before her was horribly scarred and disfigured—a burn victim from the looks of him. He wore a baseball cap to cover what looked like a hairless head. His sporadically pigmented skin was stretched tight and smooth over his face. He had no nose, only a hole for breathing, and his mouth was a gash with no lips. One arm was a stump, the other ended in a hand that curled like a claw. It was all Rayna could do to keep from turning away.

"You're Jordan Buhler?" she asked.

"That's me. Or what's left of me," he added with a laugh. His voice was surprisingly strong and melodic. "What can I do for you?"

"You're the Jordan whose screen name on Facebook is Romeo?"

"You're not here to take me to task for false advertising, I hope." Another chuckle.

The voice didn't match the man. Rayna tried not to let that distract her. "Caitlin Whittington," she said.

Jordan stared at her. His eyes were a deep, chocolate brown. "What about her?"

"You tell me."

"I've never met her." Jordan sounded wary, although with his lack of facial expression it was difficult for Rayna to judge.

"But you've written to her." Rayna took a gamble and added, "You sent her a web cam. And an iPod nano."

A beat of silence. "So?"

"What were you doing striking up a friendship with a fifteen-year-old girl?"

"There's a law against that?" Jordan moved into the room with an awkward gait and sat on the arm of the sofa. "Is this porn investigation or something? Because I have nothing to hide. It wasn't like that."

"It's a homicide investigation," Rayna said.

"What?" Again, she had trouble reading his expression, but his voice registered shock, as did his eyes.

"Caitlin was murdered."

"My God, when? How awful. What happened?"

"Where were you the afternoon and evening of Friday, March fourteenth?"

"You can't think I had anything to do with what happened?"

Rayna didn't know what to think. She felt sorry for him, of course. But who knew what looking like Jordan did might do to a person? Conceivably it could send him over the edge or turn him into a madman.

"Is that your Taurus in the driveway, Jordan?"

"It belongs to my grandmother."

"Do you have a car of your own?"

"I can't even drive. I suppose I could learn with some fancy handicap vehicle, if I could afford one, but why? I hardly ever leave the house. I live my life on the Internet."

"Seducing young girls."

"I think seducing is a bit of a stretch."

"You pretend to be someone you're not," Rayna said.

"I've read your profile. I've read the emails you sent Caitlin."

"The web is full of people pretending to be someone else."

"But in this case, the girl you were communicating with—the one you flattered and sweet-talked and deceived—was murdered. That puts things in a different light."

"So I pretend to be someone I'm not. Wouldn't you in my place? I was twelve years old when my father doused me with gasoline and set me on fire. I still haven't decided if I'm lucky to be alive."

Rayna sucked in her breath.

"I don't mean any harm," Jordan continued. "In fact, I'm very careful not to do harm. If no one is hurt, is it really so wrong? I just want to experience a little of the life I'll never have."

"What about the girls? You think it's fair to them?"

"I don't lead them on or promise them things. I just want to be a friend."

"A friend?" Rayna's tone proclaimed her skepticism.

"What? You don't think you can make friends online? You think everyone out there has some ulterior motive?"

"I think guys use 'friend' to cover a lot of territory."

Jordan ran a hand along the back of his neck. "So many of these girls are insecure and lonely, even though they have so much energy and beauty. They've got a totally distorted view of themselves. I try to help them see how special they are, to help them feel good about themselves."

Truth or bullshit? Rayna couldn't tell. "And the web cam?" she asked. "You need a camera for that?"

"No. It's for my own pleasure. I like looking at them. I don't ask them to do anything bad, although some do, all on their own."

"Maybe that's because of the phony profile and attractive photo you posted."

Jordan's eyes registered sadness. "Yeah. I know. It would be totally different if I put up a real picture of myself."

Rayna instantly regretted her tactlessness. "I'm sorry, that was mean. I had hoped 'Romeo' might turn out to be important to our investigation."

"Does that mean you don't have any leads? Besides hoping it was me, I mean."

"It's an active case," Rayna said, her voice defensive. "We're pursuing various avenues."

"What about Ty Cross?"

Rayna sucked in her breath, surprised. "How do you know Ty?"

"Like I said, some of the girls I correspond with tell me things. Private things, stuff they might not talk about with their friends."

"What did Caitlin say about Ty?"

"I wouldn't break a confidence except . . . if Caitlin is dead, it might be important. She really liked him, or maybe she liked the idea of him because he sounded like a jerk. But in Caitlin's mind, he was Prince Charming. She'd never had a boyfriend before, never been popular, and then all of a sudden she was the envy of her classmates. The other girls kept asking her if she'd done it with him yet. They sounded like a bunch of sluts to me, but they made Caitlin feel inferior. Like there was something wrong with her or like Ty didn't really care about her that much."

"She told you all this?"

"Not all at once, but over time. She made up her mind to have sex with him so she could say she'd done it. I told her I thought that was a stupid reason but her mind was made up. She wanted proof that Ty liked her. Then before anything happened, she found out Ty and another boy had something going. It totally freaked her out."

"Something going? You mean a homosexual relationship?"

"Right."

"Did she say who the other boy was? Rob Hardy, by any chance?"

"Rob, yes, that's it. He was jealous and told Caitlin about himself and Ty, probably to hurt her and send her packing. He certainly succeeded in hurting her."

So that explained the argument between Rob and Caitlin.

As well as Ty's discomfort with her questions about Rob.

"Ty didn't want anyone to know about him and Rob," Jordan explained. "Hey, do you think Ty killed Caitlin to keep her from telling anyone?" Jordan paused. "Or maybe it was Rob who wanted to get rid of her."

Or the both of them, Rayna thought, not for the first time. "Did she mention her stepbrother, Adam?"

"Some. Not like with Ty, though."

"What's the gist of what she told you?"

"It seemed like they got along pretty well. In fact, after what happened with Ty, she joked that maybe she'd lose her virginity to Adam."

"Did she?"

"Not that she ever told me. That doesn't mean it didn't happen, though."

"Does the name Karen Holiday mean anything to you?" Rayna asked.

"No."

"Terri Lowe?"

Jordan shook his head. "Who are they? Friends of Caitlin's?"

"Two more girls from Paradise Falls. Terri's missing. Karen was murdered."

"Oh, man. You think the same guy's involved in all of them? Guess I was wrong about Ty and Rob then."

Unless the killings weren't related. Why did Rayna keep coming back to that possibility? Maybe because it made sense.

CHAPTER 46

R ayna was driving back to Paradise Falls when Hank called. "Seth Robbins is demanding to meet with you," he said. "Claims it's important."

"Important to him or to us? Oh, never mind, I'll be there in about an hour." She had the fleeting thought that after her visit to his office, Robbins might show up with his lawyer to accuse her of harassment, but quickly dismissed it. Even Seth Robbins couldn't be that much of an ass.

"How'd it go with Romeo?" Hank asked.

"Not the way we'd hoped." Rayna gave Hank a quick rundown of her conversation with Jordan, including what he'd told her about Ty Cross and Rob Hardy. "I think we ought to get them both in once more and play them off against one another. Maybe we'll get some answers."

"That ought to be fun. I wonder how Ty's going to handle his dad hearing about his sexual exploits with Rob."

"Yeah, well, that's Ty's problem. Maybe if he'd been truthful early on, he wouldn't be in that pickle."

"I'll tell Robbins you're on your way."

The freeway was clear and moving at the limit, but Rayna didn't push it. She was in no hurry for a confrontation with Seth Robbins.

Robbins was waiting for her at the station. He was alone—no attack-dog attorney that Rayna could see—and looked more nervous than angry. They'd no sooner settled in Rayna's corner of the alcove than he handed her the printout of an email.

"This showed up in my inbox at the newspaper a couple of hours ago," he explained.

Rayna scanned the message then read it again more slowly.

Dear Mr. Robbins,

Kudos on your efforts to bring to light the repeated failings of the incompetent Detective Rayna Godwin. You must be a smart man, and also a brave man to point out that she's in way over her head. The woman's as arrogant as she is incompetent, a combination of traits that never fails to amaze me. But I digress. My point in writing is to say that unless the detective admits she's a failure and turns in her badge, another girl will disappear in the next forty-eight hours. I know this because I am the person responsible. In case you think this is a joke, let me offer you a bone (sorry, poor choice of words, although rather fitting in a macabre sort of way, don't you think?). Terri Lowe's body can be found three miles in from the main highway on Eagle Crest Road just before it crosses the creek. I hope that you'll publish this email in your Wednesday column. Feel free to invite comment from the 'good' detective and the public at large. It should be quite a scoop for your resume, no? You might even find yourself on Oprah.

Rayna's pulse raced. "Have you been out to Eagle Crest Road yet?" she asked Robbins, passing the note to Hank. Eagle Crest was a winding mountain road that tracked through forest land about ten miles east of town.

"No way. I'm not getting messed up in this."

"I'd say you're already messed up in it." Maybe you're even part of it. For all Rayna knew, the note could be part of a hoax, another ploy to humiliate her.

"Jesus," Hank said, looking up from the email. "I hope he's pulling our leg."

"How do I know you didn't write this yourself?" she asked Robbins.

"Me?" Robbins squeaked, managing to sound indignant all the same. "I'd never do something like that!"

"Really. You could have fooled me."

"You've got it all wrong. I'm trying to help."

"Or deflect our interest in you as a possible suspect. Gosh, the more I consider that possibility, the more likely it is. I resign, we go off looking for some unknown killer, and you wind up a hero of sorts in the press. Win, win, win for you."

"Look, I know how it might seem but that's not the case. You've got to believe me."

"Why's that?" Hank asked.

"It started out as a kind of gimmick for me," Robbins said, now sounding genuinely chagrined. "Despite what you may think, it was never personal. I rake people over the coals, that's what I do. And my readers eat it up, even when they disagree. I've gotten emails from this guy before—he's the one who told me about your daughter and husband. But this"— Robbins shuddered— "is something altogether different. I'm not going to be a pawn in a game of murder, even if it sells papers."

Well bully for you, Rayna thought. "You have no idea who sent this to you?"

"None. I swear to God."

Rayna turned to Hank. "We should have Leavitt see what he can learn about the origins of the email." She knew the sender's address would be a dead end, but she was often amazed at what the computer savvy techies in the department could uncover. "And we'd better get a team out to Eagle Crest Road."

"What should I do about tomorrow's column?" Robbins asked plaintively, literally wringing his hands. "Should I mention the note at all?"

"I'd prefer you didn't." Rayna wondered if Seth's performance was all an act, and if it wasn't, how to handle the note. Dear God, she was in over her head,

If only Cody were still here, she thought, and at the same time wondered, where the hell that came from. She didn't need Neal Cody for anything!

It took a team of officers less than an hour to locate Terri Lowe's remains. She was buried in a shallow grave behind a large boulder about a hundred feet from the road. Her throat had been slit, which was consistent with the coroner's findings for Karen Holiday.

While the crime scene investigators scoured the surrounding area for clues and the coroner prepared the body for transport, Rayna sat on a fallen log and wondered if she could actually be the cause of all this tragedy. It didn't make sense, but the emailer was certainly clear about his feelings for her.

Could it be because he thought she was getting close to discovering his identity? Hah, that was a good one.

When the media helicopters began circling overhead and the first press van showed up, Rayna headed for her car. "I'd better notify Mr. and Mrs. Lowe," she told Hank. "You stay here and keep an eye on things."

"Shouldn't we issue a warning that another girl is likely to be taken? We can't just sit on that information."

"I'll talk to the chief. Probably a generic, 'We have every reason to believe this maniac will strike again soon' will suffice. People are already nervous as hell. I can't imagine they can be more alert than they are already."

"You're not going to resign, are you?"

"I don't bow to threats." But she was already mulling over the possibility.

Rayna parked in front of the Lowes' modest house and

took several deep breaths. She'd never been comfortable delivering word of a death to family members, but ever since that devastating evening four years ago when she'd learned of Kimberly's death, the task had become especially difficult for her.

The Lowes were home, and Rayna was grateful for that. They'd have each other to lean on, and she'd only have to go through the details once.

Mr. Lowe answered the door. His face froze when he saw it was her.

"There's news," he said. A statement more than a question. "Not good news, I take it."

"I'm afraid not."

"What is it?" Mrs. Lowe asked, coming up behind her husband.

"May I come in?"

"Just tell us. Please."

Rayna took a breath. "We've found the remains of a female on Eagle Crest Road. We believe it's your daughter."

Mrs. Lowe started wailing, "No, no, no! It's not Terri. It can't be." She turned to her husband and buried her face against his chest.

Mr. Lowe struggled to keep his composure. "How could you have let this happen?" He glared at Rayna. "Why haven't you caught this maniac yet?"

"We're doing everything we can," she said. "I know that doesn't help you with your loss. You have my deepest sympathy."

His face crumpled and his body shook with silent sobs. He clung to his wife and rocked from side to side.

The rawness of their grief felt like a band around Rayna's chest. "Shall I call someone for you? A minister? A friend or relative?"

"We need time to be alone right now. Please." He reached to close the door.

"At some point I will need you to identify the body." Rayna handed them her card, although she knew they had one already. "I'm truly very sorry for your loss."

She was trembling by the time she reached her car. Mr. Lowe's accusation echoed in her head. How had she let this happen? Why hadn't they stopped this maniac already?

And now, another girl would die. This time it really would be her fault.

She gripped the steering wheel and rested her forehead on the back of her hands. If she turned in her badge, would that stop him? She had no way of telling. But she couldn't—wouldn't—be responsible for another death.

With a heavy heart, she headed back to the station, where she issued a press report covering the essentials of the crime and asking for the public's help. It wasn't likely there'd be a witness, but she could hope.

By the time she got home, she felt exhausted.

She ate a tuna sandwich for dinner then called Cody.

"I just caught it on the evening news," he told her. "What a goddamn nightmare."

"You don't know the half of it." Rayna told him about the email to Seth Robbins. "I don't even know if it's legit."

"Any idea what this is about? Who'd want you to resign?"

"No idea."

"Do you seriously think Robbins could be behind it?"

Rayna had debated that question with herself all afternoon. "Part of me would like that to be the case, but he seemed genuinely distressed by the email. We've assigned someone to keep an eye on him just in case."

"When a killer taunts the detective, Rayna, it's typically a game of one-upmanship. The creep's saying, 'I'm smarter than you.' But this strikes me as different. The email. The stuffed animals. That phone message you got, 'the fun is just beginning,' it's like he has it in for you personally."

"Why me?"

"Any jilted lovers or jealous boyfriends in your life?"

"Very funny."

"I'm serious," Cody said. "There's no one who's angry at you?"

"Not that I'm aware of. I don't even know very many people."

"What about someone you put away? Any gang arrests?"

"It's been mostly petty stuff here in Paradise Falls. What wasn't minor involved stupid perps, like the guy who tried to rob a convenience store after handing the clerk his credit card. I don't think any of them would be capable of this level of planning and organization."

"If he'd been in prison, he might have picked up a thing or two. Or even met a cohort who's been helping him. Why don't you check to see if anyone you put away in San Jose has been released recently?"

"Okay." Rayna thought it was a long shot, but she was willing to try anything.

"Maybe I should come back there," Cody suggested.

Yes. "There's no need for that."

"Maybe not for the case, but you sound like you could use some . . ." He paused. "I guess I'm the wrong guy for that." He paused again. "There's a bust about to go down here, anyway. I'd probably have trouble getting away."

But she knew if she asked him to, he would. Whatever it took, he'd find a way. "Just talking to you helps."

"I'm here. Anytime."

"I'll remember that."

As tired as she was, Rayna spent the next two and a half hours painstakingly checking the arrest and release records for cases she'd worked both locally and in San Jose. It took a lot of dialing and calling in of favors, and in some cases a sprinkling of deceit, to get the information, and even then it was incomplete. She'd been able to trace only three prisoners who'd been released in the last twelve months. She followed up with their parole officers, apologizing for bothering them after hours, only to learn that none lived close to Paradise Falls and all were employed and reporting to work regularly. After expending so much energy and adrenaline on the task, Rayna felt let down by the lack of results, even though she'd expected it to begin with.

Before heading off to bed, she logged into her police email and sent a short email to the account the killer had used.

If you have issues with me, why don't we deal with them directly?

Maybe we can work something out.

Again she thought it was probably a stab in the dark, but she sat in front of the computer screen for five minutes, hoping for a reply, before heading off to bed.

She was up early the next morning, dreading a phone call informing her that another girl was missing. She checked her email first thing—no reply from the killer—then made coffee and went outside to pick up the morning paper, removing the rubber band on her way in. When she tossed the paper on the counter, a small stuffed monkey slid free. A copy of her email was pinned to its chest, and under her words a scribbled response: *Why? I'm having fun.*

CHAPTER 47

Grace wiped the counters and filled the kettle. She hadn't been quick enough to make excuses, or convincing enough with her honestly-I'm-doing-fine response, to fend off Sandy's visit. She wasn't sure why her first instinct had been to resist—it certainly had nothing to do with Sandy herself. More likely it was because of the pervading lethargy that seemed to blanket her every move. Even her brain felt mired in molasses.

It was a bleak morning, inside and out. The morning of the day after Caitlin's funeral. A day to begin moving forward, except Grace couldn't move at all.

She'd somehow managed to get through yesterday's ordeal, although her memory of details was spotty. Today had dawned just as heavy and just as awful. Her precious daughter was in the ground. "Laid to rest" in the popular parlance, but like all the other feel-good clichés about death, it offered no solace. Dead was dead and Grace experienced no sense of closure, no peace at having Caitlin properly buried. In fact, today was worse. Yesterday she'd had a purpose; today she had nothing.

By rote, she took two mugs from the cupboard and turned on the burner under the kettle. Her friend would arrive any minute and Grace hadn't even showered. At least her kitchen was presentable, she thought, as she took one final swipe of the sponge across the countertop, and the coffee would be hot.

There was a knock at the front door, followed by Sandy's familiar "Hi, it's me," as she let herself in.

"I'm in the kitchen," Grace called out.

Sandy set a pink bakery box on the counter and gave

Grace a long hug. "I won't even ask how you're doing," she said.

"I look that bad?"

"You look great, but I know you're not."

"Everyone says it gets better with time."

"Pop psychology is overrated," Sandy said. "Sit down, I'll make the coffee." She scooped grounds into a filter and set out plates for the collection of pastries she'd brought. "It was a lovely service yesterday," she said, returning to the stove. Then she slapped her cheek with the flat of her hand. "What a stupid thing to say, like that's supposed to make you feel better. I'm sorry, Grace. I promised myself I wasn't going to spout off like some sympathy card, and now I've done it twice. It's just that I'm not very good at this. It's so hard to know what to say."

Grace ignored the pastries. She wasn't the least bit hungry but she was suddenly glad Sandy had come over. The woman was like the scent of early spring in a house long closed up and stale. "You say a lot just by caring."

"I wish I could do more."

"I'll have to take your word for it about the service," Grace said. "Yesterday's a blur for me."

"That's totally understandable. I can't begin to imagine . . ." The water came to a boil and Sandy poured it through the grounds. "You heard they found Terri Lowe's body?"

Grace nodded. "It was in the paper this morning." She'd thought about contacting the girl's parents to offer condolences, but her own grief was still too raw to have anything left over.

"It's frightening to think there's a killer preying on local girls. People are keeping their kids close, not letting them walk home or play outside. Some parents are even holding their kids out from school."

"I know. I'm picking Lucy up after school this afternoon so that she won't have to walk home."

Sandy set two mugs on the table. "That's quite considerate of you, given how you must be feeling."

"Since I more or less wrongly accused Adam of murder, I feel I need to do something to try to make amends." As if that were possible, Grace thought. Some breaches were simply too deep to be fixed. "Carl has a class he can't miss and Mimi has a full patient schedule. Besides, I enjoy Lucy's company."

"It's not painful?"

"I'm constantly reminded of Caitlin, but that happens whether I'm with Lucy or not. And she's, I don't know, needy in a way that makes me feel valued. It's kind of like being around a helpless puppy."

Sandy laughed at the analogy. "Don't let Lucy hear you say that." She reached for a croissant and broke it in half. "How's Carl doing now that Adam's okay and no longer a suspect?"

Grace sipped her coffee. It was hot and strong and soothing. "I'm not sure."

"He still blames you?"

"Not in so many words." If anything, he probably blamed Grace more for opening the door to his own doubts about Adam.

"I guess it's only natural that your relationship would be a bit rocky."

"More than a bit rocky, actually. He's trying to be supportive in light of Caitlin's murder, but he's also disappointed in me and very angry." Maybe angrier than Carl even realized himself.

He'd slept upstairs with Grace last night for the first time in over a week. He'd held her when she cried and stroked her hair while they talked of Caitlin. But there'd been a distance there too, dividing them like a wall of emotional Plexiglas.

"He's talking about moving out," Grace added after a minute.

"Moving out? As in leaving you?"

"He says it's temporary. His excuse is that he needs to have a place for Adam to live when he's released from the hospital. Carl feels Adam needs him and that Mimi's not up to the job even if her schedule allowed it."

"You believe that it's temporary?"

"I believe he believes it."

When Carl had talked about getting an apartment again

this morning, he'd pleaded with her to understand. "I suspected my own son of murder, Grace. I'm sure he sensed that. I pushed him into suicide. I'm every bit as guilty of that as you are. And I'm his father. Don't you see that this is something I have to do? I couldn't live with myself if I didn't."

She did see and that's what made it so hard.

"You're both good people," Sandy said, clasping Grace's hand. "I really hope you can work it out."

Sandy was wise enough to keep her visit short. They reminisced about Caitlin, gossiped about people they knew in common, and then Sandy said that she needed to be going. "You'll call me if you need anything?"

"I promise."

When she'd left, Grace finally took her morning shower.

Jake called just as Grace stepped out of the shower. "Do you have time for lunch?"

"I can't eat," she told him, wrapping her terry robe around her shivering body. "I'm not hungry."

"How about coffee then?"

"I just had coffee. What's the matter?"

"Nothing." Jake sighed, a ragged forlorn sound that caught in his throat. "I'm at loose ends, I guess."

"Join the club."

"Last night, after the funeral, I couldn't concentrate. Couldn't breathe. I almost went to the emergency room, but I knew the problem wasn't physical. I just felt so alone."

"Where was Starr?"

"She's visiting her sister."

"She left you alone on the night of your daughter's funeral?" That seemed a bit much, even for Starr.

"We had a fight. I told her I wasn't sure I wanted to go through with the wedding."

"I'm sorry." Grace felt bad for Jake but she wasn't in the mood to hold his hand.

"I guess we weren't as well matched as I imagined."

Grace had never seen that they were a match at all.

"I was wondering if I could get copies of some photos of Caitlin when she was younger. Of the three of us. Not right away. When you have time. I can have copies made."

"Of course."

"And maybe, I don't know, maybe I could take you to dinner some night?"

"I don't think that's—"

"I don't mean as a date. Just as a friend."

Never, in the nine years since their divorce, had Jake suggested getting together for dinner.

"It's just that I'm feeling . . . disconnected. It's dawning on me how little time I spent with Caitlin. How little I really knew her. We weren't close the way a lot of fathers and daughters are. And now she's gone. I don't get a second chance."

Although it was his own doing, Grace couldn't help feeling sympathetic. "You'd miss her no matter what," she offered. And he'd find things to regret, too. Grace certainly did. "Why are you even in town today? Did you have a meeting?"

"I wanted to visit Caitlin's grave without a lot of other people around. I wanted to say goodbye in private . . ." His voice trailed off. "Oh, God, Grace. I can't believe she's really gone."

Already noon, Grace thought, as she finished dressing. No, that was wrong. Only noon was more like it. She studied her haggard face in the bathroom mirror. How in the world would she get through the rest of the day? And the days to come.

She told herself she needed to concentrate on what was good, to find one thing to be grateful for each day. Anyone looking at her life from the outside, even knowing about Caitlin, would be able to come up with a good-sized list of positives. She had supportive friends. She had a good husband, however tenuous their relationship at the moment. She had her health, a job, a home, food in her cupboard and money in her bank account. But the gaping wound of her grief swallowed them all like a black hole.

They'll find Caitlin's killer, Grace told herself. The lunatic who was terrorizing Paradise Falls would be caught and punished. Would that bring her closure? Would she then be able to look forward?

And what about Adam? Even though she'd been wrong about him, there were questions that remained. Questions about Caitlin that only Adam could shed light on.

He was going to be moved to a psych facility in a few days, and then most likely to Carl's new apartment. Grace might never have another chance to speak with him. Mimi certainly wouldn't let her anywhere near him. Carl, too, would feel protective.

Grace put on lipstick and brushed blusher across her sallow cheeks, then drove to Pacific Memorial Hospital.

She took the elevator to the fourth floor and found Adam's room. She knew he was off the ventilator and no longer in ICU, so she was surprised to see how frail he looked. All bones and angles, skin almost as white as the sheets. His eyes were closed and an intravenous drip snaked into the vein in his arm.

She backed out of the room. She'd get a cup of coffee or something in the hospital cafeteria and come back later when he was awake. Maybe by then she'd figure out what to say to him.

CHAPTER 48

"You all finished, honey? You didn't eat much."

The nurse, whose name was Bridget, was Adam's favorite. She was a sturdy-looking black woman with smooth skin and cool, efficient hands. She spoke with a slight accent— maybe Jamaican, he didn't really know. She exuded gentleness without sounding falsely upbeat like the night nurse.

"I'm not hungry," Adam said. The food was pretty awful anyway. Who'd get excited about a soft-boiled egg and Jell-O?

"Your throat still sore?"

"A little." They'd shoved a tube down him to pump his stomach and another when he was on the ventilator. He'd been mostly in a fog when all that was going on, but he was paying the price now with a raw throat that hurt like hell when he swallowed.

"How about some ice? Or better yet, a Popsicle. Do you prefer orange or cherry?"

"Orange," Adam said, and smiled at her. "Thank you."

"I have to check on a few other patients first and then I'll be back." She patted his hand. "I won't forget you, I promise."

For some reason that brought tears to Adam's eyes. He closed them so she wouldn't see. The psychiatrist told him these ricocheting emotions he was feeling were normal, but Adam thought the guy himself was so far from normal he wouldn't know. And now they were going to send him to the nut house for a week or so.

Yes, Adam was paying the price for his stupidity. Again.

He was such a failure he couldn't even kill himself. How pathetic was that? On the other hand, there were moments when he was glad he hadn't managed to pull it off. Another sign of weakness, but there it was.

Assuming they let him out of the nut house, he was going to live with his dad—not that Adam had been consulted about the plan. His dad had rented an apartment so the two of them could spend more time together.

"You're my number one priority," he told Adam.

He appreciated what his dad was doing, but he'd miss the old arrangement. Lucy hated living in two houses. She hated that she had to shuttle back and forth between their mom and dad like some distant out-of-town relative. But Adam never saw it that way. The households were different, and they offered a nice balance.

Footsteps echoed outside his door. Hesitant, not quick and purposeful like the staff's. He opened his eyes just as Grace came through the door.

"Hello, Adam."

His heart skipped a beat. He'd known he'd see her again sooner or later, but not here, not yet. He needed time to work out what he felt. Part of him wanted to ignore her, shut his eyes, turn his back on her, and will her away. But Grace had the same gentle kindness his nurse Bridget did. He found it hard to turn away from kindness. It was a pretty scarce commodity in his life.

"How are you feeling?" she asked, moving to the side of his bed.

"Okay."

"I'm glad. I'm glad to know you'll be fine."

"You are?" That surprised him.

Instead of answering, Grace asked a question of her own. "Another girl was killed. Did you know that?"

"My dad mentioned it." Which was a big part of the reason Adam wasn't headed directly to prison. He felt grateful to the girl for being murdered and disgusted with himself for even thinking such a thing.

Grace plucked at a wrinkle in the bedspread. "I feel sort of like I let a bull loose in a china shop."

It took Adam a moment to figure out that she was talking about going to the cops with her suspicions about him.

"I don't expect you to understand," she continued. "But I wasn't out to get you, Adam. I just wanted to find Caitlin's killer."

He nodded. What was he supposed to say to that?

"I caused you a lot of pain and I can never undo the hurt."

He looked away, not sure what she wanted.

"Still, I have some questions. Things I'd like to know to settle my own mind. Like Caitlin's initials and yours carved in the log at that spot down by the river. And her ring. How did they get there?"

She knew how, Adam thought. What she really asked was why. And that was sort of embarrassing. "It was my own way of . . . I don't know, connecting with her."

"Connecting? After she was gone?"

"It doesn't make a lot of sense, I know, but her being missing upset me."

"So you buried her ring?"

"I told you, it doesn't make sense." Although it did to him.

"And her necklace? The one the police found in your mom's basement. How did that get there? Was that also part of some ritual?"

"I don't know how it got there. Truly, I have no idea." He didn't like the way she said "ritual" like he was some crazed killer or something.

"What about the photos, Adam? You took secret pictures of Caitlin. Why?"

Talk about embarrassing. If he was worried that the ring and the initials didn't make sense to others, this was a hundred times worse. He decided not to say anything.

"Caitlin was your friend, wasn't she?" Grace insisted. "Is that any way to treat a friend? To sneak around taking pictures in moments that should be private?"

Guilty as charged. "I don't think we should be talking about this," Adam said.

"Why not? If you didn't kill Caitlin, why not help me understand?"

Because she never would, no matter how much he tried to explain. "I'd never hurt Caitlin. Never, ever. You have to believe that."

"I'd like to believe it."

"It's the truth. I swear to God. I miss her too, you know. I really, really miss her."

To Adam's chagrin, his voice broke and he felt himself begin to tear up again. Luckily, Bridget came into the room with his Popsicle.

She handed it to him. "Here you go, honey." She turned to Grace. "Are you a relative? The only visitors allowed are immediate family."

"She's my step—" Adam stopped short when he saw the uncertainty reflected in Grace's expression. He knew what she was thinking. They'd once been family, but no longer.

"I was just leaving," she said. "Get well, Adam."

CHAPTER 49

"I'm not saying you should resign," the chief said, resting his arms on his cluttered desktop. "But there's a danger in fueling this guy's killer-lust by keeping you visibly involved. He's made it personal."

"So I fade into the background and he simply goes away?" Rayna shook her head. "I doubt it's that simple."

"Rayna's right," Hank offered. "I don't see him stopping."

"Are you willing to risk another girl's life to find out?"

That was the dilemma. In a sense, their killer had already won. "Of course I don't want another girl to die," Rayna said. She'd been going in circles over this all morning. "But how do we know that he won't make it personal with whomever takes my place?"

"We don't." The lines in the chief's bulldog face grew more pronounced. "You're sure it's not this Romeo fellow?"

"Almost positive," Rayna said. Hank nodded agreement.

"Or Adam Peterson?"

"He was in the hospital when Terri Lowe was killed."

"But not when Caitlin and Karen were." Chief Stoval ran a hand over the bristle of his crew cut. "Maybe this latest murder is a copycat."

"Or Caitlin's murder was," Rayna noted. "There are differences in the way she died, and her body turned up in the river rather than the woods. I didn't get a stuffed animal when she disappeared, either, although I did when her body was found."

"Christ. In the ten years I've been chief here, we had one murder, and that was a domestic dispute. Now we've got three, with another one possible any minute. And maybe more than one killer." Stoval stood up and began pacing around his office. "We've put every available officer on duty, and the eyes and ears of the community are on alert. Yet I'm scared to death he's going to take another girl right under our noses."

"We all are," Rayna said.

The chief returned to his desk. "Hank, for the time being you're going to take the lead on this investigation. I want a press conference held today, as soon as possible, and I want you to conduct it. It's not so much what you say as the fact that it's you, not Rayna, who's in charge."

"What?" Hank squeaked. "I don't want—"

"I don't care what you want, that's the way it's going to be. You're the only two experienced detectives I've got."

Rayna swallowed. "You really want me off the case?"

"No, of course not." The chief brushed air impatiently. "But I want it to look that way. If we put the right spin on it, maybe our killer will be satisfied. It might at least buy us some time."

"It's not going to work," Hank said.

Rayna silently agreed. But the chief had spoken. She was glad the decision had been taken out of her hands.

Back at her desk, Rayna fumed for a few minutes, then turned to Hank. "I'm going to talk to Ty Cross and Rob Hardy again. If what Jordan says is true and Caitlin knew about Ty and Rob, she might conceivably have been killed to keep her from talking."

"Which doesn't help us at all with the other two murders."

"Probably not."

Hank groaned. "What am I going to do about the press conference? I don't want this role. We're a good team, Rayna, but I'm just the foot soldier."

"Don't sell yourself short. Besides, I'll help you set it up."

Rayna debated going by the school and trying to corner Ty privately, but in the end she opted to do it by the book. If he did admit to anything, she wanted it to be admissible in court. She called Mr. Cross at his office, endured a barrage of insults, but refused to back off. In the end, he agreed that she could come by the house about five.

Grace wasn't the only adult picking a child up from the school. A long stream of cars lined the street, waiting to pull into the oval. Parents were scared. The whole town was on edge.

"How was your day?" Grace asked Lucy as they pulled away from the campus.

She shrugged. "How was yours?"

"Okay." Grace wondered if Lucy could see through the lie.

"It's weird how life goes on, isn't it? Yesterday was Caitlin's funeral, today I'm at school like nothing's happened. But it doesn't feel the same."

"I know what you mean."

"It's worse for you. You're being very brave, Grace."

"It's not a question of bravery. There's no alternative. The world doesn't stop just because we want it to."

Lucy slouched down in her seat. "God, look at my nails. They're such a mess. I thought I'd broken the habit of chewing them."

"Mine need help, too. How about we go get a manicure?"

"Now?"

"Sure. Maybe a pedicure, also." A little pampering appealed to Grace. "Do you have time?"

Lucy brightened. "Of course."

The nail salon was one Grace hadn't been to before, but she knew they took drop-ins. And they had big, comfortable-looking spa chairs. She'd noticed them through the window whenever she went to the camera shop next door.

"Can I get a French manicure?" Lucy asked.

"Whatever you want."

Grace settled in to the massage chair while a slender Vietnamese woman went to work on her feet. For the first time in days, she felt herself begin to relax. Lucy smiled at her across the room where another manicurist was showing her an array of polishes. She had the expression of a little girl dressed up as a princess, thrilled with the whole experience.

Grace added the afternoon to her short list of things she had to be grateful for.

"We've agreed to cooperate," Mr. Cross said as he opened the front door to Rayna's knock, "because we're concerned about these murders. But I want it known that your continual questioning of my son borders on harassment. It has to stop."

"I hope this will be the last time," Rayna told him.

"Good."

She followed him to a rich-hued wood panel den off the living room, where Ty and his lawyer were already seated in leather armchairs. Mrs. Cross was nowhere to be seen.

"Hello, Ty," Rayna said. She took a seat on the upholstered bench at the foot of the floor-to-ceiling bookcase. Mr. Cross sank into the chair behind his desk.

The boy rubbed hands together. "I don't even know Terri Lowe."

"Actually I'm here about Caitlin. And your friend Rob Hardy." Ty wasn't stupid. He picked up on the emphasis. He shot a quick sideways glance toward his father. "What about them?"

"They weren't involved, were they? Romantically, I mean."

"No way. I told you that before." He didn't hesitate, even for a second.

"How can you be so sure?"

"Because Rob's—" Ty stopped short and cleared his throat. "I'm just sure."

"You and Rob are pretty good friends, right?"

"Our families are friends," Ty said. "So we've known each other since we were in diapers." He blushed. The phrase was undoubtedly one his parents had repeated so often, Ty echoed it without thinking. "But it's not like we're close friends or anything."

"Really?" Rayna shot him a knowing smile. From the look on his face she was sure he understood where the conversation was going. "Could Rob have been jealous of Caitlin? What I mean is, you two were friends, however you want to qualify it. Then suddenly Caitlin was getting all your attention. It makes sense he'd want to be rid of her."

"Rob's not like that."

"Maybe not. But yesterday someone told me that Caitlin was really upset by stuff Rob told her."

Ty shrugged, not quite as nonchalantly as Rayna imagined he'd intended.

"Stuff concerning what you and he had done," she added.

Mr. Cross was clearly losing patience. "What's this about? So what if Caitlin was upset?"

The color drained from Ty's face. "I need to go to the bathroom," he said suddenly, and bolted from the room.

Mr. Cross sighed loudly and turned to the lawyer. "Do you understand any of this? If she's worried about Rob, shouldn't she be talking to him?"

The lawyer spoke up, addressing Rayna. "I'm not going to allow a fishing expedition."

She almost laughed. If she'd had doubts about his experience as a criminal attorney, they'd just been confirmed. The line was right off the big screen, only it was usually the judge who said it.

Ty returned, looking green around the gills. The hair around his face was damp, like he'd splashed water on it. "I'd like to talk to the detective in private," he told his father.

"What? I didn't haul my attorney over here for no reason."

"Please, I know what I'm doing."

"No, you don't."

To Rayna, Ty said, "Let's take a walk."

"I forbid it," Mr. Cross said, rising to his feet.

"Trust me Dad, it's the only way."

The attorney looked uneasy, but neither of the men stopped Ty as he left. Rayna followed him.

He led the way down the long, cobblestone driveway. Once they were away from the house, he asked, "What did you hear about me and Rob?"

"That your relationship is more than a friendship."

Ty swallowed hard. He looked like he might be sick. "What do you mean?"

"That you and Rob are lovers."

Ty cringed but he didn't deny it. "Who told you that?"

"An Internet buddy of Caitlin's. Not anyone connected with the school or the town."

"It's not like it sounds. It just happened. I didn't mean for it to. We were just goofing around, you know? Rob made it into a big thing."

"For him, maybe it is."

"Yeah." Ty kicked a stone from the sidewalk into the street. "That's one of the things I liked about Caitlin. She was safe, not always pressuring me about sex. Then Rob told her about us and she went ballistic."

"Did she threaten to go public with it?"

"No. She was mortified, like somehow it reflected badly on her. She wouldn't have told anyone."

"Did Rob know that?"

"Hell, he didn't care if word got out. A lot of kids already suspect he's gay."

"And if I talk to Rob, he'll corroborate what you've told me?"

Ty didn't respond for a bit. "He'll say it was more than once."

"Was it?"

"Yes. I tried not to. My dad will kill me if he finds out. And the guys on the team . . ." He looked at Rayna. "You won't tell them, will you?"

"I don't see why I would, unless it has something to do with Caitlin's death."

"It doesn't."

"Except that it does give you a good motive for killing Caitlin."

"Never! She would never have said anything, and I would never hurt her."

"Then maybe Rob did. Out of jealousy or spite."

"No way. He couldn't have."

"So where were you the Friday evening Caitlin disappeared? Were you really running errands?" Rayna had a hunch she knew, but wanted to cover all the points.

"I was with Rob." Ty refused to look at Rayna, addressing his words to the pavement at his feet. "There's this place we go, a friend of Rob's. He lets us use it while he's at work."

"You and Rob should have gotten your stories straight from the start."

"We didn't have a chance. You questioned me the next day."

For once, Rayna thought, something she'd done right in this investigation.

Rayna was back at her desk, finishing up for the day before she headed home, when Grace called.

"It's about Lucy," Grace said, speaking rapidly. "Carl's daughter. I picked her up after school and dropped her off at her house." She paused and took a breath. "When Mimi got home, she wasn't there. I watched her go in, and Mimi said her backpack was there, but there was no note that she'd gone out."

She paused. "And . . ."

"And what?"

Another deep breath. "You asked about stuffed animals. Mimi found one propped in the middle of Lucy's bed. A little brown dog."

CHAPTER 50

Seated on Mimi's oversized floral print sofa, Grace experienced a horrifying sense of déjà vu. A few of the players were different, and it was Mimi's house rather than her own, but the living room was thick with the same feeling of helplessness and inexorable fear as the night Caitlin disappeared.

Now, as then, Rayna Godwin struggled to put together a time line on a missing girl. "You brought Lucy home from school, right Grace? And you saw her go into the house?"

"Yes. I watched to make sure she got in safely."

"After you got your nails done," Mimi said, looking daggers at Grace. "What was the purpose in that? Someone could have followed you from the salon. If you'd come straight here from school—"

"It was a treat for Lucy."

Rayna cleared her throat. "If we can—"

Mimi pointed at Grace. "Maybe if you'd done what you were supposed to and not taken her on some frivolous escapade, this wouldn't have happened."

"If you'd been home when Lucy arrived," Grace shot back, "it would have made a difference."

"You know damn well why I couldn't be home." Mimi crossed her arms over her chest. "First you try to destroy my son, and now you're responsible for my daughter being missing. Just get out of my house. Out of my life!"

Carl shot to his feet. "Mimi, please. Stop this nonsense. This is not Grace's fault. She was trying to be helpful."

"She went to see Adam today, too. Did you know that? Grace snuck into the hospital to harass him. Your wife is a vindictive and crazed woman."

Grace rose from her seat while Carl looked helplessly between the two women. If Mimi hadn't plummeted from the height of rage to the depths of grief-stricken hysteria in the blink of an eye, Grace would have walked out. But Mimi's uncontrollable sobbing and the look of desperation in her eyes were a painful reminder of the reason they were all there.

Grace took her seat again and Carl patted Mimi on the shoulder.

"I wasn't there to harass Adam," Grace said quietly to Carl.

Detective Godwin said, "If we can focus on Lucy for the moment. What time did you drop her off, Grace?"

"About four-thirty."

"And Mimi, you arrived home when?"

She blew her nose on a tissue Carl handed her. "Six-thirty. Maybe quarter to seven."

Rayna's partner appeared at the door. "No forced locks or windows," he said. "And no footprints in the soil at the perimeter of the house."

"Who else has a key to your house?" Rayna asked Mimi.

"No one. Just the kids and the cleaning lady. She's been with me for years."

The questions went on. Cell phone records, computer usage, an inspection of Lucy's room. Grace was no longer part of the discussion. Her role as the last person to see Lucy had been covered. The emphasis was elsewhere now.

Grace wondered if Carl would be open to sympathy and comfort from her, or if he'd push her away. And Lucy. Poor, lost little Lucy. Dear God, please let her be safe. Grace recalled the pleasure on Lucy's face at the nail salon. Whatever Mimi felt about the frivolity of it, Lucy had been delighted.

"Feel free to call me any time," Rayna was saying to Carl and Mimi. She turned to her partner. "We have everything we need?"

He nodded.

"We'll be in touch the minute we know anything." The two detectives let themselves out.

"I need to call my sister," Mimi said, and headed for the phone.

"I'm going to stay here a bit," Carl said to Grace. "Why don't you take the car and I'll drive Adam's car home later."

She moved to hug Carl, but he turned away. It felt like a slap in the face.

"Doesn't the idiot follow the news?" Rayna complained to Hank, once they were in the car.

"What idiot?"

"Our killer. He wanted me gone. You held a press conference and said I was gone. Then the creep takes another girl anyway, assuming he took Lucy." Rayna wasn't sure why she expected a psychopath to play fairly, but the fact he'd gone back on his word angered her.

"Maybe he doesn't believe everything he hears," Hank said.

Rayna banged her head against the passenger seat headrest. "I don't understand what's happening. I don't understand where I fit in and what I can do about it."

"You're doing all you can."

"But it's not enough."

"Hang in there, Rayna."

"Are you channeling the poster in the break room now?" Tacked to the wall over the coffee maker, it showed a very spooked kitten clinging desperately to a precarious looking limb.

"It's good advice."

Back at her desk, Rayna shuffled through message slips then checked her email. Suddenly she sucked in a breath.

"It's from him," she said, before she even clicked on the text of the message.

Hank slid in behind her and read over her shoulder as she opened the email.

Resign means resign, Rayna. A sham isn't good enough. You can't have it both ways.

"Damn him!" Rayna propped her head in her hands. "I'm

going to do it for real. I'll tell the chief in the morning." She sat up. "No. I'm going to call him right now."

"You can't do that!" Hank sounded panicked. "I need you, Rayna. I can't run this investigation alone. Lucy Peterson is missing. We have to find her."

"Once I'm gone, maybe he'll stop."

"But what about Lucy? If you resign we might never get him. He'll win."

"What choice do we have?"

"At least think about it overnight."

"No." She picked up the phone and dialed the chief at home. He'd be waiting for a report on the new missing girl anyway. She gave him a summary of what had happened, and what they'd found, which amounted to nothing.

"Neighbors didn't see anything," she told him. "No forced entry that we can find. The only clue is the toy stuffed dog that was left in the middle of her bed."

"And the mother is sure it's not her daughter's?"

"Absolutely." Rayna took a breath. "There's something else. I'm turning in my resignation effective immediately."

"I can't let you do that, Rayna."

"You can't stop me. Say it's stress. Say I'm in rehab. Say whatever you'd like, but make it clear that I'm gone from the department. For real."

"I don't like this."

"I don't particularly like it, either."

Stoval sighed. "Is Hank there? Let me talk to him."

Rayna heard only Hank's end of their conversation, but she gathered that Fritz would be elevated to acting detective and that the chief would call in county sheriff investigators to help.

She stopped listening, slipped out the door, and drove home.

And cried.

CHAPTER 51

Rayna awoke the next morning with the dull, headachy feeling of a hangover. She'd only had two glasses of wine, but she'd cried hard and long into the night. Tears, like too much alcohol, might make you feel better in the short run, but they caught up with you the next morning. She didn't even want to think what her face must look like.

She rolled onto her back and stared at the ceiling. The bastard had beaten her. He'd succeeded in driving her from a job she loved. A job that was part and parcel of who she was. Without it, she had nothing left. Everyone and everything she cared about had been taken from her.

Outside, the wind whistled, rattling the doors. The garden gate flapped on its squeaky hinges. A good day to remain in bed. Something Rayna was now free to do. But already her mind began to race. She couldn't stay in bed. It was hard enough to stay away from her job.

Clean teeth and a hot shower went a long way toward restoring equilibrium, and a dab of foundation around the eyes did much to conceal their puffiness. She slipped into jeans and an old green sweater. Over coffee, she perused the paper while simultaneously checking the morning newscasts on TV.

True to his word, Chief Stoval had wasted little time announcing her resignation. He didn't offer an explanation, which they'd agreed was the best approach, since there was no satisfactory way to account for her leaving. The lack of a reasonable motive was bound to fuel speculation. Would she ever live it down, or would she be remembered as an overwrought woman who couldn't take the pressure?

It wouldn't be long before rumors connected her quitting

with emotional instability from Kimberly's murder.

Maybe Seth Robbins was already on it. His column in today's paper had focused on the discovery of Terri Lowe's body. His tone was more subdued and made no reference to police incompetence, but Robbins had managed to highlight his own role in receiving a message from the killer, then alerting authorities to the location of the body. Now that Rayna had left the department, maybe he'd take credit for that as well.

She turned off the TV, took a small piece of cheese in to the den to feed to Anastasia, and wondered how she would ever fill her day. There were very few people in town she knew. Very few people she was close to at all anymore. Maybe it was time to move, to start over yet again. She'd find something to do that didn't involve police work. A job where her incompetence wouldn't have such dire consequences. She couldn't imagine what that would be. She couldn't even type, for God's sake. But there had to be something she could do.

She filled Anastasia's water bottle with fresh water and then walked to the phone. She needed to tell Cody what she'd done before he picked up some fragment of the truth from others. Well, maybe she didn't really need to tell him. She supposed now that she was off the case, there was no need to ever speak to him again.

But she wanted to talk to him.

Cody answered on the second ring, which surprised her. She'd been expecting to get voicemail.

"Another girl is missing," she told him. "Adam Peterson's sister."

"Jesus. When did this happen?"

"Yesterday. And last night I turned in my resignation. It's the only way to put a stop to these murders. For whatever reason, I'm a catalyst for the killer." She told him about the note Robbins had received from the killer.

"Oh, Rayna. Sweetheart. This isn't right."

Sweetheart. The familiar endearment brought a lump to her throat. Unbidden, warm memories of their time together filled her head. Cody's naked body lying next to hers, the heat of his breath on her neck, the soft, teasing touch of his hands on her skin. God, was there nothing but loss in her life?

"Rayna? Are you still there?"

"Sorry. I guess I'm still working this through. I know it's what I needed to do, but that doesn't make it easy."

"God, no. I'm not even convinced you needed to do it."

"I couldn't live with myself if another girl disappeared because I was being pigheaded. Stoval has called in the county sheriff investigators. He may even contact the FBI again. I just hope they catch the guy."

There were voices in the background on Cody's end. "I hate to cut you off, Rayna, but I've got to go. We're in the middle of something here. I'll call you as soon as I can."

"No need. I just didn't want you hearing rumors."

"Take care of yourself, Rayna. You're a remarkable woman. The most remarkable woman I've ever met. I know you'll be okay. It may take time, but you'll figure it out."

"Thanks, Cody." Remarkable woman? Hardly. But the fact that he'd said so might have made the day seem less bleak, if only it hadn't sounded so much like a final goodbye.

Grace called almost as soon as Rayna was off the phone with Cody.

"Is it true?" she asked. Her voice registered disbelief, and something akin to betrayal. "Did you really resign?"

"Yes."

"Why?" Part question, part accusation.

Rayna hesitated. The fewer people who knew the real story, the better. "It's personal."

"How could you do that? Lucy's missing and we're in the midst of a crime wave. You can't just walk away."

"There's an entire department working on this, Grace."

"But why now? I mean, I understand it must be hard for you. Especially after what happened with your own daughter, but—"

"I can't talk about it," Rayna interrupted.

Grace seemed taken aback by Rayna's abrupt tone. "I'm sorry. I didn't mean to pry."

"No. It's not that." Rayna hesitated again. While Grace

wasn't really a friend, Rayna felt a kinship with her that she hadn't experienced with many other women in town.

"When this is all over," Rayna offered, "I'll be happy to explain. I just can't right now."

"I guess I don't understand."

"I'm sorry, Grace. How is Carl doing?"

"I'm not sure. I haven't seen much of him. He stayed with Mimi last night."

A more apt question, Rayna realized, might have been how Grace was holding up. She sounded terrible. "I imagine this is terribly difficult for you," Rayna said.

"I'm not worried about anything developing between Carl and Mimi, if that's what you mean, but I worry about our marriage. The fault lines are so deep, I doubt they can ever be repaired."

"Humans are amazingly resilient."

"But not infinitely so." Grace took a breath. "Well, I'll let you go. Thanks for being there, about Caitlin I mean."

She hung up before Rayna could respond.

By late afternoon Rayna was bored out of her mind. What the hell did people do with their days if they didn't work? She'd cleaned out her desk, which needed it badly, and the kitchen pantry, which didn't. She'd tried losing herself in a book, only to put it down again after two chapters. Probably twenty times during the day she'd reached for the phone to call Hank, to check in, only to pull back. What went on in the Paradise Falls Police Department wasn't any longer her concern.

She had tuned in to the radio news at the top of every hour. She imagined most residents of the town were doing the same thing. They were collectively holding their breath, waiting for the latest development.

None was forthcoming. Lucy was missing. Most likely dead. Dear God, four girls murdered on her watch. A terrible sadness gripped her heart. She wondered if she'd ever feel whole again.

The doorbell rang, startling her from the depths of her gloom. She opened the door to Hank's buddy Earl, wearing his trademark lumberman's jacket and blue knit cap.

"I hope I'm not disturbing you," he said.

Rayna sincerely hoped this wasn't a social call. Some misguided suggestion on Hank's part to keep her company. "What can I do for you?"

Earl seemed hesitant. "I'm kinda' worried about Hank."

That was the last thing she expected. "Worried, why?" She stepped back, inviting Earl in.

"I'd rather show you. It won't take long."

Rayna's pulse kicked into overdrive. "Is Hank hurt? In danger?"

"No, not exactly." Earl shoved his hands into his pockets and looked down at his feet, but remained outside on the porch. "I keep thinking he might have gotten himself into something. He's been acting kind of strange lately. Thing is, I don't want to cause him trouble if it's not what I think."

The man was exasperatingly obtuse. "Okay, let me get my jacket."

A steady drizzle was falling as Rayna made her way to Earl's battered and scratched old pickup. The engine coughed when he started it, and she could tell by the way they bounced along the road that the shocks were worn. She gripped the door's armrest to hold herself steady.

He turned left at the end of her street, heading away from town. "Where are we going?" Rayna asked.

"Not far. I'll explain after I show you what I found." He glanced in her direction. "So you actually resigned?"

"Right." Rayna wasn't interested in small talk.

"I don't think Hank is very happy about that."

"He's a good detective. He'll do fine."

"I'm sure he will. Unless . . . well, that's what I want you to see."

Earl turned onto a narrow country road, then pulled up in front of an old barn. He got out of the truck. "Follow me."

Rayna pulled out her cell phone. "Maybe I should let someone know—"

"I don't think so." Earl turned and grabbed the phone from her hand. Then he yanked her arm roughly behind her back.

"What the hell are you doing?"

"Shut up, Rayna. Do you want to see what I've got or not?"

His face had hardened and his eyes were icy. He twisted her arm harder and shoved her into the barn. The interior was dim, lit only by slivers of gray daylight that broke through gaps in the roof and siding. It took a moment for her eyes to adjust.

In one far corner she was able to make out what looked like a human form sprawled on the debris-laden floor.

"Guess who?" Earl wrenched Rayna's other arm behind her back and marched her closer.

Lucy! Rayna's heart was in her throat. "Is she hurt?" Rayna strained to see.

Earl spun Rayna around, struck her hard across the face, and sent her reeling to the ground. He pulled a knife from the sheath on his belt.

Pain shot through her right shoulder. She cried out and tried to move, but her leg was twisted under her and she couldn't straighten it.

She spit dirt and blood from her mouth. "What's this about?"

"You really can't figure it out?"

Sure she could figure it out. His concern about Hank had been a ruse. Earl was their killer. Her heart thundered, but she had to stay calm.

"Let's talk about this," she said.

"There's nothing to talk about. You needed to learn."

Lucy's leg twitched. Not a lot, but enough to tell Rayna that she was alive. "Learn what?" Rayna asked.

"A big lesson."

"I needed to learn a lesson?" Rayna struggled to understand.

"I'm hurt you don't remember me, detective. You've forgotten all about me while I've spent every day for the past five years remembering you."

She'd thought he looked familiar when Hank first introduced him, but Rayna still couldn't place him.

"You were just a regular cop then. You've done well for yourself in the interval."

"San Jose?" she asked.

"I'll give you a hint. And you'd better get it, or I'm carving up Lucy over there."

Think. She had to think. San Jose was a lifetime ago.

"Bethany Keeler," he said. "Does that name ring a bell?"

Bethany. The young girl who'd been killed by her mother's boyfriend a few months before Kimberly was killed.

Oh, God. It couldn't be, but it was. How could she have been so blind? "You're Bethany's father," Rayna said softly.

The man she'd helped get a restraining order against and later arrested on kidnapping charges.

"And to think I was worried you might recognize me that day at lunch. Of course, I've changed. Prison will do that to you. And I was careful, growing a beard and all. At least you remember my daughter."

"Of course I do." Hadn't she told Grace that story last week?

"And do you remember what happened to her? She was murdered! My daughter was murdered because of you." Earl kicked her in the ribs, and when Rayna cried out and curled in pain, he kicked her again in the head. "It's all your fault. If you hadn't helped my wife take Bethany from me, she'd be alive."

Rayna had trouble breathing and she couldn't open her left eye. Her lip was split. She struggled to lift her head. "You were hardly a model father. That's why your contact with her was cut off."

"She was mine! That's all that matters."

Keep him talking, Rayna reminded herself. Don't provoke him. She wiped the blood from her mouth. "Why go after innocent girls now?"

His lips pulled tight into a menacing smile. "As I told you, I'm having fun. At first, it was just going to be Kimberly. An eye for an eye, a daughter for a daughter."

Dear God, no. Rayna felt the bile rise up in her throat. "You killed my daughter?"

"It only seemed fair since you killed mine."

Rayna thought she might be sick. All these years she'd wanted to confront Kimberly's killer, and now she lay broken and bleeding at his feet.

"Thing is," Earl continued, "I discovered I enjoyed it. It's an amazing high being the instrument of that moment when life passes to death. The ultimate power."

Rayna thought of her precious daughter lying in the dirt, scared and bleeding, and Earl drunk with his own depravity. She gagged.

He smiled again. "Trouble was, your daughter's death didn't destroy you the way I thought it would. You moved on and made a life for yourself. A promotion, no less."

A life for herself? Hardly. And now she was going to die and he'd get away with it again.

"You needed to be brought down. You needed to see what a mess you make of things. What an incompetent, interfering bitch you are."

The words were like a knife in her gut. Four dead girls. Her fault. Rayna struggled to put the images out of her head. "You're killing random girls just to get at me?"

"What's the matter, detective? You haven't figured it out yet? Your observational skills are deficient. Except for Lucy here, my victims were the same age Kimberly would have been, if I'd spared her. The same fair coloring, blue eyes and straight blond hair. I'm surprised you didn't see a resemblance to your daughter."

In a way she had, but Rayna's focus had been elsewhere. "Caitlin wasn't blond," she said, tasting the blood from her torn lip.

"I'm afraid I can't claim Caitlin for my own. It worked out well, though. I owe someone a word of thanks. And now I have Lucy, Caitlin's stepsister. It's a nice symmetry, no?"

With her one good eye, Rayna glanced toward Lucy, still motionless on the dirty floor.

"You're both going to die, Rayna. Maybe people will wonder if you were in on the killings. Demented mom, gone crazy after the loss of her own daughter. Who knows how the press will play it? I'm sure there will be questions."

"Hank will figure it out."

"I doubt it. No offense, but Hank's not the brightest bulb in the pack. Good for what I needed him for, but not much else."

Earl was wrong, Rayna thought. Hank was a very good cop. But the knowledge brought her little comfort.

"To tell the truth," Earl said in disgust, "he can't even bowl worth a damn." The barn creaked and Earl looked quickly over his shoulder, then back to Rayna. "I have to tell you this has been fun for me. Did you enjoy the stuffed animals? I thought they were a nice touch. Kimberly loved the stupid things, didn't she?"

"How would you know?"

"Careful observation. Something you should have been better at."

"There was no animal when Caitlin disappeared."

"At the time, it never occurred to me that Caitlin's disappearance would turn out as it did. Ah, well, as I said, I had a lot of fun. I'd have liked to keep it up a bit longer. I had hoped you wouldn't back down quite so easily."

If Earl looked away again, maybe she could grab his knife. Not likely. He was a big man who could overpower her under the best of circumstances. With one eye swollen shut and God knew how many bruises and broken bones, there wasn't a chance in hell she'd succeed. But she had to do something.

He pulled a roll of twine from his jacket pocket and took a step toward her.

"You need to tie me up to kill me?"

"I thought maybe you'd hang yourself out of remorse after starting a fire. It's all set up. Take a look up there."

Rayna glanced up. A narrow platform, a sort of half loft, hugged one side of the barn about ten feet from the floor. A coarse rope noose hung from a thick rafter overhead. Her heart skipped several beats.

"Come on, get up."

Earl yanked her arm and Rayna cried out. The pain was quick and sharp.

"Move it!"

Somehow Rayna dragged herself to all fours and then, unsteadily, to her feet. Go for his eyes. Or his groin. Do something.

He nudged her toward the makeshift steps leading to the platform. At the bottom step she turned abruptly and aimed all ten fingers at his eyes.

He caught her wrists and slapped her across the face. When she fell, he dragged her, feet first, up the rough stairway. Each time she managed to curl her fingers around something solid, Earl yanked harder, and her grip gave way, scraping the skin on her hands.

How could she have let this happen? No wonder she couldn't protect the girls of Paradise Falls. She couldn't even take care of herself.

Once they'd reached the top, Earl hauled her to her feet, slipped the noose over her head, and pulled the scratchy rope tight around her neck. Already Rayna had trouble breathing.

Earl tied her hands behind her with twine, then grabbed a red metal can and poured gasoline at her feet. He went back down the steps and sloshed more gasoline around the barn's perimeter.

"It's your choice, Rayna. You can hang yourself and get it over with quickly, or die by fire. See, I've left you some final control. But then, I'm a thoughtful guy."

He lit a match, watched it burn for a few seconds, then dropped it onto a gasoline-soaked pile of debris. Flames leapt to life.

"Happy hereafter," Earl said as he turned to leave. "Say hi to Bethany for me."

The fire quickly snaked along the floor, fueled by twigs and debris. Rayna felt light-headed, and concentrated on keeping her balance. Any misstep and she'd plummet from the narrow loft, yanking the noose tight around her neck. When the fire got close enough, she might welcome the quick death of hanging, but for the moment she was paralyzed by fear.

If only she could free her hands. She twisted and tugged them until the twine cut into her flesh, but she couldn't break free. Then she saw an old rusty nail jutting out of the wall behind her.

Could she get to it without falling? Inch by inch, she carefully backed toward the nail. When she reached the wall, she felt blindly for the nail and began to frantically saw against it with her wrists. The nail scraped her skin as often as it caught the twine. Smoke filled her lungs and stung her eyes. Dear God, she had to hurry.

Finally, the twine snapped and her hands were free. Rayna tugged frantically at the noose, pulling it from her neck, and then felt her way unsteadily down the makeshift stairs.

Lucy. She had to find Lucy.

Fire danced along the floor. Smoke clouded the air. Pain from her head and ribs screamed at her. Fumbling, Rayna felt her way to Lucy. She tried to rouse her, but quickly gave up on the idea. There wasn't time. She'd have to drag Lucy. But Lucy was a dead weight, too heavy to manage in Rayna's present condition.

She heard the barn door rattle, and froze. Had Earl come back?

"Rayna? Rayna are you in there?" Seth Robbins pushed through the smoke toward her.

Was he working with Earl?

She picked up a nearby shovel. "Don't come near me, Seth!"

"The fire department's on its way, Rayna. Come on, you need to get out now."

Not a friend of Earl's after all? She made a split-second decision to trust him.

"Lucy's in here, too. She's tied up and drugged. Help me get her out."

Together, they dragged Lucy into the clear air. Collapsing onto a patch of dead leaves, Rayna heard sirens. As the fire engines roared down the dirt road, the barn roof caved in.

CHAPTER 52

The doctors insisted on keeping both Lucy and Rayna in the hospital overnight. Lucy was out of it enough that she didn't protest, but Rayna did. Yes, she felt like shit and yes, her body felt as though it had been through a meat grinder, but she wanted to be home.

She lost the battle and steamed silently while the nurse fiddled with an IV and plumped the pillow under her head.

By the time Hank showed up several hours later, she was glad she'd stayed, if only because the IV pain medication was much more effective than anything she could have taken on her own. Elephants danced in her head and the pain had been banished to some vague distant planet.

"How are you feeling?" Hank asked.

"To tell you the truth, I'm floating. Are you sure I didn't die?"

"Jesus, Rayna don't joke about that. Do you know how close you came? I feel responsible."

"That's silly. You didn't do anything wrong."

"Earl was my friend. Or I thought he was. I never had the slightest idea—"

"Of course not."

"He used me, Rayna. Used me for information about you, about our investigation. I feel like such a complete idiot."

Even in her fuzzy state, Rayna could tell how deeply Earl's betrayal shocked Hank. She promised herself she'd be more understanding of Hank's loneliness in the future.

"Have they caught him?" she asked.

"Not yet. That's why I'm posting a guard outside your door."

She started to protest, then realized she'd feel better knowing she had someone protecting her. She was certainly in no state to protect herself.

"Do you think he's telling the truth about having nothing to do with Caitlin's murder?"

"Yes, unfortunately. The night she disappeared we were at a bowling league dinner together. His alibi is airtight."

Rayna had suspected all along that Caitlin's murder was different from the others. "Adam?"

"That's something the two of us will have to figure out."

"The two of us?"

"The chief is reinstating you. He didn't process your resignation. Didn't even put it in the system. You'll come back, won't you?"

Would she? She wasn't sure. "Is Lucy doing okay?"

"She's going to be fine. Her mother and father are with her. One of them will stay the night."

At least she'd managed to save one girl. One out of four. Five, if you counted Kimberly. Not very good odds. And she hadn't done it alone. "What was Seth Robbins doing there?"

"From what I understand, he's been following you, hoping to get a big scoop."

"Well, he certainly got that." Rayna closed her eyes for a moment. This was one story she wouldn't begrudge him. "Earl killed Kimberly, my daughter. I told you that, didn't I?"

"Yes. I'm so sorry, Rayna. We'll get him. That's a promise."

"He knew she loved stuffed animals. He'd been watching her, following us. That's how he lured her to his car."

"Try to get some sleep."

Rayna closed her eyes again. She felt Hank brush a tear from her cheek, then leave the room.

It was the last thing she remembered until the next morning.

Grace sat at her kitchen table staring at the front page of the morning Tribune. Seth Robbins's column was at the top of page one, accompanied by photos of Rayna Goodwin, a craggy looking man, and last year's school portrait of Lucy. Carl had spent the night at the hospital, along with Mimi. He'd told Grace last night over the phone that Lucy had been heavily drugged but not otherwise harmed. She would recover, physically at any rate.

Grace had managed to patch together only bits and pieces of what had happened. Rayna Godwin had apparently found Lucy bound and drugged in a burning barn and managed to pull her to safety with the help of the columnist Seth Robbins. Grace didn't know why they were together. Robbins's column had been the stuff of adventure, not explanation.

According to Carl, Rayna had been abducted, although there was no mention of that in the news. A man Grace had never heard of, Eric Turloff, known locally by the alias Earl Tobias, was wanted in connection with Lucy's abduction and the recent murders. There was a warrant out for his arrest. She studied the newspaper photo. Grace was sure she'd never seen him. He'd tricked Lucy into opening the door to her house by pretending to be a repairman from the gas company. Grace wondered what trick he'd used on Caitlin.

She didn't understand why he'd done it. The newspaper said he was a violent man with a criminal past. Maybe that was all it took.

Just after noon, Carl's car pulled into the driveway. He looked haggard and exhausted. His clothes were rumpled, the circles under his eyes dark. Hesitantly, Grace reached out to embrace him. To her immense relief, he collapsed into her arms and hugged her tight.

"It's going to be okay," he told her. "Everything is going to be okay."

Grace wasn't sure if he was talking about Lucy or about the two of them.

"Is Lucy still in the hospital?"

"No. She's home with Mimi. She's shaken and frightened, of course, but I guess it's a blessing she was drugged. She remembers very little. By the time she came to, it was all over. We are so lucky Detective Godwin found her in time. If she hadn't—"

"She did. That's what's important. Go take a shower and I'll fix you some lunch."

Carl kissed her cheek. "It's good to be home."

Home. Grace felt heartened. Maybe there was hope for them yet.

She took some homemade chicken soup from the freezer, and while it heated, she made grilled cheese sandwiches. Comfort food. Food she knew Carl enjoyed.

Carl reappeared fifteen minutes later, eyes red from lack of sleep, but freshly shaved with clean clothes and hair still damp at the ends.

She put the sandwiches and bowls of soup on the table and they sat down.

"It feels wrong to be so happy that Lucy's safe," Carl said, "when we're still reeling from Caitlin's death. I'm not insensitive to that, Grace."

"I know. And I'm happy about Lucy. It would be too much to bear if we'd lost her, too. I just hope they find this guy soon."

"The police have roadblocks on all the major routes and his photo is in the papers and on the news. He can't get far."

"Do you think it would be all right if I called Lucy? I'd like to tell her how relieved I am that she's okay."

"You can go see her if you want," Carl said. "She was asking for you. Mimi said it would be okay."

"Thank you." The knot in Grace's chest relaxed and in its place she felt the bud of hope.

Grace waited until the next day before visiting anyone. First, she called Rayna at home and asked if she could stop by.

"I'd love it," Rayna said.

Grace took her soup and flowers, and was going to pick up the funny soft monkey she saw at the florists, before she remembered that stuffed animals had played a role in the recent murders. She decided on an oversized Peanuts card instead.

The detective's house was small, with a well-kept front yard and a cozy feel. Grace rang the bell.

"Oh, my God," she said when Rayna opened the door. The left half of the detective's face was raw and swollen.

Rayna put a hand to her bruised cheek. "It will take a while to heal."

"I had no idea. Oh, Rayna. Can I do anything for you?"

"Come on in. I'll be fine as soon as I stop hurting. Tea? Or coffee?"

"I can't stay. I'm on my way to see Lucy. But I wanted to thank you personally for all you did." Grace handed Rayna the flowers. "I brought you some soup also. I hope you like lentils."

"Love them. This is really nice. And totally unnecessary."

"Carl and I are both grateful to you."

"So you two are—"

"You were right about people being resilient," Grace told her with a smile.

They'd moved into Rayna's kitchen, which was a tidy, efficient space Grace found very appealing. She set the soup on the counter. "I thought you resigned."

"I did."

"And yet you still managed to track that awful man down and save Lucy. I can't tell you how grateful we are. How grateful I am that Caitlin's killer won't get away with it."

Grace had the distinct impression Rayna was about to say one thing but changed her mind. "I'm afraid I can't take credit for tracking him down, Grace. He came after me."

"Why?"

"Remember the story I told you about Bethany, the little girl whose father abducted her?"

"Yes, of course. Her mother's boyfriend killed the mother and girl. Who could forget a story like that?"

"Earl is Bethany's father. He blames me for her death." Rayna took a breath before continuing. "He killed Kimberly to get back at me."

"He killed your daughter?" Grace felt like she'd been punched in the chest.

"You know how devastating it is to lose a child, but to know that I was the reason she was murdered—"

"Oh, Rayna." Impulsively, Grace gave Rayna a hug. "How awful. I'm so sorry."

"Thank you."

"But he's also the Paradise Falls killer, right? That's what they said on the news."

"He killed Karen Holiday and Terri Lowe to taunt me."

"And Caitlin." Grace couldn't believe Rayna had forgotten Caitlin.

"Grace, he says he didn't kill Caitlin. We have outside corroboration that's true. He didn't do it."

Grace put a hand on the kitchen counter to steady herself. "What do you mean? How could it not be him? Are you saying you don't know who killed Caitlin?"

"I'm afraid so."

Grace felt as though she'd been struck in the gut. Adam. It must have been Adam, after all. Surely the police would pursue that. And then what?

She and Carl might have stretched resiliency to its outer limits.

CHAPTER 53

Mimi opened the door to Grace with mannered politeness, but she didn't smile.

"Thank you for letting me come," Grace said.

"I did it for Lucy. She wanted to see you." Mimi sounded both put-out and baffled that her daughter should have any need to see Grace.

"How's she doing?"

"As well as can be expected." Mimi stepped back to allow Grace to enter. "I'm going to run a few errands while you're here. Can you keep an eye on her?"

"Sure." Grace wondered if babysitting services were part of what convinced Mimi to allow Grace's visit.

"Don't let the press anywhere near her."

"I won't." Did Mimi think Grace had no common sense?

"I won't be long. Maybe half an hour or so."

Lucy was on the couch in the family room. She wore jeans and a sweatshirt, and she watched TV. Her face brightened when she saw Grace. She sat up and muted the sound.

"How are you feeling, honey?"

"Lucky. Stupid. Scared." Lucy's eyes filled with tears. "It was really, really awful. I shouldn't have let that man in but he said we had a gas leak and the whole house could blow up."

Grace sat next to Lucy, then leaned in to give her a hug. "Hindsight is a wonderful thing, but split-second decisions aren't always as neat."

Lucy held out her hands. "My nails got totally ruined."

"That's a small price to pay for being alive. As soon as you're up to it, we'll make a day of pampering ourselves. How does that sound?"

"Fantastic. Mom says I have to go back to school on Monday."

"Of course you do, if you're well enough."

Lucy twisted a strand of hair around her finger. "What do you think the kids will say about me?"

"I think you'll be the center of attention. A star. But you don't have to talk to them about it if you don't want to, Lucy. Don't let them pressure you."

"It's not just that. I'm still so scared."

"They'll catch that man soon. And you know what he looks like so you won't be fooled again. Besides, I doubt he'd come after you a second time."

Lucy wrapped her arms around herself, pulling the sleeves of her sweatshirt over her hands. "I'm scared about coming home to an empty house. I don't like being here by myself."

"Why don't you come to our house after school? I'm not ready to go back to work yet, so I'll be there."

"But I thought Dad was moving out to be with Adam."

"Adam will be in the"—Grace hesitated to use the term psychiatric hospital—"treatment center for a week or so. And I'd love to have your company, even if your dad isn't there. I'll drive you to his place or your mom's in the evening when they get home."

"If you don't mind—"

"Of course I don't mind. I'd like to have you there. The house seems awfully empty."

A news alert flashed on the TV screen.

"Turn it up," Grace said, but Lucy had already reached for the remote.

"We have breaking news out of Paradise Falls," a reporter announced. "Authorities have taken into custody the man wanted for questioning in connection with the recent murders of three teenage girls and the abduction of another."

Film footage showed a handcuffed man being led by officers to a police car.

Lucy was shaking. "That's him, Grace. That's him."

"Maybe we should turn this off."

"No. I want to see it."

Grace put her arm around Lucy and they watched in silence while the reporter delivered what turned out to be a cursory account of events leading up to the capture. Earl's truck had been spotted at a fast-food restaurant near the Idaho boarder. Local authorities, responding to a statewide alert of law enforcement personnel, had apprehended the suspect without incident.

"He can't hurt me now," Lucy declared.

"That's right. You're safe."

Lucy got up from the couch and turned off the TV. "You want some ice cream?"

"Sure." Grace followed Lucy into the kitchen.

"You must be glad they got him too, Grace. Does it help, knowing that the man who killed Caitlin was caught?"

Grace bit her lip. "If it really was him."

"Of course it was! They said so on the news."

"That doesn't make it so, Lucy. And it doesn't mean anything until he's convicted."

"But he will be, won't he?" Lucy collapsed into one of the kitchen chairs. "He can't murder three girls and get away with it."

"I'm not saying he's innocent, but Detective Goodwin told me he has an alibi for the night Caitlin disappeared."

"Alibi!" She spat the word out with disdain. "Like anyone's going to believe him."

"There are witnesses. Reliable witnesses."

"But it has to be him!" As she grew increasingly agitated, Lucy's face flushed and her feet bounced against the floor.

"Maybe it was," Grace said, trying to placate Lucy. "The police will sort it all out."

"Caitlin's backpack was right there in the Dumpster. He wanted people to see that she was just like Karen Holiday. He was like proud to be a serial killer or something."

"According to what Detective Godwin says, it wasn't the same Dumpster."

"Close enough. The other one was probably full. Or maybe there were people around."

"Could be." Grace was tempted to remind Lucy that Earl

couldn't have taken Caitlin if he was elsewhere at the time, which seemed to be the case. But the poor child was traumatized from her ordeal and desperate to believe that the only boogeyman out there was safely locked away. Grace would have liked to think that herself.

Eager to change the subject, she opened the freezer. "Which will it be? Toasted almond or chocolate chip?"

"Can I have some of both?"

"Sure."

Lucy got the bowls down from the cupboard. "Besides," she said, "Caitlin's wallet still had twenty-three dollars in it. There was money in Karen Holiday's wallet, too. I remember reading that in the paper and wondering why he hadn't taken the cash. Most bad guys would."

Although she could think of any number of reasons a killer might not take cash from his victim's wallet, Grace said, "Good point."

She took a very small bowl of toasted almond for herself, only eating to keep Lucy company, and sat down at the table opposite Lucy.

"Anyway, I'm glad it's over," Lucy said. "Thank you for coming to see me today."

"You don't have to thank me. I wanted to see you. I've been worried about you."

As she rinsed the bowls in the sink, her mind hit a pothole. How had Lucy known there was money in Caitlin's wallet? Twenty-three dollars, she'd said. The precise amount.

Had Grace mentioned it at some point? No, she was sure she hadn't. She'd forgotten all about that detail since it hardly seemed important.

She stacked the bowls and spoons in the dishwasher. A hollow, unsettled feeling swelled inside her. Had Adam told Lucy about killing Caitlin?

The sweet aftertaste of the ice cream mixed with the bile that rose in Grace's throat.

Lucy was still seated at the table, reading the newspaper comics. "Lucy, how did you know how much money was in Caitlin's wallet?" Grace asked.

Lucy looked as though she'd been stung by a bee. "It must have been in the news."

"No, it wasn't."

"Just a guess, then. I must have made it up."

"Twenty-three is an odd number to pull out of thin air."

"Maybe Caitlin told me. Yeah, I remember now. I wanted to borrow some money and she said she only had twenty-three dollars in her wallet."

A plausible explanation rendered unbelievable by its delivery.

"What aren't you telling me, Lucy?"

"What do you mean?"

"You were the last person to see Caitlin. Did you see her leave school with someone? Do you know what happened to her?"

Lucy pushed back from the table. "No."

"Were you with her? Was Adam? What happened?"

"Nothing. I don't know anything." The color had drained from Lucy's face. Her gaze darted around the room.

Grace moved closer. "Lucy, this is important. Tell me what you saw."

"Caitlin should never have taken that shortcut by the river! Everyone says it's dangerous."

"You saw her head toward the river? Why didn't you say something before?"

Lucy's hand flew to her mouth and she rushed from the table.

The obvious slammed against Grace and knocked the air from her lungs. The signs that had led her to believe Adam had harmed Caitlin pointed just as convincingly to Lucy.

Not the photos, maybe, but certainly the more damning evidence of the Garfield towels in the Dumpster and Caitlin's necklace hidden in Mimi's basement. Adam had sounded believable when he insisted to Grace that he had no idea how the necklace got there.

Was it possible that Grace had implicated the wrong one of Carl's children?

She caught up with Lucy at the door to the hallway and

blocked her way. "It was you, wasn't it? Not Adam, but you. What did you do to Caitlin?"

"I didn't mean it. I really didn't. It was an accident."

"Didn't mean what?" Grace shouted. "What was an accident?"

"I foll-followed her," Lucy sobbed. "I thought she might be meet-meeting Adam."

"Adam? Why would she be meeting Adam?"

"I don't know. He was, like, interested in her. And Caitlin teased him. I mean, like flirting. Not always but sometimes. I just wanted to see what was going on."

"Was she meeting Adam?"

"No. She was taking the shortcut home. But she saw me and we started arguing." Lucy's tears were accompanied by great gulping hiccups. "I didn't mean it. I just meant to push her a little. I was mad."

Time stood still and sped up all at once. Grace saw Caitlin and Lucy on the riverbank, the air wet with mist, the sky gray and darkening—a tableau larger than life, looming like a giant neon billboard in her brain. Caitlin on solid ground. Caitlin plunging into the raging river far below.

"Oh, God. You pushed her into the river!"

"I didn't mean to. I told you. It was an accident."

In her rage, Grace shoved Lucy. Not hard, but Lucy staggered, caught a heel on the corner molding, and collapsed into the stove. The sugar bowl crashed to the floor and shattered.

"Why didn't you go for help?"

"It wouldn't have made any difference."

"You don't know that! You might have saved her life."

Lucy's mouth trembled as she cowered near the stove.

"You let me worry about her. I didn't know what had happened. How could you do such a thing? How could you!"

Grace fought waves of nausea as she reached for the kitchen phone.

"What are you doing?" Lucy screamed.

"Calling the police."

"No one's going to believe you. Not now. First you go

after Adam, and now me. They'll think you're a nut case. Like my mom says, a bitter, spiteful, dried-up old prune."

Grace punched the phone keys.

"It was an accident but I was happy to see her go," Lucy wailed. "I hated her. Miss perfect. She never had to move from house to house. And she lived with my dad all the time. I only got three fucking days a week! It was so unfair!"

Lucy collapsed onto the floor. She pounded her fists and sobbed.

Grace made no move to comfort her.

CHAPTER 54

Grace stopped inside the entrance to Carl's study. If he'd heard her come in, he didn't acknowledge it. The room was dark but the light from the hallway cast a shaft of illumination that fell on Carl's back. Seated at his desk, he faced away from her, his head in his hands, his elbows resting on the desktop. An open bottle of whisky sat next to an almost empty glass.

"Carl?" Grace moved closer and laid a hand on his shoulder. She hadn't heard him crying but could now feel sobs shake his body.

Carl had been holed up in the tiny room for hours. Grace understood his desire to be left alone. She felt the same way. After all, what was there either one of them could say? About to retreat, she withdrew her hand.

"How can this be happening?" Carl's voice was strained, not much more than a whisper. "How could everything go so wrong?"

Because Lucy is a monster, Grace thought. But even as she silently gave voice to the accusation, she knew it wasn't entirely true.

"I was so happy," Carl said, his voice shaky. "Genuinely happy, sitting on top of the world. When we were at dinner that night at the inn, before Jake's call about Caitlin, I remember looking at you and thinking 'How can I be so lucky?' I had three great kids and a wife who loved me as much as I loved her. A wife who saw the best in me and made me want to be even better."

"I felt the same way."

Carl raised his head and turned so that he half faced her.

In the shadows his eyes and cheeks looked hollow.

"When Caitlin disappeared, I was frantic."

"I know you were." Grace remembered how grateful she'd been for Carl's support.

"There was nothing I could do to make it better. I felt like I'd reached bottom."

Grace's heart ached for Carl. She couldn't imagine the anguish he was feeling. But she couldn't forgive him either. Although what she needed to forgive him for, she couldn't say.

Carl shuddered. "And now it hurts so much. All of it. Lucy is my daughter. No matter what. I'm appalled by what she did, but at the same time I can't help loving her. I'm scared for her, Grace. A part of me still wants to protect her."

"Of course." Grace thought the romantic poets had it wrong. It was parental love that was complex and painful. That was the stuff of real tragedy.

"Do you hate me, Grace?"

"I don't know what I feel," she said honestly. There were so many conflicting emotions inside her they swirled into a muddy despair.

"I haven't stopped loving you."

"I still love you, too."

"But it's not enough, is it?"

"Not right now, no." And she couldn't imagine that it ever would be, for either of them.

Carl pulled himself to his feet. "Can I hold you for a moment?"

Grace opened her arms for a quick, awkward hug. But once locked in the familiar warmth of Carl's embrace, she had trouble pulling away.

He released her with a weighty sigh that broke into a sob. "How do I go on after this? How?" He covered his face with his hands.

Grace touched his arm gently, then backed out of the room and closed the door, leaving Carl once again in the dark of his own hell.

CHAPTER 55

Adam picked up a dart and sent it flying toward the target on the wall. It hit a fraction to the left of the bull's-eye.

"You're a natural," Dr. Passant said with a hearty laugh. "Tough competition for an old man like me." He took aim and his own dart landed not much farther from center than Adam's.

Dr. Passant, or Hugh, as some of his other patients called him, reminded Adam of a trimmed down Santa Claus. He had a white beard and cherry red cheeks, and although Adam had never heard him actually utter the words "ho-ho-ho," it sounded like something the doctor might say. Adam liked Dr. Passant. In fact, he liked living in this loony bin. He was in no hurry to return to the outside world. Especially now, when things had gone from bad to worse.

"How was your visit with your dad?" Dr. Passant asked.

"Okay."

His father had come twice in the last few days. The first time to tell him about Lucy. And again this morning, just to visit, as he put it. But looking at him, Adam decided his father needed psychiatric help more than he did. Adam was familiar with the phrase "shell of his former self," but he'd never really understood what it meant until he'd seen his dad.

"Did you talk to him about how hurt you were that he doubted you?"

"He's got bigger worries than me right now." It stung that his dad had suspected him of harming Caitlin, but he felt sorry for him, too. It was a funny thing, feeling bad for your father.

"Don't diminish yourself, Adam. You are as important as anyone else."

"Yeah, whatever."

There was a stretch of silence while Dr. Passant twirled a dart between his fingers. Finally he asked, "What are you feeling about your sister? About what happened?"

Without aiming, Adam threw another dart, barely making the outer edges of the target. "I don't know."

"Talking about it will help, Adam."

"What's to talk about? I haven't even spoken to her."

"What would you ask her if you could?"

Why she'd done it. And if it was an accident, why hadn't she tried to get help? Why hadn't she told anyone what had happened? His dad said it was because Lucy was jealous of Caitlin and that sometimes, even if you liked a person, you wanted to hurt them. Adam couldn't help thinking his dad cut Lucy a lot more slack than he had his own son. That hurt. And Lucy had been willing to let Adam take the blame. That hurt even more. No one had stood behind him. Not his parents. Not Lucy. Certainly not Grace. No one really cared about him except Caitlin.

Dr. Passant hadn't taken his turn yet. He was looking at Adam. "You didn't answer me. What would you like to say to her?"

"Does it matter? Everything's changed. Nothing's going to put Humpty Dumpty back together again."

"That's true. But you have a long life ahead of you. You can be part of that scrambled mess or you can decide to be whole."

"Like I really have a choice!"

"You want to live, don't you? To live a life that's uniquely yours."

Adam had three darts remaining. He tossed them all at once, as a handful. They bounced off the wall and landed on the floor.

"I hate Lucy," he said. "How about that? I fucking hate her. She ruined my life."

"I can see how you might feel that way."

"Can we talk about this later?"

Adam didn't wait for an answer. He strode out of the

doctor's homey office and into the sterile common room of the facility. A large window along one wall looked out onto the grounds. Adam loved looking out, even though the window was embedded with wire mesh. It wouldn't do to have an inmate jump, after all. Not that he thought about jumping. Death ended the pain but it ended everything else, too. He saw that now. He simply liked watching the world. It was more comfortable than living in it.

He did hate Lucy, but felt sad for her too. Mostly, though, he missed Caitlin. Not the Caitlin of his fantasies, but the funny, sweet girl who was his stepsister and closest friend. He should never have taken those photos of her. That had been totally stupid, even though Caitlin hadn't seemed to mind when she found out.

"You think I'm pretty?" she'd asked him, sounding incredulous.

"Yes." She was so obviously pretty, he'd thought at first that she was playing him for a fool. But the way her eyes lit up made him realize that wasn't the case.

"Sexy?"

He'd blushed. "Yeah, of course."

And then she'd started crying. Adam had been afraid he'd said the wrong thing. "But smart, too," he'd hastened to add. "And nice."

"But sexy? You weren't just saying? You meant it?"

"Good sexy, not in a bad way."

"So if we weren't related, you could see yourself maybe being attracted to me?"

Adam had felt his blush deepen. "Yeah. Depending."

She'd leaned forward and kissed him softly on the lips. "You're the best brother, ever," she said. "The only person who sees me."

They'd gone into the yard where they sat crossed legged on the grass, talking about everything and nothing. She told him about Fern, her best friend who'd moved way, about the Divas and how Caitlin didn't really fit in. He told her he knew about not fitting in, and they'd laughed.

Two days later she was dead.

Adam wondered what would have happened between them if she'd lived.

CHAPTER 56

The doorbell rang as Rayna was busy cleaning Anastasia's cage. She couldn't imagine who it could be and wasn't sure she wanted to find out. So far, she'd managed to dodge the press, except for Seth Robbins—she figured she owed him a debt of gratitude. And the only time she'd ventured outside the house, the condition of her face had drawn so many stares she was determined to avoid being seen in public for a while longer.

The doorbell rang a second time, and then a third. Her visitor gave no indication of leaving. Annoyed, Rayna finally answered it, letting in a blast of damp air.

"I knew you had to be home," Cody said with a grin. "Your car's in the driveway."

Rayna's heart lifted at the sight of him, but she'd be damned if she'd fly into his arms.

"Don't you ever call first?" She stepped back to let him in so she could close the door again before all the heat escaped.

"I take it you're alone?" He stood with his hands behind his back.

"And why do you assume that?"

"Because I want that to be the case?" Offering a quirky smile, he handed her a box of See's candy and a bottle of chilled champagne. "All dark," he said. "The chocolates, that is. Your favorite."

"Thank you." She accepted the gifts and returned the smile.

"How are you?"

"I've been worse."

"I don't see how." Cody touched her chin and gingerly

lifted her face to the light. "Ouch, Rayna. That must hurt like hell."

His touch sent a tingle down her spine.

"You had quite an experience from what I hear."

"At least it had a happy ending," she said.

"But it was damned close. When I think what might have happened . . ." Cody held her gaze until she looked away. "You don't have to always appear tough, Rayna."

"I don't." She blinked back tears. "I'm not. Not nearly as tough as I thought I was."

He traced a finger along her jaw. "I didn't mean that. You're strong and gutsy, but you're human too. You've been through a real ordeal. You're lucky to be alive."

"Anyway, it's over," Rayna said, taking a deep breath.

Cody looked at her for a moment longer, then took off his jacket and draped it over the back of a chair. "Shall we open the champagne?"

"Are we celebrating something?"

"You being alive. Can't think of anything more important than that."

He followed her into the kitchen and unwrapped the foil from around the neck of the bottle while Rayna found wine glasses. Then he popped the cork and the champagne frothed to the rims before settling back down.

"Done like an expert," she told him, endeavoring to move the conversation to lighter, safer ground.

He raised his glass toward her. "To the successful conclusion of your investigation and the capture of an evil killer."

The first taste of champagne was always the best, Rayna thought. She loved the cool, slightly sweet taste and the tingle that followed so quickly and smoothly in the rest of her body. "Let's go into the living room. There's a fire set there."

"You sure you weren't expecting company?"

"I always have one set. That way I can have a fire whenever I feel like it."

He grinned at her. "That's my girl. Always thinking ahead."

She was tempted to point out that it had been quite a while since she'd been his girl, if she ever had, but she liked the sound of it. My girl.

While Cody took a match to the fire, Rayna lit the candles strategically placed around the room. She loved the ambience of a fire and candlelight, though she rarely indulged.

They settled on opposite ends of the sofa and Rayna curled her feet under her so that she was turned toward Cody.

"It might have been my investigation," she said after a moment, "but I didn't have much to do with its successful conclusion."

"You did. You saved an innocent girl from impending death at the hands of a psychopath."

"She's not innocent."

"What do you mean?"

"You haven't heard the latest?"

"I've heard nothing since the arrest yesterday afternoon." He took a long sip of his drink. "It's been an intense twenty-four hours. We finally broke a gambling and drug trafficking ring, the focus of our operation."

"Congratulations." Rayna raised her glass in another toast. "What haven't I heard?"

"The man we caught killed Karen Holiday and Terri Lowe"—and Kimberly, Rayna added silently, but she didn't trust herself to talk about that at the moment—"and he kidnapped Lucy Peterson, but he didn't kill Caitlin."

"I'm not sure I follow—"

"We suspected Caitlin's death might be different from the others, remember?"

"What are you saying? That it was Adam, after all?"

"Not Adam. His sister, Lucy."

Cody's eyes widened. "The girl you rescued from the barn?"

"Right. She admitted as much to Grace, and then again, with some prodding, to the DA."

"Good God. Why?"

"She claims it was an accident. Caitlin took a shortcut home after her father failed to pick her up from school. Lucy followed and they got into an argument. Lucy pushed her and Caitlin fell into the river, or so Lucy says. Maybe that's what happened, maybe not. We'll never know."

"But she could have gone for help. She could have told someone what happened."

"Right. Instead, she tried to make it look like the person who killed Karen Holiday also killed Caitlin. Grace learned from Karen's mother that Karen's wallet had been found in a Dumpster in the mall, and Lucy overheard Grace tell Carl. Lucy thought if she got rid of Caitlin's backpack in the same place, people would assume the deaths were connected."

"But what about the pictures Adam had of Caitlin?"

"Like you said early on, he's a teenage boy with hormones."

Cody refilled their glasses. "What kind of sick kid lets her brother take the blame?"

"The kind who lets her stepsister drown without going for help."

"What's going to happen to her?"

"That's for the DA to decide. But she's only a child. And it might well have been an accident. There's certainly no way of proving otherwise."

"How terribly sad. For everyone."

Rayna heard genuine feeling in his voice and it touched her. For all his cocky, seemingly cool nonchalance, Cody had heart.

"What made the guy who abducted you suddenly start killing teenage girls?"

Rayna looked at the flames dancing in the fireplace. Surprisingly, her ordeal in the barn hadn't soured her on fires. She'd always loved a crackling fire and the scent of wood smoke—comfort food for the soul.

"He blames me for the death of his daughter at the hands of his ex-wife's boyfriend," Rayna said. "He wanted to make me look bad."

"Come again?"

"Back when I was working in San Jose, I arrested Earl. His ex-wife had a restraining order against him, one I helped her obtain after bouts of violence. He not only violated the order, he abducted his daughter. I arrested him and sent the daughter back to her mother. Then the mother's boyfriend killed them both."

"That's rough. But why show up now to get even?"

"He didn't wait until now." She felt her eyes tear up. "He killed Kimberly. He killed her for revenge."

"What? Oh, Rayna. Sweetheart." Cody moved closer and took her into his arms.

She cried softly, unable to stop. She'd thought she was past that. Not past the sorrow, but past the uncontrollable welling up of emotion.

" 'A daughter for a daughter' is what he told me. It's my fault Kimberly died. My fault Karen and Terri were killed, too."

"It's not your fault, Rayna. Surely you can see that?"

"Maybe it's a matter of perspective." In her own mind, she was clearly to blame. She took the handkerchief Cody held out and dried her eyes. "I used to fantasize about what I would like to do to Kimberly's killer, and then when I found him, or he found me, I was helpless. I couldn't do anything. I wish I could have beaten him to a pulp."

"He'll be convicted, Rayna. Most likely executed."

"After how many years?" Revenge wasn't the answer. Look where it had taken Earl. But in her heart, that's what she wanted. She wanted to see him dead.

"Prison's not going to be a cakewalk for him," Cody pointed out. "He'll suffer plenty."

"Not enough for me." Rayna blew her nose and took a deep breath. "On a more positive note," she said, trying to sound chipper, "the chief never accepted my resignation. I have my job still, if I want it."

"Do you?"

"Yes."

"That doesn't surprise me."

She smiled. "It surprises me."

They sat in silence watching the fire. Cody's arm along the back cushions casually brushed her shoulders.

"Tell me about this ring you busted," she said.

"Not much to tell, except that the work was intense. And satisfying."

"In contrast to a nothing case in a podunk town?"

He winced. "I told you I was sorry about that. I was peeved at the agency and took it out on you."

"So now it's back to D.C.?"

He took a sip of champagne. "I was offered a job in the Seattle office."

"One that interests you?"

"It's a good job. And the location is right. Not within commuting distance to Paradise Falls, but a whole lot closer than D.C."

Stunned, she said, "Are you going to take it?"

"Depends."

"On what?"

"You. If my being closer seems like it might be easier for us to see more of one another. If you were open to the idea."

He watched her intently, but she felt overwhelmed and confused, unable to respond.

Cody poured her more champagne.

"Aren't you having any more?" Rayna asked, eyeing his empty glass.

"I've got a long drive back to the hotel."

"You could stay here."

"No, I need to get back. There's no sense tempting temptation."

Rayna realized she did know what she wanted. She met his eyes and smiled. "Cody, the closer thing, the job in Seattle, sounds good to me. Really, really good."

CHAPTER 57

Grace waited until later that week, when she knew Carl would be at work, before going back to the house to pack up her things. Sandy had been kind enough to let Grace stay with her until she'd found an apartment—a duplex, small but bright and freshly repainted. Grace had liked it immediately.

Now, as she looked around the house, she felt nothing but sadness. She wouldn't miss living here. They'd agreed to hold off selling it for a bit, but Grace knew that Carl had no more interest in staying than she did. There were happy memories in that house, but she had trouble recalling them. Maybe with time they'd return.

She loved Carl, just as he claimed to love her. But love wasn't enough. In books and movies maybe, but not in real life. In life, obstacles were sometimes too great to be overcome.

She went through her closet quickly, selecting only those items she really liked and wore often. She packed up enough towels and sheets to see her through the short run, a few of the pots and pans she'd brought into the marriage, and then filled a large box with as much of the contents of Caitlin's room as she could. There would be time down the road to sort through and divide household items with Carl. They were both determined to be fair and even-handed.

Besides, she had to hurry if she was going to be on time to meet Jake for lunch. She'd thought he might blame her for what happened to Caitlin. If she hadn't married Carl, Caitlin would be alive. Instead, Jake seemed to gather strength from Grace's company. Gather and give. He was her lifeline out of despair.

"Caitlin was our daughter," he told her. "We grieve for her in a way no one else can."

Grace's phone rang as she placed the last of Caitlin's photo albums into the box.

"Hi, Grace. This is Rayna."

Grace had spoken to Rayna only briefly since she'd stopped by with soup. "How are you feeling?" she asked.

"Probably better than you. Am I disturbing you?"

"No. I'm at the house packing up a few things. I took that duplex I told you about. As soon as I get settled, I'll invite you over for dinner. If you want, that is."

"I'd love to come. In fact, I was calling to ask if you'd be interested in a weekend retreat."

"A retreat?"

"It won't be a touchy-feely thing, I can promise you that. A woman I met when I was working in San Jose is writing a book about parents of murdered children. There will be group discussions and she's a wonderful woman. Her own daughter was abducted and murdered eight years ago. Any chance you'd like to go with me? You don't have to give me an answer right away."

Grace looked at the box of Caitlin's belongings. Her daughter's death would be a hole in her heart forever. She'd miss Caitlin every minute of every day for as long as she lived. But she realized she couldn't rewrite the past. She could only learn to live with it. And who better to understand what she felt than others who'd been through what she had?

"Actually," she told Rayna. "I don't need to think about it. I'd like to go."

About the Author

Jonnie Jacobs is the bestselling author of thirteen previous mystery and suspense novels. A former practicing attorney and the mother of two grown sons, she lives in northern California with her husband. Email her at jonnie@jonniejacobs.com or visit her on the web at http://www.jonniejacobs.com.

Made in the USA
Charleston, SC
25 March 2013